# BOURNE
# & TRIBUTARY

*The River of Time Series*

TWO NOVELLAS BY
## LISA T. BERGREN

THE RIVER OF TIME SERIES:

*Waterfall*
*Cascade*
*Torrent*
*Bourne*
*Tributary*

BOURNE & TRIBUTARY

Published by Bergren Creative Group, Inc.
Colorado Springs, CO, USA

All rights reserved. Except for brief excerpts for review purposes, no part of this book may be reproduced or used in any form without written permission from the publisher.

This story is a work of fiction. All characters and events are the product of the author's imagination. Any resemblance to any person, living or dead, is coincidental.

© 2012 Lisa T. Bergren

Cover design: Gearbox Studios, David Carlson and Bergren Design
Cover Images: iStockphoto, royalty-free

Printed in the United States of America

*To Alexandria (Alessandra, in Italian), Amber, and other River Tribe girls, who pressed for more of the Betarrini/Forelli/Greco story... thanks for being as passionate about these characters as I am!*

## CHAPTER 1

### –GABRIELLA–

"M'lady! They approach!" the guard yelled down to us from the walls.

"Thank God," I muttered, taking my first full breath in what seemed like hours. Ever since the battle had ended the night before, Sienese patrols had circulated in and out of Castello Forelli, to drop off wounded, reprovision, rest, and head out again. As the night wore on, and the Fiorentini withdrew north, the patrols were gone for longer periods of time. But Marcello, Luca, and Lord Greco hadn't shown up at all.

Leaving me to fear the worst, of course.

"Open the gates!" the wall guard cried.

Three knights went to the massive crossbeam and slid it to one side, then opened the fifteen-foot doors. Twenty of our men on horseback arrived, but my eyes sought only one, my—

*Husband.* Marcello. I sighed in relief and then picked up my skirts and ran to him, waiting for him to wearily dismount and take me under one of his arms. I laughed and reached up on tiptoe to kiss him. "Oh, Marcello. Welcome home."

"I have to say, I think I'll grow accustomed to my wife welcoming me back, each time I have half a mind to chase a Fiorentini back to his side of the border." He winced as I gave him a full hug, making me pause in concern, but then Rodolfo Greco came around three others, leading his horse…and in an awkward moment, caught the last of Marcello's comment.

His handsome chin came up, and he stilled as if embarrassed. Not that he had any reason to be embarrassed. It was simply…awkward. The once-Fiorentini now in our castello. Marcello's brother. My captor-savior. I think we were all confused as to how to proceed, exactly. It'd take some time to figure out.

Luca came over, right next to Lia, both of them grinning. The grizzled Captain Pezzati clasped hands with Luca and the other guys, then gave me a nod of greeting and turned toward the stables. Mom came over, and I glanced in satisfaction at the circle of them, all around me. Together. At last. Everyone here, present and accounted for. Well, Dad was in his room, recovering from his own wound. But at the moment, we were all *safe*.

I was relishing the sweet relief, appreciating the feel of having my husband next to me again, when I felt Marcello begin to sink. Crying out, I got a better grip on him from under one of his arms; Rodolfo Greco came under the other. I tried to ignore his sudden proximity—and the resulting weirdness. "Quickly, let's get him inside," I said.

We eased Marcello through the Great Hall doors and into a chair, and I knelt before him. Rodolfo took a few respectful steps away. "Marcello!" I said, anxiously scanning his face and body for injury. I noticed, then, his swollen cheek, the cut at his mouth and nose, some bruising. Nothing I hadn't seen before, after taking on an enemy. But what worried me was the gray color of his skin, the way his eyes were hooded, half-shut. "Marcello, what ails you?"

"Take your ease, wife," he said in a mumble. "I am merely weary and in—"

His head rolled forward, and he slumped. I cried out again, and Rodolfo and Luca came to either side of him. "How is he injured?" I asked, my voice coming out in a strangled tone.

Luca ran his fingers through his sandy-colored hair and grimaced. "We ran into some difficulty en route home, m'lady."

"Difficulty?"

"A Fiorentini patrol. We'd parted from our men—"

Marcello moaned. I rose. "Marcello? *Marcello.*" I said, holding his head in my hands. But he was out again.

Lia brought a blanket into the room and spread it out on the floor. Rodolfo and Luca lifted Marcello and placed him on it. "Quickly," I said to the men. "Help me find his wound."

With trembling fingers, I pulled up Marcello's tunic and gasped. His belly was covered with purple, red, and green bruises. I looked to Luca.

"As I started to say…it happened a few hours ago," he said grimly, easing his cousin onto his side to look at his back. Mom knelt next to him. His green eyes met mine, and his anxious, lowered brows made my heart stop.

Nothing scared Luca.

My mom still stared at Marcello's back. "Looks like there's bruising around the kidneys," she said grimly. "He was beaten?"

Luca eased Marcello to his back again. "We'd secured the border, thought all Fiorentini had retreated. We were anxious to return." His eyes moved to Lia, who was hovering over my shoulder, then back to me. "So Marcello, Rodolfo, and I were riding home with the others when we met up with two Fiorentini patrols. We were outnumbered, two to one. And half of them went after Marcello."

Mom reached out to check Marcello's pulse at the wrist. I leaned down to listen to his heart, drawing strength from the steady, slow pounding of it, even as Luca told us the Fiorentini had driven Rodolfo, the twins and him to one side, then held Marcello, removed his chest armor, and began to do their best to beat him to death. "If it had not been for Captain Pezzati happening upon us with one of our own patrols, we'd all be dead by now."

Father Tomas crossed himself, and once again, I found myself wanting to kiss every one of our knights. If they hadn't been at the right place, at the right time—

I caressed Marcello's cheek, ignoring how Rodolfo stiffened and moved away as I did so.

"He'll be okay, right?" I asked Mom in English.

Her pause made my heart do the same. I dragged my eyes up to meet hers.

"We'll know more soon, Gabi," she said, sliding her long fingers over mine. "He needs rest. Liquids. Some medicine for the pain. There's very little else we can do for him."

*Here*, she meant. *Now*.

Once again I was longing for a phone, a quick 9-1-1 call, an ER and doctors and nurses and clean, white sheets…but we were so far from any of that. So far.

"Please," I said to Luca, panic rising in my chest. "Can you get him to my room?"

He nodded and gave a low whistle. Two guards appeared and took two corners of the blanket, Luca and Rodolfo at the other ends. Marcello moaned as they rose and carried him out, squeezing through the door and down the corridor. Mom followed us out, Lia right behind her.

They laid him on the bed in my room, and I asked them to stoke the fire and bring more wood. Giacinta appeared, telling Luca they were all needed in the courtyard, and the men left, looking relieved they had something to do. It irritated me. What could be more important right now than Marcello? Even if there was nothing to do but hang out with me and wring our hands together?

"See what that's about, would you?" I asked Lia in a whisper. She gave me a nod and followed them out.

Wordlessly, Giacinta helped me untie Marcello's tunic and slip it over his head. As battered and bruised as I was from our battle at Castello Paratore—had it been just yesterday?—it was nothing like what my man had suffered. It hurt just to look at him. And he was seriously dirty. "Can you fetch some hot water, soap, and rags?" I asked Giacinta. She set off immediately, leaving me and Mom alone with Marcello.

Mom leaned over the other side of the bed.

"What can we do for him, Mom?" I asked, my voice sounding like a little girl's, even to my own ears.

Her blue eyes ran over every inch of his chest. One thing knights had going for them after wielding a thirty-pound sword for a few years? Six-pack abs and not an ounce of belly fat. If I could transport these guys to our times, I'd have an annual best-selling calendar on my hands. Forget the hot firefighters. They had nothing on Italian knights. Not that I'd let *my* husband be in it. This one was all mine.

Mom's eyes continued to rove over his body, looking for telltale signs of what might be going on inside him. Her fingers went to his belly and probed, like she had done with Fortino. She frowned a little. "It's a little distended, I think."

I nodded, agreeing with her.

"But it's not hard, so hopefully that means he's not bleeding internally."

I let out a breath of relief. "But…you're worried about his kidneys, aren't you?"

"Yes," she said, giving me a level stare. She was always good at handing me hard news straight on. Sugar-coater? Yeah, not my mom. She pulled down Marcello's eyelids—to check out the color of his eyes? I didn't know. I thought I remembered from WebMD that yellow eyes meant there was trouble with the kidneys. Or was that the liver? From there, my brain hustled on over to Mariah, a girl in my school who'd fallen off her tube while sledding and bruised a kidney. It had been bad. Really bad. And she'd had modern medical care. But I also remembered that people could donate a kidney to loved ones in crisis…so even if you lost one, you could deal, right?

"He might have some bruised or broken ribs," Mom said. "See here?" She pointed along two of the lower left ribs, then ran her fingers lightly across them, checking as gently as possible. "We'll put a poultice together and wrap them. Let's take another look at his lower back."

I raised his arm, and then together we rolled him over.

Multiple bruises spotted his lower back, fist-wide and spreading. "They're beasts," I said. "It makes me want to strap on my sword and go hunt 'em down."

"Probably already done for you," Mom said, gently easing my man back over.

I nodded. An attack on Lord Forelli? I doubted any of those men yet lived.

Mom sighed and straightened, her hand on her chest. "I don't know, Gabi. Maybe we should summon a doctor. This is way out of my league."

"A doctor?" My last experience with one here hadn't gone so well. "So…what? They can bleed him with leeches? C'mon, Mom. You know as much as they do."

"I don't agree. The healers of this era—*legitimate* healers—had some whacky ideas, but they also had a more firm command of holistic healing, methods of diagnosis…far more than I've ever known. We can discuss his treatment before we okay it. We don't have to allow any potions or leeches or anything we don't agree with."

I stroked his face, thinking over her words. "Marcello," I whispered, leaning down by his ear. "Come on, beloved. *Svegliata,* Marcello. Please wake up."

"He's been through a great deal," Mom said. "Let's hope it's just his body trying to get on top of whatever's ailing him inside. Remember when you slept for the better part of two days after...Roma?" She sounded uneasy, like even mentioning my Losin' It moments might trigger a relapse.

"You think he might not wake up *for days?*"

Concern clouded her eyes. "I don't know what to tell you, Gabi."

My mind, of course, went directly to the time tunnel and its ability to heal. But we'd never taken five through it, and there was no way I was leaving anyone I loved behind. Could we even take five of us through? Would the healing properties work for anyone other than me and Lia? And what would happen to Dad if we went back to our own time? Would he disappear again from our lives? I closed my eyes and took a deep breath. "Okay, we'll summon a doctor." I lifted a finger of warning. "But *I* get to okay the dude as well as anything they want to give Marcello. I haven't had the best of luck with men of the medical persuasion around here."

Giacinta returned with the hot water and soap. Mom left to retrieve herbs and more bandages so we could apply the poultice and try to bring him some pain relief. Even if he was unconscious, Mom reasoned, helping his body fight pain could give him energy for other battles.

"What's happening?" I asked Giacinta as I washed my husband, wiping away the grime on his face and then his chest, wondering why Lia hadn't yet returned.

"Lord Greco left again with a patrol, and Captain Luca and Captain Pezzati with two others, all intent on making certain that no Fiorentini remain on this side of the border. The men enter our gates now, m'lady, in a steady stream, some whole and hale, seeking shelter and food, others gravely wounded. The courtyard is a mass of people…and the hallways are flooded with men all vying to claim a bit of floor for the night."

I nodded. Before, after the worst battles, we'd escaped into our own time. This was one of the first that we were present to witness the aftermath. "You're needed elsewhere, then," I said. "Go. I'll look after my husband."

"Are you certain, m'lady?"

"I am. Thank you, Giacinta. For everything…" I thought of her on Paratore's wall, so close to death. How he'd taunted me, preparing to push her over the side. How her little daughter was so narrowly spared losing her mother…

"M'lady, 'tis I who should thank you," Giacinta said, taking my hand in hers. "If you had not come when you did…"

We shook our heads at the same time, sharing a memory of pure fear. "He's gone now," I whispered, trying to reassure myself as much as Giacinta. "Lord Paratore…" I looked to the dancing flame of the fire, remembering his body pierced by many arrows, then back to my maid and friend. "He shall never harm either of us again."

She nodded, looking wan, and crossed herself. "I shall return to check on you, m'lady. You're certain you can do without me?"

"Oh, yes. My mother will soon return. Please." I gestured toward the door.

She bobbed a curtsey and left.

After I helped Mom wrap Marcello's ribs in a long bandage—strapping a funky-smelling poultice around him that she swore would help somehow, given its ingredients of goldenseal, comfrey, slippery elm and aloe vera—she looked warily over at me. "They need you out there, kiddo. The lady of the castle and all that. The She-Wolf."

I frowned. "I can't leave him, Mom."

"I'll stay with him," she said, lifting her chin in a way that said Don't Argue With Me. She sat down on the edge of the bed and looked at me. "When you married Marcello, you took on more than the responsibilities of marriage. You took on the responsibilities of lady of this castello, wife of one of the Nine. You need to confer with Luca when he returns. Find out what is next. What is expected." She shrugged. "Maybe there's nothing. Maybe there's a great deal. Regardless, your people need you."

*My people*, I said silently, trying to get my head around it. Once, that would've meant my friends on Facebook, the people I went to the movies with, the girls I ate lunch with. Now I had hundreds of people, all looking to me to lead them. I brought my hand to my head.

Mom took my other hand. "Gabi, you can do this. And Marcello"—she paused, glancing over at him—"he's strong. He'll pull through this."

"Are you sure?" I asked, my voice coming out all wonky and strangled.

She gave me a tiny, one-sided smile and nodded. "I am. Now go. Help the others in the courtyard, check in on your dad, and after you and Luca chat, come back. Okay?"

Still I hesitated. "You'll come for me? If anything changes?"

"Yes. Go. Send Lia back for updates if you need them. I'll sit here and watch your husband sleep. And pray that he wakes soon."

## CHAPTER 2

### –GABRIELLA–

Moving like a robot, I forced myself to wash my face, put on a fresh gown, and comb out my hair and wind it into a knot. I stuffed it into a little hairnet tied beneath a cap pinned to my head. If I was going to nurse anyone down in the courtyard, I didn't want my ridiculous hair getting in the way.

I paused at the door. "You're sure?"

Mom nodded. "I'm sure. Go. I won't leave him."

I glanced from her to Marcello and back, then left without another word, making myself walk down the hall. I heard them before I saw them. The moaning, the cries. The thick, stone walls and heavy, wooden door of our room had kept them mute. But once downstairs, I was in the center of chaos. I looked around in confusion. "M'lady," cried one man, clawing at my skirt. "A bit of water? Just a mite of water?"

"*Si, signore,*" I said. "I shall fetch you some." I looked up and beyond him again, focusing in on the horror that swords, arrows, clubs, and staffs left behind on human flesh. The open wounds. The blood. The brokenness. The inglorious remains of war.

As Giacinta had described, every inch of floor had been claimed by moaning and weeping men, nearly all of them filthy and bleeding, some unconscious. Others dead. Servants and the able-bodied scurried about in haphazard fashion, stopped again and again by those crying out for help. Men with treatable wounds were slowly bleeding to death as others with worse wounds got attention first.

Well, I'd seen my share of medical dramas on TV, and they weren't going to go to waste. We needed to triage this place, or whatever you called it. STAT. *Code Blue! Code Blue!* blared in my head. If we didn't have a plan on how to deal with all these wounded, we'd lose more than we had to. I glimpsed Father Tomas and called out to him. He barely heard me over the din. Gingerly, he and I made our way to the door and then out into the courtyard. While there were still a good number of wounded out in the open, too, at least Father Tomas and I could hear each other.

I paced back and forth in a three-foot square, thinking, waving the twins—Georgii and Lutterius—over to me, then Lia, then Giacinta. "This is a mess! We have able-bodied men milling about, doing little, and so many wounded! If we take the time to figure out a plan for treatment, we'll save more of them."

"What would you have us do, m'lady?" Lutterius asked. I'd come to know him by the mole on his right cheek, as well as his slightly longer, wavy hair the color of oil. Other than that, he and his brother were identical. Big men with big noses, big eyebrows, and big smiles full of crooked teeth.

"Call every able-bodied man into formation by the gates," I answered at last, figuring out my plan.

Lutterius looked at Georgii and then immediately set off.

Mom was right. A few days ago, my demands would probably have been questioned. But now, as Lady Forelli, I had power. The knowledge of it strengthened me. I looked to Giacinta. "Find a couple of men and have them bring every bag of lye we have in the storerooms out to the gates. Send three others to begin collecting every pail we have in the castle. Two others to gather bandages, needles, and uh, sinew." The last word echoed in my head, bringing back all kinds of bad memories.

She bobbed a curtsy and departed.

"Father Tomas," I said, "please—lead as many of these horses as possible to outside the gates—just for a few hours. We need the space." He nodded and moved out.

"What's your plan?" Lia asked.

"We're going to triage this place. You know, figure out who is the most wounded. Put all the people in need of sutures in a couple of the halls. All the head wounds in another. Undiagnosed in the fourth. I don't suppose any of the quacks they call doctors wandered in with these guys, did they?"

"There's one over there by the well," she said, nodding to the middle of the courtyard.

Together, we moved over to him, watching as he carefully wound a bandage around an unconscious man's leg. I took in the bag beside him, open to display perhaps twenty different bottles inside, then back to the doctor, who was about my height but thinner—I probably outweighed him by a good ten pounds. He was maybe thirty years old, of average looks but with piercing eyes. They were super dark, while his skin was the color of a creamy cappuccino.

"M'ladies," he said, rising to his feet and sweeping into a bow. "I am honored to be in your presence."

"We have met?" I asked.

"Nay. But no man of Toscana could miss the fabled Ladies Betarrini."

"Lady Forelli," I corrected him casually. "Only my sister is yet a

Betarrini."

"Of course," he said, his dark eyes moving over to Lia. "My mistake," he said apologetically, bringing a hand to his chest and giving me another nod.

"Your name, sir?"

"Forgive me," he said with a laugh. "I'm afraid my weariness has left me with half my wits. I am Physici Sandro Menaggio."

"We're relieved to have a physician with us, Signore Menaggio," I said.

I studied him, trying to ignore the tinge of warning that shot up my neck, setting every hair on end. I was just paranoid, basing my feelings off the first time I'd met up with a doctor in medieval times. With the dude who tried to kill me. This guy's clothing spoke of his relative wealth. He dressed like a merchant. So he was probably a practicing physician, making some sort of living at it, I guessed. Which had to mean he didn't kill every patient.

"Where did you learn the medical arts, Doctor?" Lia asked.

"Germania," he muttered, bending to tend to a man beside him, swiftly tearing a strip of cloth from a bundle under his arm and wrapping it around the man's head.

I shifted uneasily, and Lia and I avoided looking at each other. We weren't super fond of meeting anyone who had ever been in or near Northern Europe. There was just too much opportunity for questions about our fictional beginnings in England and "Normandy." And our safety here in Italia—as well as Mom and Dad's—was more secure if no one asked any questions of our past. Ever.

"They have a fine university there," I said, eager to fill in the gap of silence. I was guessing. But didn't Germany have some of the oldest universities anywhere?

"Indeed," he returned, to my relief, smiling to reveal a cute gap between his front teeth. It made him appear instantly friendlier. "You know of it?"

"Only by reputation." I had to move on. Georgii and Lutterius had done as I asked, and every able-bodied man was now assembled by the front gate. The twins looked over their shoulders, waiting on me.

"Tell me, Doctor. How did you come to be here inside the gates of Castello Forelli at such an opportune time?"

He shrugged. "I heard the brunt of the battle was here and anticipated your need."

"I see," I said, studying him. "And where do you reside?"

"Siena, my lady."

"There are noblemen in Siena who would recommend you?"

"I believe so, m'lady."

Still, I hesitated. Did I dare put my husband in his hands? "Did they teach you of methods to guard against infection at university?"

"Indeed. But here," he said, gesturing about, "'tis difficult to control. I fear we must leave such things to God." He crossed himself.

"I fear that God intends us to use the minds He gave us," I returned. "We would greatly value your assistance. But Lord Forelli is in immediate need of a physician's care and is my first priority. Would you kindly go and examine him, then report to me? Lady Evangelia shall show you the way."

"Of course, m'lady," he said with a genteel bow. He was so thin and moved so lithely as he gathered up his bag, I decided he reminded me of a praying mantis.

I pulled Lia a few steps aside. "We don't know this guy," I said in her ear. "Keep a dagger in your hand at all times." For good measure, I sent a fearsome-looking knight with her. He was monstrous and still had blood spattered over his face. Surely, even if Doctor Menaggio had evil intent, he would not move with our own Incredible Hulk and a She-Wolf in the room. *Please, Lord,* I added in prayer for good measure. *Watch over them.*

Moving on, I straightened my shoulders, lifted my chin, and approached the men. Beyond them, Father Tomas and the stable boys and squires led horses out through the gates. I put my hands on my hips and walked back and forth before the forty men assembled. Some were remnants of the troops that had come to our aid via Marcello's mysterious brotherhood. Some were Sienese, still wearing their red tunics with the white cross. Others were mercenaries hired by Marcello.

"We are going to organize this castello to best assist the wounded. That begins with assessing each patient and dividing them into groups. Already, there are dead in our halls. We owe each man a proper burial, respect. We will attempt to learn his name so we can see to his family. But dead men mixing with those who ail breeds illness. We must separate them and continue to do so as others pass on.

"I need ten men to immediately remove the dead, bringing them to a line here," I said, gesturing to the wall to the left of the front gates. I turned and pointed to each wall of the pentagon-shaped castle. "For those of you unfamiliar with Castello Forelli, there are five corridors, accessed via the doors at each juncture." I identified the northeast, east, south, southwest, and west corridors. "I want every wounded man brought here to the courtyard. When Doctor Menaggio returns, he and I shall tell you where to take each man. After the corridors have been cleaned and dusted with lye."

The men were frowning, clearly distrusting my plan. I knew they were reluctant to move men in pain if they didn't have to. *Haven't they suffered enough?* they silently asked me. And lye and hot water? Elements usually reserved for cleaning up, rather than as a preventative measure. "Grant me your trust, friends," I said. "I know if we do this, we shall save far more lives this day than if we do not."

I watched in satisfaction as they set out to do as I asked. And in half an hour, the courtyard was teeming with all the wounded, in misery. Including my dad.

"Dad!" I said, hurrying over to him. "You shouldn't be out of bed."

"I'm okay," he said in my ear. "Far better than most of these. I can help you. Lia told me of your triage plan."

"Are you sure?"

"I'm sure," he said, giving me a firm nod. I glanced at his shoulder, seeping blood through the bandage and his loose shirt. Even though Mom liked to diagnose problems and try out her herbal remedies, it had been Dad who'd consistently looked after our scraped knees and elbows while we were growing up. And he had that look of Betarrini determination in his eyes....

"All right," I said. "But if you feel woozy, you sit down and call for a cup of water. Deal?"

"Deal."

I straightened, suddenly feeling another's presence like I was being spied on. I turned. Doctor Menaggio, flanked by Lia and the knight. Inwardly, I cursed myself for my carelessness, using English in front of someone who might very well know a medieval form, not our contemporary dialect.

"Oh, Doctor," I said, turning fully toward him. His dark eyes shifted between me and my dad; he'd clearly heard our whisperings. Before he could ask anything, I said, "What might you tell me of my husband?"

"He still slumbers. I agreed with your mother's assessment; we must wait and see how he fares come morning. Your mother is rather gifted at the healing arts," he said, lifting a brow in admiration.

"Indeed. Mayhap it's best if I summon her out here...."

"Nay, m'lady," he said, gently. "M'lord's welfare is worth a hundred of these."

Stunned, I stared back at him, doubting Marcello would agree with that. I knew my husband would trade his life in a heartbeat for a hundred others. Ten. But what would happen if he worsened, even died? I shook off the thought, deciding to take the doctor at his word.

Giacinta called, waving at the northeast doorway.

"Good. First hallway cleared. We'll put those in need of sutures there and see how many we have left. Anyone with experience suturing wounds, report to Lady Evangelia." I noticed several men snap to attention with uncommon interest now that they knew my sister would be a part of the team. I dispatched Doctor Menaggio to identify all those in need of suturing and binding. Knights began hauling patients back inside. I turned to Lia. "You'll see to the suture teams? One can administer hemlock for the pain, another wash up wounds. One can stitch, one can bind. Good?"

She groaned, rolling her pretty blue eyes. "I seriously shoulda never stitched you up. Suddenly I'm a surgeon?"

"Hey," I whispered back with a grin, "if it wasn't for those stitches, I might not have made it. At least you have hemlock for these guys. And think about this...you didn't have to endure years of bio and chem to earn your degree."

"Methinks I'd prefer that," she said, narrowing her eyes. But she turned and trudged toward the corridor to do her duty. She'd always been better at elementary school cross-stitch projects than I. *She'll do fine.*

"Lia—"

"I *know*, Gabriella," she said, lifting a light brow. "Wash the wounds and needles before stitching."

"Thank you," I said with a small grin.

Cook came up to me next. "We have some stew and bread ready."

"Enough for them all?"

"Not to fill a man's belly," she said with a woeful tuck of her head, "but enough to put aside the ache."

"Excellent." Belatedly, I remembered the man who had reached out to me earlier. I looked around for him but couldn't see him. "Please, send some girls around with pails of water and ladles, so we know each have had their fill to drink. Then take them their stew and bread." I squeezed her fat forearm. "Thank you, Cook. That will be some of the best medicine they shall receive."

She grinned at me and waddled off.

"M'lady!" a man screamed, reaching out to me with such terror in his eyes, I froze. He stretched so hard, I could see every sinew and muscle of his neck, shoulder, arm, hand. "Lady Forelli!"

Hating that I was tentative, I moved toward him and knelt, taking his hand in mine. His breathing was coming fast and shallow, his color poor. Clearly dying. But he clung to my hand with the strength of a determined man. "My name..." he panted, "is Nuncio Mancini." He stared wildly at me, his eyes moving back and forth on mine, then slowly rolling as if he fought unconsciousness. Then they'd widen again. "I am of the village called Cavo. Please...m'lady..."

"Yes?"

"My wife...we only married...fortnight ago. Her name...tell her..."

He choked, made an awful gurgling sound. He stared at me with such intensity, the words almost rising from his open lips. *I love her. I'm sorry.* And then his eyes froze. In the span of three seconds, I felt his strength fade, his hand go limp in my own.

"Signore," I urged him, shaking his shoulder gently. "What is it you wish me to tell her? Signore!"

Swallowing hard, I set his hand on his chest and reached to feel for a pulse. *Maybe he's just lost consciousness, like Marcello.* I waited a moment, then moved my fingers to a different place, hoping I'd just missed it. *Please, please...* But I hadn't.

He was gone.

I opened my eyes and stared at him a long moment. At his dark eyes, lined with thick lashes, staring sightlessly up into the sky. He was young, as so many in this time were. The cities were dominated by people under thirty. Old people were a scarcity, killed off by infection, accident, disease that no one could treat. They fared better in the countryside. But this one—he couldn't be more than twenty. And just married…

A knot formed in my throat, thinking of his wife waiting by a window, a door, watching the horizon for his return now that the battle was over. A return that would never come.

It crystallized my fear for Marcello. What if I held his hand this night and felt the life drain from him as well?

No. God hadn't brought me all the way here to find love…just to lose it. Had He?

I looked around, trying to focus on the next task. *I am Lady Forelli. A lady of a castle doesn't get to lose it. Doesn't get to give in. She carries on. She freaks out in private if she has to. Never in public. Never, ever in public.* I shivered, remembering my breakdown after our escape from Rome. The memory felt perilously familiar, close. As if it was a chasm I teetered near…

I felt a warm hand on my shoulder, and Father Tomas knelt between me and Nuncio. He held his hand under the man's nose, waiting for breath, then squeezed my shoulder again. "He is gone. I shall see to his last rites. You shall see to another?"

Slowly, I dragged my eyes to meet his, wanting him to see the wildness in them, wanting to silently admit my fear to him.

He was safe for me. Safe.

His own look became firm. "M'lady." He lifted me to my feet, his round hands on each of my shoulders. We were the same height, and he stared into my eyes. "Fear is not of the Lord. It is of the Enemy. Do not give in to it." He gave me a little shake, willing me to hear the impact of each of his words. *Fear was of the Enemy. The Enemy.* That was something

I could grasp. Fight.

I nodded and looked down. But still he held me. Silently waiting for me to draw strength from him, solace, hope. "Our lives are in His hands alone," he said softly. "We live only the days the Lord has granted us."

"So it matters not how we live our lives? What we do?" I said, my anger choking out hope. "What we say? Whether we are good or evil?"

He gave me a gentle smile. "Nay. *Nay*. 'Tis a great matter, how we conduct ourselves. That is what gives our lives depth, meaning. Regardless of how many days we are given to do so."

I stared back at him, trying to decipher what he was attempting to tell me.

"Fight the fear, Gabriella," he said, releasing me at last. "Cling to truth and hope and love. In the end, that is all we are promised." He shook his head, a wry grin in his eyes. "Nothing else."

I nodded, confused as to why he was smiling when everything was so grim. Giving up, I numbly turned to answer questions from the servants and knights who awaited my attention as Father Tomas prayed over Nuncio. I tried to get Nuncio's bride—now a widow—out of my mind. Tried to forget that my own husband lingered in territory I didn't like at all. And after every question was answered, after every man was sent to his designated hall for care and the courtyard was cleared, I made myself move over to the line of dead men lying like tin soldiers as if they'd been toppled by the tips of God's fingers.

Slowly, I walked by each of them, looking into their faces. Recognizing each as a husband, father, son, brother, neighbor, cousin, friend.

And then I wept.

## CHAPTER 3

### –GABRIELLA–

My eyes moved up to the guards on the walls and saw that they watched me, recognized my tears. Their faces told me they noted my compassion, bonded with me further because of it. But I looked away, unable to bear it. How long until they, too, were like these before me?

"Patrol approaches!" called out a guard. "And a second, right behind them!"

Rodolfo rode in first at a canter, astride his massive gray gelding, and caught sight of me and my tearstained face before I could duck my head. His men were right behind him, two of them clearly wounded. But his attention was solely on me. He whirled his horse around and dismounted before he was fully at a stop. He hurried over to me and eased an arm around my shoulders. "Gabriella," he said, his voice a moan in shared grief before he even knew what pained me. "Is it Marcello?"

I glanced at him in confusion. His tone held both fear and hope. Which outweighed the other? "Nay," I said, shaking my head and sliding out of his uncomfortably familiar embrace. The guards...everyone would see! See his obvious attention, undue care...

"Then what burdens you so?" he asked, still holding my hand in both of his, insistent.

But then the second patrol rode in, Luca at the front, his face a mask of fury. I did a double take, so unfamiliar was his expression. Gone was the playful, fun Luca; in his place was solely a warrior on point. "Greco!" he screamed, charging toward us.

I frowned in confusion and alarm. Rodolfo took my hand and pulled me to the right to avoid Luca's horse, but this seemed to only aggravate Luca further. He jumped to the ground and ran toward us. Rodolfo eased me behind him, just before Luca struck him. Hard. A massive belt to the cheek.

Rodolfo stumbled to the side, but kept his feet. And my hand.

"Luca!" I cried, reaching out toward him with my other.

But he ignored me, his attention only on Rodolfo. "Unhand m'lord's *wife*," he seethed.

Rodolfo let go of my hand and lifted both of his to the air in a sign of submission. Luca moved so close that they were chest to chest, his face a snarl of challenge, while Rodolfo's was resigned.

"Nay! Stop!" I cried, trying to part them but failing. "What...what has transpired?"

"This man," Luca seethed, tapping Rodolfo's chest as if he wanted to pierce it, "went out there"—he gestured angrily above the wall—"with a wish to meet the Angel of Death."

I glanced back in confusion, but Rodolfo just slowly wiped the blood from a small cut in his cheek and stared hard at Luca.

"Of what do you speak?" I asked Luca, fully facing him now.

"We came across more Fiorentini," he said, pacing, shaking his head as if trying to figure it out himself. "I commanded he hold in formation, to wait, but Rodolfo *charged*, instead. But for the hand of God, they all might've been killed."

"I knew you would come to our aid in time," Rodolfo said in a monotone. I gave him a hard look, but he wouldn't return my gaze, still watching Luca as if he couldn't be trusted. Which he probably couldn't. The other men formed a semicircle around us, watching. Waiting.

"Why?" I asked. "Luca is the captain in charge of any knight that departs these gates. Even you, so new to us, understood this."

Still, Rodolfo wouldn't look at me.

Luca neared again, and Rodolfo tensed. Luca was shorter than Rodolfo by several inches, but you'd never know it by his demeanor. He got right up into Rodolfo's face again. "Because he's wracked by guilt," Luca said.

He looked over at me meaningfully, and I felt an arrow go through my heart. What was that? Guilt over my own memories?

Others neared. My Dad, with Tomas. Captain Pezzati and his patrol rode in. "Let us go to the Great Hall and speak of this in private," I said.

"Nay!" Luca shouted, making me jump. His face collapsed in sorrow. He shook his head and rubbed his neck with a grimy hand, which he then lifted to me, begging me in gesture. "Forgive me, m'lady, but permit me to see this through. In Marcello's absence..."

He took my silence as all the permission he needed. He moved toward Rodolfo again. "You are my brother." He angrily rolled up his sleeve and lifted the tattoo into his line of vision. He snorted in derision. "You may as well be my brother by blood." He dropped his sleeve and lifted both hands to grip Rodolfo's shirt. "You have sacrificed everything, *everything* for Siena. For this house. For these people." He leaned in, inches away from Rodolfo's face again. "And I shall not let you kill yourself as a means of appeasing the pain." He said the last so quietly that I wondered if only I heard it.

He backed away then, as we all seemed to be holding our breath.

"I deserve a night in the stocks," Rodolfo said.

"Shall that do it, then? Or shall we torture you as well?" Luca said. "What shall it take to free you? So that you might *live*, rather than sacrifice your very life?"

"Luca..." I said, but it came out in a whisper. How had things come to this?

Luca let out a strangled cry toward the sky, a mixture of fury and frustration and pain, his hands on either side of his jaw. He stood there like that for two seconds, then three. Then he lifted a hand of dismissal and turned away, the tension leaving him in a wave. "Put him in the stocks. Mayhap when dawn comes, he shall see that he was born to be one of us all along."

He walked away, parting the group in two as they made way for him.

"Nay," I said. "Nay! Sir Forelli!"

Luca paused, stiffened, but did not turn.

"Gabriella," Dad said, and reluctantly, I looked in his direction. Slowly, he shook his head, urging me to leave it be. To let them do this their way.

Luca looked over his shoulder, waiting on me. "M'lady?"

I glanced from him to Rodolfo. Even he didn't want me to come to his aid. I sighed and said, "I trust you to see this through to a good end, Captain."

"Thank you, m'lady," he said. "May I suggest you return to your quarters? What is about to transpire might be beyond even *your* feminine fortitude." He was remembering the night I'd come to the aid of the two men splayed out in the courtyard, one of the first I'd been here. When I didn't understand the wages of war, the price. He didn't want me to interfere again.

I turned and stumbled toward the doorway that led to my quarters, to Marcello, feeling empty. Lost. Adrift.

Dad wrapped his good arm around my shoulders. I was glad—so

glad—he was with me. Because I couldn't do this alone. I felt inside out. Like I was drowning.

But what I really wanted was Marcello. The thought of him made me desperate to see him, and I broke away from my father, scurrying to the door and flinging it open, not bothering to wait for him. I picked up my skirts and took the stairs two at a time, winding my way upward, then ran down the hall, remembering how it was just a few days ago, lit with candles and strewn with rose petals....

Mom's face didn't hold the hope, the good news I so desperately needed. She was leaning over Marcello, placing a wet cloth on his forehead. In the dancing light of the candle beside his bed, I could see he was flushed and sweating so much his skin appeared wet, glistening. "Oh, no," I groaned, rushing over to the bed and scrambling to kneel beside him. "No, no," I said, quietly laying a hand on his chest, then pulling it away, shocked by the heat that rose from him in waves. I held my hand to my chest as if it still burned, felt the knowledge like a wound.

Fever. Infection. Internal trauma.

*Please, Lord. Don't take him. Don't let his days be done...*

"Gabi, he's been burning like this for an hour. Sometimes it's the body's way to deal with whatever he's suffering from. If he can get through this..."

I looked up at her. "And if he can't?" I said. "If he can't?" I shrieked, the panic building. Mom came around, climbed across the bed and gathered me in her arms from behind.

"We have to take him, Mom," I said. "Lia and me. To the tunnel. To safety." I felt her intake of breath, saw Dad blanch, clamping his lips shut. "We could leave you two here. Return to you. After...after he is okay."

Dad shook his head. "No way. You're not going anywhere without us."

"And we can't, Gabi," Mom begged, squeezing me in a hug. "We *can't*," she said meaningfully.

I closed my eyes, feeling every weary, burdensome minute of the day we'd just endured. "We can't," I whispered back.

It was an impossible situation. Lose Marcello? Or lose Dad again?

"No," Mom said with a gentle shake of her head. "We agreed to see through life here, come what may. Together. I have hope yet, Gabi. He is strong, sweetheart. Believe in your husband. Believe in him. He can make it through this."

"You don't even know what's wrong! Not really!" I said.

"No," she said. "But look at him. Look at him."

I made myself to do as she said, searching his face. Even weakened by illness and wounds, he did look powerful. Strong.

But didn't they say the big guys were the first to faint in a delivery room? The first to succumb to the weird viruses, surprising everyone around them? The big men who collapsed on the basketball court while dribbling, their hearts refusing to beat one more time?

*Please, Lord,* I prayed, thinking of Father Tomas's words. *Grant us more days. Please, please, please give us more days.*

My parents stayed with me through the evening, insisting I down a few bites of stew, a few swallows of water, a few bites of bread, more water. Eventually, Lia arrived and Mom told Dad it was his turn to rest. She went with him, not liking his "color." She turned to us at the door. "He probably just overdid it."

"Ya think? He was pierced by a *sword*," I muttered.

"Don't worry over him," Mom said. "You'll send for me if anything changes?"

I nodded and looked over to Lia, her golden gown bearing the ruinous blood from her afternoon of suturing. "You should go too. You've been through so much. Go. Get some sleep."

"Are you sure you don't want me to stay here with you?"

"No. I'll be okay. I'll call for Giacinta if I need help. She can come for you and Mom if I need you." I prayed I wouldn't. Needing them would mean that Marcello had worsened.

Reluctantly, Lia slid off the foot of the bed and stood there. "You sure?"

"I'm sure." But then I stopped her at the door. "I need one more favor tonight, Lia."

She waited, but my hesitation made her blonde eyebrows lower with wariness. "What?" she asked in a tone that said *maybe*.

"Check on Rodolfo. It's cold out there." I shivered and ran my hands over my arms. "Feels like rain."

Her brow lowered further. "Gabi, Dad told me—"

"Please," I said wearily. "It's nothing but care for a friend. I swear it. He...he's hurting. Feeling lost." I looked over at Marcello and stroked his forehead. "I understand a bit of that. And I'm a part of the reason he's here, feeling this way." I lifted a hand, hushing her comeback before it popped out. "I know. I'm only a part. But I *am* a part. Please...just make sure he's okay?"

She gave me a long, tired sigh, a single nod, and then left.

I laid down next to Marcello, and it was then that I noticed he'd stopped sweating, even though he felt raging hot. His teeth were chattering, and he was shivering. It was weird, but I felt like it was a good sign. Whenever I'd had a fever, it'd moved to the chills right before it broke. But I remembered how I wanted every blanket available when it happened, and Marcello already had every one in the room. I tapped my lips, considering him, wishing there was something I could do for him.

Dimly, I remembered an episode of *Man vs. Wild* where the host told viewers the best treatment for hypothermia was another person's body. Skin against skin. I laughed under my breath at my own hesitation. Why not? We were married, were we not? I slid off the bed and out of my gown, tiptoeing over the cold, stone floor to hop under the covers.

I moved his nearest arm to make room for me, not wanting to hurt him. I wrapped my thigh over his, which were clad only in leggings. And I nestled into the crook of his arm, resting my head on his shoulder and my arm across the expanse of his chest, willing my own body heat to ease the shuddering within him. "It's okay," I whispered. "Shh, shh. I'm here, Marcello. You can make it through this. I know you can. You are strong. You can do this. I love you, Marcello."

And then I prayed, prayed for hours as he shivered, his teeth chattering so loudly they awakened me every time I dozed off.

*Bring him back to me, Lord. Don't take him now. Please don't take him. We need more days. More days...*

## CHAPTER 4

### –EVANGELIA–

I heard the spatter of rain outside, even before the guard opened the door, allowing me exit to the courtyard. The rain made me more reluctant to do what Gabi had asked of me. But standing in the hallway teeming with the wounded and moaning hurt my heart too. I glanced down the hall, filled with perhaps thirty men crammed in like sardines. Maids circulated with water. Father Tomas was at the end of the hall, bending over a man, closing his eyes, praying. From the look on his face, the man wasn't going to make it.

I hurriedly looked away, feeling the burden of another loss like a sack of grain over my shoulders. I'd done my share of nursing the wounded today—pushing through the horrible stitching until my skirts were heavy with blood, my eardrums dull from the sound of men's screams. There was so little we could do…so many lost to wounds that at home would be so easily fixed. I just didn't have it in me to give any more to these men, tonight. All I had left in me was to see through Gabi's request and sink into my own bed. I pulled the hood of my cape over my head, clenched the front of it closed, and nodded to the guard.

He looked down at me, eyebrows furrowed. "Raining hard now, m'lady. Sure you don't wish to pick your way through the corridors instead?"

"Nay. 'Twould take me an hour," I said, looking down the crowded hallway and using it as an excuse. The fewer who knew of my true mission, the better. Lady Forelli sending me to check on the man who had been supposed to marry her in Rome? Yeah, that would set the castle tongues wagging.... The guard opened the door for me. "Do you require escort, m'lady?"

"Nay, thank you," I said. "I think I can manage." Stepping out into the courtyard, I felt the first fat droplets hit my hood.

I took a covered lantern from the wall, taking comfort from the light of the wide, dripping candle inside, and walked around the kitchen, then to the front of the Great Hall, where the courtyard spread wide and open from castle wall to castle wall. The rain was indeed falling hard, splattering up from swiftly forming puddles, sizzling on the roof of my lantern. I felt cold water seep into my slippers but did my best to ignore it, focusing on my task. Maybe with the rain, the guards on the wall would be huddling in the towers rather than staring at Lady Evangelia hanging with Lord Rodolfo Greco.

He was in the center of the courtyard, alone. After all, he'd have difficulty escaping, even if he somehow extricated himself from the monstrous wooden block that held his neck and hands. He knelt in the water, and I could see he was wet through and through, shivering.

I shook my head. It was barbaric. And Luca had ordered it. Heck, Greco had apparently asked for it. I didn't think I'd ever fully understand the way a man thought. At least these men. But I knew that what drove Rodolfo was overwhelming guilt. For betraying Firenze to aid us, for helping Gabi escape their impending matrimony, and most likely—from what I could gather—for feeling something for her in the midst of it. It was as crazy-complicated as an episode of *Pretty Little Liars*.

I paused awkwardly, not knowing what to say, how to begin. *"Oh, hey, how are ya?"* just didn't seem to fit.

He managed to turn his head an inch and gaze at me with his dark eyes, dismissing me a second later. "You should not be here, m'lady."

"Neither should you," I returned.

"My punishment was justified." He stared straight ahead, rain dripping down his face.

Conflicting emotion warred within me. Half of me wanted to free him; half of me wanted him to suffer. If he was so close to Marcello, Luca, Fortino, and Tomas, why couldn't he have figured his loyalties out sooner rather than later? Why hunt me and Gabs on behalf of the Fiorentini? Put us through all that? Why hadn't he left the Fiorentini when he helped us bust Gabi loose from the cage that had almost killed her? Why'd he have to lose everything before choosing to join us fully?

"You're wondering why I switched my allegiance at the eleventh hour," he said, still looking forward.

I jumped a little. *Well, uh, yeah,* I thought. "Mayhap," I said.

He paused so long, I thought he didn't intend to answer.

Any sense of fear seemed to evaporate. I dared to move in front of him and squat, so he'd be forced to look into my eyes. The light from my candle lit up the lower part of his face, making him appear like the most handsome ghoul ever seen. But I wasn't concentrating on that. His answer was important for us to know. All of us.

"Even when they stripped me of my title and took my home," he said, "I intended to remain true to Firenze. I'd aided Marcello, Fortino, and your sister in good conscience. Even if my Fiorentini brothers didn't understand on a political level, I knew if I was to sit any one of them down, look them in the eye, and tell them why I made the decisions I did, they would have understood, man to man."

I let out a scoffing laugh. "Are you certain of that?"

His dark eyes flicked to meet mine. "Do not become so fearfully hardened, m'lady. I know many Fiorentini you would consider dear friends, in time."

"If they didn't yearn for my head on a platter. That, I find, disrupts a friendship."

I thought I saw the ghost of a smile.

"Many of my decisions were honorable, the humane response, even if teetering on the brink of war called for harsher choices. My friends, my truest friends, would have understood that. Supported me in that. If I hadn't allowed Gabriella to slip away in Roma, all would have been forgiven. Up until Barbato and Paratore convinced them to lay the blame squarely at my feet and use me as bait, to draw Marcello out, I had hope. Hope that I could help Firenze and Siena reach a treaty. Enter into a time of peace."

Raw grief seemed to come off him in waves. Here was a man who had been so powerful, so scary...and now he just seemed...broken. I could identify a little with him; after all, my life had just taken a drastic turn too. Forever.

"Some dreams are not meant to be," I said softly.

He said nothing.

"Mayhap, in time, another opportunity for peace shall come to pass. The point of decision is behind you, Lord Greco. Why not move forward from here? Accept your lot, and make the most of it."

It was his turn to scoff. "Take up residence in Castello Paratore, as Marcello has suggested? Await a murderer's poison in my cup of wine? An arrow through my chest as I go for a ride in the wood?"

"Have you not heard of the She-Wolves of Siena? They know a little about such things." I cocked my head with a little conspiratorial smile. "It's not as bad as all that."

He smiled then. "Yes," he said, his teeth chattering. "I imagine you do." I resisted the urge to push the wet hair out of his eyes. It had to be driving him crazy. But that little "confusion" that had happened between Gabi and him? Yeah, that wasn't going to happen between us. That would just be…messed up.

"Lord Greco," I urged, "this night in the stocks does nothing but weaken you, when we need every able-bodied knight we can gather. Let me go to Luca and convince him to—"

"Nay!" he barked, surprising me so much that I stood and backed away on trembling knees. Any sense of camaraderie evaporated. "Nay," he repeated, regret softening his tone. "Luca did as he had to do. He is captain of every man who leaves Castello Forelli's gates. I disobeyed him. Any man who does so deserves such punishment."

I studied him and felt the rain begin to seep through my cape. This was why Luca had been so furious. Lord Greco had painted him into a corner, forcing his hand. Moreover, I knew Luca had been angry because his friend had endangered his own life, as well as those in his command. He deserved punishment, truly. *Gotta set him straight.* But this?

I sighed. I knew this kind of guy. He was like the smart, talented dude on the wrong path at school. Brilliant, good looking. Money. Bright future and all that. But constantly self-sabotaging in some misguided effort to right whatever wrong he felt within himself. He'd wring out every ounce of punishment on himself that he deserved—he didn't need Luca judging his crimes too. He probably had been doing it even before the Fiorentini fully turned on him.

I'd seen my share of teen movies and TV shows. Kids wrestling with dark issues—the only thing that fixed them was a serious dose of love and kindness. And a good mentor. Maybe Tomas could help him out on that front. In the meantime…

"Lord Greco, it will be well, in time," I said softly, pulling my cape from my shoulders. His eyes narrowed as I went around the stocks, behind him. "This night, you are born anew. Into a new life."

"M'lady," he protested, anticipating what I was about to do.

I ignored him and settled the wet cloth across his broad back and over his legs. "'Tis not dry, but mayhap it will afford you a bit of warmth," I said, coming back around.

He wouldn't look at me.

"Does it wound your pride to accept assistance?" I paused. "If it does, you best get accustomed to it, m'lord. Because we of Castello Forelli live as a family, and we come to the aid of anyone who is one of us. And like it or not," I said, leaning closer, "you have become one of us."

He shook his head. "'Tis not a good idea. For me to be one of you. Already Castello Forelli is at the core of every one of Firenze's targets. My presence here only makes that core all the more enticing."

He stiffened, and a half-second later, I understood what alarmed him. Somebody approached out of the pounding rain.

Luca.

I felt the chill of the night in a new way as Luca paused beside me. For the first time ever, he didn't seem happy to see me. "M'lady," he said grimly. "Why is it that you are out without your cape?"

I felt the rain plastering my hair down on my face and tried to keep my composure, belatedly thinking about how this might look. "Gabi... uh...I..." I clamped my lips shut and squared my shoulders, opting to settle on anger rather than guilt. "I gave it to Lord Greco," I said. "If you insist on keeping him out on such a night as this, it's the least we can do for him." With that, I picked up my lantern and flounced off. As much as a wet, soggy mess of a girl can flounce.

Half of me hoped Luca would stay behind to interrogate Lord Greco. After all, his issues were with him, not me. But Luca hurried after me. "Evangelia."

I didn't stop.

Thirty feet away, at the door to the corridor that led to my quarters, he grabbed my arm and pulled me around. "*Evangelia.*"

A covered torch on the wall fully illuminated him. Lord Greco and the rest of the courtyard disappeared in the dark and rain behind him. But all I could concentrate on was his face. It was awash in confusion. Fear. Frustration. Fury. "What transpired...there?" he asked, waving behind him, into the darkness, toward Greco.

What *had* happened? "Mercy," I said simply, turning to press on the door latch to escape him.

But he slammed it shut, his arm across my shoulder, leaning into my back.

"Luca," I said, getting angry myself. I turned, but he didn't back off.

"I don't want you near him," he said, terribly close. Even with all our flirting, all our hanging out, we'd never been this close. This...intense. I found myself fighting for breath.

"That shall be somewhat difficult, don't you think?" I asked. "Given that once he's out of the stocks, he'll likely be by your side, or Marcello's, constantly? Unless, of course, you do not wish to see me either."

Okay, so it was a little manipulative. But I couldn't stop myself.

He clamped his lips shut, and he edged away. "You have feelings for him."

It took me a sec. "What? Nay!" I said. Guys could really be so ridiculous sometimes.

His eyes searched mine. "'Tis understandable. Rodolfo...he's always had any woman he wanted. I should've anticipated—"

"Luca. Look at me."

His eyes, slightly wild, stilled on mine.

"I am not in love with Lord Greco." *You big idiot! Don't you know how*

*I feel about you?* Not that I was ready to tell him.

He hesitated, seemingly reluctant to believe me.

"And he has not had *any woman he wanted*. Gabriella...well, Gabriella would have never married him in Roma. She's always belonged to Marcello."

He gave me the slightest of nods. A tiny smile edged his lips, making me breathe a little easier. "Mayhap it is but one of the Betarrini women's many strengths, resisting the legendary Greco charm."

"Mayhap," I said with a teasing smile. I was still a little irked with him for thinking anything was going on between me and Rodolfo. I shivered. "Now, may I return to my quarters? I'm as wet as a fish!"

His smile grew. "And still, even such circumstances do not dim your beauty." He reached out and took a coil of my hair, wringing it until a stream of water fell to the stones at our feet. We laughed together, and his hand moved to my cheek. "M'lady," he said intently, water dripping down over his face too. He leaned down, and for a second, I thought he was going to kiss me. But instead, he touched his forehead to mine. "Dare I believe that you have feelings for me?" he whispered, his lips tantalizingly close.

Which kinda freaked me out.

"You are free to believe what you wish," I whispered back with a teasing smile, edging away. "There is no law against such things." I turned back toward the door, intending to go in, but he held it shut, hovering close. Deliciously close again. Teasing me.

"Evangelia," he said, his lips practically on my ear, his breath tickling my neck. "How long shall you torment me so?"

"That remains to be seen," I said, smiling up at him from the corner of my eyes.

"Ahh, how you wound me! Such...is the excruciating...pain," he gasped, pantomiming injury, "of unrequited love." He stumbled back a step.

I laughed under my breath and shook my head. "Good night, Luca," I said softly. "Please. Make certain your brother-in-arms does not perish in the cold, will you? This castello has seen her share of death this day."

"I shall see to it, m'lady." He bowed and took my hand, kissing it tenderly. "Forgive me for mistaking your merciful heart as something… other. I was a fool."

I nodded, accepting his apology. Still, he held my hand.

"Some day, you shall ask me to kiss you," he said.

"Such are the dreams of men," I said with a light laugh, turning to open the door.

"Dreams of you?" he asked, shaking his head and putting a hand to his heart as he faded into the shadows again. "Only upon every dark hour of the night, m'lady."

I giggled and shut the door behind me, reluctantly entering a new hallway full of the wounded. But as I bent to pick up a pail and ladle to give each man a drink, ignoring my soggy skirts and hair—plastered cloyingly to my face—I couldn't help but smile.

## CHAPTER 5

### –GABRIELLA–

It was my husband's stillness that awakened me. I wrenched myself up so I could get a better look at him, alarm flooding my heart.

But it was then that he gave me the tiniest of smiles, slowly opening his eyes as if it hurt to do so. "You Normans have the most unique methods of providing succor to those who ail," he managed.

"Marcello? Marcello!" I lifted my hands to my mouth. Was I dreaming? Could it be true? "How do you fare? You are obviously past the fever...."

"Indeed. Wait until I tell the men how you healed me." His smile broadened. "Climbing into bed, with none but that on...."

I hit him. Not hard. But he was well enough to tease me!

He caught my wrists and held them tight, grinning through a wince when I tried to wrench away. I stilled. "It only pains me that I am not yet well enough to make the most of my nurse's care. And state of undress."

I leaned down, crying and laughing through my tears. Kissing his cheeks, his eyes, his jaw.

"Ow! Ow!" He took my face in his hands and smiled through his wincing. "Cease your kissing! It hurts!"

"I'm sorry," I said, laughing. "I can't help myself! I'm so happy you're all right!" I lifted his hand to my lips and kissed each knuckle. "Does that hurt?"

"A little. From the fighting, you know."

"Ahh, right," I said, turning it over in my hand and kissing the pads of his palm. "Is that all right?"

"Mmm," he moaned, letting his lids droop. "Yes. Gives a man good things to dream about for the near future."

"Yes, yes," I said, gently placing his hand on the covers. I needed to ease up, not push him too much.

His eyes opened, and he stared at me. The morning light was streaming through the window, and my hair rolled in waves over either shoulder. "God has smiled upon me. I have the most beautiful wife in all the land."

I swallowed hard, remembering Nuncio Mancini and my promise to go to his widow. "Marcello, I was so frightened. So, so frightened."

His smile faded, and he took my hand in his. "We were foolish, Gabriella. Forgive me. Rushing home before we knew the way was clear. We'll take heed and be more cautious next time." He closed his eyes, clearly giving in to the weariness again.

I nestled against him once more. "Better yet, let's be done with battle, war. Let this bring a time of peace. Prosperity. Rest. For us all."

"Mmm, yes," he muttered. I ran my hand lightly across his chest, and he covered it with his own. Beneath my palm, I felt his heart beat, strong, steady, true. Mom had been right. Marcello Forelli wasn't leaving me. Not for a long, long while.

*Thank you, Lord,* I prayed. *Thank you for bringing him back to me. Thank you, thank you, thank you—*

A knock sounded at the door. "One moment!" I called, reluctantly pulling away from Marcello's side. I hurriedly left the bed, saw Marcello was asleep again, pulled on a robe, and then went to the door.

It was Giacinta, carrying a tray. I grinned and pulled her in. "He awakened!" I said in an excited whisper. "And his fever seems to have passed."

Her auburn eyebrows lifted in surprise and gladness. "Saints be praised!" she returned, bustling toward the table with the tray. She straightened and glanced over at Marcello. "Might I fetch anything for you or m'lord?"

"Nay. Just tell the others that the master appears to be through the worst of it."

"Indeed, m'lady," she said with a nod. "Would you like me to fetch your white gown today? Conte Lerici and the others prepare to ride out, carrying their wounded home, after Father Tomas sees to the funeral of the masses. Your mother said you would wish to take part."

Her words made my smile fade. So many men, gone. I made myself form the words. "How many, Giacinta?" I asked softly.

"All but thirty-three have been claimed by kin," she said. She straightened. "Not as bad as it might have been, had not Lord Forelli's friends come to our aid. And, thanks to your ministrations, many more than expected made it through the night. God willing, we shall not lose any others." She shook her head. "The ground is unyielding, heavy with the wet and nearly frozen by the cold. Sir Luca intends to bury them within the old *tomba etrusca*."

I frowned. The Etruscan tombs? Surely not Tomb Two... "Does it not put us further at risk to head north to bury them there?"

"Nay, m'lady," she said softly. "The Fiorentini have plenty of their own kin to see to burial, and the border is holding a mile north of the tombs. Our men shall see to it." A silence settled between us. Almost like a moment of honor for them all, be they Fiorentini or Sienese. For the hundredth time, I hoped that this would be it, the end of battle.

I cast about for a happy thought. "How do my mother and father fare this day?"

"Already among the wounded, seeing to their care." She nodded toward Marcello. "And like Lord Forelli, your father is much improved this morn."

I perked up and took her hands in mine. "Oh! Truly?"

She grinned. "Truly. He prepares to accompany your mother to the burial site. Do you believe Lord Forelli might—"

I shook my head, cutting her off, and glanced over to my husband, who was still out cold. There was no way he was well enough to go anywhere.

"Ah, well," she said. "The others shall understand. Shall I sit with him while you're gone? Fetch that Doctor Menaggio?"

"I'd be most grateful, Giacinta."

"Good, then. I'll fetch you the gown, but mayhap your boots, given the mud?" She shook her head. "After the rain, slippers…"

"Yes, please," I said.

"Then I'll be back to see to your hair and help you into your gown. Mayhap m'lord would take a bit of broth before you go?"

"If he wakes." I nodded in agreement. "I'll try."

## –EVANGELIA–

We left the castle gates under heavy guard. Luca was taking no chances, but we had to see the dead "to ground," as they said, before decomposition really set in. Already, I steered clear of the wagons full of bodies wrapped like mummies, the smell threatening to make me sick. We were all dressed in shades of ivory and white, a medieval tradition, even if the roads were riddled with mud. I loved the elegance of it. As I crested a hill and saw more than a hundred before me, making their way through the wood, I longed to sit down and sketch the scene.

We walked in silence, Gabi and I, last among those from the castello and our friends to leave, with only a rear guard behind us. None were on horseback other than guards and scouts, and I decided I liked it. It was stately, solemn, our ranks echoing with respect and sorrow for those who had been lost. Mom and Dad had gone ahead to make certain we were not losing anything vital in the two tombs Luca intended to utilize. The last thing we wanted was to have to extricate these bodies down the line....

In seven hundred years, Dr. Manero or his archeological competition would be able to distinguish what had been original to the tomb, and when the other bodies had been added. It would add all kinds of historical mystique. Once upon a time, it would've been the kind of thing that would have kept my folks chattering and theorizing for weeks.

If the tombs were ever found at all. Had it not been for Mom and that break with a local farmer... Trying to figure out the nature of time travel and the ramifications were enough to make my head spin. So I gave up.

On the next hill, right above the riverbed that had once marked the boundary between Paratore and Forelli land, Luca awaited us, along with Captain Pezzati, who always reminded me of an Italian Sean Connery with his distinguished, grizzled gray looks. Quietly, they waited for us to gather our skirts and then took our hands to help us pick our way over the rocks to the other side. And then we finished our walk by winding our way up the steeper road to the tiny valley that held the ancient

Etruscan tombs.

When we reached it, Mom and Dad were among the many others gathered on the grassy field that held the stone mounds. I wondered if this would be what heaven looked like when that day came. So many beloved faces gathered around, everyone dressed in white. *But probably without the mud...*

We divided, forming channels to the tombs, and the knights carried the bodies in, one after another. And then, with a nod from Tomas, who stood between the two tombs, men rolled the heavy stones back into place, locking them forever away. Gabi cried then, fat tears streaming down her face. But I had nothing. It was like I was empty, worn out, wrung out. As Father Tomas began sharing a few words of comfort, my eyes moved to Rodolfo. He was on horseback—one of twelve knights assigned to guard us—and consequently, his eyes moved slowly across the northern horizon. Again, I felt his grief like something tangible. Perhaps in this funereal moment, he could put his past to rest as we had our fallen comrades, and embrace his future.

Slowly, his head turned to survey us, and he caught my gaze. But then I followed his dark gaze toward Luca. Luca was watching us both. I tried to suppress a sigh and a roll of my eyes even as I felt a blush climb my cheeks. The last thing I needed was Luca's jealousy; not when we all were trying to sort out so many other complications among castello relationships.

I lifted my chin and returned Luca's gaze with a soft smile, waiting him out. And he gave. If there was one thing having a big sis had taught me, it was how to win at staring contests. It had to do with confidence. Security. Concentrating on the right thoughts. And there was nothing in me that should make Luca worry. Greco was trouble, from skin to core, and all I wanted to do was encourage him. As a friend. Nothing more. I'd always had a soft spot for the kids on the playground who nobody else would play with. It was just who I was. And Greco…well, it was like he was totally lost.

A woman's sob made me look to the ground, remembering myself, where I was, what was happening. There were so many here who had lost friends, brothers, sons. How close had we been to burying Marcello or Luca along with them? What if we had lost both of them? The thought of it made my heart pause and then pound painfully in my chest. Gabi had been talking about how this place, this time, made us appreciate life more; moments like this brought it home.

The service was done, and the group slowly turned toward home. I was waiting on Gabi and my parents, who lingered beside the tombs, talking, when Luca came near. He gave me a small smile and cocked his head, looking totally adorable. "Walk with me, m'lady?"

"Certainly," I said, taking the arm he offered. We walked in silence for a bit, watching as stair-step children—*had they had a child every year?*—in a family ahead of us split off to walk along the top of a fallen tree, then hid around others, playing a game of tag. Already, the tone of our group had moved from somber to celebratory, as was custom here; the walking seemed somehow easier now. I tried to take it all in, to capture certain moments in my memory like a photograph so that I could draw it later.

"Evangelia," Luca said, "as soon as Marcello is able to leave his bed, I am to leave for a time."

*Leave? Why would he leave?* I thought in a panic. But I was careful to construct my answer so I didn't come off as some sort of freakishly clingy girlfriend. "Oh? What calls you away?"

"My sister is due back any day now. I must travel to Aquina to collect her and bring her here."

I felt like an idiot. I knew next to nothing about his family, his past. Not that we'd had a lot of time for such things. "Forgive me, Luca.

Please. You know all about my family, but I know next to nothing of yours."

"I would not say that I know *all* about your family," he said with a conspiratorial grin. "There is much yet I'd care to know."

"You begin," I said, easing him off that line of thinking. "Your sister. She has been away?"

He nodded, and his smile grew. "She was promised to the Church at a young age and was sent away to an abbey until the day she took her vows. The trouble emerged when she decided that she loved God and the Church but that the life of a nun was not what she most desired."

I lifted a brow and nodded. I couldn't imagine taking on a nun's vow. "'Tis difficult to condemn her for it. I hope others will not."

"Nay," he said with a shake of his head. "Adela has always made her own way, and now shall be no different. My mother and father hoped the Church would curtail her headstrong spirit, but obviously that was to no avail."

I noticed he crossed himself when he spoke of his parents. "Your mother and father…they have passed on?"

He nodded. "A good many years ago, after Adela left for the abbey. My father was head of the woolen guild in Siena, and they set off for Spain to see to their business. Their ship was lost at sea."

"I'm so sorry."

He peered at me and then shrugged. "We live, we die. I miss them, but their lives were lived well."

We walked on for a bit, each lost in our own thoughts. Time and again, I couldn't get used to how the people of this age accepted death. "How long has it been since you have seen Adela, Luca?"

He pursed his lips and furrowed his brow in concentration. "I know not. Eight, nine years? After our parents died, we lived with our aunt and uncle. Then she was accepted as a novice, and I was invited to Castello

Forelli to train as a knight."

I stared at him. *Eight or nine years?* "Truly?" I caught myself as he gave me a *you're so weird* look. "That is, I can't imagine being apart from Gabriella for so long."

"Ah, yes," he said, his face moving back into a gentle smile. "Mayhap 'tis different in Normandy. Here, families tend to live their entire lives in the same village or town or castello, or they likely live very far apart indeed."

I nodded. "So...do you hope to convince Adela to return with you here?"

"I do. It's either Castello Forelli or my uncle's country villa, which is too close to the border, and far too difficult to defend, for my comfort." He stopped to glance back, surveying the rear guard following behind my parents and Gabi. When all appeared in order, he looked back to me and then reached down to take my hand. "I'd much prefer it if *everyone* I cared about would reside at Castello Forelli." He gave me a shy smile— one of the few such smiles I'd ever seen from him—and I squirmed under his gaze. That shyness was the antithesis of his constant flirtation, telling me it was real, not an act, his fondness for me. And I thought it pretty dang enticing.

"It'd make it far simpler to keep you all in order," he said. "To have you all at the castello."

I pulled away and resumed walking, smiling over his words. "So you believe you can keep us *in order*, then? Like a bunch of chickens in a coop?"

"'Twould have to be a hen keeper worthy of Hercules' court, but a man can try." We shared a quiet laugh, and he lifted a fallen limb from the road and flung it into the woods. "I think you'll be fast friends with Adela," he mused. "If she is as I remember her."

"Since she is kin to you, 'tis destiny that we shall be," I said. It was my turn to give him a shy smile.

And it made Luca grin as widely as if I had just made it Facebook Official.

---

That night we feasted, as was customary. Marcello insisted on coming down and was carried in to great cheers. Musicians were brought in, and there was dancing in the Great Hall, but there was a subdued feeling to it with so many men missing or sitting on the side, injured. In the end, I wished we had skipped it. Especially when the baker's daughter turned up, obviously intent on getting Luca to dance with her. She was about five inches shorter than me, with sultry brown eyes and long, luxurious brown hair. Oh, and did I mention that all her curves were, uh, pronounced? As in Snooki-with-more-clothes. There was not a knight in the courtyard that didn't watch her, chat with her, flirt with her, or dance with her.

Except for *my* knight, I thought in satisfaction. I pretended not to care, not to notice, as Luca dodged her when she offered him a platter of fruit, and then again when she came by with a jug of wine, leaning suggestively over it to give him an eyeful of cleavage. She pouted that he ignored her, and turned to pour for every other man around her like she'd been assigned bar duty. They buzzed around her like bees drawn to honey.

Then *I* got all pouty that Luca hadn't asked me to dance, absorbed as he was in one intent conversation after another with the men of the mysterious brotherhood who'd ridden to our defense—Conte Lerici, Sir Mantova, and Lords Santi, Gallo, Rizzo, Colombo and Hercolani. I knew they were all heading out tomorrow, but man, didn't the guy know

I really, really wanted to dance with him? My folks were out dancing like they had to memorize every medieval dance step ever made, and Gabi was absorbed in lady-of-the-house stuff, overseeing both the festivities and her husband, who still looked pretty pale. But at least he was up and eating and drinking. That had to be a good sign.

I tried to chat with some of the village women who I only knew by name—and had little in common with—and then gave up, sinking into a big chair near the fire. I sighed, wishing for the day Adela would come home with Luca. Maybe she could be the girlfriend I needed here. Because going stag to a castello dance was pretty much boring.

"Lady Betarrini," said a man to my left. I turned, and Conte Lerici bowed. "Would you do me the honor of a dance?"

"Certainly," I said, rising from my chair, trying to not get too excited. But maybe seeing me in the nobleman's arms would light a fire under Luca. The archers in Lerici's command—who weren't already on the dance floor—watched us as though they'd been assigned to do so. None of them had been brave enough to ask me to dance, but from the looks in their eyes, they wished they had. That was the problem with being one of the She-Wolves—it seemed like only the noblemen could approach us. It was like I wore an unwanted sign: Commoners Need Not Apply.

Not that I wanted them to apply. I just wanted to *dance*. With Luca. But if Conte Lerici was the best I could do, well, I really had no complaints. He was about twenty-four—way too old for me—but pretty cute. And if he was a blood brother with Luca, then he was all right by me. Not that saving our *glutei maximi* during the battle really had to be topped.

We bowed to each other, and he led me into the dance as easily as a duck takes to water, towing me along, giving me little clues as to when we were about to switch it up. I knew most of the dance steps, but he had a little showy addition—a lift of the arm, a twist, a twirl, a bow. I'd taken enough jazz/tap in my early years to follow his lead, which clearly delighted him. He lifted my hand to his lips and kissed my knuckles as others around us smiled and clapped for us as if we were on stage.

"One more, m'lady?" Conte Lerici asked.

I glanced over my shoulder at Luca, who was bending closer to the burly Mantova to hear him, apparently totally unaware that I was even on the dance floor. I turned back to my companion. "I'd be most pleased," I said.

He smiled back at me and gestured for me to lead the way, as smoothly elegant as Lord Greco. *Which brings to mind...* I looked around but didn't see Mr. Tall Dark and Handsome anywhere. In fact, I hadn't seen him since we'd been to the tombs.

"M'lord, have you seen Lord Greco since we returned this afternoon?" I asked Conte Lerici as he turned me once, twice.

"Do you find me lacking as a dance partner, m'lady?" he mused, a smile behind his eyes.

"Hardly, m'lord. I only wondered if he returned with the others."

We went through eight more counts, drawing away from each other and then nearing again. "I believe he volunteered for patrol duty and rode out with Captain Pezzati."

*Ahh,* I thought. It made sense. Luca wouldn't have allowed Rodolfo out of his sight after what had come down yesterday...unless a man like the captain was at his side. Pezzati was one of the few that Greco respected enough to listen to. *Maybe it's his age,* I decided. There weren't a lot of gray-haired knights around.

"Will you kindly tell me something else?" I asked, giving Conte Lerici a slow lift of my eyelashes. I know, it was bad. But a girl's gotta use what she's got.

He studied me as if trying to figure me out. "Anything, m'lady."

I turned away from him, and we circled each other, back to back.

When I turned again, I said, "Tell me of the brotherhood."

The light and intrigue slipped from his eyes, leaving only concern. "That is a question for Lord Marcello or Sir Luca."

"Oh, but m'lord... Why so secretive if 'tis nothing but good?"

He studied me as he took my waist and turned with me. "There are many who would think it was more than it is...and others who would think it was less."

*Well, gee, thanks,* I thought. *Way to give me a whole lotta nothin'.* I tried a different avenue. "What brought you all together?"

His smile partially returned. "Friendship. Long summer nights spent prowling the villages for beautiful young girls to court. Finding hidden mineral waters. Feasts to which we weren't invited but sneaked into anyway."

"You didn't!"

"We did," he said casually.

"How many are there?" I asked as the music came to an end. "Did everyone that still lives ride to our defense?"

He bowed and then kissed my hand, purposefully not answering. Then he straightened, still holding my hand in his. "'Tis Firenze's own question, now." His eyes were gentle, on mine. "And best you not know the details. For your own safety."

I frowned, and then he let go of my hand. But instead of leading me from the floor, he bowed toward Luca, who took his place before me. Luca watched as his friend eased around a passel of hopeful girls still looking eager to score a dance before the night was through.

A blush climbed my cheeks. Had Luca heard me trying to squeeze Conte Lerici for information? The music began again, and the ten couples left on the floor edged into the first steps. But Luca was not smiling.

"Why were the last words from my friend, to you, 'for your own safety'?"

I forced a smile. "Oh. 'Twas nothing. I only asked about your mysterious brotherhood. Rest assured, he danced around my questions as artfully as he took to the steps of that last song."

We took a turn, and when I faced him again, he was still not smiling. "His words are true, Evangelia. You must not inquire further."

It was my turn to frown. "But why? If it involves you...Marcello, Tomas, Rodolfo...isn't it best we know?" Wasn't their business our business now?

"The brotherhood...given our success, Firenze will be keen to know more of it too."

*Firenze.* I was so sick of their lurking threat I wanted to scream at the name.

"Even in Siena—"

"'Tis hardly a secret, right?" I interrupted. "Every responsive member rode to our defense."

He hesitated, his frown deepening, and then I knew. There were some who wished to ride but couldn't, for some reason. Because they were afraid? Were others still behind Fiorentini lines as Rodolfo once was?

I rested my hand on his arm and could almost feel the triangular tattoo beneath his sleeve. I had a hundred other questions to ask about it, but it wouldn't further my cause this night. Gabi would choose to press and lose in this moment. I would give and hope to win the moment I had a more opportune chance.

My eyes went to my sister's chair as the dance ended. She'd left—probably to see Marcello back to their rooms. But the questions in my mind lingered, and I figured that if anyone knew the scoop, it'd be my sister.

"Thank you, Luca," I said. "I think I'll go and check on Gabriella and Marcello and see if they have need of anything before I retire myself." I looked over his shoulder; my parents were still rockin' the medieval dance floor like they intended to release their own version of the game *Just Dance 1345*. They'd be no help; I needed to find Gabi.

Luca kissed my hand and searched my eyes. "I shall look for you on the morrow."

"On the morrow," I repeated, and left.

## CHAPTER 6

### –GABRIELLA–

Marcello was looking like he might pass out any second, so I persuaded him to leave the Great Hall. But he refused to be carried again. *Stupid male pride...* I hated that he was so stubborn as to not accept help, but my heart leaped at knowing that he felt well enough to rise at all. Hand in hand, we left the courtyard, which was still wet with rain, and entered the corridor that led to our quarters. Moans and the stench of rotting flesh met us; fifteen men still languished inside, each battling to recover from his wounds. There were half the men that there were last night—a relief, for certain. Many had come to collect their men this day, eager to care for them at home.

I paused among those that remained, but Marcello urged me on. "They are cared for," he whispered in my ear, nodding to the servants milling about them, giving them water and soup, changing bandages... trying to settle them in for the night. Doctor Menaggio entered from the next corridor's hallway and gave us a nod.

A guard leaning against the wall hurriedly straightened and nodded as we passed. "See that no one but Captain Forelli, Captain Pezzati, or any of the lady's family is permitted upstairs," Marcello said.

"Yes, m'lord."

Marcello led me up the curving steps of the turret and then down the hall toward my room. He closed the door behind me and immediately drew me into his arms, grimacing as if it hurt to hold me close.

"Marcello," I said gently as his warm lips moved over my brow. "Maybe we should wait…"

"Wait for what?" he teased. "This?" He moved on to covering my eyelids, my cheeks, my ear with tender, soft kisses. He smelled warm and inviting, easing away my fears. But I opened my eyes and nudged him aside as he kissed my neck, tickling me. "Shouldn't you return to bed, m'lord?"

"Undoubtedly," he said, moving to kiss my lips, parting them with his own. He wrapped his arm around my back and pulled me close, grunting in pain but refusing to release me. I settled in, kissing him back with equal passion.

A knock sounded then at our door. Marcello groaned in frustration. "If it's anyone but whom I told that man to allow passage…" he grumbled, as he turned toward the door.

"Nay!" I said with a grin, moving to block his way. "Allow me." I'd deal with whoever had come to call and prevent them from suffering as a result of Marcello's frustration. I went to the door and opened it a crack.

My sister. At least the guard had obeyed Marcello's orders.

"Lia," I said, frowning. "Are you all right?"

She paused, looking suddenly ill at ease. Tendrils of hair had slipped her knot and drifted across her neck, obviously from the dancing. "I'm interrupting." She shook her head. "I'm sorry. We'll talk tomorrow. I was just checking on you. Marcello is—" She blushed. "He's better. I can see it in your eyes."

"Marcello is much better," I said, giving her a soft smile. I took a breath and slipped out the door, closing it behind me. "Are you okay?"

"Fine! Fine." She shifted her weight back and forth, telling me she was anything but fine. "Sorry. I'm, uh...not used to this whole thing. You know, you being married. I just thought...I wanted to ask..." She shook her head. "This is seriously embarrassing. Luca just... Look, let's talk tomorrow."

I hesitated, feeling torn between my sister's need and the desire to get back to my husband. "Are you sure?"

"I'm sure," she said, giving me a false smile. "Go back. I'm so glad he's doing better. Do you need anything? Either of you?"

"No. We're okay. Lia," I said, leaning forward, "are you sure you're sure? I could take five minutes."

"I'm *sure*. Goodnight, Gabs." She turned and walked away from me then, down the corridor.

Part of me wondered if I should chase after her, make her tell me what was up. Part of me wondered if I should find Doctor Menaggio and see if I could assist him with the remaining patients.

But my husband decided my course of action for me. He opened the door a crack. Finding me alone, he took my hand and pulled me through, back inside. Then he latched and locked the door, lifted my hands to the wall above me, and began to kiss me like he never, ever intended to let me go again.

---

The next morning, with all the servants in a frenzy to take care of our guests, I convinced Marcello to stay put in the Great Hall by the fire while I went to saddle horses for me and Lia. She intended to ride out with the men and see our guests properly off; I wanted to go with her. It'd give me a chance to find out what she had really wanted last night.

I entered the stables and immediately saw Rodolfo Greco brushing his gray gelding, obviously as intent on saddling his own horse as I was.

"Rodolfo," I said with a nod. I paused, nervously looking over my shoulder, wondering if I could snag a squire to do the work. But they were all busy elsewhere, franticly helping so many men, all leaving at once.

Rodolfo studied me as he continued brushing the gelding. He looked much better today—obviously he'd slept last night since he hadn't been spending the night in the stocks. *Not that I should be paying attention to such things.* "May I be of service, m'lady?"

"Nay," I said, moving past him and his horse. "I can see to it myself. The servants are all so busy—"

"You intend to saddle your own horse?" he said, looking over his shoulder, one eyebrow raised.

"Certainly."

"Allow me. I'll bring her out to you."

"'Tis not only my own. I intend to see to Evangelia's as well."

"I'll saddle them both."

"Nonsense. I can at least do one." I went into my chestnut mare's stall and reached up to stroke her nose. "Good morning, Zita," I said. I put a hand to either of her cheeks and looked into her brown eyes, wanting to talk to her but feeling self-conscious in Rodolfo's presence.

A stable hand came in and exchanged a few words with Rodolfo, then moved out. Then two knights. It was fine, I told myself. *Get a grip, Gabs. How can he relax if you don't?* It was a totally public place, and we were suitably apart. Besides, he'd soon have his gelding saddled and be gone, leaving me to my own tasks.

I quickly brushed Zita's back and then reluctantly settled a small blanket and sidesaddle atop her, reaching down under her belly for the far strap. Quickly, I looped the strap through a buckle and locked it down, then checked two others, making sure they didn't need to be adjusted. When I looked up, Rodolfo was in the stall with me, placing the bit into Zita's mouth and wrapping the bridle over her head.

"I'm all right, Rodolfo," I said. "I can see to it from here."

"I insist," he said in dismissal, moving out of the stall toward Lia's mare. "This is Lady Evangelia's mount?"

I nodded. "Yes, but truly—I am fine. Please. Go and report to Sir Luca before he places you in the stocks again."

He gave me a slight smile and began to brush the mare. "Truth be told, once is enough for me on that score. I'll see to Evangelia's mount. 'Tis not proper for the lady of the castle to do it, not when there's an able man at hand."

*Ridiculous, chauvinistic, archaic thinking!* "Yes, well, there is hardly a proper bone in my body, it seems." I turned to take the blanket from the wall, waiting for him to finish.

He frowned, his movements frustrated now as he brushed the mare's back as if intending to skin her instead. "Truly, Gabriella. Must you always be so stubborn?"

"Yes," I said, throwing the blanket across the mare's back. "I suppose I must." I turned to take Lia's saddle off the wooden horse holding it, but it stuck. I yanked, but the wooden stand threatened to come with it.

A call rang out in the courtyard. They were ready to go. I grimaced and bent to see what had snagged underneath.

"Allow me," Rodolfo said, reaching for the saddle, over me.

"M'lady, we are..." Luca said as he entered the stables. His mouth opened as his eyes went from Rodolfo—his hands on the saddle, on either side of me—to me, slowly, awkwardly rising in front of Rodolfo, caught between saddle and man.

He rushed us, grabbing Rodolfo's shirt in his hands. And once again, Rodolfo wasn't fighting.

"You misunderstand," I said, reaching out to grab Luca's solid arm, which was pulsing with fury. I yanked him aside and moved to face him. "This ends here," I ground out. "There is no need to defend my honor because my honor *has not been threatened.*"

"Of what do you speak?" Luca said. "I entered, expecting to find you alone and in need of aid, but 'tis him, with his hands all over you again!"

"All over me!" I sputtered. "Luca! Cease your silly imaginings! I am your cousin's bride. Whole and true. No other man shall ever have me." I put my hand on his chest, which was heaving in agitation, and leaned closer. "Lord Greco 'twas only assisting me with Lia's saddle. Nothing more. Please," I added in a whisper, leaning still closer. "'Tis difficult enough without you constantly coming to false conclusions. I made my decisions in Roma…forever. Do you understand me? *Forever.*"

He studied me, searching my eyes as if to see if I was lying or not. "Forgive me, Greco," he said, still staring at me. "I assumed…wrongly." Only then did Luca's eyes flick in his friend's direction.

Rodolfo, hands on his hips, gave him a wary nod. "Luca…in time, shall you trust me?" he asked quietly. "Or shall it always be this way?"

Luca pursed his lips, and I almost could hear a clock tick as seconds went by. "I know not," he said at last. "I wish to trust you, man. I do. But shadows of yesterday dim today's sun." He glanced at me. "And Gabriella…Marcello…'tis a raw place. You think I am on edge.… When Marcello is himself again, you must take the utmost care."

Greco looked at him intently. "Send me away on a mission. On castello business. Wherever you see fit. 'Tis best for all of us."

Luca rubbed his neck and stared at him in frustration. "You think I wouldn't, if I could? Nay. I shall not send you to your death."

What were they talking about? Rodolfo couldn't leave the castello? It hit me, then. He'd be more of a target than even Lia and I were, at this point. Firenze's traitorous son. Secret brother-in-arms to Lord Forelli. Newest owner of the wretched Castello Paratore.

I yanked up again on Lia's saddle, and this time it gave way. I turned and threw it over her mare's back. "Go. Both of you. Create some sort of diversion so that I might emerge with my and Lia's mounts and not attract any attention. For now that you have both been in here for five minutes, with me, there is *cause* for attention."

"As you wish, m'lady," Luca said, clearly seeing the wisdom of my words. He turned to stride out but waited at the doorway for Rodolfo.

With one long glance into my eyes, Rodolfo turned, took his gelding's reins, and followed his captain out.

Lia entered then, looking after the departing, glowering knights and back to me.

"Don't ask," I said.

✦

The men said their farewells to Marcello, who stubbornly remained in his chair in the Great Hall, rather than going back to bed where I knew he'd be most comfortable. But that was up to him to figure out—I could only encourage him so far without nagging him.

"Never without men to guard them," Marcello said to Luca, nodding toward me and Lia. "To the crossroads and back." I slid my broadsword into the sheath at my back as Lia shouldered her bow.

"As you say, m'lord," Luca agreed. But his expression said, *Are you really looking, Cousin? These girls are ready, with or without me.*

I hid a smile and left through the castello gates, surrounded by ten of the most highly trained Forelli knights, and riding alongside Lia. A half mile distant, at the crossroads, we dismounted and said farewell to Lords Santi, Colombo, Hercolani, Gallo and Rizzo, then Sir Mantova, apparently the only guy without a piece of land in the bunch. Each took my hand and kissed it. Conte Lerici was the last to draw near, but he went to Lia first. "If you shall ever deem Sir Luca wanting, you know where you may find me," he said, holding her hand and winking at Luca.

"That's quite enough, Lerici," Luca said with a smile, but there was steel behind his eyes.

What was this? I wondered. Someone was giving Luca a little competition?

Conte Lerici moved over to me and kissed my hand. "Thank you for coming to our aid, m'lord," I said. "Had you not…" I shook my head. "My family, the entire Forelli household, owes you many times over."

"Think nothing of it," he said, smiling into my eyes. "'Twas a dual honor to serve the She-Wolves as well as my brothers."

"Rest assured, it won't be forgotten."

"I hope not," he said, giving me a genteel nod. "Until the fine day we cross paths again, Lady Forelli." He nodded again toward Lia. "Lady Betarrini."

The Lerici knights rode out then, so elegant in their camel capes, their bows across their shoulders. Not a one of them had been lost in battle, and yet they'd succeeded in taking many of our enemies down. A shiver ran down my back as they grew small on the horizon, galloping now, intent on making it home before sundown.

"Luca," I said as he helped me back into my saddle. Rodolfo was lifting Lia to hers.

"Yes, m'lady?"

"Is the village named Cavo far from here?"

"Cavo, m'lady?" he said with a frown. "Nay, it's but a quarter-hour away."

"I would like to stop there. The day is clear, our guests properly seen off. And I made a promise to a dying man to speak to his young widow."

"Your husband bade me promise to see you to the crossroads and home, nowhere else."

"Yes, well, had I known Cavo was so close, I might have suggested it to him. Come, we won't take long."

Luca squinted his eyes and peered across the horizon. "What is it?" I asked, so only he could hear. "The Fiorentini are long gone, yes? Your patrols have cleared the wood of every one. Even now, there are three more patrols along the border, yes?"

He didn't answer me immediately, seemingly considering my request. "It'd be best if you sought your husband's permission before taking your journey."

I drew myself upright and lowered my chin. "I might be my lord's lady, but I am my own woman still."

Luca smiled and cocked his head. "That you are." He waved the twins forward, as well as Captain Pezzati and Rodolfo, then sent them ahead, presumably to make certain that nothing unwelcome greeted us in the village or en route. The rest of us moved out at a more leisurely pace. It felt good to be out; the sun was shining, and it was about fifty degrees—cold and crisp. *A clean sort of day*, my mom would call it.

"Can't you do something about this?" Lia asked, quietly enough that only I could hear. She gestured toward her sidesaddle. "I mean, as lady of the castle, wife to one of the Nine, can't you make a royal decree or whatever to say, 'Hey, girls get to ride in whatever kind of saddle they want!'"

I smiled over at her. "Wish I could. You know Mom and Dad's stance on that kind of thing. Avoid anything we can that might change—"

"—the course of history," she finished for me. We both had heard it ten times. "But it's kinda tough, being us," she said, with a conspiratorial grin. "When you enter into medieval times as She-Wolves, it's a little hard to change up your stride."

"I'll say." We rode a bit in silence. "Wouldn't it be cool if we could introduce jeans?" I whispered.

"Jeans? Just pave the way for pants of any sort, and I'd be happy. And a decent bra and underwear, please, while you're at it."

"Oh, Lia, *toothpaste*. I miss that most of all, I think. That baking soda mixture Mom whips up is disgusting. I'd kill for minty fresh breath again." Even Vivaro's coal and mint sticks hadn't been quite the same—

"Minty fresh breath?" she said. "I'd trade that for a roll of TP. Oh, no. I take that back. I'd trade it for tampons. This on the rag stuff is totally primeval." She looked over at me. "Can't you at least get decent latrines in order at the castello? I mean, there were latrines in Roman times, so it's not totally out of order."

"Yeah, Mom's on that track too. I think we might be able to move on that front."

A whistle echoed down the road, and we looked up to see Rodolfo on the ridge, his gelding dancing beneath him. He gave a motion to Luca, telling him all was clear and he was moving on to another flank. Then Captain Pezzati joined him, and they rode off together.

"So what came down in the stables with Lord Dangerous?" Lia asked, watching him go.

"Nothing. Luca's all freaked out any time we're in a room together." I shook my head in frustration. "Which doesn't make things easier."

"Luca's the same way with me. He doesn't trust Greco."

"I get it. I do. But the man gave up everything for us. I think we all need to just chill out and give it another go. The whole trust thing."

"He's pretty miserable," she said. "Caught. Between Siena and Firenze. And…" I met her intent gaze, and she looked away, to her horse. "...other things," she finished in a mumble.

I swallowed hard. "He'll find his path. We just have to give him a little time." But in my mind, I was replaying the scene in the stables. How could Rodolfo find the space to sort out his feelings, his direction, if even his closest friends leaped to the worst conclusions?

"That's what I was trying to tell him the other night," she said. "When he was in the stocks. It could be a new beginning for him. Kind of like coming here has been for us. Do we miss our old lives? Yes. But it's mostly the conveniences, the knowns. Could we have had good lives there, in 'Normandy'? Sure. Would it have been easier there? Sure. But that doesn't take away from the value of what we can find here."

I smiled and stared over at her. "For my baby sis, you sure are a wise old woman. Did he hear you? Listen to you?"

She smiled over my praise and then looked to the horizon, where we'd glimpsed Rodolfo. "I don't know. That man runs deep. He's like that lake in Missouri."

"Oh, yeah!" I said. A few years ago, we'd gone to some archeological symposium with our parents in Branson, of all places. And being the geeks they were, they'd hooked up with some naturalist who led us on a hike into a tiny lake. The lake ran so deep, there were sightless, colorless creatures at the bottom that had never seen the sun. But it also offered some of the cleanest, freshest water available for miles. The Indians once thought it had medicinal properties. That was totally Rodolfo—sparkling and beautiful on the top, with something else, dark and mysterious lurking beneath.

The question was: how were we to deal with what lurked beneath?

I'd talk to Tomas the minute we got back. He might have some idea on how to help our friend. *Our friend.* The phrase echoed through my mind.

"Lia, what did you want to talk to me about last night?" I asked, forcing my thoughts to other subjects.

"Oh, two things, really. One is this whole brotherhood thing," she said, dropping her tone again. "They're all really closed-mouthed about it. Do you have the scoop?"

"Not much," I said, shaking my head. "I gather it's part of the deal—kind of like a secret society, of sorts."

"Even your wifely status doesn't grant you access?"

"Not yet, anyway. Why? Why do you care so much?"

She shrugged. "I don't know. It just seems like we should know the details now that we've fought alongside them all. Or most of them, anyway. Lerici hinted that now that Firenze knows of them, there might be trouble. And I don't like being kept out of it." She shifted on her saddle. "And Luca—"

"The village of Cavo, m'lady," said the knight ten feet in front of me. I frowned, my attention swinging from my sister to our escort.

Now that I was here, what was I to say to Mrs. Mancini? I felt totally unprepared. We pulled our steeds to a stop as Luca inquired about the right house. The young girl in the doorway looked us all over, taking in the Forelli gold, then widening her eyes when she spied me and Lia. Quickly, she picked up a basket and came out to point toward the house, still a ways down the road. Luca nodded his thanks, and she gave him a little bob of a curtsy, blushing a bit.

Then she waited, eyes round, hands clutching the basket at her hip, until we moved past. Time and again, I still couldn't get used to that whole star struck thing we seemed to bring on anytime anyone recognized the "She-Wolves." I hoped that someday, somehow, that would fade.

It probably would. Something new would take our place. Something more interesting, as we settled into the normal seasons of medieval life. If we could just stay out of battle…and not get kidnapped…that kind of thing just kept growing our legend, for obvious reasons. There were some wild stories out there. Stories of me and Lia heading into battle blindfolded, just to have a real challenge. Stories of us binding our legs together like we were some three-legged monster female knight, to show off our skills all the more. Stories of me slipping out of the cage in Firenze, the mansion in Roma, using magical abilities. Stories of me swimming the length of the Arno River, underwater. The men of the brotherhood had all been trading those stories last night, partially teasing us, partially honoring us.

*Ridiculous.* It'd taken every ounce of strength we had just to survive every battle, make each escape. It was a miracle, really, that we were whole and healthy at the moment. We could've died in so many ways on so many occasions. "Let them tell their tales," Marcello had said to me when I tried to correct them. "You give our people hope. Does it matter if they garner that through truth or some variation of the truth? Hope is hope."

Luca pulled to a stop, and I focused on the young woman in the tiny front yard of a cottage. Signora Mancini. She was hoeing a garden furrow, turning over dead plants, tilling the soil. But when she spied us, she stopped, placed both hands on the top of the handle and held on tight as if it might steady her. I could read her thoughts in her wide, brown eyes.

Seeing such a party wearing the Forelli colors, seeing me and Lia, meant one thing. Her husband wasn't coming home. If he was alive, we would've sent for her or brought him to her.

Luca glanced back at me, wondering how I wished to proceed. I slipped my feet from the stirrups and slid from the saddle, ignoring decorum. I had to get to her before she collapsed. I nudged aside a nosy goat that trotted up to greet me. And I strode toward her, not stopping, until I stood directly before her. "Signora Mancini?"

She nodded numbly, her eyes wide and unseeing now. Her nose was round, bumpy, and her cheeks sunken, her arms terribly thin. Clearly, they'd had little. But the loss, the vacuum I sensed opening within her, told me they had once had much in each other.

"*Per favore*," I began. "Might we go inside to speak privately?"

She nodded again, still not quite focusing on me. But she turned and dragged herself toward the tiny cottage, dropping the hoe beside her as if she had forgotten she once held it at all.

"M'lady?" Luca said, one eyebrow cocked. He'd dismounted, come up beside me. But I waved him away. No one had thought to set a trap for me here. Unless it was one of the cats that weaved in and out of the front door, which was partially askew. "I'll remain right here," he said quietly, positioning himself by the door.

I followed the young woman inside and blinked in the darkness. The cottage was perhaps ten by ten feet, with a tiny ledge of a "kitchen," a miniscule table with two chairs, and a bed. It was old, the walls crumbling, but the bed was neat and tidily made, with a threadbare but clean, woven blanket.

"How long have you been married?" I asked her, taking a chair, gesturing to the other one, when it became obvious she was so lost in her own thoughts that she would never offer me a seat.

"What?" she asked dimly, falling heavily into the other one and rubbing her temple. "Oh. Two weeks, as of a few days ago," she said.

I waited for her to settle, to ask me why I'd come. But she only ran her fingers around her right temple and stared out the window.

"Signora Mancini, do you know who I am?" It was important that she focus. That she remember what I was about to tell her. Otherwise, I feared she'd go on hoeing that garden, day and night, dim with shock and waiting for her husband to return to her.

"You are Lady Gabriella Betarrini," she mumbled, still staring out the window.

*Close enough,* I decided. Many had not yet heard we'd wed. "And what is your name?"

"Bibiana Mancini, m'lady."

I paused. "Bibiana, forgive me, but I'm afraid I come with a hard word."

"Oh?" Her fingers dropped to her lap. She froze, waiting for me to go on. But she didn't look my way.

Gently, I reached for her hand and covered it with both of my own, pulling her to face me. I looked up into her eyes, swallowing hard around a lump in my throat. "It hurts me to tell you this, but your husband died. He was wounded in battle. In the end, the wounds were too grave for him to survive."

Her big, brown eyes stared down into mine.

"Bibiana?" I whispered.

"He can't be gone. He can't." Tears welled in her eyes, and she continued to stare at me without blinking.

For a moment I thought about Marcello—how scared I'd been that I was about to lose him forever. I remembered losing my dad—and the terrible, dark chasm of grief that had opened for all of us afterward. "I wish I came with a different word," I said. "But nay. He is buried with other knights who so bravely fought for Siena. Forgive me for not sending for you to take part in the funeral. I was…" I looked to the window. What? "Busy?" I swallowed hard. "You can come to Castello Forelli when you are ready to pay your respects. I'll take you there myself."

The tears crested then, understanding beginning to seep through the frozen facade of her face. "How did you know where I was? Where to come?" she asked.

"I spoke with your Nuncio. In his last moments, he asked me to come to you, to tell you…" I stopped, belatedly remembering that he hadn't had time to tell me exactly what he wished to say. I remembered his face so clearly, the emotion etched in every pore.

"What?" she asked, bringing her other hand to mine and squeezing. "Please. Tell me. What did he want you to tell me?"

I looked at her, remembering her husband, the earnestness of his face. His intent. I knew what he had wanted to say. What she needed to hear. He simply hadn't had time to utter the words. "He said to tell you he loved you," I said. "He asked you to forgive him for not being able to return to you. That all he wanted was a long life beside you." I smiled through my own tears.

Her eyes went back and forth, searching my own. "Bless you, m'lady," she said. "Bless you for coming to tell me."

"It was the least I could do," I said. "Do you have family within reach? A mother? Father? Siblings?"

She shook her head, a small sob escaping her throat.

"No matter. We shall see to your needs until you find your way. I don't wish for you to fret. I shall send food, supplies for your cottage, your garden. Your payment to the landlord…whatever you need, you come to me. Do you understand? Your husband paid with his life to aid us. I shall make sure his widow doesn't suffer further."

She nodded, tears still running in twin streams down her cheeks.

"I know it must feel horrible, Bibiana," I said. "But somehow, some way, someday, you shall find peace, joy. It might be a long time from now. But it will be well. I promise."

As she nodded and released my hands, as I rose, I wondered what sort of madness made me think I could promise such things. I was a She-Wolf, not God.

And somehow, I felt like I'd just wandered into territory that was His alone.

## CHAPTER 7

### –EVANGELIA–

We were riding home, sad and somber after our visit to Signora Mancini, and only the men shared quiet words between them. For Gabi and me, I think it just felt too real, too close, to be with a girl about our own age who was grieving her man. Only one thing comforted me—the guys we'd fallen for rocked this whole fight-for-your-life thing. Again and again, I'd seen Luca and Marcello escape impossible situations. As had Gabi and I.

*Don't rehearse your problems,* Dad always said. Meaning, we were only supposed to go through our problems when they were actually upon us. Which was good advice. Because thinking about going to visit Luca's grave, as Signora Mancini would eventually visit her husband's, just about made me want to burst into tears right then.

Luca caught me looking at him, my eyes actually wet with tears—of all the idiotic things—and dropped back to speak to me. "M'lady?" he asked. "May I be of assistance?"

"Nay, I was only…" I said, shaking my head, sniffing. *I was only what? Thinking about how sad I'd be if you died?* "'Tis nothing," I said, shaking my head again.

"Are you certain?"

I nodded, trying to smile brightly, assure him. He was peering at me, as if wondering if he should *force* me to tell him what was going on, when his chin lifted and he wheeled his horse about, scanning the horizon.

"Luca?"

I smelled it, then. Smoke.

"There," I said, pointing to our left. North. A curving column of black rose above the forest and continued to climb.

Luca's eyes met Lord Greco's as he and Captain Pezzati rode up from their scouting position. "That's near Castello Santi, if not the castello itself."

They nodded in clear agreement. Gabi and I shared a long look. Lord Santi? We'd bid him farewell but a few hours ago.

"Escort the women back to the castello," Luca said to the twins.

"Nay," Gabi said, slipping from her saddle and motioning for me to do the same. She quickly unbuckled the belly strap and yanked the saddle off her mare's back.

"M'lady, what do you think you're doing?" Luca said in exasperation. He dismounted and strode over to her.

"We shall ride with you. They'll need help. From all of us," she said, her tone brooking no argument. She tossed her saddle behind a big boulder. "You cannot send Georgii and Lutterius with us. You need them. And mayhap we can be of assistance too."

"M'lady," Luca said, rubbing his mouth in frustration. "Fire may mean the castello has suffered *attack*. I cannot very well lead you into that."

"Nay," she said, climbing the boulder and tossing her leg over the horse's bare back. "I shall lead *you* there."

I laughed under my breath. Trust my sister to put a man in his place, every time. I wished I could do it half as well. The others bit back smiles while I hurriedly unstrapped my saddle. Luca grabbed Gabi's reins.

"Gabriella," Luca said in exasperation, looking up at her, "what would Marcello have you do?"

"Permission, sir, to go on ahead," Lord Greco interrupted.

Luca lifted a brow and, with a flick of his chin, let them go scout it out. Greco and Captain Pezzati took off at a gallop. Luca sent two others after them.

"Marcello would ride to the aid of his friends," Gabi said. "And enlist every able body he had at his disposal. Come, we waste time. We're armed, just as you are. Cease your fretting. And *release my horse.*"

He dropped her reins, his hands lifted in resignation, his mouth in a grim line. She whipped her mare around and headed down the road after the others. Luca motioned to five knights. "Off with you, then. Stay with her."

Luca turned doleful eyes on me as I prepared to mount my horse from the same boulder Gabi had used. "I suppose it would be folly to believe you, at least, shall return with the twins to the castello?"

"Forgive me, Luca," I said. "I cannot." I nodded after my sister. "Where she goes, I go."

"I feared you would say that," he said. With one easy move, he grabbed hold of his saddle horn and mounted. "Do not let any harm come to Lady Evangelia," he said firmly to the twins. "Or you shall answer to me."

"Yes, sir," Georgii said.

Luca kicked his mount's flanks and took off after Gabi, leaving me with the brothers.

"All is right with my world," Georgii said, trotting beside me.

"How so?" I asked.

"The She-Wolves are back in the wild."

I laughed under my breath. But I quickly sobered as I caught the tension of the men beside me. The smoke was thick in the woods, making it appear almost foggy. As we slowed, I eased my bow from my shoulder and nocked an arrow, my eyes burning as I scanned for enemies. Where were Gabi and the others in our party? Still ahead?

We heard a woman scream, and then the keening of someone crying in grief, perhaps a quarter mile distant. But the sounds came to us as if ghosts carried them along in the smoke. The crack of a branch brought all our heads around, the men moving to guard me. It was then we saw the deer, running away. We all let out uneasy laughs and sighs of relief.

As we neared the end of the woods, the smoke grew thicker. And when we finally exited the trees, we saw the small castello, her lone tower engulfed in flames. A servant milled about outside, hand over her mouth; another knelt between the bodies of the dead, weeping.

At first, I thought it had just been a fire. Fires started all the time, given all the candles and fires for warmth and kitchens that relied upon wood-fueled stoves. Castello Forelli had a whole "fire brigade" pantry filled with buckets and blankets to wet down. But as we got closer, I saw an arrow through the chest of one man, a knight, and another man with a clear sword wound. And other knights dead in the courtyard now visible through the gates.

"Stay close, m'lady," Lutterius said, seeing it too.

"I shall," I said dimly. "But we must find the others." Where was Gabi? My eyes scanned the rest of the crowd. I spotted Ziti, her mare, munching at a hay pile, seemingly unconcerned about the fire. Then Greco and Captain Pezzati's mounts.

I slid from my horse, as did the knights, each coming to either side of me.

A woman stumbled out of the front gate, her face black with soot, a small child in her arms. She let out a sob, gasping for breath—from the smoke? From grief? Tears washed away twin tracks down her cheeks.

"Oh no," I said, rushing toward her. I took the boy from her arms, wondering if I might resuscitate him with mouth-to-mouth—deciding Mom and Dad could just deal with me using twenty-first-century emergency care—but then I saw the long, thin, bloody line across his throat.

The child had been murdered. I nearly dropped him.

I fell to my knees and hurriedly laid him down and backed away, staring at him in horror.

"Ezio Santi," choked out the woman. "M'lord's only heir."

Gabi, Greco, and Captain Pezzati came out then, helping men and women, and behind them came our other knights, carrying bodies or helping others escape. Last came Luca, carrying a woman's body. All of them were coughing, faces covered in black.

All of them wept. Every one.

Luca gently set down the woman, and I rushed over to him, wrapping my arm around his shoulders as he shook. She, too, had been murdered.

"You knew her?" I asked, crying now, myself. Never had I see him cry before. Never.

He pulled up the bottom of his tunic to wipe his eyes and nose. "Lady Nerina Santi. Marcello and I grew up with her."

"Where is Lord Santi?" I asked, reliving memories of last night, seeing him laughing, drinking.

Luca shook his head. "The fire...it was too hot. He was..." He rose and went to the servant weeping over the little boy. "Who were they? Who attacked you?"

The woman looked up at him. "They came disguised as merchants. And once inside, they poured out from their wagon, eight men. I'd never seen so many men, so bent on killing. We ran and hid after the first knights fell before them. God help us," she said, choking back a sob. "We ran and hid!"

He reached out to touch her shoulder. "Had you not, you'd be dead too," he said. "Be at peace. Lord Santi would have wanted you safe."

I looked past him. He was right. There were five dead maids laid out, several footmen, several more knights. In a castle this size...how many more had been lost? But Lord Santi had departed Castello Forelli with a good twenty men, just hours ago. "Where are the other knights?"

"Most of them dead, inside," said the maid bitterly, glancing over her shoulder at the fire licking away at the timbers between stones. "They surprised us so. The men had just disarmed and went to their barracks—"

"Most?" Luca asked, his brow furrowing. He was wondering the same thing as I—how had eight men overcome so many trained knights?

"Most, m'lord. Others fought the fires. A few gave chase but they have yet to return." She looked over to the woods, her expression bleak.

"Were the men Fiorentini?" Luca asked.

"'Twas impossible to tell," she said, her eyebrows curved into an anxious arc. "But they left this mark on the servants they killed." She rose and, sobbing, pointed to a maid's ankle. On it, was a bloody cut in the shape of a triangle.

I swallowed hard.

*A triangle.*

Luca stared at it for a long moment, and then to the woods, as she had done. "How long ago did they depart?" Luca asked, turning a hard gaze back on the servant. "In which direction did they go?"

She shook her head. "I'm sorry, sir. By the time we left the gates, they were long gone."

Luca swore under his breath and paced, his eyes moving back and forth as if his mind was whirling.

I took his hand. "Retribution?"

His eyes met mine, and the fear I saw made me shudder inside. He nodded a little. "By all appearances."

Gabi, Lord Greco, and Captain Pezzati neared us. Greco knelt by the maid's ankle and then looked up at Luca. "Every one of us, as well as any we love, are in grave danger," he said.

"You know who did this?" Luca asked, his brow lowering.

Lord Greco gave a slight nod. "I believe so."

"Who? Who are they?"

"An elite force of Firenze. Like none you have seen. Barbato's men." His dark eyes flicked to the woods. "I'd heard talk of them. But I've never seen them."

Luca paced away, hand on his head. "They intend to murder us all. If they cannot kill us on the battlefield, they shall hunt us down where they can reach us. Eradicate the chance that we might draw together again to defend one another."

"Weaken us from within," Lord Greco said grimly.

"How can they be so foul?" I asked. "To kill even a small child?"

"No future heir to pick up his father's sword," Luca mumbled, looking over at the boy, the woman. He shook his head. Fresh tears ran down his face. "But I thought even they were incapable of such brutality."

Clearly, our enemies wished to send a message. No one was immune to their wrath.

"We need to warn the others," Gabi said. "Get ahead of any other Fiorentini, if we can."

"I think not," Luca said, laughing under his breath without a hint of joy. "You and Evangelia are to return to the castello without delay," he said. "From there, we shall send our fastest riders."

I shifted my weight from one leg to the other. I couldn't deny it. Looking at the slit throats of the woman and child, the bloody ankle of the maid, I suddenly wanted nothing more than Castello Forelli's solid gate shut between me and the world. The Freakiness had just reached a Whole New Level. But my eyes went to this home's flaming towers, her open gates. They'd let them through. Would someone be able to steal into Castello Forelli, too?

No, we had to rout this enemy. Take them down. Before they found their way to us. Ours. My eyes met Gabi's, and I knew we were thinking the same thing.

"We reached out to ten of your brothers during the battle," Gabi said. "Seven answered our call, but it stands to reason that all ten may be in grave danger. How many more of their women and children might die this day?"

"They do not know the identity of all in the brotherhood," Luca said, shaking his head, his mind clearly whirling. "They were but some of many who rode to our aid in the battle."

"You do not believe so," I said, "but what if they tortured Lord Santi before they killed him?"

"He wouldn't divulge such information. Even unto death." He gave me an irritated look. "We are brothers. Willing to die for one another."

"But what if they were threatening his wife? His son?" Gabi asked quietly.

Luca lifted bleak eyes in her direction.

"Do we need to go to all ten, Luca? Without delay?"

He gave her a slow, grim nod.

"We need to divide and ride ourselves, as fast as we can, if we are to save them."

Luca was shaking his head, hands on his hips. "Nay. By no means."

"Luca," she pleaded, "We have no time for this! You cannot spare the men to escort us back to the castello. Assign Lia and I each to a different guard." She reached out to touch his arm. "If we do not try and warn them, and they are attacked as the Santis were," she said, shuddering, "if *more children* die, I could not live with myself. Could you?"

He stared into her eyes, chewing on his lip, debating for a long moment. "Marcello shall hang me," he groaned.

A small smile tugged at the corners of her mouth. "He shall not," Gabi said, striding toward her mount.

"And if he does," I said, "I shall cut you down."

"Small comfort, that," he mused, rolling his eyes. "You shall ride with me, Evangelia. I don't want you out of my sight."

"And Gabi?" I asked, wishing she could stay with me too.

His eyes immediately moved to Lord Greco and then onward. "Captain Pezzati shall attend her. The others shall ride out alone."

He put out his hands in stirrup fashion, and I stepped into them. He easily lifted me up, and I wrapped my skirts around my legs, trying to protect them from the chafing of riding bareback. It was one thing to do so for a short ride, another to plan on riding miles that way. Luca's eyes lingered on the skin of my ankle.

But there was no lust in them.

Only fear.

## CHAPTER 8

### –GABRIELLA–

"I'll go north to our brother there," Rodolfo said, giving Luca a meaningful look. "I know it best."

*So there are still some on the wrong side of the fence. One of the missing three?*

I looked away. Of course Greco'd volunteer for that. Crossing the border. Risking his life. Him and his stupid Death Wish.

But Luca merely clasped hands with him. "Go with, brother. And return to us."

"If it be His will," Greco said, eyeing me for just a second. Then he whirled and galloped down the western road at breakneck speed. Apparently he'd head north at some point down yonder.

Georgii went tearing down the same road after him, intent on warning Conte Lerici, who lived in the northwest of Toscana. Could he reach them on the road before they were ambushed? Even with their astonishing archery skills, if they were surrounded in a wood, attacked where bows would not be adequate defense… Rodolfo's form was already small in the distance, his cape flying behind him. *Help him, Lord,* I prayed silently. *Help us all to save them.*

"We shall go to the two southernmost contacts. I shall take Lady Evangelia to Villa Gallo, and you, Captain Pezzati, shall take Lady Gabriella to Castello Colombo. Obviously, if there are men who dare to steal across our border and commit such atrocities," he said, waving at the dead and wailing servants, "they would dearly love to capture or kill our She-Wolves. Keep close watch."

"We shall see to our task and immediately return to Castello Forelli," the older man said in solemn promise.

Castello Forelli. My heart skipped a beat. I thought of Marcello, Mom, and Dad. "Need we not warn our own?" I asked.

"Baldovino shall go to them," Luca said, his mount prancing back and forth, sensing the tension. We all looked at the youngest, most inexperienced knight in our company. Luca was clearly sending him home to get him out of harm's way—but couldn't risk sending one of us with him. "The guards have likely seen the smoke in the distance and closed the gates." He lifted his hand, shushing my fear before I spoke it. "We've been infiltrated once," he said firmly. "Our men know that they need to be extra vigilant about any 'merchants' attempting to enter in covered wagons. But Baldovino can also alert Marcello, and he shall send out additional patrols to come to our aid."

The others were all quickly dispatched, half beginning their trek on that western road. With Castello Forelli lying on the far northeastern border, most of our allies of the brotherhood were to our west and southwest. Matteo, a young archer, was sent to Castello Rizzo. Lutterius was sent toward the only contact in Umbria. A shiver ran down my back.

It'd been my idea to summon the brotherhood when we were on the brink of demise. But had coming to save our lives only resulted in the end of theirs?

*What's done is done,* my dad said. I straightened and wrapped my skirts around my legs as my sister had done. Dad was right. I had to focus on what we could do, not what we couldn't go back and change. Those men had saved us. And I aimed to repay the favor.

### –EVANGELIA–

Gabi and I held hands a moment before we parted.

"See you soon," she said meaningfully.

"See you soon," I agreed. There was never a good-bye between us. Only the promise to reunite.

Then she and Captain Pezzati entered a narrow trail—a shortcut through the woods—and Luca and I left to find the village of Gallo. We took an old Roman road for a time, heading directly south and then, like my sister, entered a smaller trail that climbed steeply over three hills and dumped us into an abandoned village, little more than a courtyard and crumbling well and the remains of five buildings. We paused at the well, hoping to bring up water for our horses and ourselves, but it was dry.

Luca groaned, and I tried to gather enough saliva in my mouth to swallow. Not that I'd been able to manage that in the last hour. "Forgive me, m'lady," he said, turning miserable eyes up to me.

"For what?" I asked with a wry smile. "For allowing the well to run dry?"

"For not stopping sooner. You must be parched."

"No more than you. I'll drink my fill at Villa Gallo. How much farther is it?"

"A half hour or so."

"Let us be on with it, then."

But he didn't move to his horse. He turned and looked over his shoulder, northward, squinting.

"Luca...what is it?"

He looked at me, surprised, as if he'd forgotten I was there. "Luca," I said. "You're frightening me."

He shook his head. "Forgive me." Quickly, he mounted and turned to resume our journey.

But I remained where I was. "Tell me."

"'Tis nothing," he said.

"Clearly 'twas something," I insisted.

He sighed and rubbed the back of his neck. "'Tis only that I was thinking about Lady Gabriella's fear for our own, back at Castello Forelli."

A shiver ran down my neck. *Mom and Dad.* "And?"

"And I am confident they will be well," he said, reaching a hand out to me, apology in his eyes. "Nay, 'tisn't that. It's *my* sister. My aunt and uncle."

I held my breath. *Oh.* "But are they Forellis?" To my knowledge, I'd never met a Forelli beyond those outside the castello.

"Nay. But my sister is. And if word spreads of Adela's return...even though I haven't lived alongside her in a decade..."

"They might come after them."

He nodded gravely.

"Quickly," I said, nudging my mare in the flanks. "Let us warn our friends at Villa Gallo, and once we borrow a proper saddle for me, we shall go at once to your kin."

He caught up with me. "We shall warn our friends, and when you are properly guarded, *I* shall see to my kin."

I stared straight ahead. *We'll see about that.*

So I was totally relieved when we rode up to the sprawling villa surrounded by a rather meager wall and saw that clearly all was well. No smoke rose from her rooftop; no soot-covered servants stumbled out. "Sir Luca Forelli and Lady Evangelia Bettarini, here to see your lord at once!" he called up to two guards who looked down at us with a dubious expression.

At our names, the two shared an alarmed glance and immediately disappeared to let us in. Were only the two of them on guard? We'd have to insist that Lord Gallo's family flee to the safety of Siena for a time. Or bring on more mercenaries to help guard their flanks. I looked around. They were at the top of a hill, but the woods crept close on two sides. I shivered, remembering the flames atop Castello Santi's towers. If our enemies could enter and destroy our friends there, how much more vulnerable were these?

I laughed at myself, then. When had I become a battle strategist?

My days of thinking about a date for the Snowball dance or my desire for a new smartphone never seemed so distant as they did in that moment.

The gates opened, and Lord Gallo and his lady strode toward us across the small courtyard in front of the villa. Luca dismounted and then came around to help me. "Close the gates!" he called to the guards. Hastily, they obeyed.

"My friends!" Lord Gallo said, his round face marked by confusion. "To what do we owe the favor of your visit so soon after parting?"

"'Tis most grave business, I fear," Luca said. "Gavino, I cannot tarry long. Might you water my horse and send someone to fetch provisions? I must be away at once."

"My horse as well," I said.

Lord Gallo looked at us in further confusion. Luca shot me an irritated glance, and I returned one of determination. "Of course," the young lord said, pretending not to notice. He waved to a squire, and the boy ran up, retrieved our horses, and led them away. The noblewoman, about twenty-two and with plain but dignified features, wrapped a wary hand through her husband's arm.

"M'lord, m'lady," Luca said, "we've rushed to warn you of grave danger. Castello Santi was attacked this morning, and both Lord and Lady Santi, as well as their little son and servants, were murdered."

Lady Gallo gasped and brought a hand to her mouth. She looked over her shoulder. On the villa steps were two little girls, one holding a baby. None of the children was older than five.

Luca eyed Lord Gallo. "There was some indication that the attack was retribution for the brotherhood coming to our aid. If Castello Santi fell, your villa may very well be indefensible," he said. "You must retreat to Siena for a time."

"Impossible," Lord Gallo said, looking dazed. "They would never come this far south. And how are they to know which lords are of the brotherhood and which are merely loyal Sienese answering the Nine's call?"

Luca paused. "I asked the same question. But Gavino," he said lowly, as Lord Gallo's wife glanced over her shoulder to the children again. "These were trained killers. They may have very well used Santi's loved ones as bait to find out what they wished to know."

Lord Gallo looked offended, angry. "He would not have betrayed us. Not Santi."

Luca returned his grim stare. "They entered Castello Santi and murdered everyone they could catch, then burned her. There shall be little left of her walls come nightfall. They cut Nerina's ankles, Gavino—

as well as some of his servants—with a triangle, to send us a message. No one knows what Santi did or did not divulge before it ended for them." He swallowed. "Do you wish to take such risk with your own? Here?"

Lord Gallo looked from Luca to his wife, then his children, visibly shaken. Some of his knights were beginning to appear, summoned by the servants. "I shall get them to the city," he said slowly, deliberately. "Mayhap it's best, for a time. Until this ends."

"Mayhap," Luca agreed. "Can you pack and go at once? And take Lady Evangelia with you? Deliver her to Palazzo Forelli in Siena?"

I bit my tongue. It wouldn't do to argue. Not yet.

"Of course, of course," Lord Gallo said.

"I've forgotten myself," Lady Gallo said, taking my arm. "Would you not like to come in, Lady Betarrini, and take your ease for a bit?"

"Some water would be most welcome, and a bit of bread if you have it. But truly, m'lady," I said, putting my grubby hand on hers. "You must gather your kin and be away from here at once. What we've seen this day…" I shook my head and then looked at the kids again. "Please," I whispered. "Trust me when I say you must find safety in the city."

She met my gaze, fear in her brown eyes, and nodded once. Relieved, I followed her into a sprawling sitting room and washed my hands in a basin, then immediately poured my own silver goblet full of water, gulping it down before pouring another. A servant stood by, looking chagrined that I'd beaten her to it. But I didn't care. "Pack your things," I demanded, summoning every bit of my lady-ness I could. "You're to go to Siena within the hour. Tell the others, too. No one but fighting men are to be left behind."

Her eyes widened, and she scurried off.

Luca entered then, following the maid with a curious expression, then looked back to me. He poured himself a goblet full of water as well and drank it down, wiping his lips with the back of his hand. "Will you go with them, to Siena?"

"Nay. I go with you, or I return home to Castello Forelli."

He sighed and looked to the window. "'Tis gathering dark out there, Evangelia. Go with them to the city. There will be Forelli knights there who can see you to the castello come morn, if that is what you wish." He set down his goblet and took my hands in his, love and fear alive in every line of his face. "Please," he whispered. "Please."

My heart softened. He was so sweet. And all he wanted was for me to be far from harm. You had to admire a guy who wanted to keep you from death. I studied him. Maybe he'd move faster without me. Maybe he'd have a better chance to reach his aunt and uncle, his sister. Be safer, if he didn't feel he had to protect me rather than watch out for himself. "If I must," I said, resignedly.

"Thank you," he said, lifting my hands to his lips. He kissed my knuckles and looked like he was having serious thoughts about leaning in for a real one on the lips, when Lord Gallo entered.

"Pardon me, Luca, m'lady," he said, ducking his head.

"Nay," Luca said, dropping my hands. "Come."

"We can be ready within ten minutes," he said.

"Your servants, too, Gavino," Luca asked. "Leave none but a few knights."

Lord Gallo gave him a momentarily confused look and then nodded once. A servant passed by him, a tray full of bread, cheese, and fruit in her hands. She set it beside me and Luca. "Eat your fill," Lord Gallo said to us. "Fetch them some cloths," he added, speaking to the servant. "Sir Forelli shall need additional provisions for the road."

The girl bobbed a quick curtsy and scurried out to do as he bid.

Outside, Luca took my hands in his and kissed them again as the others milled about, shouting and chatting excitedly. "Do not wither as you pine for me," he said with a grin.

I was so glad to see him smile—something that had been spookily rare in recent days—that I grinned with him. "Miss you? What shall I miss? You ordering me about?"

"Nay, me following your every move, wishing I could be holding your hand every time you were in the room, wishing I could hear every word you speak, taste—"

"Enough of your idle prattle!" I said, pushing him away. He was being silly. But I immediately felt the distance between us with a shiver and wished I could pull him closer again. "You come back alive, Luca Forelli," I demanded with a pretend glower.

"Now who is ordering whom?"

"I am ordering you," I said, stepping forward to grab hold of his tunic in my fists, as if I intended to shake some sense into him. But then, before I could talk myself out of it, I pulled him closer and kissed him on the lips.

Lady Gallo gasped. One of the little girls squealed. But I ignored them. I could only look up and into Luca's beautiful green eyes.

He didn't move as I eased away, only stood there with shock and love and hope and triumph in his gaze. "I shall wear that kiss, m'lady," he whispered, "like a tattoo on my heart."

"Yes, well," I sniffed, releasing and smoothing out his tunic. "See to it that you return to me with more fervor than you show even to your sacred brothers."

He grinned as I started to back away, stepping forward and wrapping an arm around my lower back. He pulled me to him, swift and sure, making me softly gasp. Then he gently tipped up my chin and kissed me so softly, so longingly, that I closed my eyes, giving in to it. It was his turn to release me, leaving me in a daze. Gradually I looked around the courtyard and saw that everyone was staring at us, most with grins on their faces.

"Be it known," Luca said loudly, still looking nowhere but at me, "that Lady Evangelia Betarrini is my lady." He raised his arms like a triumphant wrestler in the ring of the WWE arena, and I giggled. Even if he hadn't asked me.

"Really, Luca," I said below my breath, feeling the heat of a blush rise up my neck and cheeks. "Must you act so...victorious?"

"Oh yes, I must," he said, with a nod, grinning. "I most certainly must." He leaned closer. "I shall count the hours until we are reunited. And then we shall practice that kiss," he added in a whisper.

"You hope," I chided.

He raised his eyebrows. "I do." His grin faded as concern again overtook him. "Take close care, my love."

I took those last two words in. *My love.* And then I nodded. "You as well."

His impish smile returned. "First the kiss," he whispered. "In the days to come, the mad profession of love."

"Is that how it shall transpire?" I asked, raising a brow.

"Oh yes," he said, tossing me a cocky grin. He settled his hands at my waist, and I resisted the urge to pull him in for another kiss. "How else *would* it transpire?" He lifted me up onto my mount, this time on a *real* saddle, regardless of Lady Gallo's disdain.

"Until we meet at Castello Forelli," I said, reaching down to take his hand, after he settled my feet into the stirrups.

"I shall hasten to your side as soon as I can," he said, kissing my knuckles. He reluctantly left me and mounted in that arcing swing I so admired. Then with a hand over his heart, he broke our gaze, said farewell to the Gallos, and rode out of the villa gates.

## CHAPTER 9

### −GABRIELLA−

Under guard of a Forelli patrol who'd run across us, Captain Pezzati and I rode through the castello gates just as the sun set in the winter sky. I wearily dismounted and took Mom's hands and hugged her, then Dad, seeing in their expressions echoes of my own grief. Marcello emerged from the Great Hall doorway then, limping as he hurried over to me. "Ah, Gabriella, Gabriella," he said, holding my head and kissing me on both cheeks before pulling me into his arms. But his body was rigid, angry. "How could you have taken such risks?"

"I am well, Marcello," I soothed, taking his arm and urging him back toward the Great Hall. He paused to clasp hands with Captain Pezzati. But I pulled him toward the warmth of an evening fire in the fireplace. The last thing he needed was such stress as he battled to recover. I wanted to at least sit down as we figured out our next steps.

"Are they all back?" I asked. "Everyone from our party?"

He glanced down at me and shook his head. "Nay. Luca, Evangelia, Rodolfo, Georgii, and Lutterius are still out."

I frowned. It made sense that Rodolfo and the twins were still absent—they had the farthest to go. But Luca and Lia? I looked toward Captain Pezzati, and he looked equally puzzled. He'd wagered that they'd beat us home.

"But there is no word from Villa Gallo?" he asked. "No smoke from that direction?"

"Nay." He shrugged and gave me a wink. "Mayhap the two of them are merely lingering on their way home."

"Mayhap," I said, knowing he was just trying to distract me, give me something to hope for. It was fine with me if Lia and Luca finally got on with things. And to be fair—their absence didn't *have* to be the equivalent of life-threatening danger. Maybe they were just hanging out, grabbing the rare chance to chat, hold hands, flirt…without all the castle gossips watching it unfold. But…would they? After what we had witnessed at Castello Santi? I couldn't imagine it. Lia would know we'd be worrying.

Captain Pezzati was waylaid by other knights, who reached out to clasp hands with him in greeting. I went to the fire crackling in the mammoth stone fireplace and lifted my hands toward the flames, realizing that I'd become chilled in the evening air. "What report from the others?" I asked, partially turning toward my husband as he took his chair with obvious pain.

His brow furrowed. "They attempted to infiltrate Castello Rizzo, too, but were turned away by wary guards. Matteo reached her gates ten minutes after they left, and went after them, but lost their trail."

I nodded, rubbing my temples between my thumb and middle finger. When Marcello fell silent, I looked his way again and knew immediately. Mom and Dad looked stricken too. "Oh, no," I moaned. "Nay, nay. Who else?"

It was Marcello's turn to rub his temples. "Lord Hercolani. God be praised, his wife and baby were away."

I put my hand over my mouth and turned back to the fire, feeling ill.

"No one else?" I asked, my strangled voice sounding foreign to my own ears. "Everyone else is safe?"

"So far," Marcello said.

"You saw nothing suspicious on the road?" Mom asked, rising to stand beside me, wrapping her arm around my shoulders.

"Nay. All was calm. Some farmers. A shepherd. Not even another knight, besides Captain Pezzati and our own men."

She took a deep breath. "Good, then. I'd take that as a good omen that Lia and Luca will soon be home too."

"I hope so, Mom," I said, covering her hand with my own and leaning my head toward hers.

### –EVANGELIA–

We were nearing Siena as the sun grew low in the sky. I shivered and wrapped my cape more tightly around me, wishing I'd taken my heavier one this morning when I set out or thought to ask Lady Gallo for a spare one to borrow. But the city was getting closer, visible in the distance. Soon enough we'd be inside her walls, weaving our way toward the palazzo, where I could settle by a merry fire and later sink into a soft feather bed, beneath piles of blankets to warm me....

But first I'd send a messenger pigeon to Castello Forelli, so that my family did not freak out over me all night. And I could—

A commotion near the front of our traveling party—which numbered over thirty—stole my attention. I shifted my mare to the right, straining to see over the bobbing heads of the Gallo girls' maids and others ahead of me.

Three of the Gallo knights were beneath a tree, circling. I edged out of line and urged my mare to a trot, passing the others. One of the knights saw me coming, said something to the others, and all three turned toward me. One moved forward to stop me. "M'lady…"

But I was already close enough to see. My eyes went wide as I stared up into the cradling branches of an ancient oak, a man hanging ten feet above my head. I stifled a gasp and bit my lip, circling him, trying to get a look at his face. It was the color he wore that alarmed me most—Forelli gold.

"M'lady," said another knight, trying to block my way. "'Tis truly not a sight for feminine eyes."

"'Tis obviously not a sight for *anyone's* eyes who loves the house of Forelli. Who is it? I must know!" I turned again and then abruptly pulled up just before I could finally see his face. Slowly, his big body spun on the rope. I froze, wondering why I hadn't thought of it before. There had only been so many men with us with that dark, wavy hair.

And when I saw his face, I knew for sure.

*Georgii.* Eyes bulging, tongue protruding. And a triangle cut into his ankle, blood still dripping to the soil below.

"Cut him down," I gasped. "Please, cut him down." My voice breaking, I slid off my mount, rushed to the tree and vomited. Georgii, sweet, fun Georgii, so willing, so young. And Lutterius's twin… What would happen when his brother found out? I braced myself against the tree with one hand and wretched again, the last bits of food from Villa Gallo leaving my stomach.

I spit, gasping for breath. Then I straightened, put my hands on my head and turned, trying to think about my next steps. What next? Who to tell? Where to go?

"I wager they surprised him on the road back to Castello Forelli," said a Gallo knight to his master, as he rode up. "It appears they chased him to a spot around the bend, where his horse came up lame. He was surrounded."

My eyes went to the knight. "They chased him down?"

"Yes, m'lady," he said, sorrow in his eyes. "Mayhap he rode for Siena, hoping he could make it in time."

*My mind whirled. Georgii had come from the northwest, where Conte Lerici resided. If he'd run across the assassins, they had been somewhere up there.* The knight's face dimmed before me, and I could see only one other.

*Luca.*

He was heading north. What if he was trapped or tracked as Georgii had certainly been? Surrounded? Hanged?

I strode over to the knight who I'd seen Luca talking to and conferring with about the best roads toward his uncle's villa in Aquina. He shifted his weight from one leg to the other, looking as though a real wolf stalked him. Me. I looked up at him, hands on my hips. "Sir Luca Forelli went to his uncle's villa. Which way did he travel?"

"By this very road, m'lady. This road intersects with another—"

The knight to his side slammed the back of his fist into his belly, making him gasp. "Quiet, fool. M'lady, you cannot go after Sir Forelli. Not now. Not at this hour. He made us swear we'd see you safely to Siena."

But I was already running for my mount. As I'd watched Luca do over and over, I grabbed hold of the saddle horn and swept up into an arc, almost settling myself neatly into the saddle, but just a little shy. *Okay, that's a little embarrassing. Next time, I gotta pull up a little more as I swing....* I stubbornly clung to the side and scooched myself the rest of the way on before sitting up, a bit out of breath. I reached for my reins and whipped my horse around.

"Wait, m'lady, we shall accompany you!" said a knight.

"Nay," I said, summoning every bit of princess-ness in me I could. These weren't Marcello's men; they were Gallo's, giving me half a chance. *And besides, I'm a She-Wolf. The sister-in-law of one of the Nine. Surely I can make this happen.* "The more of us there are together, the more likely we'll draw our enemy's eye. I must do this alone."

"You're mad!" said Lady Gallo. "She's mad!" she repeated to her husband, shaking her head in total confusion.

"You cannot!" said the second knight. Several of the others grumbled their agreement.

"I must go to Luca," I said to Lord Gallo, ignoring all but him. "Get your family to the safety of Siena's gates. And then send Forelli knights immediately toward the villa, along this same road. Understood?"

"Yes, m'lady," he said, fear and wonder warring in his eyes. "Go with God."

*God and a thousand of His angels,* I hoped, as I tore down the dimly lit road.

---

An hour later, just as I was losing the last of my light, I met up with the road that the knight had mentioned and turned north. There was a good, long stretch in front of me, and at the very end, I thought I glimpsed a man in a dark cape, and a flash of yellow beneath his saddle. But it was really too dark to tell if it was Luca for sure. Seconds later, the rider disappeared into a dark wood. But hope surged within me.

Determined, I pushed my weary horse down the road. With luck, I'd gain on him. If it wasn't Luca, I told myself, I could at least find out from the traveler if I was heading in the right direction. And I'd have more road behind me than ahead, once total darkness overtook me.

Ten minutes later, I reached the forest and pulled up, circling as I studied the deep, dark shadows of the trees ahead of me. Would I be able to pick my way through as nightfall came, or was I likely to get lost within? *I'll help nobody if I get lost.*

Movement ahead caught my eye. But then was gone. "Luca!" I called, covering my mouth too late. *Way to go, idiot,* I said to myself. *Why not announce to the whole wood that you're chasing Luca Forelli? Hey, everybody! Forelli Peeps, right over here! Come and get 'em while they're hot!*

I shook my head, frustrated with myself—both for the shout and for all the negative self-talk. *Mom wouldn't allow that to go on, if she was here. I shouldn't either.* I nudged my mare forward, my eyes sweeping warily left and right, trying to discern anything out of the ordinary. But all I saw were trees and more trees and the winding road, which was covered in pine needles and cones and small branches. It was about the width of a Ford truck but relatively straight, so I was heartened. Surely, even in the dark, I could find my way.

When it grew too dark to be certain of the road, I dismounted and tapped the toe of my slipper, paying attention to the sound of the dirt and stones beneath it, so different from the soft cushion of the forest floor, which was riddled with more branches.

I glanced up, seeing that the tree canopy closed above me. Was there a moon to come? I hadn't been paying attention lately. I listened, the hairs at the back of my neck standing on end. No birds called. There was little sound at all. I pressed forward, telling myself that I'd only scared them off, or that they'd all flown south for the winter. Like the moon, I couldn't remember birds in recent days. *I've been a little preoccupied,* I thought, cutting myself some slack. *No negative self-talk, no negative self-talk.*

I froze. I'd definitely heard rustling to my left. I stared and stared, but by that time, it was so dark, I was pretty much blind. More rustling sounded to my right. I whipped my head that way and eased my bow from my shoulder, nocking an arrow.

My pulse thundered in my ears.

"Luca?" I said softly. But no one answered. Several seconds ticked by.

When I heard rustling again to my left, closer this time, I let the arrow fly.

But as I was reaching for another, someone tackled me from the other side.

## CHAPTER 10

### –EVANGELIA–

It felt like we were airborne for a full minute. Which we weren't, obviously, but it felt like that...like my whole life was suspended in time. And when we crashed to the earth, the air was knocked from my lungs with such force that I was in full-on panic. Growing dizzy. I writhed, struggling to leave the man's grasp, to right myself, hoping my lungs would begin working again. But he stubbornly held on to me.

He rose with me still in his arms. I was like a limp rag doll, desperately trying to will my lungs to work, wondering if I was about to die, hearing their voices all around me like I was underwater. Like they were Charlie Brown teacher voices. *Mwah, mwamwah, mwah...*

*Please, God. Help me breathe. I cannot fight if I cannot breathe!* The figures danced in front of me as my vision tunneled to a dot.

My lungs snapped open then, and as I sucked in one ragged breath and then another, my vision immediately steadied. I was surrounded by six men who appeared as little more than silhouettes in dark tunics and leggings, one with an arrow through his shoulder. A seventh man still behind me held on, one arm wrapped around my upper chest, the other around my waist. "That's it, m'lady, breathe. That's a good girl."

Then the eighth man entered the circle, a lantern in his hand. They parted for him, and he raised his lantern, lifting it until it was inches from my face. He was nondescript. A little taller than I, but not much. Strong and lean, with the coloring of a thousand other Italians, a bulbous nose, strong chin. The others clearly deferred to him.

He broke out in a huge grin as he studied me. Another brought my mare closer, and they lifted the saddle to show the blanket of Forelli gold. I groaned within, still trying to catch my breath. I'd never escape them if I kept feeling like I was going to pass out at any moment.

One of the men laughed, and the others did then too. "'Tis a very good day, my friends," said the leader, lifting a tendril of my hair and fingering it. "And so the day is redeemed." He turned then, leaving the way he came. "Bring her."

My captor let me go, and I stepped forward. But his hand clamped down on my shoulder. "Not too fast, or too far, She-Wolf."

I clamped my lips shut. So they clearly knew who I was. This was not good. Not good at all. Were these the assassins who had murdered the Santis and Georgii? Or some other enemy? We were still deep within Sienese territory. Of all the rotten luck... *Seriously, God? Really? Couldn't You have cut me the tiniest of breaks?*

We moved around a rocky outcropping and entered a clearing. The leader set the lantern down in the center and turned to await me.

But I saw him then. "Luca!" I cried, breaking free of the man's grip and running toward him, past the leader.

He was tied, spread-eagled, and barely conscious, hanging from the ropes. His shirt was torn to the waist, hanging open. It looked like he had a spreading bruise across every one of his six-pack abs. His beautiful face had been beaten, one eye already swelling shut, blood dripping from the corner of his lip, a bruise gaining ground on one cheek. He opened his good eye and squinted at me, then groaned. "Nay, nay!" he said, groaning again. "Evangelia, why did you come?"

I laughed then, feeling like I was losing it, nearly hysterical. "I'm here to save you," I said with a little shake of my head.

"Excellent," he said, wincing as if speech hurt him. "And how do you fare at your given task?"

"Not so well," I admitted. "But grant me a moment. I only just arrived."

He laughed then, a little, his grin even more lopsided than usual.

I reached out to touch him, but the leader took my hand and pulled me around to face him. "Enough." He turned me closer to the lamp and looked me over again.

My eyes scanned the group behind him. *There*. One man with my bow and arrows, admiring the Lerici heads. I had to get to it, somehow.

The leader followed my gaze. "Ah, nay, m'lady. You shall not be getting your hands on those. You've already robbed me of one knight." He nodded toward a man sitting on a rock, another behind him and cutting away the fabric of his tunic, preparing to pull out the arrow. The wounded man glared at me.

"You are Fiorentini," I said, needing to know for sure.

"As certainly as you are Sienese," the leader said with a slight bow. "Forgive me if I do not introduce myself." He crossed his arms and brought one hand to his lips, tapping them. "Tell me," he said, stepping past me and then crossing back. "How is it that you and Sir Forelli are so far from home? And yet apart? To where were you heading?"

"Tell them nothing!" Luca cried, right before one of the bad guys punched him in the belly. I felt it like he'd punched me instead.

I stared silently at the leader and those around him. They were not nearly as big as our Forelli knights. More like the track team in school than the football players. Or in Colorado, the climbers. Lithe, but crazy-strong. *Ninja assassins,* I thought grimly. Able to slip in and out of places we least expected them. Greco had known something about them. Said something about Barbato...

My enemy squinted at me. "Come now, Lady Betarrini. Everyone knows that the She-Wolves rarely go anywhere unaccompanied." He leaned closer and whispered, as if sharing a secret. "There are enemies about."

"So I've heard," I said stiffly, staring straight ahead.

He lifted his brows and straightened. "Impressive, even under duress." He circled me. "So I take it the rumors are true? Sir Forelli is your intended? I am guessing he forbade you to come and you followed him anyway."

I gave him my best death glare from the corners of my eyes.

"You She-Wolves are the most odd sort of women. That is, if you are *truly* women..."

He reached down to lift my skirts, and I slapped his hands away. "Stop!"

The men erupted in guffaws and laughter.

"Better make sure, Captain!"

"That's the way!"

"Show us, She-Wolf!"

Behind him, Luca wrenched against his ropes, but they held tight. There was no trace of humor left in his eyes, only fear and frustration.

*What have I done?* I looked around the circle of men. Could I possibly fight my way out, escape into the darkness? But then what? What about Luca?

"Are Lord Forelli's men coming behind you, Lady Betarrini?" my enemy asked.

"Of course! These woods are their territory, not yours." *At least, I hope they've set out...* "And when they do reach you, they shall show you what happens to men who steal beyond their proper borders and murder innocent women and children."

His hand whipped out faster than I was prepared for. His fingers squeezed on either side of my throat. In seconds, I was on my knees before him. "Your men robbed countless women and children of fathers and husbands," he said with a grunt, close to my face. "We are here to make certain such atrocities do not transpire again." He released me, and I dropped to my hands and knees, gasping for breath.

He strode over to Luca and took out his knife.

"Nay!" I gasped, reaching out, begging. *Not Luca. Please, Lord. Not Luca.*

But he did not move to slit his throat as I feared. He moved to Luca's shirt and finished cutting it away, exposing the triangular tattoo above his elbow. "This," he said, pointing into the tattoo with the tip of his knife until blood formed and ran down the blade. Luca grimaced and took heaving breaths but did not cry out. "This is what you chase, seeking to warn them."

He rushed back to me and picked me up by my upper arms, dropping his knife as he did so. He shook me, his eyes wild. "I shall know which of their cursed brothers is ahead. Who? Where?" He shook me again. "Where?"

"I know not! It is as you guessed. I was merely following Luca!" I pretended to break then, summoning tears for the Santis, for Georgii, to aid me in my act. Big crocodile tears rolled down my face. *They didn't know. They didn't know!* At least, not about all of them. Lord Santi had not broken confidence. Despite the cost.

My enemy grimaced and, with a groan of disgust, let me go. I fell like a ragdoll to the ground, my skirts covering his dagger. I clenched the bodice of my gown with my left hand, crying and trembling as if I was a total wimp who'd lost it. And in my right, in the folds of my skirt, I clenched the knife. "Please, just let me go. To take me, or kill me, shall only bring about more bloodshed, not less. Surely you recognize that."

He took hold of my left hand and leaned down. "It appears that you are female after all. Mayhap you need a bit of food, a bit of wine. I have forgotten my manners. We shall begin again after you collect yourself."

I looked up at him, giving him a little-girl look that I hoped would soften him up even further. And then I rose. But as I did so, I whipped around him, bringing my blade up beneath his chin. The men around us erupted in shouts of alarm and movement, swiftly sidling around me.

The leader tensed and lifted his hands up. "M'lady, what is your course of action? Slay me, and then what? There are still six fully able men to corral you again."

"Cease! Cease speaking!" I cried. I urged him backward, away from the light, but the men followed us. "Tell them to stay put!"

"Come and take her," he said. "If I die, I die. Kill her, too, if necessary, and take her body back to Firenze."

Did this guy never shut up? Luca was wrenching madly, trying to free himself while the men were distracted. But his bonds held. I pressed harder on the knife, and the man came with me, back deep into the shadows. He lurched backward, clearly not caring if I slit his throat—on purpose or by accident—and wrenched my arm away as we twisted and fell.

I cast about as he rose, until I was able to grab hold of a piece of wood and swing it toward him, desperate to hit him before he got ahold of me.

But the stick broke in half as it glanced off his skull, obviously rotten in the middle. He grinned, frustratingly unharmed, and dived toward me, but I rolled to the side. He barely missed me, falling to the ground with an *ooph*, his hand scraping my shoulder. I turned, found my footing, and ran into the darkness, my plan to arc around and get back to Luca to free him.

Which pretty much didn't work out.

One man grabbed hold of my skirts, which were flying behind me, and I fell again, cursing wretched medieval gowns and wishing for the thousandth time that I had just *one* pair of decent jeans. I picked myself up, ready to flee again, but the leader caught up with me and grabbed hold of my arm. He turned it behind my back, which brought me up short. "Back to the clearing," he grunted, panting. "Now."

We marched back to Luca, who took a deep breath, clearly frustrated that he was seeing me again.

"Tie her up," the leader said. "Beside him. But not too close."

In short order, I was spread-eagled beside Luca. The men hung out at my ankles overlong, pantomiming caressing my leg, but with one look toward the leader, I knew I had nothing more than that to fear. He wanted me for something bigger.

"This a part of your plan for rescue, m'lady?" Luca asked out of the corner of his mouth.

I laughed under my breath. "Indeed. I find that if one gets herself tied up, completely vulnerable, they let down their guard. And that is when we can strike."

He laughed then, and the sound of it heartened me, but then he lifted his chin, as if the action hurt him. I looked over at him in concern, remembering Marcello and how sick he had become after his beating. "Luca?"

"Be at peace," he said, wincing. "I shall survive."

"Quit your banter," called the leader. They were building a fire in the center of the clearing now, bringing in water and unwrapping food. He eyed me for a long moment and then glanced over at Luca, then back to me.

"I'll have your name," I called back.

The men all laughed. "She has courage, I'll give her that," said one.

The leader stared back at me. "You are She-Wolf, in our presence. You may call me He-Wolf."

"That, I fear," said Luca, "is my title."

"Not this night," said the man. He rose slowly, and the look of lust in his eyes made my mouth grow dry with fear. Luca tensed beside me. My stomach clenched. *So much for not being scared about that...*

The leader approached, running his eyes over me from head to toe. Not since Paratore had I been so freaked. I fought to ignore him, to not allow him to feel my fear.

"You touch her, Fiorentini," Luca ground out, "and I shall flay the skin from your body while you still live."

The man's eyes flicked from me to him. "You are hardly in a position to threaten me," he said calmly. "But what is to keep me from skinning you here, in front of your lady?" He moved over to him, his face an inch from Luca's. "I bet she would tell me about your brothers, even if Lord Santi refused." He eyed me. "What would it take, m'lady? Watching me cut off his fingers, one by one? Would it take one? Five?"

"Luca Forelli would never forgive me if I betrayed him," I said.

The man laughed. "Be that as it may, we'll have weeks to test the theory, once we get you to Firenze. I cannot decide which my people would favor more—watching Lord Forelli's dearest cousin and captain slowly put to death, or his sister-in-law." He threw up his hands. "I best take you both back and allow the people to decide. Surely one of you shall break, sooner than later."

"Why not kill us now?" Luca spat. "As you did the Santi family?" I figured he was visualizing what I was—Gabi up in that cursed cage, weak with hunger and thirst. We could not be taken back to Firenze. *We could not.* There surely would be no escape for us, no rescue. Not this time.

I wrenched against my bonds, but they held true, as they had for Luca. Our captor laughed. "Why not kill you now? Because I need the secrets you hold. We know of the brotherhood—Lords Marcello and Fortino, Hercolani and Santi. Rizzo evaded us, but he shan't be so fortunate next time." He tapped his chin. "Then there is you, Sir Luca, the once-priest, Tomas. The traitor, Greco. Who else?"

Luca stared back at him, his lips clamped in a line.

"Regardless, you shall ensure our safe passage back across the border on the morrow, should we not evade your men. And even if you do not break, we shall continue to steal across the border until we are certain that every one of your brothers is dead. On the way home, I simply need to secure but one more target." He pulled his dagger from his belt and ran the tip along my throat and down toward my sternum, all the while staring at me. "Which you *shall* help us identify, beginning with where you were heading this night."

I stared into his dark eyes. "Never."

He smiled a little. "Never say never, She-Wolf. Everyone has a price. Everyone. Don't they, Sir Forelli?" He slid the dagger into his waistband and then, with a playful grin to his men over his shoulder, rubbed his hands together as if in anticipation and went to the hem of my skirt. He began easing it up, his hands on my ankle, then calf. The men behind him hooted and hollered.

I forced myself not to cry out. I only stared at him, hating him more than I'd ever hated anyone in my life. Even Paratore. And that was saying something.

*It's not good to hate,* Mom's voice said in my head. *Hate the action, not the person.*

Which was all well and good in theory. In reality, it was a lot more difficult.

A whole lot more difficult.

## CHAPTER 44

### –EVANGELIA–

"Nay," the man mused, pleasure in his voice, "these are not the legs of any man. The wolf is surely female after all." His hands moved past my knee, and I bit my lip.

"Stop," Luca ground out at last, his voice strangled.

The leader paused, his warm hands lingering above my knee, and slowly he cocked his head in Luca's direction.

"I shall lead you to where I was going," Luca said. "But you shall leave the lady be. *At once.*"

I couldn't believe what I was hearing. Surely he didn't intend to lead them directly to his family...not after what we'd seen this day. What this guy had threatened! But I also wasn't anxious to let the jerk in front of me continue to feel me up. So I stayed quiet.

The leader straightened, slowly, his eyes on me. It was with some relief that I felt the skirt of my gown fall back down into place. "You'd say anything to protect this one," he said to Luca, still staring at me.

"It is as you say," Luca said. "But I am a man of my word."

The leader was still looking into my eyes as if he could read my thoughts, discover the truth there. Then he moved over to Luca as if reluctant to do so. "Swear it on this lady's life."

"I swear it."

Our captor squinted, aware now that something was off. "You were en route to one of the men in the secret brotherhood?"

It was Luca's turn to remain silent.

"It matters not," said the leader. "Whatever location is vital enough for Sir Forelli to try and warn is likely advantageous for us to conquer. Eat, drink, see to the horses," he said over his shoulder to the others. "We ride in an hour."

---

I kept freeze-framing scenes as the minutes passed, like I was going to put it down in graphic novel format when I was back and safe at the castello. Not that Mom and Dad would ever approve. Talk about messing with history. I was pretty sure that there'd not been any graphic novels prior to the twentieth century. It just was my method of coping—putting into art what I couldn't quite process in reality.

*If* I could ever draw or paint again. My arms had long ago gone numb, stretched out and up as they were, and felt so thick and static that I figured they might just crack away at any point like old, dead tree limbs.

The men ate, offering us none, and I salivated over the smell of dried meat warming in some wine over the fire, which only made me furious with myself. As if my very body was betraying me. More than anything, I wished for water. It'd been since late morning that I'd had anything to drink, and I'd vomited it all up.

Worse, we could hear the burble and *glup* of a nearby brook, from which the men were clearly drawing water, filling skins, and drinking their fill in front of us. Along with wine. They toasted their success of the day. For the sacking of two castles, the murder of a Forelli knight, and the capture of us.

*Two castles.* Who else had been lost this day? How many?

I loathed them. I shot them looks that I hoped would say *Die, scum,* regardless of what my mother would say. They were heartless, truly heartless. Demons, devils. My mind went back to the little Santi boy, his throat slit. How could they? *How could they?*

And yet my body screamed for water. I thought of dying here, this night. Limp in my bonds. Never returning. Gabi, Mom, and Dad hearing the news for the first time. The gasps, the pain in their eyes—it was like watching a movie in front of me. If I hadn't been so dry, I might've wept. For the first time, I understood, truly understood, a bit of what Gabi had suffered in that cursed cage. And it'd been another day, more, from now, when we'd freed her. How had she managed it? The hours of tortuous thirst?

"Please," I whispered, hating myself for my weakness. "Please."

The leader's head pulled up and turned toward me. He raised his hand and shushed the men, who were laughing. Slowly he rose, and I shoved back a shudder of fear. "Yes, m'lady?" he asked, if he was nothing more than a man in the castello, seeking my approval.

"A bit of water," I managed to say, my tongue thick and dead in my mouth. "May I?"

He sidled closer to me. "Beg me for it."

"Evangelia," Luca warned from my side.

But I could not help myself. *Water, only a bit of water,* was all I could think about. "Please," I said.

He smiled. "A She-Wolf, begging me for anything. I never thought I'd see the day." He stared at me a moment longer and then sidled back to the fire, lifted his skin, which was fat with liquid, and returned to my side. Making sure his companions were watching, he lifted it high and let the stream pour from its mouth, watching me open my lips like a hungry bird, swallowing even as I closed my eyes against the splash. The water washed over my face and ran down my neck, but all I could do was open my mouth and beg for more, swallowing and swallowing. The liquid ran down my parched throat, but it still felt raw, like sandpaper, soaking up every drop, deep within. I ducked my head away, trying to grab a breath even as he still poured.

Luca wrenched and shouted, "Cease your abuse, man!"

"What? The lady thirsts! I only mean to sate her desire." He ran out of water, but there was another right behind him, dousing me. I could drink no more and still breathe, but a third let the water from his skin fall over me, enjoying the game, until I was soaked through, the winter chill then seeping in. Two more stepped forward, their breath forming clouds before their faces.

I stared at one after another, refusing to cry out even as they poured. Blinking, staring hard at them, hoping they knew the depravity of their own miserable existence as they messed with a defenseless woman. And as I did so, I dreamed of sinking an arrow into the blackened heart of every one of them.

"So help me," Luca shouted, wrenching against his bonds again beside me, "I shall—"

"Enough," said the leader at last, eying us from the edge of the fire five feet away. "Fill your skins again and mount up. We ride shortly." Immediately, the others did as he bid, still laughing under their breath. I was pretty sure Luca was riled up enough to cut down three on his own if he could get ahold of a sword. And I'd take the others.

But the leader came up to me and cut me free, and as my arms fell to my sides, I realized it was as bad as I had anticipated. I wondered if I'd ever be able to hold a bow or sword again. I could feel the weight of my arms, like lumps of dead flesh, but nothing from the shoulders down. He cut the bonds at my ankles and easily turned me around, tying my hands behind my back. At least, that's what I assumed he was doing. I could not feel any of it, only the tug and strain across my chest.

He looked up at Luca. "Try nothing," the man warned him. "For this one shall ride behind me, and if you do anything out of order, my first task shall be to slit her throat. All I need is her head to bring victory to my people. Tragedy that it might be, I have no need to bring the rest of her along, if pressed."

Luca stared back at him, loathing in his eyes, and nodded once. My captor shoved me down to my knees, then went to work, cutting Luca down. Luca fell heavily, his face crumpled with pain. Again, I worried about the beating he had suffered, wondering what was happening inside his lean torso...or was it only that he had hung there longer than I?

Another man brought horses alongside us. Gruffly, I was lifted up and onto my horse. The leader shoved my feet into the stirrups, all business now, and tied my reins to his saddle.

"How am I to hold on?" I asked, fighting the desire to scream as feeling began to enter my arms again with all the fun of a thousand needles.

"Use those fine She-Wolf legs of yours," grunted the leader, mounting his horse.

Two men lifted Luca up into his saddle and handed his reins to a third. In seconds they were all assembled. They were fast, I'd give them that. And clearly lethal. But two things gave me hope as we rode out.

They'd been deep into the wine. Hopefully it would ease their guard.

And by now, surely, the knights of Siena were hard on our tail. *Please God, let them be on their way.*

But what if they'd chosen to wait for daybreak?

## –GABRIELLA–

We all sat around the tables that night at the castello, trying to choke down some food as we awaited word from Lia, Luca, Lutterius, Georgii, and Rodolfo. And we jumped every time the Great Hall door opened. Halfway through our roast venison, a servant arrived with a message. He hurried over and offered it to Marcello.

Marcello wiped his mouth with the edge of the tablecloth—something I still wasn't used to—and then took the paper from him. He unrolled the tiny scroll, and I knew it was a message via the dovecote. Once Marcello had become one of the Nine, he'd established a colony of homing pigeons that flew solely between the palazzo in Siena to the castello here. It was one way he secured more time outside the city's walls than within…the medieval version of a cell phone.

He glanced at me and then leaned to one side, toward the torch on the wall, in order to read it. His mouth became a grim line, and he rose, his eyes wild.

"Marcello," I said.

Lutterius entered the Great Hall, just home, his face in a customary grin. The other knights shouted their greetings, lifting goblets in a toast as he passed. He approached with a jaunty step and ducked into a short bow before Marcello. "M'lord! Glad tidings from our friends in Umbria. All is well, and her occupants on guard."

His smile faded as he noticed, at last, the chagrin on his master's. "M'lord?"

"Lutterius," Marcello said, clearly stricken but trying to cover. "We welcome your return. 'Tis happy word indeed. Please...take your ease. Sup. Drink. You have done well."

"Thank you, m'lord," Lutterius said, concern still knitting his brow. I could tell he wanted to ask other questions but dared not, not when he'd clearly been dismissed. Reluctantly, he turned, and a bench full of knights made way for him, patting him on the back, shouting his name again.

"Marcello," I said again.

His eyes met mine, then Mom's and Dad's. "Come," he said, gesturing to the fireplace on the far side of the hall. We quickly followed him. Marcello paused by Captain Pezzati, put his hand on the man's shoulder, and said a quiet word in his ear, and the man rose to follow behind us. I could feel the curious eyes of everyone else at the five tables as we passed. But it wasn't until we were out of earshot that Marcello turned to look at each of us.

"Luca and Evangelia reached Villa Gallo. The family is safe in Siena. But Luca went north to his family's villa, probably fearing the worst. His sister is due home any day now, and after seeing what he did at Castello Santi..." He paused, chin in hand, pacing, then looked back to us. "Evangelia was to rest at Palazzo Forelli overnight, then travel back to us under guard."

"But she didn't reach it," I said, my voice sounding dead in my own ears.

He shook his head gravely. "They discovered Georgii," he whispered, "hanged."

Mom gasped, and I covered my mouth. Slowly, I slid my eyes over to Lutterius, Georgii's twin. *Impossible.* The brothers were as hard to imagine separated, forever, as Lia and I were.

I looked to Marcello. "She went after Luca," I said.

Clearly miserable, he nodded.

"So you're telling me that my daughter is somewhere out there," Dad said, his voice rising, gesturing toward the dark window, "alone? With a band of killers about?"

The Great Hall had fallen silent. Marcello cleared his throat. "Hopefully not alone, Lord Betarrini," he said quietly. "I pray to God she is with Sir Luca."

"Small comfort, that," Dad said.

I laughed under my breath. *So much for a 10:00 p.m. curfew...* But fear choked any crazy sense of humor right out of me. *Lia...*

"A contingent of Sienese set out," Marcello said. "One portion a patrol from our own men at Palazzo Forelli. They are good men."

Dad shook his head and rubbed his neck. "*We* shall ride after them," he said, pointing at Marcello in a way that I'd not seen anyone else get away with. "Without delay."

"Agreed," Marcello said. He raised a hand. "Full contingent, two patrols. Ready in the courtyard in five minutes." The knights rose as one, as fast to action as a fire station crew scrambling after hearing the alarm. "Lutterius, wait," Marcello called, agony in every syllable.

My folks and Captain Pezzati left to prepare for their departure. I felt a thousand years old as I turned to face Lutterius, who approached us with a wary look etched across his face. For the first time, I wondered if being Lady Forelli meant more weight and responsibility than I might be able to bear. *How many more, Lord? How many more must I tell that their loved ones are lost?*

Marcello took my hand in his, and I squeezed it, knowing he felt twice the burden. The least I could do was to stand, to support him. To love him. Any way I knew how.

"Lutterius," Marcello said gently, putting a hand on his shoulder, "you shall remain behind. Rest. 'Tis been a long day for you, and my sorrow is deep...."

## –EVANGELIA–

I could do little but hold on to my horse's back, my thighs aching, begging for release. A man in front of us held up the lantern before him, leading the way through the dark night, but the light was scant, the shadows deep. The band of Fiorentini seemed able to see in the dark, unperturbed by the curving road, the branches that we narrowly ducked in time.

Gradually, I understood that they felt braver under cover of night. Without aid of moon and especially deep within the forest, there was little likelihood that they'd meet up with Sienese patrols. Plus, they were moving north, back toward home, which was undoubtedly making them breathe more easily. Last, they had *us*. A most excellent bargaining chip.

I tried to look over my shoulder, make out where Luca was, but the men behind me were nothing but dark, bouncing forms. I sighed. I wasn't psyched about being anyone's hostage. This had to end before we reached Luca's aunt and uncle, let alone his sister. We didn't need another young chick in the hands of these jerks. But truth be told, the main reason for my desperation, at that stage, was my body. My legs were seriously about to give out, whether I wanted them to or not.

I heard the whinny of another horse, and I glanced forward to see the lantern-guy's gelding rise up, in silhouette, while another nearly crashed into him, racing by. The lantern fell and was extinguished. The men shouted. The leader, the guy with my reins, shied to the left.

Under the sudden cover of darkness and commotion, I instinctively rolled. On my way down, I belatedly realized I had to find a way to use my arms and break my fall. But then I hit the ground at an angle, tumbling unexpectedly to the left, down a small ravine, over and over again. For a moment I feared I was going over a cliff, it was so steep. But then I came to a stop with a grunt, against what felt like a huge fallen tree, and I froze, listening to the commotion ten feet away.

I heard a sword meet another. Two horses crashing through the brush, five feet away from my head. The cry of the leader, recognizing I'd escaped.

Only then did I dare to take a breath. Quickly, I scrambled to my knees and tentatively raised my head, trying to see something, anything. It was too dark. Anything I thought I saw was clearly in my imagination. The guy would look for me—I knew it. He'd told Luca his first task would be to slit my throat. The best I could do was hide.

So I sidled over the old, fallen tree—three times wider than me—to the far side, and settled down, partially shielded by the lower portion of its round bulk. My pulse thundered in my ears as I tried to make out all I heard. The soft cry of one man, the grunt and moan of another, men wrestling, crashing through the brush, breaking branches. Who had dared to venture in? Where was Luca?

I found a ragged knot on the tree trunk and sawed it against the rope on my hands, back and forth, hoping against hope that it might cut me free. How was I to make it out of the forest with my hands bound behind me? But my movement only made a desperately loud cracking and scraping sound. I grit my teeth, hoping the fighting above me would cover my noise. But when I heard someone approaching the other side of the tree, down the bank, I dropped my hands and tried not to breathe. I scooched deeper into the crevice beneath the tree, trying not to think about all the creepy crawlies that I'd be joining. Tried to forget the winter chill through my damp dress, threatening to set my teeth to chattering.

The man paused, took another few steps, and then stopped—it sounded like right above me, right across the tree. I wondered if he could hear my heart pounding. It almost hurt in my chest, so hard was it thumping.

I could hear the crunch of the bark above me as the man edged over it, pausing to listen, then pushed off. His boot landed inches from my face, sending dust into my eyes. I closed them, willing myself not to sneeze, and sucked in my belly, fearing he might back up and discover me by chance. He paused, as if listening again.

The entire forest was silent. All sounds of scuffle, fight, had ended.

Slowly, he squatted and turned my way. I couldn't see him. Just sensed his movement.

"It's true then," he whispered. "Wolves can become one with the forest."

*Luca.*

My tears took me by surprise as he pulled me into his warm, strong arms. "Shh, shhh," he said. He ran his hand down my shoulders, my back, my arms, finding my bonds, and gently turned me. Then he cut me free and pulled me back into his arms, settling me back into my hiding place, cradling me close beneath the curve of the giant log, lengthwise, his back exposed, guarding me. "They are still about," he whispered in my ear, caressing my hair, trying to ease my tears. "Hunting us. Rodolfo and I only took three of them."

I nodded, not trusting my voice. *Rodolfo.* It'd been Rodolfo who came to our aid. But with three down, where were the five that remained? And where was Rodolfo now? All remained silent above us. Maybe all who were left sat in silence, waiting for another to move first.

Luca picked up his head, his hand stilling on my hair. "Hear that?" he whispered.

But I heard nothing for several seconds. Then I did. Many riders.

"The Sienese," I whispered. "I told Gallo to send them after me."

He squeezed me. "A fine, fine idea," he said, kissing my forehead as if in congratulations. He held on tight to me, waiting as they approached, growing louder and louder. "Now you stay here," he said firmly. "I shall be right back."

He rolled out of our hiding spot as dancing lantern light came sliding through the forest in fits and starts. I couldn't help myself. I rose and peeked over the edge of the log, watching as Luca crept up the bank. It was like seeing the scene with the aid of a very slow, clunky strobe light. Every half second I caught a glimpse of a knight, the approaching patrol, decked out in Siena's finest armor, Forelli gold tunics beneath.

"Forelli and Greco in the field!" Luca cried at the last possible second, to warn our men that there were friendlies in the mix. "Five enemies about!"

A man rose from the brush and threw a dagger at Luca. He ducked, and I did the same behind him. It ended in a tree above my head. When the light next came my way, the knife was still trembling from impact.

The patrol didn't waver. They split into two lines, shouting directions to search the forest for the enemy, relaying word about Luca and Rodolfo. Luca tackled the man who had sent the dagger our way, and they wrestled, but then two Sienese knights came running. Luca raised his hand when one of our men raised a sword over his head. "'Tis I, Sir Forelli!" Luca called.

The man only narrowly missed him. If there was one thing more difficult than medieval battle, I decided, it was medieval battle at night. Because in the melee, Luca's adversary had slipped away.

As had the others. Only our men seemed to be about, roving, combing the brush, hoping they'd run across them. Luca turned back to me and then hurried down the embankment, helping me over the log, constantly looking about.

"Did you see which way they went?" asked the captain of the patrol.

"Nay," Luca said, wiping his mouth with the back of his hand. "They are as subtle as shadow and as lethal as poison. They likely head north," he said, looking left along the road.

The captain lifted his chin and immediately mounted. "Twelve of you remain with Captain Forelli and Lady Betarrini. The rest with me."

The others circled around us, forming a barrier. I melted into Luca's arms, and he held me close a moment, kissing my forehead, my hair. "Evangelia, I am so glad you are well." He pulled away a bit. "You are well, yes?"

"Yes," I said. My shoulder was killing me, and my legs would be screaming bloody murder come morning—but I was well enough. Whole. And so was he.

He hugged me again and then released me, turning toward another. Greco.

They shared a smile and clasped hands. "Thank you, brother," Luca said. "You saved us from an uncertain end."

Lord Greco gave him a small smile and rubbed away a trickle of blood at the corner of his lips. "I trailed them for a while, then lost their trail. God be praised, I found it again."

I studied him, remembering how he and the tracker had chased me and Gabi down, once. *Apparently he learned something of the art. It made me glad he was on our side now.*

"Unfortunately, when I was again able to steal close, I discovered they held you and Evangelia captive. I knew I'd have to surprise them… in a more dramatic fashion, were I to have half a chance of freeing you."

"And you succeeded," Luca said. He shook his head. "We really must speak further about your willingness to die."

"In time, Luca," Lord Greco said with a gentle smile, laying his hand on Luca's shoulder. "Leave it be for now."

I reached out and touched his elbow. "Thank you, Lord Greco. Had you not dared to come alone...I think they would've heard the patrol behind us, and mayhap evaded them. We very well may not have escaped."

Lord Greco turned tender eyes upon me. In them, I saw flashes of the familiar struggle—the guilt, the compassion, the hope, the fear. "Mayhap this night has granted us a more intimate use of names. Please...call me Rodolfo?"

I smiled. "Rodolfo, then. Thank you."

"I am glad to have been of service, m'lady. Unfortunately, with some still about, we best get you out of this wood and to safety."

"Agreed," Luca said.

A knight came trotting up, my bow and quiver of arrows in hand. "I believe these belong to you, m'lady?" he asked, offering them to me with a shy smile.

"Indeed," I said. I shouldered the quiver of arrows and then the bow. Instantly, I felt better. More ready. More myself. More the She-Wolf. Far less the captive.

"There is only one way I shall take cover," I said.

Luca turned narrowed eyes in my direction. "Evangelia—"

"One way only," I said, taking his hand in mine. "And that is when we know that your family is safe. Come. Let us go and retrieve them... and see them *all* to Castello Forelli."

## CHAPTER 12

### –GABRIELLA–

I didn't know if I'd ever get the look on Lutterius's face out of my mind. The disbelief, the horror, the breaking, the loss. It was like half his own life slid from his body as he sank to a chair before the fire. We left him there, knowing that the remaining Forelli knights, Father Tomas, and Cook would make sure he was offered food and wine and led to the barracks. But would sleep come for him tonight? Would he cry himself to sleep?

It was too real. Too close. As we rode, I prayed with everything in me—for Lia's safety, for Luca's, and then for Lia's again. *Please please please please please, Lord,* I prayed. But had Lady Santi offered such pleas to God? As her child was killed? As she herself was murdered? If He didn't answer her prayer, why would He answer mine?

We rode hard and fast at a full gallop along the road, only easing our pace when the road became a forested path we had to pick through for a quarter mile in utter darkness before we met another wide, straight road again. Marcello figured we were four hours distant from Luca's uncle's home. And what would we find when we reached it? Another home burned to the ground? Nobles and servant alike marked with the triangle?

*Please please please, Lord,* I prayed again, resuming my silent pleas. I didn't know why God answered some prayers and not others, but I figured if it counted, I was sure going to make sure He heard me.

We paused at a creek to let the horses drink. Marcello pulled me a small distance away. "How do you fare, wife?"

"I grieve for Lutterius. For us. For everyone who has lost someone they loved this day."

He nodded and took my hands in his. "As do I," he said with a sigh.

"Marcello," I said. "How do you fare, riding so soon?"

"Well enough," he said, giving me a small smile, realizing that he didn't fool me.

He was driven. Beyond anything I'd ever seen before. "Tell me, Marcello. Tell me of this brotherhood."

He looked at me, miserable. "It is best if you do not know."

"I already know seven of them," I said, lifting my hands. "Do not tell me the others' names. Just tell me what drew you together in the first place."

He glanced to the others, who were beginning to pull their horses away from the stream, mounting up. "The Republic was at peace with Firenze. Trade was good. For ten years, our fathers enjoyed good trade, and we gathered to run like"—he ducked his head in a smile—"wolves." He led me over to my horse and helped me mount up. "We were dear friends, brothers, truly," he said in an undertone. "And we wanted…we wanted to hold what we all felt that final summer, forever. It was almost as if we knew that it was all about to change. We swore to serve one another unto death."

He turned and mounted his gelding, drawing up alongside me.

"Why the triangle?" I asked softly as we moved to join the others.

"The symbol of the Trinity," he said. "As the Father serves the Son, as the Son serves the Spirit, as the Spirit serves the Father. Never-ending service. Unending self-sacrifice. Unity. Each one, stronger together. So we sought to be too."

"Even when borders once again divided you," I said, thinking of Rodolfo Greco, of the man in Umbria. Of the two others who had not answered our call.

"Even more, then," he said. He looked over the twenty-four knights and my parents behind us. Then we rode out again.

Toward Lia. Toward Luca. And my prayer turned from a plea for preservation to a request that we might reach our loved ones in time to serve. That our Maker would strengthen us all, even while we were yet apart.

## –EVANGELIA–

It took us forever to get out of that forest, with Luca reluctant to use lanterns, fearful it might make us easy targets. I could see his point. My eyes already moved left and right, waiting for our enemies to attack again. My shoulders ached, not from being tied up anymore, but from being all tensed, an arrow nocked on my bowstring. It was a comfort that the first group of Sienese knights appeared to have passed this way without trouble. At least, there was no sign of them.

The tiniest bit of a sunrise was easing the darkness to east, casting a faint lavender to the blue-black sky, when our rear guard raised a cry—"Riders approaching, Sir Forelli!" We pulled over to the side, into the brush, to await them, every man with his sword drawn. Since they were coming from the south, Luca wagered they were Sienese. But still, our knights moved to surround me, Luca to my right, Rodolfo to my left, two others before and behind me. I tried not to get scared. *I'd rather face anybody but those assassins again,* I thought.

It only took a few passing by for us to make out their silhouettes in the predawn light. "Forellis in the wood!" Luca yelled, seeing what I thought I'd seen too—Gabi and Marcello racing by.

She and Marcello pulled up—and behind them, the rest of the patrol.

Gabi and I each slid to the ground, crying out, and raced to hug each other. "Boy, am I glad to see you guys," I said. Mom and Dad were there then too, encircling us with their arms.

"Lia, we were so frightened," Mom said, kissing my hair. "Thank God. Thank God you are all right."

"But we still have to get to Luca's family," I said, scared they'd want to hustle me back to Castello Forelli. I wanted to see this through. For Luca. For his sister.

"Let's get on with it, then," Dad said. He turned and clasped hands with Luca, who gave me a weary smile of triumph. Like he'd captured Dad's favor and therefore had me all the more. Which I suppose he did.

Quickly, Luca told Marcello and the others about what had happened to us the night before, about Rodolfo and the Sienese patrol saving us. About the five men still about.

"Nay, our men must've chased them north. They must be crossing the border by now," Marcello said. "They dare not stay on this side of the border. All of Siena is already turning out to hunt them down."

I shook my head. "These men...they are unlike any we have yet encountered."

Luca nodded, backing me up. "Truly. They were sent to counter the brotherhood. And they seem frightfully dedicated to their task."

Marcello gave him a long look. "Very well then. Let us see to your family and come up with a plan to rout these enemies out once we're safely back to Castello Forelli."

"Yes, m'lord," Luca said, lifting me to my saddle as Marcello lifted Gabi.

We rode out, and I felt stronger, whole, with my family again by my side. The studly Forelli knights, out en masse, as well as the dark giving way to day, didn't hurt my mojo either. We finally left the woods and urged our steeds into a full gallop down the road among the rolling hills, heading directly north for a good half hour.

Luca led the way, turning sharply left down a valley. But then he was pulling up, his face a mask of fear. Smoke was billowing just over the next horizon.

"Captain," Marcello barked, seeing what I did—my man tensing to ride off on his own. "You shall stand, Luca."

"*Marcello.*" Luca grimaced, turning away in utter frustration, but Marcello ignored him. My brother-in-law—it was still *so* weird to think of him that way—gestured to his scouts. "Ride around the villa at a distance and find out what you can. Return to us. We shall continue our approach."

The men set off immediately.

"We must *steal* our way forward," Marcello said firmly.

"Why?" Luca cried out in frustration. "They know we approach!"

"They do not. They did not know for certain where you were headed, correct?"

"Correct," Luca said reluctantly.

"Let us make our way up this hill and peer over. See what we can."

I fought the urge to reach out and grab Luca's reins. I was so worried he'd tear off. Go all-commando trying to rescue his family by himself in his agitation. But he appeared to take some comfort in Marcello's plan.

We left our horses in the care of two knights and crept up the hill, staying hunched over. At the top, among boulders, we carefully peered toward the family villa. I swallowed hard. Smoke was rising within. A servant ran out the open gates but fell, an arrow in her back. The other Sienese knights were nowhere in sight.

Marcello snaked a hand out and took an iron grip on Luca's arm. "Hold, Luca," he grunted as his cousin struggled and then gave in. "Give me a moment to think."

"There," I said, looking beyond the villa. "See? To the west."

We could see our scouts dipping around the hills on either side, but in the distance, on the far side, dust rose from a group of twelve riders in camel tunics and capes. "Lerici's men?" I asked hopefully.

"I hope to God you're right," Marcello grunted. He eyed them in the distance. "In thirty seconds, we shall stride down this hill like we own it. Lia, I want you to take out any of them you can. You too, Matteo," he said to another archer.

"And then what?" Luca said. "They shall murder them all before our eyes."

"Nay, they shall not," Marcello said, his eyes moving to Rodolfo for the first time. "Because they'll want us more. We are of far greater value than your aunt and uncle—even your sister, if she has returned. They'll entertain a trade—your family for three of the brotherhood."

Marcello turned to me, pulling off his tunic, strapping on a back sheath, shouldering a sword, and then settling the tunic back over it. "You shall follow us, you and Matteo, and yet remain just out of range for any arrows sent our way. Obviously, you must not allow the men who come out to retrieve us actually lay hands on us. Shoot over our right shoulders. When I snap with my left hand, we'll dodge left, and your arrow, Evangelia, as well as Matteo's, shall take out the two men in front of me and Luca. We'll draw our weapons and take care of the one in front of Rodolfo, as well as any others."

Matteo paled. I'm sure I looked a shade closer to gray than even he.

"Nay, Marcello," I said. "I cannot! What if I miss?"

He gave me a small grin. "Do not."

Luca took my hand and kissed it. "Please do not."

"Surely there's another way," Mom said.

"I don't see it," Marcello said, already striding down the hill. "The Lerici knights shall soon be upon us. If the Fiorentini see no way out, they shall murder everyone they can before giving into death themselves. Our only hope is to make them think they are about to claim victory—without delay—as well as escape." He turned to face us, walking backward. "Our only hope."

"I myself look forward to the day," Dad said, "when men can sit down and settle their differences across a table."

"When does that occur?" Mom asked softly. "I don't remember that ever happening for long in the history books."

He sighed and nodded. "You're right, of course." He looked to me. "You've got this, Lia. You've shot a hundred birds from the sky. You can do this."

I shook my head as we trudged down the hill behind Luca, Marcello, and Rodolfo. A shout went up from within the walls. A man in dark clothing pointed in our direction. So we'd been seen. This was really happening. They wanted me to shoot a man, directly over one of our guy's shoulders.

"Don't overthink it," Dad said, putting a hand on my neck. "You have the Lerici arrows," he said, looking at my quiver. "They fly straight and true."

So, yeah. My dad was talking me up on how to assassinate an assassin. Talk about your alternate universes.

Three more servants ran out, so far that I thought they'd make it, when arrows brought them down. I groaned and nocked an arrow, Matteo doing the same beside me. Were my hands shaking as much as his?

I shifted the strap of my quiver, getting it set just right, then felt back to settle the arrows, separating them so that I could grab and nock another as fast as I could.

Marcello, limping as if in pain but covering it, stopped just shy of an arrow's reach, fifteen feet ahead of us. "I am Lord Marcello Forelli!" he yelled. "Release your prisoners and show yourselves, Fiorentini scum! This ends *here*."

The leader immediately rounded the corner, a young woman in his arms. I saw Luca falter and Marcello ease his hand to his cousin's shoulder.

*Adela Forelli.* Luca's sister. Marcello's cousin. It had to be, for them to react so.

Two other men emerged, an older woman in one man's arms, an older man directly in front of the other. Two archers appeared on the walls beside the gate. Matteo swore under his breath, beside me.

Marcello, Luca and Rodolfo couldn't see them, from below. Higher on the hill, we could.

"Take your ease," I said, handing him a Lerici arrow. "Use these. They fly faster, truer, and farther than any of our own." Thinking it through then, I handed him four more, leaving me a good ten, and he dropped them into his quiver. We stepped forward, together, and each took a knee, about five feet from the other, the same distance as Luca and Marcello were. Behind us, my parents, Gabi, and the other knights stood, weapons drawn.

How long did we have? Until the Lerici knights were here and the Fiorentini recognized that death was upon them? "Go on, boys,"

I muttered as I took aim at the archer on the wall. "Force him to it. Hurry."

The guys moved forward a bit, taunting their nemeses. "Take us instead," Luca called, tossing his sword aside. "You want us most." I knew his waistband was filled with daggers.

"Is that the traitor Rodolfo Greco?" called the leader, dragging Adela forward.

"It is I," Rodolfo called, stepping closer to Marcello.

"Cease your approach!"

My eyes shifted from one Fiorentini to the other. All five. Or had another survived? "C'mon, c'mon, c'mon," I whispered. Our guys were getting closer to the killers.

"You intend to trade yourselves for these?" said the leader, bringing his knife blade tighter against Adela's throat.

"For innocents such as these," Marcello said. He and Luca stepped forward, Rodolfo right behind them. They began to spread out, giving us room. "But we only give ourselves to you as prisoners if you release them unharmed."

The Fiorentini leader hesitated, considering.

Marcello snapped, expecting us to take out the men in front of them. But he hadn't known about the men on the wall when he first set out.

"The archers, Matteo," I grunted, and let my first arrow fly just as the defenders drew back their arrows, taking aim at our men. Mine reached my target, the force of it knocking him backward, out of sight. Matteo's man dodged at the last moment and took it through the shoulder. *Good enough,* I thought, nocking another arrow as I strode forward.

I needed to be in closer range, because now our men had drawn their hidden weapons. With a nod from the Fiorentini leader, the two men holding Luca's aunt and uncle threw them to the ground and charged toward Marcello and Rodolfo. Luca eased toward the leader and Adela, hands up, as if trying to talk him down.

I was close enough to see the leader's expression falling from glory to fury-filled panic. I could see the muscles on his arm tighten, could read in his eyes that he was about to slit Adela's throat as he had so many others in the last day....

Sounds of the battle faded, my concentration solely on the man about to take the life of someone my man loved.

"Not this one," I whispered. I aimed, adjusted a hair's breath, and let the arrow loose. It sailed from my bow, and I could do nothing but watch it fly as if it moved in slow motion. It just missed Marcello as his attacker drove him backward. It was almost stopped by Rodolfo's arm as he drew back to punch his adversary. It passed over Luca's shoulder.

But it ended in the forehead of the leader, five inches from Adela's own.

His fingers splayed, dropping the long dagger. He stumbled backward, a hand starting to move up to his forehead, as if he wondered what was bringing him down, as if he couldn't quite believe it. But then he fell, dead.

Adela whirled, hand to mouth, and then looked up the hill to me. But I was focused on the others fighting our men. "Come," I grunted to Matteo. As he did so I drew another arrow, walking toward them, taking aim at one, then another, considering their movements, seeking the first clear opportunity.

One of the men turned and kicked, surprising Marcello—still not at his best—sending his sword flying. He dodged his adversary's strike, the blade brushing past his neck by half an inch.

I knelt, forcing myself to wait through the man's next strike, knowing I needed just a bit more focus, concentration. Marcello caught his arm as he brought his sword toward him. They stood there, chests heaving. But the Fiorentini's left hand was drawing a dagger, his intent quite clear. In another half second, he would drive the knife into Marcello.

I let the arrow fly.

It rammed through his leather armor, knocking him backward. He dropped his sword and fell hard, to his rear end, his hands coming to his chest. At that moment, as Rodolfo took out his target, the Lerici knights took down the second.

It was done. Over. Our men were safe. Adela and her aunt and uncle were safe. I stumbled toward Luca, who lifted one arm and welcomed me into the curve of his embrace.

Gabi screamed, behind me. I whipped my head back to see what alarmed her, then followed her gaze to the wall. The wounded archer, the one Matteo had winged, was back. And he aimed his arrow at me.

Five Lerici arrows flew over our heads as Luca dragged me toward two horses. But as soon as we reached them and looked back, we saw that the Lerici had taken him down.

"Oh, Luca," I said, tears starting to flow. "Thank God. Thank God you are well."

"And you, Evangelia," he said, bringing his other arm around me. His chest still heaved for breath, but he held on to me, caressing my neck, my back. "You did well, love. Shh." He kissed my hair, my forehead. "Please do not cry, Evangelia. Please. It is all right. It is over."

"Over?" I asked, looking up into his eyes. "For how long?"

"For as long as God grants us peace." He brought my hands to his lips. "Come. We must go to my sister."

He led me back toward her. Mom and Dad were already beside Adela, greeting her aunt and uncle.

Adela turned to watch our approach and, seeing Luca, hurried to him. He dropped my hand to embrace her. Together, they cried, tears of joy mingling with relief. Luca grinned at me, over his shoulder, then picked up Adela to turn her around in the air. I teared up again too, in spite of myself.

Gabi wrapped her arm around me, and we nestled our heads next to each other. "It's over," she whispered. "And look. Look at that guy, so in love with you," she said. "That's life, in his eyes. Hope. Isn't it?"

I looked over at Luca, beside Adela, pride and joy in his eyes. Mom and Dad stood nearby, smiling and waiting.

"That's a whole lotta good you can grab, Lia, in the midst of the bad. A whole lotta love. Right there. In front of you. In front of us." She took my hand. "Are you still in?"

"For better or worse," I said resignedly. "When you took your vows with Marcello, the rest of us pretty much did the same, signing on for life."

"Then let's do that. Sign on for life. For every day God grants it."

Rodolfo sidled near, hearing that last part. "Every day, a gift."

Luca led Adela up to greet us, his arm around her shoulders. She wiped tears from her cheeks with the back of her hand and gave us a small smile as we stopped, three feet from one another. "Lady Evangelia Betarrini," he said, "I'd like you to know my sister, Adela Forelli." She was several inches shorter than I, with mousy brown hair, but the same, lovely, kind and merry green eyes as her brother.

"Adela," I said, offering her my hand. She took it but didn't shake it, in the manner of medieval women.

"Lady Evangelia," she said. "I owe you my very life."

"Not I, but God alone," I said, with a glance toward my sister. "And 'tis I who owe a debt to you for remaining so still," I said with a little smile.

Her grin grew wider. "So this is the one?" She said to Luca. "The one they say has stolen your heart?"

"Is that what I've done?" I asked, my eyes moving to Luca. "Stolen your heart?"

"Undoubtedly, m'lady," he said. "You've marked me forever." His hand went to his chest, and he gave me a meaningful look, silently reminding me of our kiss.

And in that moment, I glimpsed hope again, like a shaft of light piercing the darkness of my soul. Felt a lifting deep within, as if I'd been turned from the end of a bottomless cave, back toward the exit.

And I knew that somehow, some way, most everything would be all right. For all of us. Gabi and Marcello. Luca and Adela. Mom and Dad. Rodolfo. And me.

Day by day. In time.

# TRIBUTARY
A NOVELLA

## CHAPTER 1

She was gaining on him. She leaned hard, pulling on the reins, leaning around a giant oak to pick up his trail again. *There!* She glimpsed his brown, furry rump, the speck of hooves as the boar dived into the bramble, hoping to lose her.

But he would not lose her. She'd tracked him for hours, losing his trail and then picking it up again. Through two woods and a creek. All she could think of was bringing him back to the villa, tied over her gelding's back. Cooking fat chops over the fire, Papa curing the hocks. Eating their fill, for once.

Ever since the battle, times had been terribly hard in their house. Her brothers, gone. No beau, coming around to court her. She and Papa circled each other, uneasily, neither of them sure how to proceed as family, alone. But summer was almost upon them. Hope surged. And this boar was a symbol of that new beginning.

She ignored her thirst, nagging at her for hours, and leaned forward, urging her gelding to give his last to the effort. She knew the horse was weary, desperate for drink, but they almost had him! The boar grunted and then squealed as she closed the distance between them. He had to know that his moments were short.

She pulled the brim of her father's hunting hat low, and lifted her spear in hand, concentrating on naught but the boar, seeing it on a roasting spit this very night, her family washed, ready, eyes bright with hope...

## –EVANGELIA–

"A rider approaches, hard," Luca said, glancing over at me and Gabi.

"Only one?" Marcello asked. "Are you certain?"

Luca and Lord Rodolfo Greco listened, together, and then shared a long look and brief nod. Still, they edged over to me, Marcello and Gabi, slowly drawing their swords in a protective stance. We were in a clearing, the woods fading for a moment, the shock of a threat startling us all. Things between Siena and Firenze had died down. A skirmish here and there, but nothing like last year. We'd settled into the peace, like a new snow covers the ground.

As the rider drew closer, we tensed, bracing ourselves. I ran my hand over the curve of my bow, but resisted the urge to nock an arrow. It was only one rider. What harm could be coming our way? That three of Siena's finest couldn't handle? Not that I was really ready to shoot anyone again. Not since—

I heard the snort of a boar, then glimpsed the hunter, a bit of a man—a boy?—but still coming at a full gallop, long spear in hand, heading straight toward my sister. Did he mean to—

"Gabi!" I shouted, as the men shouted too, moving to intercept him.

But the boar emerged then, running between our horses, making Gabi's mare rear and Luca's shy, whipping him around in a circle.

"*Aspettate!*" I screamed. *"Sta solamente cacciando!" Wait! He's only hunting. No assassin*—

But I was too late. Rodolfo charged, angling himself so that the hunter would hit him instead of my sister. He swung his sword, hitting the tip of the intruder's spear, sending it flying. The hunter's horse collided with his, faltered, then went down, while Rodolfo held his seat.

"He was hunting! Only hunting!" I yelled, as all three men dismounted and approached the slight man, swords drawn. Confusion filled their eyes. The hunter lay frightfully still.

Gabi and I dismounted.

"Stay where you are," Marcello growled at us, eyeing the forest beyond the hunter suspiciously.

"Marcello, he's alone," Gabi said. "A boy on the hunt. For boar, not for *wolf*." She edged past him and I followed her lead. We hurried over and crouched next to the hunter.

Gabi paused and then reached out. "It's a woman," she said quietly. She eased the hat off and gently lowered the huntress's head back to the ground, grimacing when her hand came away wet with blood. My sister was right; the huntress was filthy, but clearly all-girl.

"A woman?" Rodolfo said in shock, sheathing his sword, his face a mask of confusion.

It was scary, seeing her lying still. "Is she alive?"

"For now," Gabi said. She leaned back, considering. Greco bent and ran his fingertips through bright red blood on a small boulder a foot away. Her gelding was back on his feet, nuzzling the girl, as if urging her to move. Luca ran his hands down his hocks and legs. "The horse is in better shape than the girl."

Gabi pushed the horse's head away, like he was a big, nosey dog, and went to the girl's other side. Gently, she ran her fingers along the girl's neck and head.

"How bad?" I whispered.

"I don't know," she returned. "I'm no EMT. But I'd guess we need to put her on a stretcher and get her to the castello. Keep her steady, quiet, until she wakes. Mom might know more."

"To the castello?" Rodolfo said, picking out the lone Italian word among our English. He moved to pick the girl up.

"Nay!" Gabi shouted, reaching out her hand. He pulled back, his dark eyebrows lowering over his eyes. He really was one of the most beautiful men I'd ever seen, and was still trying to get over his crush on my sister, more than a year after she'd married Marcello. There was this low-lying tension between them you could feel anytime they were in the same room. And proximity didn't help.

Her tone and face softened. "Moving her might hurt her further. We need a flat surface, a stretcher, to transport her back to the castello."

"I'll go," Rodolfo said. "I can be back fast."

Gabi and Marcello nodded, and Rodolfo mounted and raced out of the clearing as if this girl was his own sister.

Gabi and I shared a long look. The mighty Lord Rodolfo Greco had been through a lot in the last year. He basically made a play for Gabi and lost her for good to Marcello. All his holdings in Firenze had been taken and he'd been banished from ever entering the city again, an enemy of the republic.

All because he chose us over the city of his birth.

Marcello had done what he could to mitigate the pain. He granted Castello Paratore, and most of the land we'd won in the battle, to Rodolfo. But that put him perilously close to the border. While the castle was in his name, he was forced to remain with us, a little farther south, for protection. Hanging out at Castello Greco merely invited assassins to try and bring him down. But hanging out at Castello Forelli brought its own kind of tension. Which was probably why he was so on edge when the huntress raced toward us...

And now he'd be wracked with guilt. We'd seen many die of far lesser injuries in this era. If the girl was paralyzed, even partially, she was unlikely to live long. Even I knew that the stress on her inner organs would be something we'd be ill equipped to handle. Mom had tried to save a paraplegic man last month, to no avail. It was one of the hardest parts of living here...to know that medical conditions readily handled in our own time often proved impossible in medieval Italia. Infection was our biggest enemy. As scary as this girl's unconsciousness or potential paralysis was...it was the blood that really freaked us. An open wound.

"Lord Forelli," Luca called. We all looked up. He'd lifted the saddlebags across the hunter's horse. Beneath was a blanket. Even muddy, it was clearly embroidered.

With the emblem of Firenze.

We all froze, staring. Marcello broke first, turning, hands on his face, looking up into the new green leaves of the massive oaks high above us.

"The Fiorentini," I muttered in English, toward my sister, "they won't like this. They won't like it at all."

"No they won't." Slowly, she lifted her brown eyes to meet mine.

"I can't do it, Gabs." *Not again.* Not after last year's battle. The Santis, the Hercolanis, all murdered. Not after so narrowly escaping ourselves. It couldn't all be starting again, could it? Because I couldn't. *I can't I can't I can't.*

Gabi reached out and put a hand on my shoulder.

But she had no words of comfort for me.

Rodolfo paced for hours outside the Fiorentini girl's room, chin in hand. Marcello tried to talk to him, persuade him to retire to his quarters, but he refused, somehow believing the whole incident was his fault. Sighing, Marcello left him to continue his pacing, and pulled up a stool on the far side of our patient. Gabi reached across the girl to take his hand and squeeze it. "*Hai fatto quello che potevi,*" she said. *You did what you could.* Mom nodded her agreement.

I leaned against a wall, waiting to be sent on whatever errand Gabi needed done, wishing Adela, Luca's sister, was here, rather than in Roma, visiting friends. She'd received some training in the healing arts—such as they were in medieval times—and was pretty good with concocting foul-smelling herbal blends that actually seemed to work.

Luca was dozing at a table, his head on his crossed arms. I shook my head. The guy could sleep anywhere it seemed. And wake as chipper and happy as if he'd had eight hours in a Marriott king-sized bed.

It was completely aggravating.

I closed my eyes and thought of fine hotel sheets, silky and smooth to the touch. I was homesick. Seriously homesick. Like none of my family seemed to be. Everyone else seemed to have settled in. Each of us had had our speed bumps, but generally, they all seemed pretty content. Meanwhile, I was a mess. Becoming more grumpy and agitated with every passing day. Torn between my family, my adorable boyfriend, and the longing for home. Meaning twenty-first century Colorado.

A knight appeared at the door. "M'lord, there are two men at the gates, asking if we've seen a girl matching this one's description." He nodded toward our unconscious patient.

Luca was up, rubbing his face. "Want me to see to it?"

"Nay," Marcello said. "I want you to see them in."

Gabi looked at him in surprise, and I saw that Rodolfo had paused outside the door.

"You want us to allow the Fiorentini in?" Luca said.

"They are two men," Marcello said. "What harm can they do? It will create much more difficulty for us if they know she is here and they cannot see that we're doing our best to care for her."

"Understood, m'lord. I'll show them the way," Luca said.

We all glanced at one another. Rodolfo finally came in and went to the girl's bedside, taking her hand in his. "Wake, friend, from your slumber," he urged. We all know what he was thinking—if she could regain consciousness before her people saw her...

But she did not stir.

They arrived shortly thereafter, two men, one burly, one slight. Luca and three knights followed them in. "Alessandra!" said the smaller one, rushing to her side, kneeling and stroking her head.

"You know her, friend?" Marcello said.

The man continued staring at her, caressing her forehead. "My daughter, Alessandra Donatelli." His eyes hardened. "What happened to her?"

"She was hunting, and ran into us," Rodolfo said, stepping forward. "We were startled. She fell from her horse and struck a rock."

The bigger man stepped forward, his eyebrows lowering in a combination of confusion and recognition. "I know you..."

Rodolfo ignored him, focusing on Signore Donatelli. "She came at us so fast, wearing a hat...we didn't know—"

"Why...you are Lord Greco!" said Donatelli's companion, taking another step to face him and clenching his fists as if he meant to strike.

"Nay!" Marcello said, stepping between them. "Be at peace!"

"I served in your contingent, before you turned traitor!"

Rodolfo finally met his eye. The muscles in his jaw tensed. "There were many nuances of my decision of which you are unaware—"

"Should have figured that you would hide here," the big man sneered, glancing over at Marcello with hatred. He said the word *here* as if we were living in some sort of swampy pit rather than Castello Forelli. Luca and another knight came up behind Marcello, ready to move with but a word from their lord.

"There will be no good end to such a conversation," Marcello said, keeping his tone calm, his voice low. "Let's speak only of Alessandra. She is what you are here for, correct?"

"Yes," Signore Donatelli said. "What is the matter with her?"

Marcello eyed him. "She came at us with a spear. One of my knights intercepted her, and their horses collided. She went down to the ground, and hit her head on a rock." He frowned and shook his head. "She has not awakened since."

"We shall take her," Signore Donatelli said, rising. "Back home where we might see to her ourselves."

"Nay," Mom said, rising with him. She reached out a hand. "Please. Let us watch over her. I've had some experience with—"

"You propose we leave this man's daughter *here*?" barked his friend, looking at her incredulously. "When we've spent two days trying to find her?"

"Hear me," Mom said, focusing on Alessandra's father. "I have some knowledge on how to treat your daughter. She shouldn't be moved. And you can see that we've treated her as one of our own, can you not?"

"She is not *your own*," spat the big man, again stepping forward in a threatening manner. Marcello gave up and turned away, while Luca and the other knight restrained the man by each taking hold of an arm. "She belongs with us!" he bellowed.

"Cease your threatening tone," Marcello said, "or you shall be escorted out to wait on your companion." He sighed. "We only want her to remain here until she is well."

"We shall see to her healing," said the big man. "Release her at once!" He tried to wrench free, but the men held on.

Marcello took a deep breath and clenched and released his fists, trying to control his temper. "What is your name?"

"Signore Motini."

"Signore Motini, you and I both know that if we release her, and the worst happens, we shall be held accountable. Our only choice is to treat Alessandra as a welcome guest. Not a prisoner," Marcello's eyes shifted to Signore Donatelli. "You are both welcome to remain here, with her, until she is—"

"We cannot stay here!" spat Motini. "We'll be considered the likes of *him*," he said, jutting out his chin in Rodolfo's direction. "Banished from Firenze!"

I had to hand it to Rodolfo. They were about the same size, but I knew he could take this Motini dude in seconds. I'd seen him in battle. But he merely glowered back at him, his dark eyes frightfully steady, his arms crossed over his chest.

"Remove him," Marcello said.

The men did as he asked. But it took all four of them.

Alessandra's father looked stricken as his friend was taken away. The hall door slammed and we were finally left in silence.

"I know that this is a most confusing situation," Marcello said, staring into the older man's eyes. "Upon my life, no further harm will come to your daughter. Give Lady Betarrini but five more days to tend to her."

"*Marcello,*" Gabi whispered. He couldn't make such promises. We didn't know if the girl would ever regain consciousness. What would happen if she died?

But Marcello only focused on Signore Donatelli. "She must stay here. To move her shall certainly only invite death near. If I thought it was best for her to leave, would I not send her off with you, gladly?"

The man looked up and into Marcello's eyes for a long moment, while we all held our breath.

Signore Donatelli considered him, then nodded. "Upon your life. You shall return her to me in good stead."

Marcello reached out his arm, and the girl's father took it. "Upon my life."

## CHAPTER 2

Alessandra heard the men talking, at first, as if they were in another room. Then gradually, she realized they were close. Right beside her. Gradually, her head stopped spinning. But try as she might, she could not make her eyes open, speak, or move her arms.

*What ails me?* She thought in a panic. *Why can I not move?*

She redoubled her efforts to move, to speak, all to no avail.

Swirling in terror, she forced herself to listen to the men, to try and place their voices. To draw comfort from them. Why did they sound like strangers?

"You cannot continue to punish yourself so, Rodolfo," said a kind, male voice.

"Punish myself?" scoffed the other. Rodolfo? "There is no need. God is doing a fine job of it."

"You had come so far. Then this bit of a Fiorentini arrives and you fall back into your whirlpool of doubt."

"Mayhap I've only deluded myself," Rodolfo said. His tone was dark, tortured. "Convinced myself I belong here. That I belong anywhere, now. I only draw Marcello's enemies closer, by my presence."

"Nay. You made a choice. An honorable choice. Truly, our sails were set long ago, when we took the mark of the brotherhood. Can you not learn to go with the wind?"

The screech of wood on stone told Alessandra that one of the men stood, or brushed against a chair. "And what if I cannot forgive myself?"

The second man let out a scoffing laugh. "You place yourself in the Savior's position alone, man! What a preposterous notion—to forgive oneself? He has done the task. Forgiven all sins, past and present and future. You accept the power of it or you do not."

Rodolfo paused. "Surely there is something I can do...some pilgrimage I must make..."

"You want a task? Here 'tis. Commit this girl to your care. To see her restored to her family."

"The girl? What good would that do?"

"Come now. She's a Fiorentini in need. Vulnerable. And since your betrayal of her people chafes you, mayhap caring for her will be the balm you need."

The other remained silent.

"Surely a female as comely as this isn't difficult to—"

"You're speaking nonsense, Tomas."

"You wanted penance. I'm suggesting a path. And while you're keeping an eye on our pretty guest, ask God to chip away at the pride that holds you captive, so wrapped in chains you can't reach the gifts that are at your feet."

"Pride?" Rodolfo sputtered. "What is left of my pride?"

"Apparently enough to keep you entrapped."

"You do not know of what you speak," Rodolfo said, suddenly sounding dangerous, powerful, angry.

"Nay? Are you certain?" answered Tomas, unperturbed.

His companion fell silent again.

"Mayhap this one has been sent here to help you find the resolution you seek." Tomas said, and by the sound of his voice, Alessandra was sure he was turning to look upon her. "Seek the Lord's guidance, Rodolfo. You'll find life is far less a struggle with the wind at your back."

Alessandra wanted to keep listening. To understand. To find out if these two would find resolution, but her mind was spinning, disconnected visions coming to her, as if in dreams. She heard pages turning, smelled the distinct odor of parchment and ink, lambskin—a book. The man, Tomas, was speaking in Latin while she struggled to cling to this unseen world. *He must be a priest,* she thought. *And he is praying over me.*

And then she could not fight it any longer, lulled by the priest's gentle prayers, she succumbed to the pull to rest, rest, rest...

–EVANGELIA–

I shivered as the chill of deep night settled in. Gabi, feeling ill, had gone off to bed, and since Mom hadn't slept in a couple of days, I'd persuaded her to let me take a turn, watching over our guest. *Alessandra. A beautiful name for a beautiful girl,* I thought as I sketched her profile on my parchment, mounted on a board. She was quintessentially Italian—about five-foot-four, olive skin, long, dark lashes, lovely cheekbones, bigger, Roman nose, lush lips. As entertaining as it was to sketch a Tuscan Sleeping Beauty, I just wished she'd wake and go home...And kill this seed that promised to turn into a whole new crop of Forelli-hate.

Firenze didn't need much more of a push to come calling again. We'd been in an uneasy truce for more than a year now. But none of us truly believed it'd hold. And I just wasn't ready to take up my bow against anybody else. There'd been enough killing. So, so much killing last year...and the year before that...

Rodolfo stood at one end of the room, like a silent, brooding archangel, one boot propped on the stone wall behind him, chin in hand, half-dozing. *The man refuses to give in to sleep*...He was so dang intense about everything. Someday, he had to find a way to lighten up or he was never going to get a girl.

Luca, noticing me shiver, picked up a wool blanket from a rack in the corner and wrapped it around me, leaving his hands on my shoulders in silent encouragement. A smile tugged at the corner of my lips and I reached up to lay my fingers over his for a moment.

Gabi, Mom and Dad—over the last year, they'd settled into life here in Medievalville like it was some exotic vacation destination. If it wasn't for the fact that I was crazy-wild to be a family again—and for cute Luca always nearby, ready to try and make me smile—I might've run into the Tuscan forest screaming, convinced I'd gone mental. Some days I could just live my life. Enjoy it even. Other days I'd pause and stare at half-dressed knights sparring, maids hauling up water from a well, smoke coming from the kitchen chimney, and try to get my modern brain and my ancient surroundings to match up. But there was a serious sort of disconnect between the two.

For a while, Gabi worked hard at helping me along, aware that I'd sacrificed a lot to stay here, so she could stay here. But ever since she'd gotten married, all she really had time for was Marcello. *Marcello, Marcello, Marcello. Blah, blah, blah.* It was kind of nauseating, really.

And totally sweet.

And epically romantic.

So yeah...I was a little conflicted. I'd kinda gained my dad and lost my sis. Not to be a whiner or anything...I know that sisters have close times and distant times...but I wasn't expecting the my-sis-permanently-left-me-for-a-guy feelings until I was in my twenties or thirties, you know? Not when I was just about to turn seventeen.

"Lia," Luca said, edging closer again.

I shook off my dream-like thoughts, my eyes focusing on our patient again. She was shifting, turning her head. I sensed Rodolfo move from the wall, instantly shaking off his doze. He'd become a little obsessed with this girl, feeling responsible for how he'd endangered Castello Forelli with this latest fumble.

Our worst fear was that when her dad came back for her, he'd come with Fiorentini soldiers. And she wouldn't be alive when they reached us. Now, seeing her move, hope surged within me. All would be well! No new battle would be upon us! Only a new, potential act of peace, passing a wandering Fiorentini daughter back into the arms of her father, in better health than when we met her. Surely that'd be worth something...

Alessandra squeezed her eyes shut and waved her head back and forth. Then her eyes, wide and brown and beautiful, blinked and opened, searching the ceiling of the room first, then, sensing us, roaming over our direction.

She gasped and scrambled to rise.

"Whoa, whoa, whoa," I cried, putting out my hands like I was trying to calm a frightened horse. *Don't let her move around if she wakes,* Mom said, as she parted. *Sorry, Mom. Blew that one—*

"*Aspetta! Piano, piano...*" Rodolfo urged, coming to her other side. *Wait. Easy, easy...*

But Alessandra was having none of it. She sat up, glancing down in confusion at the luxurious, soft night gown we'd put her in, then pulling the covers to her chest. Her long brown hair edged over her shoulder, making her look soft and rumpled and sweet, in spite of the fear and anger that rumbled under her lowered brow. "Where am I?" she asked. "Who are you?"

"*Siamo amici.*" *We are friends,* I said, reaching out my hands in a manner that said, *it's okay.* "You are safe. You were injured. On a hunt. There was a misunderstanding. But you are all right. Your father was here. You'll soon be home with him."

Her brow furrowed in confusion, her eyes shifting back and forth, as if trying to remember. "The boar," she said, catching the tail of a memory. "I was hunting..."

"And then the boar led you straight into a clearing, where we were," Rodolfo said, helping her piece it together. He hovered at the foot of her straw tick, keeping a respectful distance. "M'lady, I owe you an apology. You had the spear—I blocked you—"

"And was unseated," she mumbled. Her eyes met his. "I don't remember anything beyond that moment."

"No. You've hovered on the edge of death these past two—almost three—days."

She studied him and then looked at the far wall, as if a window to her missing memories might open there. "Three days," she whispered, clenching the blanket in her fist all the harder. She looked to me with urgency. "My father came?"

"Yes," I said, nodding in encouragement. She was plainly scared and disoriented. "He'll be back soon for you. We convinced him to leave you here. My mother—she's fairly adept in the healing arts. And you've been gravely ill."

"It was no easy task," Rodolfo added with a tender, caring smile. "Your father was reluctant to leave you behind."

Alessandra studied his face and then let a little smile soften her own. "I am a woman grown. But he is a bit over-protective, really. I lost two brothers in the battle," she explained. "He only has me left."

Rodolfo froze and visibly paled. I held my breath, as did Luca, beside me. Alessandra looked from one of us to the other, reading the tension immediately. Silence hung in the air. "You never said where I was," she said, suspicion dawning in her eyes. "Nor who you are."

"M'lady, you—" Rodolfo said.

"I am no high-born lady of the court," she said in agitation. "I am Signorina Alessandra Donatelli. Now, pray tell, who are you and where am I? Exactly."

"Signorina Donatelli," Rodolfo began again. I admired his steady, calm tone in the face of what was to come. "You'll remember your hunt plainly led you across the border. You are in the care of Castello Forelli."

She stared at him, hard. She struggled to swallow, as if her mouth was dry. "And you are…Lord Forelli?"

"I am Lord Rodolfo Greco," he said, after a moment's hesitation.

"Lord…Greco," she repeated numbly.

His dark eyes searched hers. "Yes."

"I lost my brothers, *as well as my intended,* the night Castello Paratore was taken," she mumbled, her brow lowering in pain. "Because you turned your back on Firenze. Because you wanted the castle for yourself!"

"There are two sides in any battle, Alessandra," I said, my voice trembling a bit at the memory. "As I remember, Lord Greco was in chains, nearly hanged, alongside our priest and many of our people. Lord Paratore was a monster—"

"M'lady," Rodolfo said, giving his head a little shake, shutting me down. He turned back to Alessandra. "I am sorry for your losses. Clearly my presence upsets you, Signorina. And Evangelia's mother wished for you to remain calm. 'Tis best for your healing. I will return come morning." He rose, and stiffly walked to the door, quietly closing it behind him.

Luca and I shared a quick glance.

"There are many things you do not know, Signorina," Luca said.

"Clearly," Alessandra said, in a measured, drawn-out way. "But I do know that that man," she said, pointing out the door Rodolfo just exited through, "and all of you, the *Sienese,* destroyed much of my life, my future." Her hand was trembling.

"We all lost in that battle. I lost friends myself. Men I considered brothers," he said. "Rodolfo lost everything in Firenze. All he'd worked very hard to gain."

"Luca—" I intervened, trying to ease him away from his own rising agitation.

"Men you considered brothers," Alessandra interrupted. "But not flesh and blood. Kin. Your husband-to-be." Her last words sent ripples of pain through the room.

Luca paused a moment. "We could have left you out in the woods to perish," he said, gesturing north. "But we did not, even after we knew you were Fiorentini. Consider what sort of people would act in such a manner, and decide for yourself if we are the animals you've made us out to be. *Buona sera,"* he said with a slight bow.

With that, he strode away, not even pausing to say goodnight to me. I'd never seen him so agitated. Probably because she was accusing one of the brotherhood. And nothing ticked off the guys around here more than messing with one of their boys.

Well, right. They didn't like it if anyone messed with one of their girls either.

Alessandra and I shared a long look and then she closed her eyes, as if she had the mother of all headaches.

"You must rest," I said softly.

She gave me the slightest of nods and pulled up her blanket. But her big, brown eyes popped open a second later and she studied me. "You are one of the Ladies Betarrini."

"I am," I said, pouring a cup of water and then offering it to her, realizing we hadn't quite gotten around to introductions. "I'm Evangelia

Betarrini. My sister is Lady Gabriella Betarrini Forelli. And that was Sir Luca Forelli, cousin to Lord Marcello and captain of his guard."

Her expression betrayed her confusion, as if she were torn between contempt and awe and fear. Like she was meeting Darth Vader. Or Loki. Or Damon Salvatore. She slowly took the cup and rose on one elbow to drink it down, waving me away when I moved to help her. "You do not appear as fierce as they say you are."

I laughed under my breath. "Not all is exactly as they say."

"They say you can kill five men with one arrow."

I frowned, her words making me feel slightly nauseated. Maybe I was catching Gabi's stomach bug. "I've killed far too many men in battle," I muttered. "But never more than one at a time."

She paused, continuing to stare at me. "The memory of their deaths pains you?"

"Greatly," I said without hesitation. "I haven't as much as shot a rabbit in more than a year. I cannot seem to bear it." I shook my head. "As soon as I lift my bow, it all comes back." I looked up at her. "And I'd rather not remember."

She frowned, hesitating. "The Sienese won the battle. Yet you do not rejoice in your triumph?"

I considered her words. "Let us say that my future's path changed as abruptly as your own during the battle and afterward." *We decided to stay here, and Gabs got married…and I left Castello Paratore, covered in my enemies' blood. Oh, and yeah, then I was almost killed by the assassins…* Bile rose in my throat at the memory of it. Yes, I'd lost in that battle—my dreams, as well as the last vestiges of my childhood. But what if I'd lost Gabi or Mom and Dad? Luca? Or all of them? As Alessandra had lost brothers and a boyfriend?

She looked away, rubbing her forehead.

"I can give you a tincture, for that headache," I said, rising to fetch a bottle Mom had left.

"Nay," she said. "I will not accept potential poison from you."

Her words stung, as well as her sudden coldness just when I thought she was beginning to warm. "You think we've nursed you for three days, washed you, taken care of your *necessities,* only to poison you? When we know your father will return in a few days and call upon Firenze forces to rise if you are not well?" I let out a little laugh. "Lord Marcello pledged his *life* that you would be safe here."

Her brow furrowed, and a tinge of red climbed her cheeks, but she said nothing, only turning her back to me.

I sighed and considered downing Mom's precious potion myself. Because my head felt as if it was in the middle of a vice clamp. I needed to give her a little leeway—a measure of God's own peace, Father Tomas would say—but I was dead-tired too.

So, yeah. It was bound to be a rough few days.

Now that we knew she'd live, we'd all be counting the hours until Signore Donatelli came to collect his daughter.

I was still agitated that afternoon, still churning over my conversation with Alessandra, while Luca'd returned to his easy-going manner. I paced back and forth in the courtyard, hands on hips, while Luca reclined in a hay wagon, hands behind his head, watching me. "You seem upset. Shall I fetch you your bow and arrows, my love? Mayhap sticking a few arrows deep into a—"

"Nay!"

"What about some of Cook's special pudding for a special treat?"

"Nay!" I repeated, tossing out my hand in dismissal.

"A walk, along the ramparts?"

"Nay, Luca…" I put my hand to my head and paused, looking up at the sky, then over at him.

He rolled to his side, his shoulder-length hair flopping half over his face, chewing a piece of straw. I stared at him, considering sketching him there, my own lounging, gorgeous, medieval knight. But even that wasn't what I needed. I pursed my lips and tapped them with one finger, still looking him over.

"Why stare at me with such intent?" he asked, his brows lowering. He cocked one brow and grinned. "Could it be that you wish to join me, here, in the hay wagon?"

"Your hair," I said, ignoring his flirty suggestion. "It's gotten long, of late."

"The barber hasn't been through in some time." He reached into his mouth, probing with a finger. "I have a tooth that's giving me fits too—"

I sucked in my breath, suddenly knowing what would make me feel better, and smiled. "He'll come through, soon enough. But before he does...Luca, may I cut your hair?"

He stared at me a moment. "You wish to cut my hair."

"Oh, yes! May I? It would ease my agitation to...to do something. Something constructive."

He considered it a moment and then shrugged. "I don't see why not. You are adept with the shears?"

"As adept with the shears as I am with the pen and ink."

"Then, by all means, let's get on with it," he said, making a gesture in the air, completely relaxed.

"Draw closer." He obediently sat up, on the edge of the wagon, letting his boots swing over the side. I stepped closer, reached up and ran my fingers through his hair, just long enough now on either side to tie back—not that he ever did—and slightly wavy. He closed his eyes and smiled, as if my touch made him want to go to sleep. Then he opened his green eyes and looked at me. "What say you? How shall you shear this sheep?"

"I shall shear you short," I said. I lifted sections of his hair. "Here, and here, and here. All around. Might you live with it as such?"

He pursed his lips and wrapped his hands around my waist. "'Tis uncommon, as you describe. Would you not prefer I grow it a little longer and wear it banded at the nape of my neck, like Marcello?"

"Nay," I said quickly. That look was for my brother-in-law. And my sister too. Not for us.

"Truly?" he frowned.

"Truly."

"Well, then, fetch the shears, woman, and do what you wish with me. For God knows," he said, leaning closer to me, his lips almost on mine, "I am yours to do with as you wish."

I smiled, stood on tiptoe to give him a quick kiss—which elicited a hoot of approval from the guards on the wall above us—and then left for the stables, where I knew there was at least one pair of scissors. I also picked up a basin, a pitcher and a knife—as sharp as a razor—then a towel, soap and an ivory comb from my room. I waved at Luca to follow me into the Great Hall.

It was long after supper and the big room, full of long tables and benches, was vacant, except for the two of us, standing alongside the dying embers of a fire in the massive hearth. I took his hand and pulled him to the nearest table and bench, seating him with his back to the table.

"Now lean back," I said, easing his broad shoulders to the edge, so that his head hovered over the basin. I lifted the pitcher and poured it over his scalp, dousing it thoroughly, then lifted the bar of soap, lathered it in my hands and began rubbing his hair, working the suds through.

"Saints in heaven, woman," he moaned, "what are you doing to me?"

"Washing your hair," I said, as innocently as I could. But I was grinning. I used my best spa skillage, not only giving him a thorough shampoo, but also massaging his head, moving my thumbs in tiny circles, easing away tension, stress. At least I hoped that was what I was doing.

His fingers ran down my arms, looking up at me. "I want you to wash my hair this way, every night of our lives."

I grinned, rinsing his hair out now, intentionally letting a little splash in his eyes. His hands sprang away to rub them. "We shall see, won't we?" I said.

I lightly towel-dried his hair, then moved him to a chair, right by the fire. Once he was situated there, I combed it out, and set to work. I had a distinct look in my mind—lots of layers. Short on top. A little longer at the nape of the neck—just long enough to play with. Slightly longer sideburns. To play up his impish green eyes.

But I was working with some whacky kind of scissors. They were broad and flat, with a very stiff coil at the end and a wicked edge. The end result was...less than perfect.

So I cut. And cut. And cut.

"Is there to be nothing left?" he asked, as the embers burned low in the hearth.

"Mayhap," I said, finally smiling at what I was seeing. I ran my fingers through it, helping it dry, and he quieted. Then I tilted his chin up toward me and smiled. "Very nice, Luca. Very, very nice."

He ran his fingers through it. "The men will never let me hear the last of it," he moaned, lifting a silver platter to try and get a bit of reflection, as if he was very much having second thoughts.

"Until you tell them your woman thinks it most handsome," I said.

That made him still, then smile. He wrapped a hand around my waist and drew me close. "So is my lady finished with me?" he asked, looking up.

"Oh, I think not," I said, giving him a quick kiss. "We have yet to finish your sideburns."

"What? You mean to shave me?"

"Do you not trust me?" I pretended to pout.

"Nay, nay," he said, sounding not at all convinced. Before he could say more, I moved to the basin, poured more water in it, grabbed the soap and razor, and came back to him. "Shall I put another log on?" he said nervously. "So that you might better see?"

I pulled up a stool, close to him, and straddled it, caressing his face. "I see very well, Luca. Trust me."

He turned his face toward me and covered my hand with his. "Evangelia Betarrini, by now, you must certainly know that there is not another woman I trust more in the world."

"With anything?"

"Anything," he said.

And that lone word made me smile more broadly than I had all day.

That…and his killer new haircut that made him look all kinds of hot.

## CHAPTER 3

Alessandra watched through slitted eyes as Lord Rodolfo Greco returned in the earliest hours of morning, and saw Lady Betarrini sleeping on the settee. He reached for a blanket and covered her with it. His every move spoke of respect and care, surprising Alessandra.

He straightened and quickly looked over to Alessandra, as if he'd felt her gaze.

She dropped her eyelashes and assumed the heavy, rhythmic breathing of sleep, hoping he'd leave then, as was proper. But instead, she heard him stride over to the empty chair beside her bed and sit down. "You need not pretend you slumber," he said quietly.

Alessandra debated continuing her ruse, potentially convincing him in time, but she felt like she could feel every hour of the four days she'd had her eyes shut. She was ready to be awake, moving, despite the murderous headache she suffered. She let her eyes flutter open.

"Ahh, yes, there you are," he said, triumph in his brown eyes.

"Isn't there a maidservant you could send in to watch over me, while the lady sleeps?" Alessandra asked. "Your presence in my makeshift bedchamber is hardly proper."

"Agreed," he said easily, but only settled back in the chair and placed a casual boot on the opposite leg. "Be at ease—you've nothing to fear from me. I've been charged by Lord Forelli and our priest to see to your safety—until your father returns to fetch you. Lord Marcello pledged it, upon his life, that you would be well, and well you shall be. Think of me as your personal guard. Your protector."

"Or jailer," she bit out. Even as she said it, she knew it wasn't quite true.

A tiny smile crossed his handsome face. "You wound me, Signorina. 'Tisn't *quite* like that…"

She slowly sat up, her head throbbing, but she tried to hide it. "Why tarry? Let us rise and ride. You may escort me home. My father will be nothing short of pleasantly surprised."

"Alas, Lady Betarrini, Evangelia's mother, would hear of no such thing. She'll allow you to slowly resume your previous activities on the morrow, bit by bit. She says that those who have hit their head must move forward with utmost care. And if we neared the border, let alone crossed it—there'd be misery to pay from the Fiorentini. With or without one of their own in tow. Particularly, with *me* towing her."

Alessandra frowned. "I would tell them of your succor."

Rodolfo raised one brow in surprise. "Which would be most kind. Unfortunately, the Fiorentini might twist even good will into something more beneficial for them." He shrugged. "Even now, your father has surely gone to the Grandi in Firenze. He shall return with a contingent of knights to ensure you are as well and whole as Lord Marcello pledged. And if you are not, you must know that the Fiorentini shall demand justice. In fact, they'll almost hope you are not, so they can be justified in extracting it."

She remained quiet, thinking through his words. She didn't want to believe it. But she'd learned enough to know that the ways of war and politics were more complex than she'd believed as a child.

"Something tells me that a woman who hunts with as much determination and focus as you might try something ill-conceived." He lowered his head, all trace of ease gone from his face, and in its place, only a man determined to see through his task as charged. "And signorina, you shall not be leaving this castle until my lord places your hand in your father's."

She looked toward the ceiling. She really hadn't decided what her next steps might be. But if Lady Betarrini went on sleeping, she might be able to rise, escape…

Alessandra felt a heavy weariness slide over her again, claiming her as it did again and again, her lids begging to close, even after all those hours of sleep. But as she let them fall, the throb behind them kept her from settling into slumber.

"Lord Greco," she said, but stopped when she saw he'd risen and was already pouring another tincture bottle into a goblet.

"The pain is plain in your eyes," he said knowingly, a look of compassion in his own. "And Lady Betarrini is quite adept at fashioning medicines." He lifted the cup to her. "This will bring you ease."

Alessandra paused, sniffing the swirling liquid, wondering if it was anything more than medicine. But Evangelia had been right—as was Lord Greco. Their master had sworn upon his life that Alessandra would be well in their keep. So why poison her now? Quickly, she drank it down, puzzling over the flowery taste.

But in minutes, she slept, blissfully freed of the pounding ache in her skull.

The rising sun was lifting the sky from periwinkle to pink through the window when the elder Lady Bettarini stirred and sat up, tossing her long braid over her shoulder and rubbing her face. She looked from Rodolfo to the sleeping girl. "How does she fare?"

"She awakened for a time last night. She seemed more alert."

"Might you stay, m'lord, and keep watch over her while I see to my morning toilette? I can send a maid…"

"A good plan, m'lady," he said, rising, gesturing to the door. "Until she arrives, I'll remain right here."

She gave him a gentle smile. "Thank you, Rodolfo." She edged over to Alessandra, laid a gentle hand on her brow, then felt for her pulse at the wrist. She smiled at him again. "I shall return shortly," she whispered.

He took the chair and gazed out the window, watching as the sky warmed in color, turning now to peach, until he felt Alessandra's eyes upon him.

He glanced down at her, slowly, carefully. She did not blink. He thought she might be only a couple of years younger than he, an age most women were married and with children, unless they had no beau… He refused to back down from her stare, steadily meeting her probing eyes.

"Why?" she whispered. "Why turn your back on all who had ever loved you, were behind you?"

He considered her words, grudging in his admiration for her forthright, honest question. "Because not all were as you describe," he said with a sigh. He cocked his head and leaned forward, forearms on his knees. "I do not expect you to understand, Signorina Alessandra."

She waited, unmoving, as if she hoped he'd try to explain.

"Do you remember when we were children? When Siena and Firenze were at peace?"

She nodded.

"My father and Lord Forelli's father were friends. They traded, in the spring and autumn, both for their own households as well as the surrounding villages. We came here, every year, and in turn, the Forellis came to us six months past. We were two of a number of families who gathered as such, each with sons about our own age. Marcello and I… Luca…" he added, casting a smile over his shoulder, "we were friends too. And over time, it was almost as if we were brothers. Kin."

He let the word settle, knowing she'd remember her own use of it. She closed her eyes as if she felt it as a wave of pain, and turned to her back, staring up at the ceiling. "Go on," she whispered.

"We made a pact. A lifelong pact. To serve one another when any of us called. We swore it upon our lives. We swore it as an oath to God."

She remained silent and he wondered if he'd said too much. But the brotherhood was no longer a secret. Not since Firenze sent their fiercest knights to track down those they'd discovered and murdered them. Rodolfo's teeth ground together, remembering.

"You know as well as I that relations between the republics gradually soured, and escalated swiftly toward ongoing strife. Battle. And what once were boys became men of age, but on opposite sides of the line that had been drawn between us."

She let her head fall toward him again, folds of shiny brown hair beneath her face. She was truly beautiful, and at the thought of it, Rodolfo made himself look away, to the window. "It was naught but a boyhood pledge," she said. "Your loyalty belonged with your fellow Fiorentini."

"Nay," he said, staring back at her. "It was an oath of boys, witnessed by God, who foresaw that we'd grow to manhood, divided. To not honor my oath to them ultimately tore more deeply at me than turning my back on my Fiorentini friends. Make no mistake. I love my city. I loved my life among our people. But long ago, my life became inexorably entwined with those who love Siena."

He looked at her, feeling ragged, raw. "And then the Fiorentini..." He shook his head, rubbing his neck. "They committed such heinous acts...Trust me when I say you do not know what lengths some will go to in order to accomplish their goals."

"No more than the Sienese."

"On the contrary," he said. "They went to far greater lengths than the Sienese. Stooped so low it appalled me. Not all of them. But certain men among the Grandi—"

"I don't believe it."

He sighed and sat back in his chair. "You are free to believe what you wish."

She paused. "Why tell me all of this?"

He took a deep breath and leaned forward, elbows on knees, his hand cupping his cheek. "I know not. Only that...only that I wish for you to understand. To know that at least one Fiorentini understands why I did what I had to—"

"But you accepted Castello Paratore, lands, as bounty from Lord Forelli," she said.

"I'd lost everything, signorina. I had little choice. If I was to begin my life anew, I had to have resources."

"Convenient, that," she said, her tone hardening. "That your oath was to one of the Nine. Someone capable of rebuilding your holdings within a fortnight."

"My oath was not traded on future power. Only upon loyalty, whether we be prince or pauper."

"I'd wager that none of those boys of your brotherhood became paupers."

He hesitated. Was he to be blamed that he'd been born to a powerful merchant rather than a farmer too? "Nay, not all are rich, but none became paupers."

"Who are the others? Are there others, yet, who swear fealty to Firenze, but might turn at any moment?"

He considered her. He could detect no evil intent, but this woman was still considered a potential enemy in Marcello's keep. "That is not for me to tell."

He rose, already feeling as if he'd said too much. "I have only told you what I have so that you might understand what draws a man to make decisions as I have."

The maid arrived then, chirping her good morning, a basket of food hanging over her arm, a pitcher of water in her hands.

With a nod toward Alessandra, Rodolfo turned and strode out of the room, suddenly needing some fresh air.

---

Lady Betarrini, startlingly tall and blond—like an older version of Lady Evangelia—came around the bed and knelt in her elegant gown at Alessandra's feet. "Oh, my friend," she said, taking her hand, "what joy it is to see your recovery. Truly, I've prayed day and night for little else." She smiled and Alessandra tried to hide her surprise. The woman had every one of her teeth! She'd seldom seen a woman of her own mother's age that looked as well as Lady Betarrini. *Proof that the rich truly do have more than we.*

"Thank you," Alessandra said, remembering her manners, and a little stunned at the lady's overt friendliness. "You have been most kind in your ministrations. I may have perished if not for you."

She smiled again. "I hardly saw to you alone. Gabriella, Evangelia, Rodolfo, Luca…you might say we saw to you as one of our own."

Alessandra stiffened. She was not one of them. To even mention it was akin to calling her a traitor, even if the woman had clearly not meant it that way. "Lady Betarrini—"

"Please, call me Adri."

Alessandra paused again. What sort of lady asked to use her Christian name, so soon upon meeting? With a girl half her age and not near her social status? *Most strange.* "Lady Adri, might I go home this day? I awakened in the night with a terrible headache, but this morning I am nothing but famished."

"I believe you," she said. "But you must take it very slowly, and gradually experiment with movement. Your head suffered a terrible blow." She lifted her long fingers to Alessandra's face and hesitated. "May I?"

Alessandra nodded and the woman moved her face toward the sun streaming through the window and lifted one lid and then the other, studying her eyes. "There is no trace of headache this morning?"

"Nay."

She rose and bent Alessandra's head forward, examining the wound on her scalp. "That's not looking half-bad."

Alessandra puzzled over her odd wording. Did that mean half-good? "Are you a physician, m'lady?"

"Me?" she said, a smile in her tone. "Nay. I simply like reading of the healing arts, and on occasion, I'm called upon to see to those in need. Like you."

The lady's hands moved down to hold one of her own, and she set two fingers against Alessandra's wrist, closing her eyes...counting? Alessandra couldn't tell.

She ceased and looked into Alessandra's eyes. "Today, a bath. Food, of course. Mayhap a walk about the courtyard on someone's arm. But nothing else," she said firmly.

"And on the morrow? On the morrow I may return home?"

"Nay," Adri said. "Do you find us so abhorrent that you are eager to leave our keep?" she said with a wry grin. "Your father returns in two days. If God smiles, you shall be right as rain by then and we will happily send you off."

So the others spoke the truth. Or simply had agreed on the same story to keep her here. "What does this mean, 'right as rain'?"

Adri smiled, her eyes as blue as Evangelia's. "An expression from our homeland. Is rain not always quintessentially right?"

"For a farmer, yes," Alessandra said. "Until there's too much of it."

Adri's smile widened. "My grandfather always said there was always too little or too much rain. But it's always such a warm feeling to be inside by the fire, when the rain comes down, is it not?"

"Your grandfather…he was a farmer?" She tried to get over the shock of it. Weren't ladies and lords always born to other ladies and lords?

"Indeed," Adri said. "He grew potatoes. They do not have them here." Her long fingers formed a ball. "They're a root vegetable that grow into ovals, about the size of my fist, here. Baked, with some butter, some salt and other spices…" She closed her eyes and moaned, clearly wishing she had one right now. "Mmm, now I'm famished too. Mayhap I'll go about and fetch us some food to break our fast."

"Would you like me to send a maid for it, m'lady?" asked a tall knight with short hair, as he entered. Alessandra struggled to remember which one he was, from the night she awakened in a fog. *Sir Luca Forelli*, she decided. The dreaded captain of the Forelli knights, looking decidedly less than dreadful.

His green eyes came to rest on Alessandra. He did not look away, as was proper. He stared at her as if he could read her thoughts.

She closed her eyes and turned over, her back to him. She might have to remain here for a bit longer, but that did not mean she had to allow them into her head or heart. No matter how kind they were.

No. She was a Fiorentini. And God had allowed her through gates that no other Fiorentini had passed through, since they'd briefly taken the castle in war. What could she discover, while she was here, that might aid her people? Could she discover something that would be worthy of a reward, from the Grandi, rescuing her and her father from another winter of starvation and struggle?

The thought made her smile a little. Papa would be furious with her, likely beat her for hunting where he had forbidden her to go. For crossing the border. For getting into this mess. If she could not only find her way out, but discover critical information as well...Mayhap it would turn out for the best, after all.

# CHAPTER 4

Lady Adri had been true to her word. After breaking her fast, Alessandra had enjoyed the deepest, warmest, longest bath of her life, then a maid had combed out her hair and tucked it into an elegant bun at her neck, wrapping the heavy coils in a net that was hooked to a tapestry-covered band in her hair.

Then she helped her into a luxurious, soft gown in an olive color, trimmed with a gold ribbon. Never had Alessandra been in anything as fine. In spite of herself, she stared at her image in the speckled mirror. Dark rings still haunted her eyes, testimony to her trauma, but never had she felt more beautiful. It was as if she were again a small child, pretending to be a lady of the castello. Except now she was actually in the castello.

Lady Gabriella and Lady Evangelia entered then, ooing and ahhing over her transformation.

"Oh, Giacinta," Lady Gabriella cooed, walking around Alessandra, "you've done your customary magic. Look at her! We bring home an unconscious huntress, and in four days' time, she's become a lady."

Alessandra knew she was blushing furiously. Never had anyone made much of her outer beauty. Even Valente, her husband-to-be. But she'd also never donned such finery...

"*Bellisima,*" Evangelia said, smiling into her eyes. Alessandra was struck again by how much the girl looked like her mother. Who did Lady Gabriella take after? Mayhap her father. Because she looked like the most beautiful of the Tuscan people, whereas Evangelia was clearly foreign, standing out with her fair hair and blue eyes. Viking blood? Or had she heard they were once of Normandy?

"Ready for a turn around the courtyard?" Lady Gabriella asked. "I assume you'd like a bit of fresh air, and an escape from this old library."

"It'd be welcome, yes, m'lady."

"Good, then follow me."

Lady Evangelia offered her arm and Alessandra took it. They went through the door and into a hallway, where a knight stood guard—probably left in Sir Luca's stead—then toward a turret and spiral staircase leading upward. But Gabriella led to the right, out a larger, armored door. Once through, the lady of the castello took her other arm. It only took a quick glance to see that the knight, tall and brooding, followed them.

Alessandra squinted into the bright morning sun, hearing the men before seeing them. The ladies politely paused with her, letting her set the pace. There were shouts, laughter, commands, the sound of metal upon metal. As they edged past the main building in the center of the castle walls—a meeting hall of some sort, with the kitchens in back, judging from the smoke and smell rising from a chimney—they came upon them. The knights of Castello Forelli. Most wore loose shirts, open at the neck. A few had taken them off and sparred only in their leggings, belted at the waist, and boots. They panted from their sparring efforts, sweat dripping down the faces and chests.

Alessandra hurriedly looked to the ground. Never had she seen so much raw, masculine power in one place. And she was walking along with the She-Wolves of Siena. Again and again, she wondered if she'd stumbled into a nightmare. And yet each time, she admitted to herself that there was no omnipresent sense of fear among them. Only care. Camaraderie.

As they walked, she could sense they were gathering more and more attention. "M'lady, might I assist you?" called one to Gabriella. "Yes! Mayhap our visitor is an uncommon burden upon you!"

Alessandra dared to look their way, blushing furiously, and saw that indeed, a good half of the group had abandoned their drills and stared in their direction in open admiration.

"Best you pay attention to what your captain has to say," Lady Gabriella called, "Or you're liable to end up in the stables with unpleasant tasks before you."

"Knights at attention!" a man called, irritation lacing his tone.

It was Sir Luca, up on a small platform, and to his right was what had to be Lord Marcello Forelli. They had yet to formally meet. He stared at Alessandra, between his wife and sister-in-law, while Luca stared solely at the men. "Allow your attentions to wander like that again," Luca shouted, "And you all shall be plowing the Widow Giannini's fallow ground through the night!"

He hopped down and weaved among the fifteen pairs, as they quickly returned to their two rows. They stood, three feet apart, swords held in both hands, point toward the ground. And now, chastened, they all stared solely at their opponent, awaiting their captain's command. *Thirty knights.* Clearly, Castello Forelli was still on guard, despite the truce. Or had Lord Forelli brought in more, in light of her arrival?

"This will be an excellent exercise, gentlemen," Sir Luca yelled, humor returning to his tone. "Three of Toscana's beauties wander our court as I speak," he paused to give them a flirtatious nod, looking mostly at Evangelia, "but where are your eyes? Solely upon your opponent! Do not let them drift to anyone but the man before you, or there shall be repercussions! Concentrate, men, *concentrate*. Ready yourselves. Attack."

Lord Forelli remained on the platform, hands on hips, as the men set to striking and parrying, laughing when, here and there, they managed to swat their opponent with the flat of their blade. Alessandra's brothers had sparred with sticks, but had never done so with swords. Mayhap that was why these men yet lived while her own brothers did not return home. Beppe, a year younger than she. Ilario, but a boy of fifteen…She missed them. Oh, how she still missed them. But it had eased from the hourly, to the daily sort of missing. Mayhap, in time, it'd become weekly. *Life has a way of healing the wound,* her mother once said, *even if you'd choose to keep it raw and seeping.*

The sisters on either side of her paused to watch as Lord Greco stepped up on the platform and circled Lord Forelli, sword drawn. Lord Marcello smiled, nodding in acceptance of his challenge, and rolled up his sleeves, just as Lord Greco did, several steps away. On Marcello's arm, just inside and above his elbow, Alessandra spied a triangular tattoo, a most uncommon marking. He unsheathed his sword and tipped his head forward, signaling that he was ready for the sparring to begin.

Lady Gabriella pulled them to a stop, directly behind the platform, continuing to watch. Alessandra glanced over her shoulder. Behind them was the guard who tracked their every move, and beyond him, the towering front gate of the castello, firmly closed. Above, on the wall, were additional knights, keeping watch on their companions below, as well as the road and forest outside the castello.

Alessandra's attention returned to the noblemen before them.

Greco did not pause, immediately turning and bringing his sword down in a harrowingly fast arc, toward Marcello. But Marcello was ready, blocking the strike and letting it slide down the length of his sword, even as he turned. As soon as his weapon was unencumbered, he whipped it around, narrowly missing Greco's chest. Alessandra gasped. "Do they intend to kill each other?"

"Nay," Lady Gabriella said. "Somehow, they emerge from these exercises with little more than bruises and scratches."

Greco blocked his lord's next strike above him, and rammed his left fist into Lord Marcello's belly. The man bent over in pain and then a second later, barreled into Greco, pushing him off the platform. They fell onto the dirt before the women, Marcello on top. He rose, panting, his fists full of Greco's shirt. "Pushing it a bit today, aren't you?" he asked. "Could it be our pretty audience?" His eyes flicked up to the women.

With a growl, Rodolfo managed to unseat him, and they rolled over and over in the dirt. When they neared the platform, each surged toward their weapons again. And this time, Luca stood there. He began to attack Marcello and then turned on Rodolfo, mayhap giving both men training in taking on more than one opponent. He was much more lithe and elegant than the larger men, bending low to avoid swinging swords, turning in the air like a dancer.

He stepped out of the fray after several minutes, staring only at the men, studying them. He glanced over at the other knights, all still steadily at their task, more and more of them crying out in pain and anger, while some began to grudgingly call for mercy. Then, when Marcello and Rodolfo clashed, holding their swords in a cross above their heads, panting, Luca rolled up his own shirtsleeves, revealing defined muscles and...a triangular tattoo on his arm.

Alessandra considered that. Both men with the same tattoo, in the same place. She remembered then. It was the mark of the brotherhood. In Firenze, after the battle, she and her father had seen the mark on flags, being burned in the city piazzas. Had they all taken them as boys? Did Lord Greco have one too?

With a shout, Sir Luca came charging after the tall, dark-haired knight.

Lord Greco turned just in time to block Luca's strike, and lifted a hand to catch Marcello's wrist as he brought his own sword down. He dropped his weapon and tried to punch Marcello, but this time, Marcello blocked it. Luca brought the tip of his sword to the back of Rodolfo's neck. "You're dead, brother," Luca panted, wiping the sweat from his upper lip.

Slowly, Rodolfo lifted his hands. "Mercy," he said.

"Let's go again," Lord Forelli said, turning to take up his ready position, "except this time, with you both against me."

"Come," Lady Gabriella said, urging them forward again. "I really cannot stomach much of that. It's too close to how it really is on the battlefield."

Alessandra glanced over at her. The lady did appear a bit peaked. Surely she did not truly worry for her husband's safety? He appeared to be one of the finest knights possible, with others in his command that were nearly as good. And wasn't she one of the She-Wolves of Siena, capable of taking ten men on at a time?

"Alessandra, are you still feeling well?" Lady Evangelia said. "Or shall we walk you to your quarters?"

"Nay. Please. Let us resume our stroll. It feels good to be outside again."

"'Tis a most beautiful day," Gabriella said. "I love it when spring begins to give way to summer."

"As do I," Alessandra allowed.

"Tell us, Alessandra," Evangelia said, "Where did you get such a pretty name? It is uncommon, in Toscana, is it not?"

Behind them, more of the sparring men were calling mercy, one by one. The loser sat down on the ground, the victor above him. Apparently until Sir Luca called for another round. Only three sets of men remained fighting, the rest watching their lords on the front platform.

"My grandfather once read of a woman named Alessandra in a book."

"Your grandfather is a learned man?" Gabriella asked. She caught herself, looking contrite. "Forgive me. It is rather uncommon...I thought...Do you not live on a farm?"

"Indeed. My grandfather was a merchant, but never quite successful at it, and eight of his ten sons are farmers. My papa knows how to read and write, but he says it is not a woman's place to know such things."

"Oh, that's a shame," Evangelia said sorrowfully. "There is much to discover in the pages of a good book."

"I imagine so..." She paused, aware that she'd said too much. What was she doing, allowing these women into her head? Her heart? They were the enemy!

"Oh, we could teach you!" Evangelia said. "Might we, Gabi?"

"We hardly have time, before she departs. But we could begin, yes. Remind me, Lia. When the book merchant travels through next, or we get to Siena, I need to buy some books. We are in sore need of something new."

Alessandra looked from one to the other, considering the wealth required to purchase books. "You both read?"

"We do," Gabriella said.

She supposed that she shouldn't be surprised by the revelation, but in her village, she'd never known another woman who knew how to read and write. Mayhap it was part of the privileges of the noble class, to school their daughters as well as their sons. Or simply part of the mystique of the Ladies Betarrini. The She-Wolves of Siena.

Although, so far, she'd seen nothing in them that smelled of female knighthood. Only genteel femininity. Not that they didn't have the stature of warrior queens. They were certainly both tall enough. Evangelia was a good four inches taller than her, and Gabriella two inches beyond her sister. She felt like a mere girl between them.

"Alessandra is entirely too long a name among friends," Gabriella said. "May we call you Ali? My friends call me Gabi, and we call my sister Lia."

Alessandra stared up at her. "I suppose so," she said. She'd never been called anything but by her given name. But the nickname felt somehow warm, light to her, like she'd shed a heavy load.

"Or Sandra," Evangelia said.

"I-I think I prefer Ali," she said carefully, not wishing to offend her hostess.

"Good," Gabi said, squeezing her arm. "I like it. So tell us, Ali. How old are you?"

"Twenty," she said. It was odd, strolling arm in arm with them, having this girlish chat. Almost dreamlike.

"Ahh!" Gabi said. "I shall be too, in a year. Lia is almost seventeen."

"And your husband?" Alessandra dared.

"He's twenty-two. Lord Greco is twenty-three, and Sir Luca is of your own twenty years."

Alessandra considered that. Lord Greco was only three years older than she. It seemed impossible that anyone near her own age had been so pivotal in the great battle. But he had. More than a year ago now… She shook off her reverie, aware that she was thinking about him, sparring with Lord Marcello, his power and prowess clear in every move, even if he had lost. Grudgingly, she admitted to herself that he was the most handsome man she'd ever seen, even if she despised everything he stood for. Now she understood why women used to speak of Lord Rodolfo Greco as the most desirable bachelor in Firenze, and why their voices became shrill when they spoke of him now, as if he had broken all of their hearts.

His words from last night came back to her. The way his eyes pleaded with her to understand. She felt the pull to empathize with him. But was a man divided any sort of a man at all? Her father had always been so stalwart, so sure in his loyalties. He'd become mean and surly, dull in the eyes, but that was due to their losses, their struggles. Never could she remember him hesitating, or changing his mind. He was single-minded, and had taught her to seek others who were similarly single-minded. *Life is far more simple when one knows his mind,* he said.

And wasn't Rodolfo's tortured speech testimony to that truth? It was as if he'd been torn in two, within, and continued to roil in the guilt and frustrations of his decision to come to Lord Forelli's aid.

Outside the kitchens, when the stench of rotting bone and sinew met their noses, Lady Gabriella pulled them to a stop, visibly paling again.

"Gabi?" her sister asked, dropping Alessandra's arm and turning toward her. "Are you all right?"

Gabriella bolted away from them then and vomited near the wall, one hand braced against it. Evangelia went to her, as did the knight, while Alessandra froze, unsure of what to do.

"Nay, it's all right," Gabriella said, waving the knight away with an embarrassed look. He backed off to a respectful distance.

"This is the third day in a row you've been sick," Evangelia said lowly, laying a hand on her shoulder. "Mayhap you need to rest in your room. Get past this."

"Nay, nay," she said, pushing back her shoulders, and taking a deep breath. "I am fine. 'Tis only in the mornings."

"When is your baby due, m'lady?" Alessandra whispered.

Both women slowly dragged their eyes up to meet hers.

Alessandra frowned. *Oh no.* They'd not yet come to it. She'd seen her own mother pregnant eight times, four of those pregnancies leading to her brothers, the others lost at various stages. She'd learned to recognize the signs. But mayhap these ladies, with all their learned ways, had not. "Forgive me," she began rapidly. "Mayhap I misunderstood—"

"M'lady," said the knight, daring to near them again. "Might I fetch your maid? Your mother? Are you in need?"

"Nay," Gabi said, lifting a hand to him, leaving another on her belly. "Please. We are well. I simply ate something that did not agree with me this morning. Mayhap it was Cook's porridge?"

He smiled, plainly relieved. "Better not allow her to hear such words, so near the kitchen's door," he warned, with a nod.

"Agreed. Come," she said, turning to Alessandra and Evangelia. "Let us resume our stroll." They resumed their easy pace, and the knight fell back behind them.

"It is not possible," she whispered.

"It's not?" Evangelia asked, pacing ahead, turning to walk backward. Anger made her eyes stormy. "Really, Gabi? Do you not share a bed with your husband?"

Why was Evangelia acting so oddly? Was this not welcome news? Were not babies always welcome? Heaven knew death stole so many of them away…'Twas best to have as many as one could.

"I thought you were taking precautions," Evangelia said, cold fury building in her pretty face.

Alessandra's mouth dropped open, utterly confused.

Gabriella's hands were on either side of her face now, massaging her temples. "I was…but there was one night…" She began to blush furiously.

"Gabi!" Evangelia rubbed her face in agony. "You were going to wait…Just a few more years…"

"I know, Lia!" Gabriella bit out, now turning angry eyes upon her sister. "You think I forgot?" She stepped forward again, leaving Alessandra behind, pushing past Lia.

*A few years...* What were they talking about? Why would they wish to wait?

They both seemed to remember her presence again, as one. Gabriella looked down, took a deep breath, and then turned toward Alessandra, taking her hands in hers, while sending a reassuring smile over her shoulder to the guard. "I know we've only just met," she whispered. "But please. I beg you. Speak of this to no one."

Numbly, Alessandra nodded. Never in her life had she been with women who did anything but celebrate new life, budding within. Did not every married woman pray for babies? Certainly every woman she knew. Again, mayhap it was an oddity of the noble class...or the Sienese.

"I think it best if we get you back to your quarters," Gabriella said, "and I to mine."

## CHAPTER 5

Lord Rodolfo Greco entered the library after a quick knock and Alessandra guiltily shut the lambskin-bound book and slid it back on the shelf. His dark eyes, lined with thick lashes, went from her hand on the shelf to her and back again. "They are there for us all to read," he said, pulling a cloth from his waistband and wiping the sweat from his brow. He turned a chair backward, and straddling it, sat down. "Do you read, signorina?"

"Nay," she said, aware that he was looking her over now, undoubtedly admiring her in her borrowed finery. "Evangelia and Gabriella...they spoke of teaching me, but there's not time."

"You could always return for lessons," he said. Was that the hint of a smile in his eyes?

"I hardly think that would be advisable."

"You're likely right. Please," he said, giving way to a crooked smile, gesturing to the settee. "Sit, if you'd like."

It was more a command then a request, and Alessandra did as he asked, fighting the urge to chew her lip. It would have been far easier, loathing him, if the man weren't so dreadfully handsome. And...*winsome*. There was something about him that drew her. A quiet ache, deep within him, she longed to relieve. An itch she longed to soothe. Was it being here, being part of the Sienese, when he was…not?

"You must feel better today, signorina. You look…well."

She folded her hands in her lap in an effort to keep from wringing them, every nerve on edge with him so close. It was different, today. His attentions. More as a man with his eyes on a maid, rather than a guardian keeping watch. "I am better. A slight ache, behind the eyes, an ongoing weariness, but much improved over the last several days."

He studied her a moment longer, then rose, went to the desk, drew out a piece of parchment, uncorked the ink, and dipped in a quill. Swiftly, he wrote for a couple of minutes, reached in a cup for a pinch of powder, and sprinkled it across the parchment. He gave Alessandra a long look, leaned down and blew, a cloud of powder rising and then disappearing in the air. "Come," he said, gesturing for her to approach.

She did as he asked and sat in the chair before the desk, directly in front of him. A shiver ran down her neck and spine as he leaned over to point at the parchment. "If you wish to learn to read, these are the primary building blocks," he said, his warm breath washing over her bare shoulder, almost as if a kiss. "'Tis the letters of Dante's Tuscan, a language we should all learn to read and write, whether we be Fiorentini or Sienese."

She forced her eyes to the parchment, from one crisp letter to the next. His script was lovely, precise, even if she didn't quite comprehend what she saw.

"These are a few words," he said, pointing to the bottom of the sheet. "The letters form words, which become sentences, which become paragraphs, which become pages of script, which eventually become books. 'Tis best to take reading one step at a time. First the letters. Then some words. But I wish to ask…Do you know what this word says?" He leaned closer to her again, making every hair on her neck stand on end.

He smelled of leather and clean sweat and juniper, and she fought the urge to turn toward him. To look at him.

She looked to where he pointed.

"'Tis my name."

He cocked his head to look at her, terribly close, but she did not meet his gaze. "'Tis indeed," he said with some surprise. "Do you recognize any other words?"

"Nay. My grandfather wrote my name for me, once. That is why I recognize it."

"Ahh," he said in appreciation. "A learned man of Firenze. What was your grandfather's name?"

"Singore Marco Donatelli. He was a merchant of silver."

Rodolfo half-laughed and he walked around the desk to face her. He smiled, and her stomach tightened, because when he smiled…when he truly *smiled*, he was the most handsome man she'd ever seen. "I knew your grandfather! I met him!" He thrust out a hand in excitement and then let it rest on his hip. "My father took me to his shop, once. It was a block from the Duomo, yes? We went there to purchase a gift for my mother."

Alessandra found herself smiling up at him and quickly looked to the parchment again, as if intent on studying her letters. Because she didn't want to notice the sparkle she'd just glimpsed in his dark eyes. The curl of his ebony hair at the nape of his neck. The way his broad shoulders came down to a narrow waist. She didn't want to linger in this new-found camaraderie, between them. The draw. The pull.

She wouldn't. She couldn't. Because she was leaving this enemy fortress. Just as soon as possible.

## –EVANGELIA–

I stood by the window, looking out to the southern wall, tears streaming down my face as I listened to my sister sob.

Gabi wept as if the child was already dead in her arms.

Our parents had made it very clear. With the plague upon us in 1348, two years from now, the fewer we had to look after, the better off we'd all be. We already loved every person in the castle and beyond. But children? A little niece or nephew? A toddler when the plague truly began savaging Italy's population, city by city, stealing one in three lives?

Even the *idea* of it struck terror in our hearts.

Their plan had been to wait until after the plague eased, to try for children. But birth control in medieval times was hardly what it was in the twenty-first century. "It's an art, of sorts," our mother had said, disappearing behind closed doors to explain what she could to Gabi.

*Too bad I'm the artist of the family,* I mused, numbly counting limestone blocks to try and get my mind off of it.

After a while, her awful sobs eased, and I went to sit beside her on the bed. I reached out a hand and laid it on her back.

"Oh, Lia, what am I going to do?"

She turned over, her eyes red and puffy, one arm resting against her forehead as she looked to her bedroom ceiling, frescoed with stars. I stared at her, momentarily tongue-tied. You have to understand. My sis never cried. I'd seen it maybe ten times in my life, as much as this. She was a suck-it-up-and-deal kind of girl. I was the crier in the family.

"Well, Gabi," I said, trying to ease the moment, "once you stop vomiting your guts out, you're going to get hugely fat."

She giggled and wiped her eyes.

My voice dropped. "And in nine months, you're going to have the prettiest baby we've ever seen."

Her chocolate brown eyes shifted to me, welling again with tears. "It's crazy, so crazy, Lia. I just figured out I was pregnant. And I love it already. It's...a part of me."

"I know," I said, reaching out to stroke her hair. "A little niece or nephew." I shook my head. "It wasn't part of the plan, but you and I know that life is kinda hard to plan, right? All kinds of things we couldn't quite imagine have happened, even before this baby."

She and I shared a meaningful look. We hadn't been back to the tomb and the time portal that had brought us here in more than a year. "If things get bad...if the worst happens..." I said. "Gabs, we could take the baby back. Heal it. And return."

"And leave Mom and Dad here? Marcello?" Her eyebrows lifted. "Luca?"

"Let's deal with it when we have to. Right now we're just borrowing trouble, as Dad would say. And you...you have all kinds of fun ahead of you."

"Like what?" she asked, shoving herself up to a sitting position. "Having a baby without an epidural? Varicose veins? Stretch marks?" She frowned and massaged her head. "What am I gonna do about prenatal vitamins? To say nothing of prenatal care...Do you know how many things can go wrong in a pregnancy?"

I laughed, under my breath. "There's the hypochondriac I know and love." I covered her knee with my hand. "It's going to be okay, Gabs. Thousands upon thousands of women had babies in this era. And you're going to be one of them. We have Mom with us."

"Just don't tell her yet. Or Dad. I have to figure out the right way to tell them."

"Okay. But Mom will find the best midwives to bring in; together they'll handle anything you and this baby throw her way." Please Lord, let it be true. A servant had died in labor just last year. Another had died right after giving birth because Mom and Gabi couldn't stop her bleeding. I shoved away a shiver, not wanting my sis to see it.

Gabi leaned back against the headboard, lost in thought.

And then Marcello was there, striding in, his face awash in worry. "Gabriella," he said, coming directly to the bed, on her other side. "I was told that you have taken ill."

"Nay, Marcello. I am well."

"But Dario said you were sick, outside the kitchens…" He took her hands in his and I moved to go, to give them their privacy.

"Nay, Lia, stay," she said, and I reluctantly sank back to the foot of the bed. "Trying to keep it a secret is futile." She looked back to her husband. "Marcello, I am not ill. I am going to have a baby."

He stilled, his eyes shifting back and forth across her face to see if she was joking. "Truly?"

She nodded, her eyes so earnest and hopeful, it hurt to look at her. "Truly."

After a moment's hesitation, he gathered her into his arms, and then tenderly kissed her forehead, her cheeks. "It is grand news, Gabriella," he said, still holding her close. "Grand. I know it is not what we intended, not now, before…but we must trust in our Lord. All will be well."

"I hope so," she said, her voice cracking again.

"A baby," he said in wonder. "A baby! Baby Forelli."

Tears were streaming down Gabi's face again, fear alive in her eyes.

I slipped off the bed then, and out of the room. Together, I knew my sister and brother-in-law would find their way through this. But I was anxious about the challenges it would bring, too.

Because things that affected the lord and lady of Castello Forelli, affected us all.

---

After looking in on Alessandra, dozing away under Mom's watchful eye, I accepted Luca's offer of going to the new construction site and for a short ride beyond. I was eager to avoid any prolonged conversation with either of my parents; ever since we'd returned here together, we shared a bond we'd never had before. It wouldn't take long for them to detect that something was up with me…and I'd crack.

Despite my pledge to Gabs not to tell our parents about her pregnancy, there was no way I could deal with Mom or Dad peppering me with questions. I'd never been able to stand long, against them; I was always the first to cave. But now, here…I was pretty much worthless. We'd been through too much to be anything but totally honest with one another. I hoped Gabi would tell them soon.

Luca gave Dario strict instructions to follow Alessandra anywhere she went—and to never allow her outside the castle walls—then offered his arm and I laid mine over it, letting my fingers rest on his chapped hand, as we walked to the stables. For weeks now, the men had been at work, clearing and plowing new fields, and building the foundation for an expansion of the castle wall that would increase the size by half, and include a vast, new warehouse, as well as apartments and latrines for more people. No one had been told why. They all assumed it was merely strategic. What nobleman so near the border would not wish to be able to better survive a sustained attack?

Only Luca and Marcello had guessed what was ahead of them, with the plague. But my parents had insisted they keep it to themselves. Every move we made here, in this era, was undoubtedly changing the future. We'd seen it ourselves, in our visits back and forth. When we left at first, Castello Forelli was little more than rubble. When we returned the second time, it was in amazing condition, a tourist site. I didn't remember this extension being there—but maybe it just hadn't been in view when we swung through. All we knew was that our presence in the past had impacted the future. And Dad constantly preached that we had to limit that.

But even he couldn't avoid the desire to try and spare us all through what was to come—and in this time and place, the threats came, one after another, from a variety of sources. Marcello's intent was to have enough room, and enough supplies, to keep us all for a year. Mom and Dad reasoned that if we could remain inside, and keep the world out, essentially living in quarantine, that we had a good chance of riding it out. A good chance...

"Ready?" Luca asked softly.

He looked down at me and I shyly looked back up into his eyes. I nodded, and he placed his hands on my hips. But he didn't lift me up and into the side saddle as expected. "Luca..." I said with a grin. "This is hardly the place."

He smiled back at me, and lifted a teasing brow. "Nay. It is not." He took my hand and pulled me into a horse stall, shielding us from two knights chatting at the stable entrance. Then he caressed my face and bent to kiss me, softly at first, then deeper, pulling me close. I gave in willingly, as glad to be in his arms as he was to have me. There, I felt guarded, safe, comforted, even as my heart was threatened with news of Gabi's pregnancy. I didn't want to think about her. I wanted to think about him. The spicy, clean smell of him. All leather and crisp linen and juniper soap...

He closed his eyes and groaned, pulling slightly away, after we'd kissed for a long minute. "It's been far too long since I was able to kiss you, Evangelia."

I laughed under my breath. "A day? Two?"

"Any day without a kiss from you, beloved, seems as weeks." He leaned in for one last kiss, sighed and then led me back to the horse, quickly lifting me to my saddle and settling my feet in the stirrups. He lingered, staring at my slippers.

"What? Is there a hole in one of them?"

"Nay," he said, pulling one foot back out of the stirrup and lifting it, baring my ankle. "Even your feet are lovely." Then, making sure he was unseen, he bent to brush aside the hem of my skirt and kiss the top of one foot in an act of reverence. As if I were a princess and he my loyal subject. "Luca!" I whispered. If he were seen doing that… Such silliness from the captain of the Forelli guard! The men would tease him forever about it, and worse, me too.

He tossed me an impish smile, gave my foot one last, longing touch, and then mounted his horse. I shook my head and took a deep breath, relieved we were on the move, and had been undiscovered.

The knights had left from the front entrance. A young squire, perhaps eight years old, opened the doors for us, his expression doleful as we passed. He was all about seeing to his task as instructed. Every squire was assigned to a knight, who saw to his training, so that he might someday become a knight himself. Many poor families offered their children as we passed, holding them up, their cries desperate. Because, while they had to give up their kids, they knew their children would receive a bed, care, food, and a future within the castello walls. In the year that we'd been here, eight had come to live with us, and they followed my dad around like puppies, recognizing that he loved children, and wasn't as rough on them as the knights.

Guards opened the heavy front gates and we rode through, an older teen at the top shouting, "Mind yourself with the lady, Captain!"

"Watch *yourself*, whelp," Luca called back with a grin, "or I'll assign you latrine duty."

"Lady? What lady?" called back the boy, without hesitation. "All I saw was my cap'n, heading out!"

Luca laughed, the sound of it joyful and welcome to my ears. I loved how the guy smiled and laughed over everything, even in the face of severe difficulty. I mean he could be serious when he needed to, but he often reminded me not to be too serious.

"Latrine duty is a most effective threat," he said.

"For good reason," I said with a smile.

It hadn't taken Mom long, with all the people who now lived at the castello, to convince Marcello to dig a rudimentary sewage system. We still used chamber pots in the night, if necessary, but now, toward the back of the castle, where the hill fell away, were eight latrines, as well as a way to dispose water, straight from the kitchen, without hauling it out in buckets.

The latrines were like a castle's version of outhouses. I groaned at the memory of how cold those stone seats were in winter. They were bad enough as the weather warmed. But at least it was something. Dad had worried about the long-term repercussions of one of the Nine introducing something like it in this time period, but Mom was pretty clear—it was a non-negotiable. Her rationale was that the Romans had something like it in empirical days—why couldn't we? We were not introducing something new, we were resurrecting something that had already been. At least that was her reasoning, which Dad had debated endlessly as faulty logic.

But Mom had won.

And it had become a favorite threat among the men—to be assigned cleaning duty, since Mom also required they be washed out several times a day in order to avoid spreading disease and infection.

"Mayhap the guard was right," Luca said over his shoulder, bringing my attention back to him. "Mayhap none but me exited the castello gates, minutes ago."

I smiled. "Forgive me, good sir. My mind is in a tangle this afternoon."

"Is that the source of your tears?"

I looked toward him, but he wasn't looking back at me. Was it so obvious on my face? Or was he merely that attentive?

"In part."

"And Gabriella? Dario said she was ill…" This time, he glanced back at me over his shoulder, as he swayed in his saddle, following the easy gait of his mount.

"She is well. Just feeling a little sick to her stomach. It shall pass."

His green eyes pierced mine and then he looked away. "Glad am I to hear it."

I knew I'd probably not fooled him. Luca was uncommonly keen, picking up things that I often missed. It was part of what made him a brilliant captain for Marcello. Between the two, they were pretty amazing in battle, and even in just leading the people of the castello, day to day. Managing the knights alone was tricky; all that testosterone in one place was like a simmering volcano, especially with the relative peace that had settled upon us the last fifteen months. That's why this current building campaign was brilliant. The men sparred all morning, and worked on the wall, warehouse or in the quarry all afternoon. The heavy, physical work only made them stronger, a more fearsome fighting force. By nightfall, they were too weary to do anything but shove ample amounts of good food and wine down their throats and drag themselves off to bed, which kept them out of trouble.

We edged around the second corner of the castello and the work site opened up. The forest had been cleared from about a city-block's worth of land. I was sad for the trees to go, even though I knew that the growth posed tactical dangers, and we needed this space for what was to come. The men had cut the trees' branches off and stacked the logs in enormous piles. The wood would be further cut, in time, stacked and dried—used all winter and winters to come, in Cook's kitchen. "And we'll cut the best of it into beams for the new apartments," Luca explained to me.

Here on this edge, the hill began to fall away into a second valley, and the plan was to make rooms, three stories tall. The Romans had housed guards and firemen in such a way, and the plan had Dad's fingerprints all over it. As an archeological specialist in Etruscan and Roman topography, he'd dragged us around to every site possible. We'd hung out at Hadrian's Villa, south of Rome, for a full week, the summer before he died.

*Before he died.* It was weird to think about that, seeing Dad come into view now, so alive and well. He was beneath a small tent, open in the front, only there to shield them from the wind, rain and sun. Chin in hand, he studied a parchment, tacked to a table, beside Father Tomas, pointing to a section.

I knew I couldn't deny it—I'd do it all again to get Dad back. Go back in time. Stay here, even if it only meant we got to keep him. He looked up, then, and smiled at me and Luca as we approached. Whereas I favored Mom in looks, Gabs totally looked like Dad, all Toscana, from head to toe.

Before...back home, we'd have to jump up and down to get his attention. Here, we always came first. As we did with Mom. That, too, was a cool thing about living here. It was another thing that would make me take the leap again. *The Path to Improved Family Dynamics,* I envisioned a title on a modern book. *By Evangelia Betarrini.* And inside, there'd be one sentence: *Find a time portal and travel back to medieval Italy.*

"*Buon giorno, figlia mia,*" he said, coming closer. *Good morning, my daughter.* He still got a nerdy kick out of the medieval, formal phrasing we used around others.

"What's up, Coolio?" I returned, in English, smiling back at him.

He chuckled. "Good to see you out of the confines of the castello." He helped me free my feet from my stirrups and reached for me, easily lowering me to the ground.

"So, your task is about done here, Lord Betarrini?" Luca said, laughter in his eyes. All around us was chaos, the very first stages of raw construction.

Dad smiled back at him. "Undoubtedly. We might even have it completed tonight."

"Excellent, excellent," Luca said, taking Dad's outstretched arm of greeting in his. He turned when Father Tomas waved him over, and after silently asking my permission to leave my side, strode over to the priest and three men, pondering a wagon full of three mammoth, freshly hewn limestone blocks.

Dad wrapped his arm around my shoulders and led me over to the small tent. "So, what will it be, honey? Want to work in the quarry? Dig a trench? Take an axe to some logs?"

I laughed. "Not quite dressed for that," I said, picking up my silk skirts.

"Ah, yes," he said. "I have another task for you, then. He shuffled through the stiff parchment sheets in a stack and pulled one out. On it was an architectural schematic of the new castle wall. "Think you could give this a more artistic perspective, as a gift to Marcello? I think he'd enjoy it."

"Sure," I said, taking the sheet from his hand and studying it. "You're looking for something a bit more 3-D?"

"Not only that. Softer. Romantic."

I smiled up at him from the corner of my eye. "Dad. This whole castle life thing is really getting under your skin, isn't it?"

"Maybe," he said, looking a little sheepish. "I just want to show Marcello—and the others—where we're going. You can help them envision it."

"All right. I'm in."

"Excellent." He turned away and grabbed a fresh sheet of parchment, ink and charcoal. "What's your poison?" he said, offering both in his hands.

"The charcoal, I think. To start." Parchment was precious. Each sheet was about as expensive as a sheep. And charcoal was a bit more forgiving than ink.

"Here you go," he said, "feel free to take over my table and stool."

"Thanks."

He bent to kiss my temple, squeezing my shoulder, and left to greet six more wagons pulling in, hauling what looked like sand and stone.

※

I worked for hours, constantly consulting Dad's drawings, ultimately producing three different views—one from the outside, with the tall tower showcased fifteen feet above the others; one from the inside, looking up at the guards' apartments, with a cutaway to show three, side by side; and another outside the warehouse, exposing a portion of the segmented stalls and levels.

Luca came by frequently, trying to get a glimpse of what I was working on, but each time, I practically laid across them, blocking his view. "Nay, you must wait to see them! I'm not finished!"

He muttered under his breath about women and their unreasonable demands, clearly curious as all get-out, but he always walked away with a wink or a bow.

Dad got to see them first, as the day drew to a close, and Father Tomas clanged a bell, summoning the men in. He picked up one drawing after the other, whistling in admiration. "I do believe you have a future as an architectural artist, Lia."

"Yeah, sure," I said, pleased by his praise, but recognizing the folly of his words. "Huge demand for those here in 1346."

He cocked a brow in my direction. "You never know. Seriously, babe. These are beautiful." His eyes ran over the sketches again and he shook his head in admiration. "They show great care and skill. Marcello and Gabi will be so pleased."

Marcello and Gabi. All afternoon, I'd been able to forget them and their baby…

"What?" Dad asked, his eyes narrowing as he studied me.

"Hmm?" I shook my head and looked down. "Oh, nothing. Nothing. I'm glad you like them. I think Marcello and Gabs will like them too."

He considered me a moment and then Luca was there, and Dad was all about showing off the product of my afternoon's work. I had a flashback to middle school, and Mom and Dad being in the halls on art night, finally recognizing that I had a little talent of my own…

"These are inspiring, Evangelia," Luca said. "They'll encourage the men at their long task, as well as Marcello as he empties his coffers to complete it."

"There's always the She-Wolf gold we can tap into, if we need it," I said.

"Yet another reason I need to wed you someday," he whispered as he walked by, just out of Dad's hearing. He moved to my other side, and when Dad looked away, added with a cheeky grin, "So I can get my hands on all that lovely gold as a dowry."

I edged away, feeling the heat of a blush. Because from the way he said *gold,* I had the distinct understanding that he spoke of something else.

Me.

I had to admit, I liked his pursuit. He was dogged and dedicated. And in Gabi's shadow, back home, just emerging from a belated puberty and braces, I'd really never experienced that with boys. Here, the boys were men at an early age, just as the girls were declared women. And Luca...well, Luca was a man that no girl could ignore for long. And he clearly wanted me. I couldn't get over that.

"I see the truth of it now. You're only interested in my wealth," I taunted as he bent to lift me into the saddle.

He paused, his face perilously near my neck. "Why yes, m'lady," he said, consciously letting his warm breath wash over my bare skin. "What else could it be?" I started to edge away, laughing, but he took firm hold of my waist and lifted me up. He put my feet into the stirrups and grabbed hold of the reins, still smiling, as was I. That was happening a lot lately. The two of us, grinning like idiots, as I gave into what I assumed was inevitable.

*Inevitable.*

I finally admitted it to myself, then.

I wasn't only falling for Sir Luca Forelli.

I'd been his all along.

## CHAPTER 6

Alessandra asked to join the sisters in the morning, to break their fast. Mayhap she'd learn something today about Castello Forelli. Her father would demand every detail, and be sorely disappointed if she returned with only stories of their fine food and kind company—especially if her mind continued to linger over Lord Rodolfo Greco. One never knew what knowledge might be useful…and the elder Lady Betarrini seemed ready to let her venture farther afield today.

They escorted her into the Great Hall, and Alessandra's eyes widened at the sight of table upon table of men and women eating bowls of porridge and cutting slabs of cured ham onto each plate. Her mouth watered. Trays with rounds of cheese were passed around, along with loaves of bread. The castello held far more people than she had imagined, and the meal, despite the early morning hour, was more akin to a feast than merely breaking one's fast.

"A good morning to you, wife and sister!" called Lord Marcello as he spied them. "And to you, Signorina Donatelli. My friends, please greet Signorina Alessandra as one of our own. She will abide with us until the morrow."

The women they passed nodded in friendly welcome, and the men shouted and smiled in her direction. Alessandra blushed furiously, called out in the midst of seventy others, but she had to admit she felt their warmth. It surprised her. She thought they might be wary, cold even, with one of the enemy among them. Mayhap their sheer numbers made them feel invincible.

Alessandra took a seat at the head table between Evangelia and her mother, across from Lord Betarrini, Luca and Lord Greco. Alessandra reached for the pitcher of water, her mouth suddenly dry at the mere glimpse of Rodolfo. Did she feel the heat of his appraisal or did she imagine it? She dared to look up as she set the pitcher down.

He lifted a cup as he swallowed a bite of bread. "*Per favore*, signorina," he mumbled, asking her to fill it. There was no way out of it without appearing rude.

Warily, she took hold of the pitcher handle again and poured.

He gave her a wise smile and lifted the cup in a silent salute. "How do you fare this morning, friend?"

Her headache was inescapable, worse again. But she was weary of taking the medicine and sleeping the days away. "Well enough to cross the border," she said.

Action around her ceased for a moment, and then hurriedly set in again to cover the tension.

"You shall be back among your own soon enough," he said easily, sipping some water. "Why not take the opportunity to join me in envisioning a fully realized peace between our republics while you yet abide with us?"

Alessandra turned her attention to the steaming porridge set before her. A maid came by and poured thick cream on top of it. Lia offered her raisins. Lady Adri offered her sugared walnuts. Alessandra accepted both. And when she took her first bite, she closed her eyes in wonder. Never had she had anything atop her porridge but cream. And the porridge at home was always pasty. This had an altogether different texture, nutty and glorious, intermingling with the sweetness of the raisins.

"You like it, Signorina?" asked a round woman, from over Luca's shoulder.

"Cook, this is Signorina Alessandra," Luca said, gesturing toward her.

"Glad I am, to know you," Cook said.

"And I, you," Alessandra returned. "Truly, this is the best porridge I've ever eaten." What harm was there in complimenting the cook for her fine meal?

The cook smiled in pleasure, lifting another spoonful to fill Luca's bowl again. "Be sure to get a bit of that ham as well," she said, gesturing down the table. "Looks like you need more meat on those bones."

"Leave her be, Cook!" called a knight from the nearest table, obviously listening in. "Her bones appear in fine order to me!"

The other knights around him guffawed and hit him on the shoulder.

Luca sent a warning look over his shoulder, but when he turned back around, he clearly hid a small smile.

"Ignore them," Lia whispered. "They're like a bunch of children in the morning, all full of Cook's good meal and a night's slumber."

Alessandra nodded and took another bite. She was as hungry as she was after a full day's hunt, and yet she'd done little but lay about. Mayhap it took more sustenance than she imagined, to heal from a wound such as hers, and fight the constant headache. A thick slice of ham was set upon her trencher, as was a chunk of bread. Then some soft, creamy cheese. She ate and ate…until she became aware of Marcello and the others gazing over drawings on parchment.

"These are extraordinary, Evangelia," Marcello enthused, perusing one after the other. "Thank you."

"My pleasure, m'lord," Lia said with a single nod. "It's thrilling, is it not? To envision what is to come?"

"Indeed. I think we'll put them up on the wall so all can see what we labor toward."

Alessandra didn't know what they were talking about, but she ached to find out. Undoubtedly, it was something else her people needed to know about.

She felt it then again. The heat of his gaze. She looked up to find Lord Greco's eyes upon her, and they blazed with alarm. Did he sense what she was after? She frowned and took a defiant bite of bread, even though her belly protested it was more than full. Mayhap he'd done the very same thing—tried to obtain information his people could use. But he had turned away from their own, from the Fiorentini, the people of his ancestral home. She chewed until the bread became paste in her mouth, watching as the drawings were passed from man to man, the women sidling in for a peek and squealing, until someone took them and nailed them into a panel that another had brought in.

"Do you wish to see them?" Lia asked, when half the men had left the hall, and the nobles at their own table rose.

"Nay," Lord Greco said, loudly, drawing the attention of their table. "She is not to see them."

"Rodolfo," Marcello said, frowning in confusion. "We have no secrets from our new friend. And she is our guest. Be at ease. Anything she discovers will be known by her kinsmen soon enough. Our expansion is far from secret."

Rodolfo opened his mouth as if to disagree, then abruptly shut it. "As you wish, m'lord," he muttered, with a bow of his head. A young priest, round and bald, set his hand on Lord Greco's shoulder. "Brother," he said, "might you assist me with something outside?" Rodolfo sighed and reluctantly followed him out, never looking back in Alessandra's direction.

When he was gone, she felt able to take her first full breath.

"Forgive Lord Greco," Lia said. "Your arrival has brought up old difficulties for him."

"He needn't feel conflicted," Alessandra said. "Unless he regrets his traitorous acts." It was out before she could stop herself. "Forgive me, m'lady," she blurted. "Clearly, I am as conflicted, being here among you, as Lord Greco finds himself."

"Pay it no heed," Evangelia said softly. "Castello Forelli…coming here for the first time brings up all sorts of contrary feelings. Until it doesn't."

Alessandra puzzled over her words, but rose and followed her out. Lia either had thought twice about showing her the drawings, or their exchange had made her forget. Servants buzzed around the tables, clearing trenchers and bowls and knives and mugs. Others grouped around the sketches, now pinned to the panel. From what she could glimpse as they passed, Castello Forelli was in the midst of a major expansion; the footprint of the property would be half-again as large, if she'd judged it correctly.

There could only be one purpose for such action. The Sienese intended to make the castello stronger than ever. And launch an attack on Firenze from the security of her walls.

She glanced at Evangelia, her head throbbing more than ever. These people spoke of peace and acted as friendly hosts. But she could not forget who they truly were. *Sworn enemies.*

***

Alessandra strolled alongside Evangelia and Lady Betarrini in the courtyard, puzzling over what she might learn that could aid her people.

Such information would help shield her from her father's wrath when he came to collect her. She shivered at the thought of his fury. He'd never cared for her independence, her "mannishness," as he called it. Ever since her mother had died of the fever, he'd never known what to do with her. And his frustration frequently dissolved into yelling. Since her brothers died, things had become much more dire...One thing might change their future. If she could only do this one thing...

Lord Greco sparred with a younger knight, clearly training him, and did not give her a glance as they strolled past.

"M'ladies, do you not spar yourselves?" she asked Evangelia and Adri, walking on either side of her. "With Lady Gabriella?"

Adri gave her a half-smile, half-frown. "On occasion. Since the battle and the skirmishes afterward, we've tried to avoid it, practicing the ways of women more than warriors."

So the Ladies Betarrini would no longer take to the battlefield? This would be welcome news. Regardless of what they could or couldn't accomplish on the front lines, most agreed that the mere idea of them among the knights, spurred the Sienese on.

"Might you teach me," she asked Lady Evangelia. "How to be a better archer?"

"Ahh. I have not picked up my bow and arrow in a long while," she said.

"Is there nothing I can do to convince you?" Alessandra pressed, reluctantly following them when they resumed their stroll. "You might help me become a better huntress." She glanced over at the platform again. "Assist me in killing the next boar, before he crosses the border."

Lia looked back at her, confused why she pressed so rudely, then followed her gaze to the platform. A look of quiet knowing entered her blue eyes. She lifted her chin and a small smile edged the corners of her lips. She plainly thought Alessandra wished to show off for Lord Greco.

"Do you wish for the lesson out here, in the courtyard?"

Her mother looked at her in surprise. "Truly? Are you ready for that, Lia?" she whispered.

"I think so. It's naught but a little fun, right Ali?"

Alessandra nodded, trying to appear the light, flirtatious girl. If it kept them in the immediate vicinity, so be it. She wanted to know if Greco bore the mark. Surely that meant that any remaining traitors in Firenze could be found, with a simple examination of every man's arm. If any more like Greco remained, on their side of the border, disaster might be upon them. After all, Rodolfo had not said no, when she asked if there were others…

And if Lady Evangelia had lost her skills with the bow…such news would greatly encourage her people.

As the men finally stepped into sparring formation, Lia edged over to the knight who guarded Alessandra, Dario, and asked him to send for the appropriate weapons and targets to complete the lesson.

Dario hesitated, his eyes flicking over to Alessandra. "Give the Fiorentini a weapon?" he said, lifting a brow, while folding his arms. "I think it unwise, m'lady."

"What can she do, here, surrounded by our finest?" Lia said in wry amusement. "I will take responsibility for her. And if she proves troublesome, all our knights are within reach, no?"

The tension eased, then, from his face, and he turned to call for a servant to do as she bid.

"Two lances, too," Lady Adri called after the servant boy. She smiled down at Alessandra. "I'd wager you're best with one of those, since you were hunting with one."

"I am fairly adept with it in the hunt," Alessandra hedged. She'd grown up sparring with her brothers. "And yet I doubt I could truly be a reputable adversary to the fabled Ladies Betarrini." She'd find out just exactly how skilled they were...or if they were no longer a threat. *One thing to report back...*

"Mayhap," Lia said, her voice soft. She was staring up, toward the sky, apparently lost in thought. Alessandra felt a wave of regret wash through her. She was pressing the woman, pressing her into something she didn't really wish to do. And Evangelia had been nothing but kind to her since she arrived. Her words came back to Alessandra...that she'd not so much as shot a hare since the day she set down her bow. Had she returned from the fields and forests damaged? Had she truly lost her will to fight?

Guilt and glee warred within her.

*You are Fiorentina,* she reminded herself. *These are the people who took your brothers' lives. Valente's. No matter how they appear.*

She owed it to them. To Beppe and to Ilario. As well as the countless other boys who would be lost in the next battle if she did nothing. She had to learn what she could, here, now. Had not God himself set her inside Castello Forelli's gates? Who was she to turn away from such an unprecedented opportunity? If Lord Greco was right, and her father returned with the Fiorentini knights behind him, and if she could provide them with critical information, mayhap she'd be given a treasure as a reward. She and her father could add on to their tiny house, this summer, and replace the decrepit roof. Purchase some cloth for new clothes. Have some extra food for the winter, rather than rationing out every morsel, chasing every boar in sight for miles...

The knight returned with three servants, all carrying various materials. Three targets were set up, to the right of the massive front gates, and to one side of the group of knights. Evangelia took her quiver of arrows, holding the slender case in her hand as if unfamiliar with the weight. She didn't seem to see the other servant offering her the bow.

"Lia," her mother said, softly. Both she and Alessandra had

already accepted their own bows and quivers of arrows, while servants buckled on their leather arm guards. Dario had placed himself a foot to Alessandra's left, directly between her and Lord Marcello, burly arms crossed as he stared at her. He appeared ready to strike her down if she attempted to do anything but a little ladylike target practice.

Evangelia seemed to come out of her reverie and slowly took her place between her mother and Alessandra, her mouth set, her eyes determined. She nocked an arrow and drew the string back, letting it fly without hesitation. It went sailing thirty paces, directly into the center of the target.

Men whooped and hollered behind Alessandra and she glanced over her shoulder. They were elated. Uncommonly excited. By an arrow.

"Our Lady of the Arrow has returned!" called one.

"As sure in her aim as if she'd never ceased," crowed another.

"Go ahead," Evangelia urged Alessandra, as her mother took her shot, hitting the lower left quadrant of her target. "Nock your arrow, staring at your goal as you do. See it in the air, the arc necessary to cross that distance."

Alessandra did as she said, holding the end of the arrow against her bowstring, studying the target, the distance. Then she lifted the bow and, trying to emulate Evangelia—and yet not—let it fly.

It went high and to the right.

The men erupted in delight. "True to the Fiorentini, she has no aim!" called one.

"Pay them no heed," Evangelia said, aiming anew. "Study it. Imagine your action before you take it. See it in your mind, from your bow to the target." Beyond her, her mother sent another arrow flying, hitting the top right side of her target this time.

Alessandra reached for another arrow, so focused on the target and Evangelia's coaching, that she didn't hear his approach. Only when he was wrenching her bow from her hands did she see Sir Luca, towering over her. "Are you mad?" he ground out, toward Evangelia. "She could have killed you with that first arrow!"

Lia reached for him as he frowned at Dario, the guard. "Release her bow, Luca. The girl is doing nothing but target practice. And from what I saw in that first round, she needs quite a bit more if she is to become a *murderer* in our midst."

"She is Fiorentini. A huntress. Do you *know* what the Fiorentini have offered in bounty for any one of us?" he said, gesturing in agitation. Marcello and Lord Greco came up beside him then. Dario appeared so contrite that he might be ill.

"I am not about to kill any one of you," Alessandra said with a little laugh. "Would I not be forfeiting my own life if I did so?" She looked up at Sir Luca in defiance, turning to face him.

He peered at her, his green eyes searching hers. "Mayhap you'd consider it an honor. To die for your Fiorentini cause. To avenge your lost loved ones. Who knows what you might be planning?"

"Heavens, Luca," Lia said with a sigh behind Alessandra. "She's not a soldier. She's our guest. What has come over you?" Alessandra could hear her nock another arrow and then the rustle of it slicing into the tightly tied haystack at the end. She was trying to cajole him out of his dark fury. Show him that she trusted Alessandra and he should too.

But Luca stood his ground.

"Tell Dario to draw his sword," Alessandra said. "And if I do anything but aim at the target Lady Evangelia indicates, strike me down."

Luca stared down at her. "Don't think I won't."

"Good, then."

"Good." With that, he allowed her to wrench her bow away, and she turned back toward Evangelia, hating that she trembled now.

Behind her, she heard Rodolfo murmuring to Dario. He was issuing the order as she dared! Lord Greco! He, too, feared she would attempt a rash act. And in that moment, God help her, Alessandra considered it. Evangelia studied her, their eyes locked, and then tellingly turned her back to her, effortlessly letting another arrow fly. It edged in, right next to the previous three.

She was as good as the legends said. There was no indication that she was out of practice. And with each progressive strike, the guards atop the walls cheered. The knights behind them were absorbed in their sparring exercises, and Alessandra imagined the sparkle on Dario's blade behind her.

"Up here, ladies!" called a guard, setting a shield to one side and stepping away.

Lia moved her aim upward, letting the arrow fly in another smooth motion. The arrow struck the center whereas her mother's went high.

Alessandra felt the stiff pull of the bow, getting used to it compared to her flexible old yew bow at home. The arrows were longer, too. Foreign in her hands. But somehow right, in keeping with the bow. She aimed at the shield, wishing she could try and emulate Lia's strike, but it wasn't time. She didn't want them to know her skill. It was best if they did not think of her as a threat. Only a lowly villager, come to stay for a turn, soon gone. She aimed low, and pretended to be downcast when it struck the very center of the stone she'd targeted.

"Over here!" called another guard, on the top left of the wall. He set up another shield and Lia immediately struck it. This time, her mother did too. Again, Alessandra went low. The bow had uncommon reach and she found herself wishing she could keep it, take it home. With this, she could strike a hare on the far side of the field from their home's front step.

They went on, aiming for one target after another. The guards laughed about "the Fiorentini's poor aim," but she ignored them, glad for how their banter ate up the time. She could feel the trickle of sweat roll from her hairline down her back, but she refused to turn and look at the men. She didn't want Greco to see anything more in her eyes. Suspect anything. Not until she knew more…

About fifteen minutes later, Lady Adri asked if they might switch to lances. She tossed one over to Alessandra and she automatically caught it with one hand, then belatedly pretended to drop it. She reached down to pick it up from the dirt, stealing a quick glance at the men.

Sir Luca was staring intently in their direction, arms crossed. Alessandra hurriedly turned back to the women, wishing they'd go back to sparring, giving her the opportunity to spy a certain triangle on Lord Greco's arm…

She lifted the lance in both her hands, feeling the balance of it. It was longer than her hunting spear, but had been sharpened at either end.

"It's likely too long for you," Lady Adri said, twisting her own lance in her hands, as if she were getting the feel of it too. "We can have the master at arms fashion a shorter one for you."

"Please. Don't bother," Alessandra said. "I'll be gone before he could begin."

"When you came into the clearing," Lia said, "you had a spear in hand."

"Yes," she said. She turned toward the target, and taking a few steps, heaved it over her head. It went sailing through the air and struck the very bottom of the target.

"It's too big for a sprite of a woman like you!" called a knight.

Others muttered more ribald comments, making their companions laugh.

"A bit heavy, that, to use as a spear," she admitted to her companions, ignoring the men.

"Indeed," Lady Adri said, arching a brow. "But you still managed to almost reach the target."

Lady Adri took three steps and hurled her pointed lance down the length of the yard. It hit the castello wall above the target and cracked. She groaned. "Clearly, my lack of practice has harmed my aim much more than my daughter's." She went off to retrieve her lance and see how bad the damage was.

"Do not let her fool you," Evangelia said. "In a few more throws, she'll regain what she's lost."

"I do not doubt it, m'lady."

But Alessandra was nervously watching Sir Luca, now down near the target, peering at her with suspicion in his eyes. He was picking up her lance, talking to Lady Adri. The tall, blond woman appeared to argue with him, glancing her way. Arguing about her.

Luca had guessed her secret. Suspected her. Alessandra's heartbeat tripled as he strode toward them.

Lia took a step closer to her.

Without warning, Luca tossed Alessandra her lance and again, and she automatically caught it, staring at him in quiet defiance.

"Luca," Lia began.

"Please, m'lady," he said, holding a hand up to her while staring at Alessandra. "I beg you attend your mother and give me a few minutes with our *guest.*"

"What is this about?" she said, stepping between Alessandra and the knight.

"I aim to find out why the girl *pretends* to not have as much prowess with weapons than she truly yields."

"What? She just emerged from her sickbed—"

"Two days ago. Trust me, Lady Evangelia, this one is fully healed. And concealing something. I intend to find out what that is. Please, go with your mother."

"Come, Lia," Lady Adri urged, sorrow etched in her face.

"Nay!" Evangelia said, wrenching away from her mother's hand. "I will remain here."

"Fine," Luca said. "I bid you not interfere." He paused and leaned his head toward her, looking into her eyes. "Trust me."

But then he turned and came after Alessandra.

Alessandra studied the tall man as he circled her, taking another lance from a servant. She'd only seen him looking this serious, this intent, when he was sparring or drilling the men. He let out an unearthly cry and came at her, hurtling his lance down toward her head.

She didn't think. She lifted her own and blocked his blow, then turned, striking at his legs.

He jumped her swooping lance and smiled at her in triumph. *"There 'tis."* He struck again, and she blocked it, then the next two, in quick succession, up high, down low, in the middle. Then she turned and rammed her lance toward his back, belatedly seeing that he'd tossed his own aside, and caught her wrist with both of his hands. He swiftly twisted the lance from her grasp and swung it back around, directly at her head. She crouched, sliding one leg to the right, feeling the *whoosh* of the lance brush past.

"Do you intend to kill me?" she sputtered.

"Not yet," he said, ramming the lance down again, missing her by inches when she whirled away.

She rolled and grabbed hold of the other lance and quickly gained her feet. A knight—many encircled them now—whistled in low appreciation. Marcello and Lord Greco were there too. Luca came after her again, fast. Striking, striking, striking. She parried, parried, parried, until her strength gave out and she stumbled backward, only rising as far as her elbows before Luca had his lance at her throat.

"Luca!" Lia cried. But Marcello physically held her back, as deadly serious now as his cousin.

"Tell us, Signorina Donatelli," Luca said, panting, and taking a knee beside her. "Why did you hide your prowess with weapons? So that you might plunge a dagger, sink an arrow, when we least expect it? Might you have only been waiting for access to our armory?"

He stared down at her with squinted eyes, trying to decipher the secrets she held back from him. And for the first time, she feared the captain of the Forelli guard. Feared he'd figure out what she was after, her intent. And then she feared for her life.

"I know not of what you speak," she tried, using her most plaintive voice, staying still. "I only wish to return home, to my family."

"Luca—"

He lifted a hand to Evangelia, cutting her off. Slowly, he lifted his lance and then knelt beside her. "We saved you, woman," he said quietly. "Lord Marcello extended you and your family friendship, binding his life to your own. But if you intend to harm the very hands who nursed you to health, you will not find mercy in us again."

His green eyes locked with hers, waiting.

"I understand," she whispered. She remained perfectly still, fearful he might turn and pierce her with the lance, if she dared move.

Then he rose. "To the barracks to change, and then the hall for your noon meal," he said to the men, still staring at Alessandra like he couldn't tell if she were a snake about to strike, or slumbering in the sun. "Be ready to ride out to your afternoon's assignments within the hour."

He turned from her then, walking off with Marcello as if nothing at all had just transpired. The others gradually peeled away, doing as he bid. She closed her eyes, feeling alternately hot with fever and bitterly cold, as if she were about to faint.

"Rise," commanded a voice.

Her eyes sprang open. Lord Rodolfo, offering his hand. With a quick glance to her right, she saw Lady Evangelia with her mother's arm around her shoulders, apology in her eyes, as she was led away.

Alessandra sighed and accepted the nobleman's hand, coming to her feet.

"You are no spy," he said softly, still holding her hand. "But you were foolish, thinking you could deceive us. The Forellis have not held this castle for generations by being fools."

She said nothing for a moment, only pulled her hand from his to brush the dirt from her green gown's soft sleeves. It irritated her that he drew her in some visceral way, even in this moment. "What does it matter, be I adept or weak with weapons? I have none at my disposal."

"It matters," he said, following her as she trailed the others toward the living quarters of the castello. "There is no cause for your actions unless you have devious intent."

She picked up her pace, scurrying across the yard. Dario, shadowing their movement, gave her an odd sense of security with Lord Greco in such close proximity. Right now, all she wanted was to be away, away from this towering knight who sent her heart to hammering. She reached for the latch of the turret door and heaved it open, but he slammed it shut. She could feel his chest behind her, his head to one side of hers. But it was his arm, and the sleeve that fell down past his elbow that drew her attention. Just peeking out was the faded blue ink of a tattoo. So he was marked too—

He saw her staring at it and with one swift move, grabbed hold of her arm and whipped her around, pinning her against the wall. *"Are* you a spy? Were you sent here to infiltrate us?"

She huffed a laugh, even though her whole body stiffened with fear. "Nay! How could I possibly do that? How could I orchestrate a fall that took me to death's door for days? Whatever his intent, God himself sent me here. To you." She stared back in his dark eyes. "I am Fiorentini.

Make no mistake about it. Will I tell my people that Castello Forelli intends to expand? Certainly. That Lady Evangelia is as good with her arrow as they claim, but hesitates at shooting a hare? Yes. Not *all* of us wander from our loyalties, Lord Greco. *I* will remain true to my people."

His dark brown eyes narrowed and his nostrils flared, for several breaths. "Your people—some of your people..." He abruptly dropped her arms and paced in front of her, rubbing his face. "Signorina, you do not know of what they're capable. What extent they'll go to, to bring these people—my people now—to the *gallows.*" He raised his hand and waved over the entire part of the castello that held the living quarters. "These people who *saved* you. Fed you. Tended to your every need. Those in power in Firenze would gladly kill every one, given the chance."

"The men I know are honorable and true. They shall meet you in battle. But they will not try and kill innocent women...and children." She paused, considering. The Ladies Betarrini? The child Gabriella carried? Would they be spared? A shaft of doubt pierced through her.

"I know good and true men among the Fiorentini too," he said, softening, as if remembering people he loved. "But the men you are about to know are far from honorable. Trust me. You *must* trust me. You arrived as a farmer's daughter, a misplaced huntress. But you shall leave our gates a *pawn.*"

"Nay," she said, shaking her head. "I do not believe you. You have been soured in your thinking, in your beliefs. They've turned you completely against us."

"If only you knew," he said, such sorrow in his face that Alessandra fought an unreasonable desire to try and comfort him.

He searched her eyes, and his expression took her breath away. There was no trace of threat left within him. Only dread. Fear. Longing for understanding...

A shiver ran down her back and she wanted to run, she was so confused. What was he doing to her? Making her feel for him? Confusing her? Forcing her to question everything she'd known, trusted, believed?

He stepped aside, looking over at Dario, standing several paces away, then back to her. "See Signorina Donatelli to her room. And make certain that she does not leave it until I come to fetch her for supper."

## –EVANGELIA–

I left my mother and followed Luca into the stables, barely able to stay silent until we were alone, but then, once we were, too furious, too confused to figure out where to begin.

"You're angry." He lifted a gentle hand to brush aside a strand of my hair, but I batted it away.

"Yes!"

"You do not understand why I had to be so harsh."

"Nay!"

He put his hands on his hips and waited for me to look up at him. "Evangelia, if you wish to put weapons in that woman's hands, I had to be certain you and the others were safe. That is my charge. If I cannot do that then I do not deserve to be captain of the Forelli guard."

"I understand that," I said, pacing back and forth in front of him. "But did you have to be *that* harsh with her?"

"Yes," he said calmly, leaning back against the wall. "I could see she was hiding her ability. Deliberately missing her targets. And that alarmed me more than if she'd hit them as well as you. She's clearly not as swift, but I'd wager she has aim that rivals yours, my love."

"Don't call me that!" I said, angry still, but his words made me begin to question her too. Why had she hidden her ability? Why not use the moment to show off? Unless…

"Don't call you what?" he said, moving away from the wall, toward me. He lifted his hand to my face again, as if approaching a skittish horse. I hated that I shifted away, but not out of reach. I felt powerless to avoid the draw to him. Gently, he edged over to me again and cupped my cheek. And slowly I looked up to meet his eyes. But I did not lift my lips, did not offer him the awaited kiss. I was still too angry for that.

"Just as I have to see through my duties, I also must claim what you are to me, Evangelia. And if someone endangers you—or anyone else in Castello Forelli—you shall see my ire sparked beyond all measure."

His green eyes hardened and I grabbed hold of some of his fury, using it to pull away. "There could have been another way to get the information you needed."

"Was there?" he asked quietly.

I couldn't think of any suggestions, and that only infuriated me all the more. I stalked out of the stables, hoping my anger at least made Luca think twice the next time he decided to take down one of our guests.

## CHAPTER 7

Gabi'd heard. She met me in the halls and together, we walked down to Alessandra's quarters.

Dario stubbornly stood between us and the door. Gabi looked at him steadily. "Stand aside."

"M'lady, I do not think Lord Greco intended for the woman to see anyone until supper."

My sister drew herself up, every inch the lady of the castle. "Lord Greco can speak to me directly if he takes issue with it. Now stand aside."

Reluctantly, Dario did as she bid and we entered.

We stared at the empty room as seconds ticked by. "Alessandra?" I tried, hoping against hope that she was under the bed, or hiding behind the settee, but my voice echoed about the empty chamber.

"Lia," Gabi whispered, nodding to the high, small window. Alessandra had dragged a table beneath it. Was it even possible to squeeze through? Reluctantly, I allowed the truth to settle. She was small. It would have been tight, but possible.

"She was probably frightened. Maybe she was worried the men did not intend to release her now. If she gets home and reports that—"

"Or if she broke her neck coming through the other side..." I added in a whisper, staring at Gabi. Terror waved through me.

"Or if the Fiorentini find her, fleeing from our men..." Gabi said, bringing a hand to her lips.

"We have to find her and bring her back," I said. "Fast."

"Before supper," Gabi said. "They come to get her tomorrow. And if she's not here..."

I nodded. "Alessandra, please allow us to help," I said a tad loudly, feigning conversation for Dario's benefit.

Gabi smiled, looking a bit like her old self. "Come now," she added, equally as loud. "Surely you can see—"

"Very well. Mayhap you'll feel better after a rest." I lumped some blankets under another, roughly forming a body in case the guard peered in. "You've been through a great deal."

"Are you certain you do not have need of anything else?" Gabi said, by the door now, not quite as loud, gesturing for me to hurry. Who knew how long she'd been gone?

We slipped out the door, giving Dario an exasperated look. "There's no reasoning with her," Gabi said. "The best thing for her is rest. See that she is not disturbed."

"Yes, m'lady."

We walked away down the hall, fighting not to appear hurried or harried. "The guys are gonna so kill us when they find out."

"They'd better not," she returned. "It's their fault. If they hadn't pushed her, pressed her as they did..."

We paused in the courtyard. "I'll get the horses ready. You fetch your sword?"

Gabi nodded, understanding my reluctance to enter the armory. We divided, trying to act as natural as possible. But adrenaline surged through my veins. If we didn't take care of this fast, we were sunk.

I entered the stables, cautiously looking around for Luca, and relieved to find him gone, gestured to two squires. "Lady Gabriella's and my mount, quick as you can."

The boys ran off and I moved to the saddles, thinking about ditching them, but then deciding we had to depart on side-saddle, as if we had all the time in the world, or the guards would know something was up. Just an afternoon ride out to the construction site...I rehearsed it in my head, practicing tone, phrasing. Second-guessing myself.

Gabi arrived then, her sword already in its traditional place; in a sheath at her back. But when she turned, I could see she'd also brought a bow and a quiver full of arrows.

"Gabs..." I shook my head. "It's one thing to mess around in the courtyard but another to—"

"C'mon. Take them. You know that we're going to get hassled, trying to ride out without a posse. Put it across your shoulders. A costume, of sorts. We'd be idiots to head out unarmed."

She was right, of course, and precious minutes were passing. I shouldered my bow and quiver, then helped the squire toss the saddle across my mare's back, as Gabi did with her own. Then, as I was about to mount, I stopped cold.

"What are we doing?"

"What?" she asked.

"You can't come with me," I whispered. "Gabs, your preggers, remember? And I'm pretty sure riding a horse at a gallop, chasing someone down, isn't on the list of recommended exercises in *What to Expect When You're Expecting*."

She paused and frowned. "I'll be okay. It's so early—"

"No, it's not," I said, mounting, gathering confidence when she still hesitated. It was so un-Gabi, I had to be right. "You stay here. Get me through the gates. Cover for me. I'll bring Alessandra back."

"I can't send you out alone," she said.

I gathered the reins and urged my mare forward, passing her. "I won't go far. I'll surely catch up with her, long before the border. And with our patrols out, the woods have to be clear."

She reached out and grabbed hold of my reins. "No, Lia. You can't even get yourself to use that bow these days. You might talk me into going solo, but I'm not sending you out, *unarmed.*"

"No, I'm okay," I said, my hand running over the smooth surface of the bow. I clenched it in my hands, striving to make her believe what even I couldn't quite accept in my heart. It was one thing to shoot at some targets, but was I really ready to take up arms against another?

*If they endangered me or mine, yes,* I decided.

"Let me go, Gabs. I can do this. For us. For all of us. We're wasting time!"

She still looked unconvinced as I bent to retrieve the reins from her hands. Then, before she could argue with me further, I called out to the nearest squire to go and open the doors. *"Vai! Apri le porte!"*

He scurried away, and I trotted through, then slowed my pace as I neared the front gates, waiting for my sister to stride up behind me. A guard, Patrizio, peered down at us. Mostly me, shouldering the bow. I knew it'd bummed the guys out in the last year, with me avoiding any time with the arrows. "Ah, out to do some hunting, m'lady, now that you've greased the wheel?"

"A good suggestion," Gabi called. "But Lady Evangelia merely wishes to see the progress that has been made beyond the wall."

I looked down, trying to hide my smile. She wasn't lying, directly.

"No escort?" he asked doubtfully, clearly pondering his options. He knew as well as we did that we never went out without our own version of Secret Service.

"Most of our guard is directly round the castello wall," she returned.

"And the rest out on patrol. What shall happen between here and there? You can watch Lady Lia every step of the way. Let us not trifle with this any longer. Open the gates."

He paused for another nanosecond, but there really was no arguing with the Lady Forelli. She had nearly as much power as Marcello. Only Luca outranked her. *Thank God he's not around right now,* I thought. I shivered, remembering how harsh he'd been with Alessandra. The only people I'd ever seen him act so tough with were enemies. And Greco, when he was bent on killing himself. But Ali wasn't our enemy. Was she?

The guards opened the gate and Gabi followed me to the center. "The guys are so gonna kill us," I said under my breath. "Right after Mom and Dad work us over."

"They'll be more freaked if you don't find Ali and get back here before her father arrives. Then we'll all be in a world of hurt."

I hesitated. "Maybe I should go get them now, Gabs. Tell them what's up."

"We can't. Don't you see? Then Firenze might really see our guys as evil stalkers."

"Is it any better if they find *me* out here? Chasing her down? A She-Wolf of Siena?"

"Not really." Gabi's lips thinned into a thin line. "There's a good three miles between us and the border. If you don't find her straight off, promise me you'll come back for the guys. Okay?"

"Okay."

"Take this," she said, lifting a long dagger up to me.

"No."

*"Take* it. Just in case."

I sighed and did as she asked, just to get her off my back, slipping it into my waistband.

"Go get her, Lia. I'll be watching for you, up on the wall."

I moved out, circumventing the castle, half-hoping I'd discover Alessandra below her window, with a sprained ankle or something. But the road was empty. I let out a heavy sigh.

I paused beneath the tiny window of her quarters, twenty feet above the ground, and whistled, amazed she could squirm through, and make it down alive. At the bottom were two deep footprints in the dirt that softened as she obviously took off. I traced the path with my eyes, marking her direction in the forest.

What was I doing? I was no tracker. My eyes shifted over to the few men in sight, wishing I could ask Rodolfo to help me. But Gabs was right. If the Fiorentini found Alessandra with Lord Rodolfo Greco after her, they'd really come down hard on us. All of us.

I casually moved out and into an arm of the forest that had not been cleared, hoping Gabi had thought to go to the wall and distract Patrizio or whoever else had it in their head to watch me. I pretended to have spotted a rabbit and pulled my bow from my shoulder. But as soon as I was hidden from view, I found a place to double-back and hit the path that Alessandra had taken.

It was fairly easy for a while, finding clues of her path. It'd rained a couple days ago, softening the ground. And she was obviously moving fast. A turned rock here. A broken branch there. *Maybe I'm learning how to track,* I congratulated myself. But as I got farther away, it became less obvious. And I began to wonder if she had even come this way at all.

I had to make better time. If I got too close to the border and an enemy patrol saw me...well, let's just say Alessandra wouldn't be the biggest issue. What would Gabi do?

*She'd ditch the stupid saddle.*

In under a minute I'd stepped up onto the boulder and swung my leg across, bareback now. Free to ride at a gallop like my stubborn, willful sister would do, if she were here. And, you know, unpregnant. *Here we go,*

I told myself. *I am a She-Wolf of Siena.*

Part of me exhilarated in the sense of freedom and adventure. The chance to save our people from certain trauma.

The other part of me screamed that I was heading into big, big trouble.

---

Alessandra paused on the hill, listening to the forest, the sudden loss of chatter among the birds. Her eyes scanned the horizon. A quarter-mile distant, she saw ten birds abruptly rise, as if startled. Was somebody following her? She could just glimpse a corner of Castello Forelli in the distance. Castello Paratore—now Castello Greco—was closer, and quiet too. Her eyes scanned the wall, watching as bored guards made their rounds. If Castello Forelli raised an alarm, there'd be an entirely different feel here. Somehow, she was as yet undiscovered.

Or was she? Her eyes returned to the birds as they flew off, settling on another tree. She edged through a boulder field, hovering in the shadows, not wishing to catch the Castello Greco guards' eyes. Once under the trees again, she resumed her run. She had to get to the border. From there, she'd only be an hour's walk from home.

*It must be close,* she told herself, panting as she ran in a slightly lurching fashion. She could usually run for hours. Often did, hunting, preferring the quiet. But the squeeze through the window had strained a long muscle across her back that hurt every time she moved, and in the frightening drop outside the castle wall, she'd twisted her left ankle. Both were slowing her down.

She studied the bit of forest where the birds had risen, wishing she had her horse now. But she wouldn't have been allowed through the gates on her two feet, let alone on horseback. And now her path had been chosen. She just needed to get across it, to safety. To home. To her people.

---

It caught Luca's attention immediately. The patrol riding into the building site, in half the number he'd sent out. He dropped the parchment to the table and strode toward them, leaving the foreman sputtering behind him, shocked at his rude departure. But Luca's eyes were on Vanni, the leader of the patrol.

"Three Fiorentini contingents on the border, sir," he said, dismounting. Luca took his arm in greeting, but frowned over his words.

"So Donatelli went to them. Reported his daughter is here."

"It appears that way, sir."

"You left the others to keep an eye on them?"

"Indeed. They're at the old watchtower."

Luca looked to the trees, considering. The old watchtower stood in crumbling remains at the old border—a border they'd reestablished last year when they pushed Firenze back. Three contingents. A hundred and fifty men.

Lord Greco approached, casting him a look asking silent permission to listen in. Luca waved him in closer. "The Fiorentini," Luca said. "They've assembled as we feared. On the border."

Rodolfo's dark eyes scanned his and then looked over to Marcello, talking with Ben Betarrini and Father Tomas. He'd just spotted them and they hurried over. Together, all three men entered their circle and were told of what had transpired.

Marcello shook his head and lifted a placating hand. "'Tis only a show of force. They'll return back to Firenze. Once the girl is in hand on the morrow. They merely wish to remind us of their slumbering might. And press their hand, if we give them just cause."

"'Tis likely, m'lord," Luca returned. "But let us err on the side of caution. We must send for reinforcements."

Marcello met his gaze. "We have done nothing wrong. Only saved the woman. Even the Fiorentini shall see that there's nothing to quibble over if they have her back."

"Or they shall concoct a false tale and use it as rationale to escalate to battle again," Rodolfo said.

Marcello shook his head. "The people are still weary. Just now recovering. Not as many will rise to our call to battle. On either side. Surely they understand that as well as we."

An alarm bell began clanging, high above them. Their heads rose as one, and two knights came running around the perimeter of the castle, Dario and Patrizio. Luca and Marcello turned, hands on hips, waiting.

Panting, Dario began speaking as soon as they neared. "M'lord, our guest has escaped."

Luca's heart skipped a beat. "Signorina *Donatelli?* How?"

"Through the window, it appears."

Rodolfo swore under his breath, taking a step away. "Impossible. How long ago?"

"An hour. Mayhap two."

"There is something else," said the second, hesitating. He looked around the clearing, as if looking for someone.

Luca resisted the urge to throttle him. "Well? Out with it."

"Sir," he said, sending a last, desperate glance around the yard, "Is Lady Evangelia with you?"

This time, Luca stepped forward, tension clamping down on his chest. "Clearly not, man. Are you saying she left the castello?"

The guards shared a miserable look then glanced back to him. "An hour past, Captain."

Ben Betarrini groaned and turned away, his hands on his face. Marcello, Father Tomas and Luca shared a long look. But Greco was advancing on the guards. "On horseback?" he asked.

"Yes, m'lord. We thought she was coming here, to you. That's what the lady intimated…"

Rodolfo flung his hand out, dismissing the man's excuse, then pointed at Patrizio's chest. "Surely somebody was watching her from above."

"Indeed, m'lord. She disappeared in the forest, just over there. She appeared to be hunting and—"

"Lady Forelli," Marcello interrupted. "She is yet inside?"

Dario nodded, a little relief in his eyes that he needn't report further bad news.

Greco's eyes went from the castello to the forest and he put his hands on his hips, pacing. "She's gone after Alessandra," he breathed, looking to Luca. "Intending to stop her before it was too late, no doubt."

"After the Fiorentini girl?" Ben asked, dark eyebrows knitting together. *"Toward* the border?"

Lord Greco simply returned his look until he understood. That was exactly what she had done. The men immediately moved toward their horses, tied to trees at the edge of the clearing. Luca shouted for all knights to assemble and await orders. He shoved down a wave of aggravation. *Why would she not come to me? After all this time?*

"She must believe she can get to her," Marcello said, striding between Luca and Ben. "I wager they were concerned that if the Fiorentini scouts saw us all chasing Alessandra down, then the battle would be reignited."

"But she does not know of the contingents on the border," Luca said.

"Right. That's why we shall have to intercept her, just as she intends to intercept Alessandra. Bring them all home." He paused. "Leave our men behind. The fewer of us there are, the better. If the scouts see our men moving out—"

"Understood," Luca said.

They quickly mounted and rode over to where Lord Greco was already examining the footprints beneath the high window. He rose. "She hurt her left foot when she landed," he said, following her trail across the road and into the loamy forest. "See? She's favoring it here."

The men—Marcello, Luca, and Ben—followed him, letting him get his bearings. He looked up, into the trees ahead and fingered a broken leaf. Then he mounted. "This way. As suspected, Evangelia is on Alessandra's trail."

"Can we catch up to them before they reach the border?" Ben asked.

Rodolfo looked back, regret in his eyes. "I know not."

## CHAPTER 8

### –EVANGELIA–

I pounded down an open road, urging my gelding faster, but then had to slow to pick my way through the forests. And I had to entirely avoid the winding riverbed and boulder field that left me exposed. I couldn't risk the guards at Castello Greco spotting me and riding out to find out what I was up to.

The border was just a mile distant now, across an ancient creek bed that the Nine had defined as the new dividing line between Firenze and Siena, reclaiming territory that had been in Fiorentini hands for two generations. Trees had been felled on either side, widening the line. Castello Forelli sent groups of six men to spend three days at a time up here at the old watchtower, but Gabi and I had only visited once for a celebration, and when we did, we'd been surrounded by fifty of their best warriors.

I shoved down another shiver of fear as I rounded a bend in the road. I wished she could be here, with me. Beside her, I was stronger. I touched the bow on my shoulder. Especially now…

When my mare stumbled a bit, I renewed my focus on the old

Roman road, knowing I had to concentrate. *Just get through this and—*

I saw them, then. Two Fiorentini knights, staring dolefully back at me, a thousand paces away. *Scouts.* My heart set into a triple-time beat as I muttered a word I'd never say around my future niece or nephew.

Because scouts, often heading into enemy territory and forced to fight for their lives, were some of the fiercest among knights. And they were on two of the most beautiful, strongest horses I'd seen in a while. *Can't outrun them.*

I touched my bow again, searching my heart. *Surely now...*

But I couldn't. Couldn't take another life. Rob another mother of her son. A wife of her husband. A child of his father...

The "Survivor" mantra came back to me. *Outwit. Outplay. Outlast. Outwit, outplay, outlast, outwit, outplay, outlast...*

Panic washed through me as the scouts dug their heels into the flanks of their mounts, charging toward me. I immediately wheeled my own horse to the left and trotted down a trail, into the brush and trees. I had no idea where it led. I only hoped to God that it would provide an escape rather than trap me in.

I didn't look back, forcing myself to concentrate on the path ahead. Soon it was weaving beside a hill that became a cliff. *Maybe an old goat trail,* I thought. The forest was thick to my left, and the cliff rose steeply to my right. With limited options, all I could think was *hurry, Lia, hurry.* Terror at the thought of a scout's arrow piercing my back surged through me. I had trouble concentrating, I was so scared.

But even that thought couldn't make me take my bow from my back, nock an arrow, shoot another man. I was so done with that. So done. *I can't, Lord. I can't. I can't I can't I can't. Help me.*

I pulled up, sure now that I couldn't outrun them. *Outwit...* I glanced back down the path behind me. Any sec, the scouts would appear. How could I escape them?

Quickly, I slid to the ground and slapped my gelding's flank, setting it off running, farther along our path. Then I carefully lifted the thickly leaved branch of a scrub oak and moved into the forest, forcing myself to be careful, slow.

Scouts were good trackers. They themselves had to avoid upsetting rocks, breaking branches, betraying their presence. But the soil was sandy, and my slippers sank so deeply that the dirt came over the edges. There was nothing to do but hurry and hope the branches would cover my tracks. I could hear them now, speaking in low voices. Studying my trail as they rounded the corner. Confident in tracking their prey.

I crouched, pretty well hidden by the scrub oak, closing my eyes and listening, praying the scouts would see nothing but the continued evidence of my mount's progress forward. *Away. Please, think I went on. Go. Follow the tracks of the horse. Get scared I'm getting away.*

But they were pausing right where I had. I heard the metallic slide of a sword leaving its sheath and slowly lifted my head to peer through the leaves. I was terrified, because I still couldn't seem to force myself to slip the bow from my shoulder. A year ago I could've taken care of these two in seconds. But that was then.

Flashbacks from Castello Paratore cascaded through my mind, blinding me, deafening me in memory. So many cries of pain, of anger. So much blood. So many dead. Dad, pierced by the sword. Gabi, going over the edge. Mom and me, fighting our way forward, too late, too late. Then the assassins, bent on taking the brotherhood down, one castello at a time. The murdered women and children. Luca and me narrowly escaping a similar fate—

I ducked, just in time, as the knight's sword came ramming into the scrub oak and stuck in the trunk above my head. Acting on impulse, I shoved against him, as hard as I could, and surprised, his foot caught, and he fell over an exposed root to his back. We both heard the sickening crack of a breaking bone and he screamed.

With him temporarily down, I ran back the way I'd come, as fast as I could, the branches whipping my face, scratching me, until I reached several boulders. I kept running, aware I had about a minute's lead, the other maybe checking on his buddy. When I was through the boulders, making sure I'd left some clear clues of my passing, I circled around, slipping between them. Hearing him come now, I slid the dagger from my waistband.

I held my breath, knowing he was just a foot away. I saw a pebble skitter past, kicked from his boot. Any second...

As soon as he was past, I leaped onto his back, pulling the dagger to his neck. "Do you know who I am?" I said in the lowest, most menacing voice I could muster.

"I am fairly certain," he said, deadly still, hands up.

"Then you know I shall not hesitate to use this," I grit out. "Drop your sword." He didn't know I was struggling with some sort of weird PTSD. And I figured it was sorta vital for me to keep him from finding out.

The sword clattered to the ground and I smiled a little. *Outwit.*

"Why not kill me now, She-Wolf?" he asked, half-afraid, half-infuriated.

"Because I intend to take you back to Lord Forelli and he shall find out why you are scouting on Sienese land. That is not a part of our treaty agreement."

"The treaty is dead," he spat. "When you kidnapped Signorina Donatelli—"

"That's utter nonsense," I growled and slid off of him, my dagger still at his throat. "Lie down on your belly."

Reluctantly, he did as I asked and I pulled his wrists together behind him, casting a worried glance down the path behind us. His companion was silent, which scared me. If I was lucky, he'd passed out from the pain. If I wasn't...

I was tying his hands when he twisted, trying to buck me off his back. I went flying, but I was up in a flash, the dagger to his throat. "Do not attempt that again," I spat, willing him to see the fury in my eyes. "Now lie *down*."

His lip curling, he did as I asked and I completed my task, looking down the path and around the woods again, freaked his partner was sneaking up on me.

"I shall track you down and slice your pretty head from your body," said the scout, as I wound the rope around his ankles, hoping to really leave him stuck. I tied him up so tight, his fingers were turning blue. "Then I shall take your head to Firenze and we shall celebrate for days."

"That sounds unpleasant," I muttered benignly, already leaving him behind, my dagger out. I bent and grabbed hold of a grapefruit size rock in my left hand, and crept down the path, eyes open wide, ears pounding with my own pulse. Maybe the dude was waiting for me around a tree, a rock, as I had awaited his companion...

But then I saw him, pretty close to where I'd left him. The bone had pierced through his leggings, white and splintered among blood. I winced in spite of myself as he moaned, gripping a sword.

"Let go of that, and I will assist you," I said, gesturing toward the sword.

"You're mad," he spat.

"Agreed. No woman with her wits about her would offer to aid you. Now do as I say."

His chest heaved, and his face paled. He had clearly lost a lot of blood. Maybe the bone had pierced an artery or something.

"Trust me. I shall not kill you. I seek only to be on my way, unhindered. Truly, I could walk around you and be away from you, could

I not?"

"You would allow me, a Fiorentini, to live?" he asked, his eyes narrowing.

"I allowed your companion the same," I said, glancing over my shoulder.

He let his head drop back to the earth, panting, sweating now. Then with a cry of frustration, he dropped his sword and watched me approach with wary eyes.

I paused, just out of his reach, and crouched at his side, studying his wound. I looked to his eyes. "You shall bleed to death if I do nothing. This will hurt you more than I," I said, then I whacked him upside the head with my rock. I felt for a pulse, hoping I hadn't killed him. He was out, but not gone. *Outlast.*

I took my dagger and ripped open his legging. It was bad, really bad. The best I could do for him, and still have a chance at finding Alessandra, was to stop the bleeding. He'd likely lose his leg, in time. But he'd have a better chance of living. I cut a strip from his tunic and then tied it tight around his upper thigh, using a stick, as Mom had taught me, to tighten the tourniquet.

Then I ran up the rest of the path, to the one that edged the cliff above me. I looked one way and then the other. Now what? I had no horse. I didn't know for certain where I was. So I began climbing. If I could get high enough, I could determine where I was. Maybe spot Alessandra. And any other enemy scouts.

I scrambled upward, choosing my handholds and nooks for my toes, while struggling with my skirts. None of the Nike ads ever showed climbers in medieval gowns. For good reason.

Ten minutes later, I reached the top, crouched and moved through the brush and scrubby trees that spread across the ridge. And froze.

Below, across the babbling creek, were a ton of Fiorentini knights.

Some of them sparring. Others gathering to talk and laugh. Still more, shooting targets. It looked like a scene at Castello Forelli. Except five-times that many men. *Five-times that many…*

*I gotta warn the guys.* They were here! Ready to attack. Tomorrow, *tomorrow* if I didn't get Alessandra back to them.

But then I knew our own scouts would've seen them by now. Warned Marcello and Luca.

"So they're coming," I whispered, half-ecstatic at the thought and half-freaked. Because when our guys found me here, so nearly stumbling into the enemy's hands, they'd be mad. So. Mad.

I edged backward, further into the protective shrubs again. On the other side, I set off, hunched over, down the ridge, back toward the road. Now that I knew where I was, I knew there was a scouting path, down at the end. Maybe that's what the other scouts had been intent on doing—taking down anyone who might spot their assembling forces.

A minute later, I heard a woman's cry. I paused, cocked my head, listening, and then crept through the brush again. I'd rounded a bend, the Fiorentini troops completely hidden from view here, but I dropped down and army-crawled forward, wincing as I felt the fine embroidery of my gown snag and tear. *There goes another dress…*

Cautiously, I peered over the edge of the cliff. Four knights were surrounding Alessandra, who limped over to them. She seemed to collapse, and one lifted her in his arms. The other three immediately took a protective stance around them, swords drawn, warily watching the length of the creek as they edged back.

*Oh no. I'm too late! Too late! Outplayed…*

Two nobles emerged from the forest, striding toward them. It was then I saw the flash of color deep between the trees—a tent.

Why were they so far away from the rest of their knights? Was it not foolish, dangerous even?

But then I saw him. Barbato.

The little, evil lord who'd tried to marry Gabi off to Greco, effectively making her Fiorentini. Using her. If he was here...

Then something really sneaky was about to go down.

I watched as the noblemen greeted Alessandra, smiles wide. But as soon as the knight carrying her was past them, their smiles faded and they joined the others in watching the opposite bank of the creek, as well as down the creek, where their men were. They scurried backward, heading toward the tent.

"Something's off," I whispered to myself. They were acting weird. Why hide her?

Then it happened. When the others were hidden by the forest canopy, and I could barely see them, the knight in the center turned on his comrades. Swiftly, he rammed his sword through the neck of the man at his side, yanked it out and turned to chop the head off the other. I stared, stunned, and choked, vomit rising in the back of my throat.

I gasped, as panic flooded my chest. Why? *Why, why, why?*

*Because they want no witnesses*, I realized. Alessandra had walked into a trap. They intended to steal her away. And use her disappearance, undoubtedly, to incite war again. If Marcello couldn't deliver the promised prize...

I stumbled to my feet, seeing the man's head fall to the ground and roll, over and over in my mind, half-blinding me. The other Fiorentini... they'd find the dead knights.

*And claim our men have stolen across the border and murdered them.*

I laid a hand on my belly. A knot was there, growing, making me feel nauseated all over again.

*Oh, God. God! God! Help me! I need to get past this, Lord. This barrier. I need to be able to rise! Use my bow! For Mom. Dad. Gabi. Everyone I love...*

But inside my brain, it was as if synapses were firing left and right, creating tiny explosions of light, fireworks in my head, and I ran then, as if I was five years old again, tearing out of a dark and scary room, afraid of the monsters beneath my bed.

## CHAPTER 9

Alessandra heard the cry of a man behind her, and twisted in the knight's arms to see. But his hold tightened, and he bent then, to duck through the folds of the tent's opening. The noblemen followed, looking like they'd heard nothing, their faces only masks of concern for her.

"I am Lord Barbato," said a small man with a closely trimmed beard, as the knight set her down on a lounge covered in a rich tapestry. "And this is another of the Grandi, Lord Foraboschi." The other was taller than Barbato, more gray, regal in his stance.

Lord Barbato took her hand in a fatherly way. "You have no idea how glad we are to find you, my dear."

"And I you, m'lord. All I want is to get home to my father. He'll be worried."

"Of course," he said soothingly. "Of course. We shall move in haste." He motioned to a servant in the corner and the man brought a tray with bread and cheese, as well as a pitcher of water. Lord Foraboschi poured her a cup and Alessandra sat up to drink greedily from it. Her nose wrinkled. It wasn't the freshest water, despite being so close to the creek, and tasted vaguely of something odd. But she was so thirsty that, when her host poured again, she quickly drank it down too.

She leaned back against the settee, so happy to feel the relative safety of her Fiorentini overlords and be off her aching ankle. A wave of relief went through her, and she fought off a dizzying sensation of weariness. Her run over the last miles must have robbed her of more strength than she realized.

"Tell me, Signorina," the little nobleman said, stroking her hand. "How many men are within Castello Forelli?"

"Thirty or more, within her gates," she said. She frowned. Why could she not make her mouth form the words right?

"Good," he said, seeming not to notice. "And how many do they send to watch the border?"

She shook her head in apology, but then abruptly stopped when it sent another wave of dizziness through her. "I know not."

"That's all right," he said. Behind him, a knight entered. His face was spattered with blood and his mouth was grim, but he didn't seem alarmed. He nodded once at Lord Barbato.

Alessandra frowned, trying to figure it out. But then her mind went back to what had brought her north in the first place. She had been in such a rush...so intent on telling them something. What was it? Why couldn't she think of it?

"They must have threatened you, Alessandra," the man said gently, more fatherly than her own papa had ever been. "For you to run, it must have been awful, indeed."

She nodded. But inside she wondered, had it really been a threat? Lord Greco, Sir Luca Forelli...they had merely warned her from hurting their own, right? When shadows of her enemy intent were uncovered? She remembered the kindness of the Ladies Betarrini, the sisters' warmth.

But then she remembered Luca, narrowly missing her with the lance...Lord Greco, turning her around so roughly...They were her enemies. *Enemies.* People responsible for her brothers' deaths. Valente's death.

And she was on a mission. The expansion, she remembered, her mind finally settling like a rolling ball in a crevice. She gripped the lord's hand. "They're building, m'lord. Expanding. Intending to make Castello Forelli even mightier," she said, feeling like her tongue was expanding, her lips swollen. She let go of his hand to touch them, wondering if it were true. Distantly, she decided they felt normal. On the outside.

"That is hardly a secret, sweet girl," he said, narrowing his eyes. "We need something else from you. You feared for your very life," he guessed, studying her. "They must have tortured you."

"Nay," she said, with a confused shake of her head. "Only—"

"Then what else, woman?" he asked, brusquely casting off her attempt to explain. "What else did you learn?"

The blood-spattered knight bent at a basin in the corner and after rolling up his sleeves, splashed his face. *Rolling up his sleeves,* Alessandra thought groggily, now fighting off an overpowering urge to sleep. She thought of her dead brothers, and that seemed to settle her careening mind for a moment.

"Do you know of Lord Forelli's brotherhood?" she murmured, forcing each word out now. "Lord…Greco. A tattoo…"

Lord Barbato leaned forward, his small eyes narrowing. "Of course we know of it. And Greco, too, has the tattoo, you say? On the arm, as with the others?"

"Here," she said, brushing the inside of her arm with her fingers. "They all have it. All of them."

"How many, Alessandra?" he asked urgently. "How many are there? What are their names?"

"I know not, m'lord." And then, though it was only midday, she closed her eyes and could not summon the strength to open them again.

"Saints above, Evangelia," Marcello said, pulling me roughly into his brotherly arms and kissing my forehead, "if I wasn't so glad to see you alive, I'd throttle you right now."

"Well I know it," I said, apology thick in my tone. "Forgive me. I only thought I might resolve it. Cut Alessandra off, before things got out of hand…"

I hugged Dad, drawing strength from his warm arms around me, and saw Greco behind him, scanning the ridge we'd just descended.

Luca stood two paces away, arms folded, the muscles in his jaw clenching. He stared at me, waiting. "Evangelia," he said, with a little shake of his head. "We so feared for you…"

"I know," I said, shyly hooking his fingers with two of mine, feeling like a jerk for not going to him in the first place. "I was wrong to go without you, Luca. But I shall find a way to make it up to you. For now, there is much to tell you."

Quickly, I filled them in—about the scouts I'd narrowly escaped, about seeing the contingents of knights, just a half-mile down the creek, and Alessandra, intercepted by Lord Barbato.

"Lord Barbato," Rodolfo repeated, stepping forward and cocking his head, as if he'd not heard right.

"Yes," I said, my eyes shifting to my brother-in-law.

He and Greco stared at each other until Marcello lifted his chin, a vein in his neck now working overtime. "Why do you believe *he's* here?" he asked.

"Some political intrigue, I'd wager," Rodolfo said.

"Indeed," I said, remembering. "Just outside Barbato's tent, I saw one knight kill the two at his side. Suddenly, without provocation, without warning. He *executed* them."

Luca stared at me. "His own men?"

I nodded. I tried to not remember the head, tried focusing on the stabbed man instead, as if that was a whole lot better. And somehow, it was.

"'Tis as we feared," Rodolfo said, stepping away, chin in hand, staring up at the ridge as if the answer was up there on a neon sign. "He intends to steal her away. The Fiorentini shall storm up to Castello Forelli on the morrow, demanding Alessandra's safe return, as promised."

"But there shall be no Alessandra to turn over," Marcello muttered.

"Giving the reason they seek to attack," Luca said.

"They shall hurt her, claiming it was us," Rodolfo said softly, looking over his shoulder at Marcello, quietly asking permission. "Or worse."

"Unless I send one of my best knights to retrieve her," Marcello said, as if weighing each word.

Greco nodded, once.

"By your leave, I shall accompany him, m'lord," Luca said. My heartbeat sped up at his words.

"Nay, Luca," Marcello said. "We need you back at the castello."

"Forgive me, m'lord, but don't we need the girl to reappear just as dearly? Greco and I will bring her back. Together. 'Tis not a task for one man, in enemy territory."

Marcello considered them both a moment, arms folded. "Very well. Go."

Luca hid a small smile.

"Marcello, I might be—" I began, but he cut me off with a raised hand, already moving toward his horse.

"You and your sister shall go immediately to Siena with your parents, accompanied by a healthy number of guards. The last thing we need is one of you held hostage, too. You came perilously close to that, today."

"I'll give you two a moment," Dad said to me. Greco had already mounted his grey gelding, but Luca waited nearby. For me.

"What of the scout I tied up?" I asked Marcello. "The other, with the broken leg?"

"Let their own discover them this night," he said with a grin, mounting his horse. "Let them consider what happens to those who wander into She-Wolf territory." His gelding turned in a tight circle, sensing our agitation.

Luca took hold of my hand again and I dragged my eyes to his. "Don't get killed," I said, only half-joking.

He lifted my hand to his lips and planted a gentle kiss on it as he smiled at me with his eyes. "What shall you give me if I return to you alive? A promise may give me the strength to run all the way back to you."

I smiled at him, aware now how much I didn't want him to go. How much I didn't want him in enemy territory. In danger. A wave of nausea passed through me again as I thought of the knight's head...

"Lia," he said softly, edging my chin up. As I looked up into his eyes, my vision cleared. "You need not make any promise. I will forever—"

I halted his speech with the tips of my fingers. "Return to me, Luca, and we shall speak of a certain request that would require me to don a blue dress."

His grin broadened and he kissed my hand again. "Until then, m'lady."

"Until then," I said, finding it impossible to do anything but grin back at him. Despite the fear and the threat and the dread.

Because Luca had that effect on me.

Dad offered his arm and I went to him, feeling the warmth and the shelter there. It was a different kind of strength than Luca's. A daddy's strength, nearly as welcome now. "You had good intentions, didn't you, Sprite?" he asked, leading me toward his horse.

I glanced over my shoulder as Greco and Luca galloped away, Luca sending a little flirty salute to me as they disappeared around the bend. I listened as the sounds of their horses' hoofbeats faded in the distance, and prayed that no Fiorentini scout spotted them as they crossed the river and stole their way to the Barbato tent.

With luck, they'd have the girl back within the hour, and they'd all be safely back at the castello before we had to leave for Siena.

*Please Lord,* I prayed, as Dad helped me up onto the horse, remembering Father Tomas's admonitions against hoping for luck when we had God himself on our side. *Please, please, please, Lord. Be on our side. See us through this. Oh, and it'd be really cool if you'd bring Luca back to me. Amen.*

---

Luca and Rodolfo crept closer and closer, pausing behind trees, moving forward, swords drawn, daggers in their other hand. They saw the dead knights, telling them they were heading in the right direction. But as soon as the tent fully came into view, Rodolfo's heart sank. *No guard.*

Had they missed them already? He ignored Luca's grunt of disapproval and ran directly toward it. Luca was right behind him. They burst inside, immediately back to back, ready to face their enemy, but it was as they'd feared. They were gone.

He met Luca's stern gaze and dashed outside again, directly to where their adversaries had mounted up. Luca said, "I'll get the horses," and ran off, disappearing between the trees. Rodolfo's eyes returned to the tracks, tracing one set of hooves and then the other two. "Three men," he whispered to himself. "This one carrying the woman." Had they told her they were taking her home to keep her quiet? How long would it be before she realized she was in danger?

*Stupid, stupid girl,* he thought, cursing her decision to run. He paced, his hand on his head. If she'd only waited but another day, all would have been well! And yet...and yet, if he'd been in her position, he could understand. The Fiorentini were as poisoned in their thinking about the Sienese as the Sienese were about the Fiorentini. He'd been around both long enough to know that neither side was fully innocent.

And now Alessandra would be a pawn in the game. How long would it take for Barbato to decide he was safer killing her and simply utilizing her absence at the appointed time of trade? Half of him was surprised they hadn't found her dead already, beside the knights outside, waiting for the rest of the Fiorentini to discover them all, fueling their charge upon Castello Forelli. No one would stop to ask questions.

*Unless he has more dire intentions. Intentions that would make her welcome death, instead...*

Luca moved through the trees, leading his mount. He was moving slowly, obviously hoping to avoid drawing the eye of any Fiorentini scouts.

"We best be away from those two," Luca said with a nod toward the bodies. "If we're found on this side of the creek even, their Fiorentini brothers shall tear us apart." He looked up at the tent. "Why not bother to take it down?"

"They're not Barbato's colors," Rodolfo said. "Even the knights do not wear his herald. They must have been mercenaries."

"Clever little man, isn't he?"

"As well as ruthless," he said, meeting Luca's gaze. "Once he has what he needs from Alessandra..."

"He'll not be suggesting a game of tric-trac?"

"Nay."

## CHAPTER 10

Alessandra awakened as the horse entered the river, splashing her face. She blinked, forcing her eyes to remain open, although they begged to shut again. What was wrong with her? She felt ill. A horrible ache pounded behind her eyes, different than the one she'd suffered at Castello Forelli. And she was so desperately weary... Not since the time she had the coughing sickness as a child, or the fall that landed her in Castello Forelli, had her head felt like this, so thick and groggy.

The horse entered deeper water, barely touching bottom, by the feel of it. It dawned on her then that she was lying, facedown, across the girth of a horse, and she couldn't remember being placed there. But she remembered who she'd been with last...

She forced herself to look up, into the face of the man in the saddle behind her, but was blinded by the setting sun. "Lord Barbato?"

"Ah, signorina," he said nervously. "Please, stay still. Lord Barbato is directly behind us. I am but his hired servant." Gradually, she placed his voice. The servant from the tent.

"Where...where are we going?"

"To safety, signorina. You appeared...unwell, and m'lord wanted to make certain you were behind defensible gates before the night was through. He thinks the Sienese poisoned you!"

"Might…might you not simply take me home?"

"Nay, signorina. You must be defended. M'lords wish to speak with you further about Castello Forelli and those within. You may yet have information that may assist your brothers-at-arms."

"Anything," Alessandra said, meaning it. But what else did she know that might help them? She wondered what she'd told them and what she had not. Mayhap she'd dreamed their entire conversation, due to her fever. Or the poison. Whatever plagued her. It felt dim in her memory.

She could not fight it any longer. She gave in to the sway of the horse, letting her head flop alongside its sweaty flank. A length of her hair drifted beside her face and into the water, but she couldn't summon the strength to lift it out, or truthfully, even to care. In the morning, she'd be better. And she could figure it out. In the morning…

---

Happily, Barbato's party seemed as eager to avoid the Fiorentini as Rodolfo and Luca were. They made good time for a while, alternately breathing easier, the more distance they put between themselves and the knights assembled at the creek, and growing more dismayed at how deep they were traveling into Fiorentini territory. By the terms of the truce, none of the Sienese could venture into lands held by Firenze, without written safe rights of passage. While both men carried a signed letter from Marcello in their saddlebags, there was no corresponding wax seal from Firenze. If questioned, it would do little more than buy them a few minutes.

It was their good fortune that they'd been dressed for work on the construction site today, rather than in their uniforms displaying the

Forelli gold. But even dirt could not fully conceal the wide stripe of it on Luca's horse blanket.

They made good time for a while, but lost precious minutes every time the trail faded or other travelers forced them into hiding. When the men they were tracking decided to cross the river, rather than take the bridge that would lead them to the main road north, Rodolfo breathed a sigh of relief. *They're not heading to Firenze.*

But that left him wondering where they were going. Northwest, he decided, glancing up at the last vestiges of the setting sun, down to the shadows.

"Where do you think they head?" Luca asked.

"Barbato has a summer estate, a manor out toward the sea. Three or four hours from here."

"The perfect place to question the girl and dispose of her body," Luca said bitterly. "Bind her up. Release her to the fathoms. Meanwhile, you and I get farther and farther from our people." He looked back over his shoulder, southward. "We'll have no hope of returning to them in time, before battle is upon them. Lia…"

"Come now, Luca—"

"You saw that she elected to capture those scouts rather than take them down as she used to. If she is under fire…And I am not there to defend her…" He turned partially away, his profile a mask of anguish.

"She's strong, Luca. A She-Wolf, even if the fight within her now slumbers. If the enemy comes to our gates, she shall rise. And Marcello intends to cart them off to Siena anyway."

Luca looked off to the horizon and then back to him. Never had Rodolfo seen him so devoid of humor and hope.

"The battle will likely begin," Rodolfo said. "Our only hope is to get to Alessandra and bring her back alive. Swiftly."

"Then what say you and I do just that?" Luca said, his usual bravado slowly sliding back into his tone. "You know, rather than take our ease at the next town's inn, putting our feet up, demanding the finest Parma ham and bread."

Rodolfo laughed under his breath. "Agreed." He paused, circling around a section where their adversaries' trails merged with several others, then separated again. The two of them moved on, cautiously cresting a hill, as if they were nothing but two noblemen, out for a leisurely afternoon ride.

"I assume 'twould be far easier if we rescue our misguided friend before Lord Barbato reaches the villa?" Luca asked.

"Indeed. The difference shall be fighting the four or so who have her now, versus a good number of knights at the villa."

"Hmm. Let us opt for the foursome option. The other may prove messy."

Rodolfo smiled. "Agreed."

But as he said it, a patrol of six men crested the hill to their right. The first man carried a red and white flag on a pole. *Fiorentini.* He returned to looking forward, as if there was no reason to pause.

"Mayhap they won't see us," Luca said lightly. He didn't turn to look at them.

"Too late," Rodolfo returned, spying out of the corner of his eye, the patrol leader turn his horse in their direction. "We'll present our papers, letting them take their ease a moment, then before they discover the missing Fiorentini seal—"

"Take them down," Luca said under his breath, as the knights surrounded them, demanding they come to a halt.

Rodolfo and Luca did as they asked. "Greetings, friends," he said.

"I am Captain Severino de Firenze," said the short, stocky patrol captain. "Who are you and what is your business upon this road?"

"We are nobles on our way north," Rodolfo said easily, as if it weren't entirely obvious. "We have letters of safe passage here," he said, reaching into his tunic and pulling the parchment sleeve from a pocket. He tossed the leather packet to the captain and the man caught it, still studying them.

"What are your names?" he asked, his tone a little more respectful as he untied the packet's string.

"It's all there," Rodolfo said, his eyes shifting over the other knights around their captain. Standard arms...

"You do not know your own names?" asked the man, sliding out the papers.

"Oh, yes. Forgive me," Rodolfo said. "I am Lord Rodolfo Greco, and this is Sir Luca Forelli."

"We thought it high time for a proper visit," Luca said.

The man's eyes stilled on the papers and shifted up to meet his, but Luca and he were already in action, cutting down the nearest two of the six. The group erupted into shouts and grunts, two horses rearing up on hind legs, the rest surging into motion. A minute later, Luca was pulled off his horse and Rodolfo jumped off his gelding, so they could fight back to back, when he belatedly saw the Fiorentini captain duck under his horse's neck.

Rodolfo narrowly missed impalement, and stumbled to his left, lost his footing as well as his sword, and went to one knee. He threw himself to the right to miss the man's next strike. The man was strong, even if he was short, Rodolfo thought grimly, pulling his dagger as he rose to face the captain, sensing another approach him from behind.

"So the traitor dares to cross the border," said the captain with a sneer. He was attempting to cover the sounds of his man behind Rodolfo. But Rodolfo was watching his eyes. Waiting, waiting for the moment they—

There. He bent and rammed his dagger backward, praying he hadn't guessed wrong at the man's move. He hadn't. He heard the surprised gasp of his enemy, felt the dagger plunge into his belly and turned to wrench the sword from his hands, whirl and meet the captain's next, furious strike. With a growl, he attacked, striking and striking and striking until the captain's sword went flying. They faced each other, hunched over and panting. Luca stood to one side, hands on the end of his sword handle, watching.

The captain looked from Rodolfo to Luca and back again. He raised his hands, his face a mask of fury. "Mercy, m'lords."

*Mercy.* The word echoed his mind a moment, as if foreign. Unknown. Rodolfo paused. He knew that given the opportunity, the man would have sliced him from neck to navel, and left him to the birds. But it was the honor code among knights—some knights. And he knew this one would never have granted him the same.

Some men were best disposed of before one had to meet them on the battlefield again.

"Rodolfo," Luca said, when he raised his sword. And in that one word, his conversation with Father Tomas came back to him. Of penance. And forgiveness. Of going with the wind, rather than against it.

He lowered his sword and considered the captain. "Mercy is yours," he spit out, feeling none of the word. "May you remember this day the *Lord* spared you."

They threw the dead bodies over their horses' backs and hurried down to a ravine, dragging the bound captain behind them. There, hidden in a deep gully, they left their adversaries' bodies, and forced the captain to strip, binding him to an old, fallen tree. The naked man stared at them with seething hatred. "I shall find you and kill you both," he said.

"Ah, that is no sort of gentlemanly response to the mercy we have shown you," Luca said, mounting his horse. "You should be promising us your finest cask of wine!"

"Only if I watch you drown in it."

Luca looked dolefully over at Rodolfo. "He is a rather unpleasant sort, isn't he?"

"Indeed." They turned and galloped up the hill again, and when they found Barbato's trail, rushed onward, praying that they hadn't fallen too far behind.

---

Alessandra was fully awake by the time they rode up to the walled mansion. As soon as the horse came to a halt, she slid off, belatedly remembering her injured ankle, staring at the servant, who gazed back at her in surprise. "Signorina—" he began.

But Lord Foraboshi trotted up beside them then. "Ah, Alessandra. You have recovered. Good. Good. Please, Eobroni. Take her arm in case she faints again."

Alessandra wavered on her feet, feeling weak from hunger, thirst. And her head still throbbed. She felt confused. Lost. "M'lord, if you only would allow me to go home—" she said.

"In time, my dear. In good time," he said, taking her arm as his servant took the other. The creaking gates of the villa swung open and four knights emerged to welcome them. The other knight, the towering Celso who had accompanied them from the border, followed behind her.

She really had no option. Despite her growing sense of dread, she could do nothing but take the steps before her. *It will be well,* she told herself. *They only wish to ensure my safety.*

But then the big knight put a bag over her head and covered her mouth with his hand. He picked her up in his arms when she struggled, and bodily carried her forward.

She pretended she'd fainted again, hoping he'd release her mouth, allowing her to breathe, and it worked. He paused, shifted her in his arms and kept moving. Her heartbeat sped up when she realized they were avoiding the large, loud courtyard, apparently full of men and horses, and were heading away from the noise. As if hiding her. Why would Lord Barbato hide her from her own people? She frowned, trying to think, wondering if she might be asleep, suffering through a nightmare in which nothing made sense...

The guard deposited her on a straw tick, covered in a rough blanket. She moaned and moved her head, as if just awakening again.

Lord Barbato pulled the bag from her head. The big knight was right behind him. "Forgive me, my dear. 'Twas best if the others not yet know you are here."

"M'lord...I am well enough to speak to my Fiorentini brothers," she said, forcing herself to rise, to show him. *Mayhap that is why he's not eager to introduce me.* "If you might just give me a moment. Some water. A brush. I can make myself presentable."

"Not yet," he said, folding his arms. "Sit down, Signorina."

Slowly, she sank to the edge of the straw tick and folded her hands in her lap.

"I must be certain I know of all that you wish to say to the Grandi. First. I want no surprises."

"I...I have told you all I know. Of the construction. Of the men with their triangular tattoos denoting the brotherhood."

"Yes," he said, pacing before her, chin in hand. "Tell me more of those. None of the other knights had them?"

"None that I could see."

"Intriguing," he said, his eyes narrowing. "We've noted that mark on other Forelli allies. How many are there?"

"I tried to find out, m'lord. But they would not say."

He tapped his lips, thinking, then eyed her again. "What else? Surely you gained other knowledge while inside the gates of Castello Forelli. Or did they keep you chained to a wall?" She laughed a little at that, then quickly sobered when she saw his stern expression. "Nay, m'lord. For the most part, they treated me most kindly."

"Nay," he said. "I do not wish for you to say that ever again."

She frowned in confusion. "M'lord?"

"They beat you," he said, striking her across the mouth before she saw it coming.

She was too surprised to cry out, and only lifted the back of her hand to her split, bloody lip. She stared at him from the corner of her eye, fear mounting in her heart. Lord Greco had warned her...tried to warn her...*Nay. Only this one is bad.* If she could go to the others...she'd be certain to meet good men. Upstanding men.

"I wish to see another of the Grandi," she said firmly, squaring her shoulders. "Lord Foraboschi."

But he only hit her again, this time knocking her to the floor. For a small man, he was terribly strong, she thought, trying to get her head to cease its dizzying spin.

"You were raped repeatedly. Hit. Slapped. Choked. Chained. Threatened," he said, leaning down beside her.

"But that 'tisn't true," she said, cradling her head in her hands, trying to get the earth to return to its normal slant so that she might rise.

"It shall be if you do not tell me what I need to know," he said, winding his small hand cruelly in her hair and wrenching her head back. "You're a beautiful woman, Alessandra. It shan't be a chore for Celso, here, to serve the republic..."

"M'lord, please," she gasped. "I am a loyal servant of the republic," she pleaded. "I know nothing else."

*Except of Lady Evangelia, and her inability to lift an arrow against the enemy,* she thought.

*Nay. Not that. They need not know that!*

*Or of the babe in Lady Gabriella's belly.*

"What is it, my dear?" he said. "You've thought of something."

"Nay, m'lord."

"Why do you protect them? Our enemy?" he seethed, tugging at her hair.

"I know nothing else. I swear it."

He released her hair then, making her think he was changing his mind, seeing he'd acted in error, when he kicked her in the stomach.

Alessandra panicked, needing breath, yet unable to take it. She writhed on the floor. When she was finally able to take a half, gasping, lurching breath, he again wound his hand in her hair. "Tell me and this ends," he whispered in her ear.

She didn't believe him, but she had to give him something.

What? Anything she thought of made her feel the cold wave of betrayal. There was knowledge that fueled forces of war. But then there was knowledge that could only lead to very private pain…

He was sawing at her hair before she fully realized what he was doing. She screamed, watching long waves of it fall to the floor, to her skirts. "Stop! Stop!"

"Come now," he said, as she felt the last of it lift from her shoulders, the pull of strands at her neck. "'Twill make your story all the more effective." He tossed the last handful to the ground and Alessandra couldn't help it. She was so confused, she gave way to tears, lifting her hands to her head to feel her shorn hair.

He leaned down beside her ear again. "They sheared you like a spring lamb," he said. "That's what you shall tell the Grandi. It was horrifying. They laughed as they did it."

"Nay," she said, shaking her head as tears streamed down her face. "Why must I lie?"

Lord Barbato slapped her again. This time, as she went to the ground, she stayed there. The cool stones gave her an odd sense of comfort. But he took her arm and wrenched her upright, leaning her back against the bed frame.

"Do you not see?" He shook her, an odd smile on his face. "Do you not *see*? You are our own Helen of Troy, inciting our battle." He laughed under his breath. "Well, not quite the same. But you shall serve the same purpose."

He rose and stared down at her. "You may feel poorly at the moment, Alessandra, but you shall always know that you gave it all to serve your republic. And once the men see you, abused, shorn, used, no man in Firenze shall fail to rise up and beat the Sienese dogs into submission." He paused and stared at her. "Only your dead body might make them more furious. So, dear Alessandra, I suggest you consider the benefits of quiet compliance." He leaned down. "Now tell me. Tell me what you know."

*Castello Forelli*

"I shall be with you soon," Marcello said to Gabi, taking both her hands in his and kissing them. "Take close care. No foolish decisions," he warned her. "You act on another's behalf now," he whispered.

Only I was close enough to hear it. Mom and Dad were busy getting settled on their own horses.

"You swear it? You'll be with me soon?" she pressed.

"I swear it," he said, bringing her hands to his chest and putting his forehead to hers. I didn't think Marcello could look any more in love when it came to my sister, but this whole baby thing had him looking like he was ready to sing her a Taylor Swift song or something. He looked like it was killing him, sending her away. And suddenly, I remembered his face when she was so close to death, and he dragged her palm down to the handprint in the tomb...

"M'lord," said a skinny knight, Este, entering the stables. "Scouts have located enemy soldiers, venturing across the border. We must get your family to Siena, or commit to keeping them here."

Marcello nodded and turned to help Gabi up on her horse, gently settling her feet in the stirrups and tying her reins to Otello's, already mounted ahead of her. He was one of Marcello and Luca's most trusted men, a linebacker sort of dude, with a ton of meat on him, and most of it muscle. Beside him, Falito, a regular, 5'10" sort of guy, looked kind of freakishly small. But I knew he was just as fine a fighter. As were the other twelve in attendance.

"You make certain our scouts let us know if any cross the border," Marcello called to Este. "One is to come here, to alert us, and the other is to find our party on the road and alert them."

"Yes, m'lord." He disappeared through the open stable doors.

"Any difficulty in bringing Pio and Sandro with me?" my dad asked Marcello, glancing at the two cute stable boys and back to his son-in-law.

Marcello smiled and ducked his head. "You really must cease adopting the children about or they shall never become the men we seek to make of them, sir."

Dad smiled, but only stared back at him, waiting him out.

"Fine, fine," Marcello said. "We shall make due without them." He looked at the squires. "Go! Get your knapsacks and stuff a clean shirt in them. You must be presentable if you are to represent the Forelli household in Siena."

The boys scurried away, even as another man slid a bit into the mouth of a mare. They were so small, they could ride together.

Marcello lifted me into my saddle. "Don't fret, Evangelia, over Luca. He shall see this through as he has all other battles."

I sat up straight, wanting to kick him instead of allowing him to place my heels in the stirrups. "I know," I said in irritation. "Or I'll simply be forced to go and rescue him again." Was I so easy to read? Did everyone know that I was falling for the guy?

Marcello laughed. "I'll be most eager to tell him you said that."

"Please. Do so. Mayhap it shall keep him from further harm."

"Take care of your sister too," he said. He turned to a servant and took hold of my bow and quiver. He stared into my eyes as he handed them to me. I was obviously fooling no one. Every one of my companions knew I was struggling with it, even though I thought I'd been hiding it pretty well over the last year. I shouldered the bow, choosing to watch a servant as he silently handed Gabi her sheath and sword, rather than meet my brother-in-law's knowing eyes.

"Ready, m'ladies?" asked Otello, looking back at Gabi.

Gabi nodded, granting him permission to head on out. Falito gave a low whistle and we moved out of the stables, joining our guards. I hated that we were taking men away from Castello Forelli, but understood the importance of it. Firenze specialized in using kidnapped victims for their cause, and if the wrath of our neighbors to the north was about to descend upon us again, it was best if Gabi and her baby were behind far more impenetrable walls. Me too, I supposed. Our contingent of knights would see us to Siena, and then most of them would ride back tomorrow. Hopefully before the Fiorentini arrived.

Gabi and I rode side by side, the knights ahead of us towing us along like tugboats with barges. I still hated the whole side-saddle thing, but at least it required little effort. I could daydream, or stare at people and places along the road in the hazy twilight, cataloguing them in my head for future sketches.

The last I'd sketched was Alessandra. Did Luca and Lord Greco have her yet? Were they heading home, even as we left the gates? If so, Marcello would hand her off in the morning to her dad, and the Fiorentini would have no rationale to attack. We'd be back within the week. The pang of missing the castello, before I'd even left, surprised me. Slowly but surely, maybe this place and these people were taking over my heart as they had, long ago, for my family. I wrapped my hand around the shank of my bow and looked up at the guards. They nodded back at me in silent farewell. *Be safe. Be well,* I thought, sending good wishes up to them. *Be here when I return.*

But as my eyes returned to the road ahead of us, I had one particular man's face in mind.

*Luca, oh, Luca. Please don't be in trouble...*

---

"That is *not* what I wished to see," Luca said, sliding down again beside Rodolfo. "They have guards on every corner. It's a nest of vipers."

Rodolfo peeked over the top of the hill. "By the colors, vipers I know well." He crept back and turned over, looking up to the darkening sky. "Mayhap we could steal in under night's cover."

"As much as I love the opportunity to increase the legend of Sir Luca Forelli, I fear we'd be diced into small cubes of stew meat before the night was over."

Rodolfo rubbed his face, trying to think of a solution. Come morning, the Fiorentini would arrive at Castello Forelli's gates. Luca hoped their horses would be safe, back in the wood a half-mile distant. Otherwise, it'd be a long walk home...

Luca pulled some dried meat from his pack and handed Rodolfo a portion. "Eat. It shall help us think." He pulled a skin of water out and drank greedily, then handed it to his friend.

Rodolfo ignored his offering, still searching the skies as if the emerging stars held the answer. "There are too many. We have no choice but to wait and hope they take Alessandra with them. Mayhap there shall be a juncture where we can move and rescue her."

Luca quit chewing and grimaced. "What if they kill her tonight? Bury her within the villa's walls?"

A wave of pain moved briefly through his friend's face, then was carefully hidden. Rodolfo's dark eyes met his. "We move before daybreak if they do not. If they intend to use the woman, if she still yet lives, they shall move out with her before morning dawns."

Slowly, Luca nodded. "First watch is yours, brother," he said, settling down happily in the grass, his hand over the hilt of his sword. He pulled a branch over him like a blanket. "For I am weary beyond dreams."

## CHAPTER 44

Alessandra still struggled to accept that what she yet endured was real. "Please, m'lord. All I wish is to go home."

"In time, my dear. In time. Right now," he said, turning again to face her, "I want you to consider every minute of every day you were in Castello Forelli. What did you overhear? Think, Alessandra. Mayhap you overheard something…a guard…a maid…something that may have seemed like castle gossip."

She shook her head again and this time, took a step back, the ball of potential betrayal in her belly now getting bigger, making her feel ill again.

He advanced, frowning now, his face moving into a sneer. *"Think,* Alessandra. Think. There is something else in that pretty head of yours. I'm certain."

"M'lord," she gasped, as he cruelly pinched her arms.

He shoved her backward, pinning her to the bed, one hand clamping down on her throat. "Tell me."

She choked, writhing, struggling to get free, to breathe.

*"Tell me all you know."*

She nodded then, giving in.

He immediately backed away, sitting up straight, brushing his tunic and straightening his leggings, patiently waiting while Alessandra struggled to calm herself, to take one breath and then another and then still another. She rose, sitting against the wall, her legs drawn up under her skirts like a protective wall. Celso stood morosely at the door, staring straight ahead, arms crossed. Barring her exit, any hope of escape.

"Tell me, Alessandra, and your agony shall soon come to an end."

"Lady Evangelia Betarrini," she began, hating each word as it left her mouth. "She cannot summon the strength to take up arms against another."

Lord Barbato stared at her for a long moment, and then smiled, laughed. He clasped his hands together. "Truly?" he asked in amazement. "A She-Wolf, hobbled? Maimed?"

She nodded, unable to look at him any longer. She felt sick to her stomach. And she was already praying that such information would never cause Lady Evangelia harm. She was safe...safe behind the walls of Castello Forelli. With Sir Luca and Lord Marcello and all those fierce knights—

"What else?" he asked, leaning toward her again.

"Sir Luca Forelli. His heart belongs to Lady Evangelia."

"Oh, that is not new information, my dear," he said, cocking his head and sliding his hand up her arm, up to her neck, hovering where he'd so recently choked her.

Alessandra swallowed hard, tensing for attack, but refusing to drop her gaze.

"What else?" he whispered, squinting at her. "There is something else."

He dug his thumbs in, just enough to send terror through Alessandra again. If she didn't tell him, this would simply go on all night. All night... If she survived it. And from what he said, he didn't truly care if she did.

"Lady Gabriella," she whispered. "She is to bear a child."

He lowered his head, so low she could feel his breath on her shoulder. "Now that...that is truly joyous news, is it not?"

She shivered as he backed away. How could she have done it? Betrayed the ladies who had treated her with nothing but kindness? But then, how could such things be a weapon in this man's hands? As Lord Marcello had said, she knew nothing that wouldn't be public knowledge in time...

She closed her eyes, ashamed of herself. Despite her attempts to rationalize, she'd acted only to save herself.

Lord Foraboshi rose and straightened his tunic, soothed back his hair. He poured water from a pitcher into the basin, cupped a hand and drank, then looked up at Celso. "That is it. We shall move against the She-Wolves of Siena. End it once and for all. With Lady Evangelia hobbled and Lady Gabriella with child...it might be our only opportunity. Our greatest opportunity. We shall bring them to Firenze. Bring them to their knees. And behind them, their republic shall be brought to their knees as well."

"A fine plan, m'lord."

Lord Barbato steepled his fingers in front of him. "Marcello will have sent them to Siena, to the palazzo. Thinking them safest there."

"Undoubtedly."

Lord Barbato paused beside Celso as he passed. "See that 'tis done by the time I return. You have ten minutes."

"M'lord, the others are certain to recognize her wounds as recent."

Lord Barbato squinted up at him. "My brothers shall see what they wish to see. They shall see the advantage of backing up my claims, allowing us to attack Castello Forelli and distract the She-Wolves' protectors. Now...must I find another to see to this task?" He cast a lustful glance in Alessandra's direction. "It shall not be difficult to find a willing—"

"Nay," growled the knight. "I shall see it done."

Lord Barbato left then, closing the door behind him, and the knight advanced.

Alessandra tried to run away, dodge him, but the man grabbed hold of her arm. She screamed and dropped like a dead-weight, trying to wriggle free. "Nay! *Nay!* Unhand me!"

He dragged her up to her feet, practically off the ground, and she screamed again in terror, half-crying.

"I am your friend," he whispered in her ear, pulling her terribly close. *"Alessandra.* You are safe."

She cried out, confused, thinking she'd misheard. He took hold of her upper arms, holding her still. "Alessandra," he whispered again.

"Come here!" he yelled upward, as if she'd escaped him.

"I shall not harm you," he whispered, looking steadily into her eyes. "You are safe. But all will be lost if you don't help me make him think his orders are being carried out. Scream." He gave her an urgent look. "Scream," he whispered, shaking her.

Alessandra cried out, tears still streaming from her eyes, trying to make sense of it. *Why? Why is he coming to my aid? What does he want? What shall be his price?*

"Cease your complaint!" he yelled toward the door, his eyes containing none of the malice his master's had. "Just give in, woman. You cannot escape me."

He let go of Alessandra and slid toward the door. She fell against the wall, trying to stop trembling so violently. He listened for a moment and then looked over his shoulder at her. She let out a little involuntary yelp. Closing his eyes a moment, he took hold of the latch and eased it open, peering outside. He pulled a dagger from his belt then and fully yanking open the door, disappearing through it. A moment later, he dragged in a dead guard, dropping him to close the door. He immediately began stripping off the guard's boots and leggings. "Quickly. Out of your dress," he said.

She stared at him in horror. Did he intend—

"I shall not look. Please. Do you not yet see? I can't escort a woman out of here. But a squire?" He nodded, with the hint of a smile.

She nodded, numbly, finally understanding.

He yanked off the man's boots and leggings as Alessandra turned and unhooked the back of her gown. She supposed it foolish, her reluctance to leave the gown behind—it'd been a gift from the Betarrinis, the finest she'd ever worn. The Betarrinis. *Betrayer,* she chastised herself. She slipped the dress from her shoulders and looked back. The knight was offering her a shirt, averting his eyes.

She wrenched it from his hand and slipped it over her shoulders, then reached for the leggings, pulling them up and securing them with the belt that came next. They were ridiculously long, as was the shirt and tunic, but at least the man had not been as large as Celso. She hurried over to the boots, pulling one on after the other. She'd not be able to run in them, but she might be able to manage a shuffle.

Celso went to the door again, peering out, before glancing back at her. He scowled and then dragged her over to the basin, wetting his big hands and then hastily slicking back her short hair. He growled. "You do it. You're still looking far too…womanish."

She dipped her trembling hands in and did the same, wetting it down thoroughly, then glanced back at him. He groaned. "As well as can be expected," he said, taking her hand. They slid out of the room and down the hall. She winced at the heavy sound of her boots, but they were largely disguised by the more frightening sounds—voices, laughter, animated conversation, among fifty or more men, but steps away.

"Come," he said, after peeking around the corner. "Walk as if you belong here. As if we simply head toward the stables."

She nodded. But he was already moving. She struggled to keep up, wondering if anyone would shout, call to them, or worse...

But no one did. They made it to the relative safety of the next, dark hallway, only lit by the occasional torch.

"Walk like a man," he said with a grunt of disapproval.

She frowned. Simple for him to say, when he wasn't wearing boots too big for him. And he'd been a man all his life! What if she asked him to walk like a woman? Still, she attempted to do as he asked, using the boots to her advantage. Her head ached again, as did her side where she'd been kicked, her neck...

They turned another corner and then through a doorway, and they were outside. Alessandra took a breath of clean, sweet evening air. The knight pulled her between two wagons, crouching down, watching as a group of knights paused beside the door, talking and laughing. He reached in the open back of the nearest wagon and took out a coil of rope.

"Why are you doing this?"

"What?"

"Saving me."

"'Twas the right thing to do."

"But you are Fiorentini. They shall hang you for your treasonous acts."

He gave her a small smile, barely discernible in the faint reach of the nearest torch. "They'd hang me anyway, in time, on suspicion." He pulled up his sleeve and showed her. Even in the dim light, the tattoo could clearly be seen on his fair skin.

She gaped. How many were in this brotherhood? She'd imagined them all to be nobles, not knights in the ranks...

"These are times of shifting sands when it comes to loyalty to one's republic, are they not?" He didn't wait for an answer. The knights had moved indoors. And they were on the move again. He stumbled over a ladder, backed up, ran his hand the length of it and then looked up at the wall. It was but a minor defense, nowhere near the height of a castello's. But it was patrolled by men they could see, as dark silhouettes against the starry sky.

Alessandra glanced back toward the mansion doorway, concerned now. Precious minutes had evaporated. How long until Lord Barbato returned? Found out they had disappeared? Sounded an alarm?

Celso urged her flat against the wall, looking up. Above them, a knight casually walked by. She prayed his attention was mostly outward. But she knew the laughter and noise within was probably drawing him too. She closed her eyes, hoping against hope they would not see them, that it wouldn't be at this moment that Lord Barbato discovered he'd been betrayed.

*Move on, please move on. Lord, help us!*

Gradually, achingly slow, he moved on.

Celso didn't hesitate. He pulled up the ladder. It was missing a couple of rungs, but Alessandra figured she'd be able to get past them. "Go," he said, as soon as he had it upright.

She hurried up it, but within a few steps, knew she was about to lose her boots, and if she didn't let them go, they might make her fall. She let them drop to the side and scrambled up the rest of the ladder, Celso right behind. At the top, they crouched, each looking in opposite directions as Celso hauled up the ladder as quietly as he could and lowered it over the other side. He almost had it settled again when they heard the shrill cry of a man from within the villa.

Alessandra jumped on the ladder, almost sending it to one side, but Celso held tight. She hurried down, half sliding, wincing as deep splinters entered her palms. But inside all she could think was *away. We must be away.*

More alarmed shouts rose. The guards were running in their direction, from either side, having spotted their ladder.

"Make haste!" she cried, not bothering to disguise her voice. An arrow came singing by her head and she crouched, watching in horror as Celso's tunic got caught on the broken rung and he struggled to free himself. She reached up and pulled, as hard as she could, and ended up bringing the man down with the ladder. He was immediately on his feet and took her hand.

Together they ran.

---

"Luca," Rodolfo said, nudging his friend. *"Luca."*

He was instantly awake, shoving aside the branch and turning to his knees. "What is it?"

"Two men just came over the wall. The Fiorentini are in pursuit."

"Well, we needn't wade into that scuffle," Luca said. But his eyes were tracing the dim form of the two, disappearing down a shallow valley to their left.

"Mayhap they know of what has transpired with Alessandra," Rodolfo said. The villa gates were opening. "And now, we cannot stay here. They shall discover us."

"Yes, well," Luca said with a sigh. "Sleep is not fully necessary, is it?" He rose and pounded his chest. "Not for a Forelli knight."

Rodolfo shook his head and they set off in a steady run toward the wood where their horses were hobbled. With luck, they'd intercept the two on foot on their way there and question them. In any case, they didn't wish to stay where they were, not with enemy knights out looking for those hidden in the slopes and gullies about the mansion.

Minutes later, they reached the wood. Looking back, knights were just now cresting the hill where they'd hidden, lifting torches high. They entered the trees and padded forward, pausing to listen every few minutes for the two who had escaped the villa. It was difficult, so dark that Rodolfo could barely keep track of Luca in front of him, as well as dodge trees. He ran with one hand in front of him, ducking left and right to avoid the trunks and branches.

Luca stopped so suddenly, he almost ran over him. Luca laughed under his breath and steadied him. Slowly, he slid the sword from his sheath, as did Rodolfo. "We know you're here," Luca said, just loud enough for anyone in the immediate area to hear. "Come out, or we shall be forced to hunt you down. If you're against those who inhabit that villa, you shall find aid and protection in us."

Judging from the sounds, a large man moved toward them.

"Be you friend or foe?" Rodolfo barked, moving to stand beside Luca.

"Neither," said a deep voice. "But rather, a brother, long lost."

Rodolfo wondered over his words. But then he was closer.

"If I remember voices correctly, I'd wager I face Lord Greco and Sir Luca Forelli."

"Celso?" Luca said, a smile of greeting in his voice. "Celso Costa?"

The man laughed and the two embraced in the dark. Rodolfo took the man's hand. But then sounds of those in pursuit drew them up short. "What of your companion? Who is the boy?"

"It is I," said another, moving softly through the branches to stand right behind Celso. "Alessandra."

"Saints be praised," Luca said, his voice numb with surprise. "Now let us make our escape before we become the latest swine to be skewered and roasted on a Barbato spit."

## CHAPTER 12

They hurried through the forest, the light of torches at their backs. They managed to keep just ahead of their adversaries for a while, but Alessandra was moving painfully slowly, holding her side and limping. It wasn't until Rodolfo looked back in agitation that he saw her face and groaned. In the flickering, filtering light, he saw that her hair had been shorn. Her face and hands were bleeding. And she was hurting, barely able to stand.

He turned toward her and reached out, grimacing when she flinched, swaying weakly on her feet. "Mother Mary, what did they do to you?"

Celso paused just ahead, glancing over his shoulder at them. "He beat her. He wished it to look like she had suffered by your hands. Or the Forellis'. And he left her with me, to make it far worse. That is when we made our escape."

Rodolfo shared a brief look of fury with Luca, then turned and swept Alessandra into his arms. She buried her face in his chest, clinging to him in a manner that melted the anger within. She was an innocent. Played as a pawn in far worse ways than he feared.

They reached their horses and Rodolfo lifted Alessandra up and into Luca's saddle. "Do you have the strength to hold on?"

She nodded. He mounted his horse, while Luca and Celso silently took up the front and rear guard. They ran, as best as they could, spooked that they no longer saw bits of light behind them. Either their adversaries had given up, or worse, they'd elected to try and go around, cutting them off from the road south.

At last, they emerged at the far end of the wood. Rodolfo thought he knew where they were, but couldn't be sure. It simply was too cursedly dark, the stars too feeble. There would be no way to ride the horses, not if they didn't wish to break their necks or simply let them pick their way forward. He dismounted and pulled Alessandra back into his arms.

Luca stopped beside them. "Send off the horses? Use them as a distraction?"

"Agreed. 'Tis far too dark for them to be of much use, especially if we need to move quickly."

Luca slapped one horse on the flank, then the other, sending them trotting away. The group continued to make their way.

"I can walk," Alessandra said. "Please. Let me try."

"You have no slippers," he whispered back, making his way down a path as quietly as he could, hoping it led to a creek bed that should be dry, if he had the right place in mind. Luca and Celso were right behind them.

They reached the bottom, and by the feel of the rounded rocks, Rodolfo grew more confident in his surroundings.

*"Down,"* Luca growled, and immediately, Rodolfo turned and sank against the soft, eroded bank, Alessandra still in his arms. The bank was just a bit taller than his head, but formed a small alcove. Loose soil crumbled over his shoulders. He tried not to move, well aware of the swiftly approaching torches and hoofbeats. Luca and Celso were to their left and right.

"Four men," Luca whispered, closing his eyes, hands on the hilt of his sword.

Rodolfo glanced down at Alessandra. She was plainly terrified. And in the growing light... He pulled her closer, desperately trying to provide some sense of comfort.

A horse paused above them, and dirt crumbled over Luca's head and shoulders. Rodolfo feared the whole bank might give way, burying them alive.

*Stay still,* he told himself. *We must stay still.*

Flickering, bright light flooded the creek bed.

"Any sign of them?" hissed one.

"They had to have come this way, sir."

"Unless they went East."

"Sir! Tracks from two horses, this way. Fresh."

The men wheeled their horses away and more dirt rained down on their heads. Two counts later, Luca and Celso disappeared, chasing after the men as stealthily as they could.

"Where are they going?" Alessandra whispered.

"To overtake them." He rose and gently set her down. "When they find the horses, they'll guess it's a ruse and come back for us. Best for us to surprise them." He took her hand. "Come. I think I saw a small pool of water, just over here."

He made his way across the rocks, reaching down again and again, until his hand met cool liquid. He urged her to bend down beside him, placing her fingers in the pool. She drank, eagerly, while he kept watch, willing Luca and Celso to return. The minutes were sliding by, and if they tarried here much longer, another patrol was liable to come hunting.

"'Tis too dark for us to make it to Castello Forelli before my father arrives at her gates," Alessandra said miserably.

"Indeed. The battle shall be upon them, justified or not."

"And if you arrive with me in hand, looking as I do..."

He let the silence stand.

"And yet, I cannot go back there," she said, her voice crackling with fear.

"Nay," he said, seeking her hand, finding it. "You cannot."

"So…Barbato has won. The battle shall be upon the Sienese, swords raised to defend my honor. Honor compromised by none but my Fiorentini brothers."

He sighed heavily. "Now you understand what I tried to tell you."

"I…I simply couldn't…" She coughed and pulled her hand away, rising. "I have created nothing but trouble, m'lord. You must loathe me."

He rose and wished he could see her face. "Nay, signorina. I feel nothing but kinship toward you. Understanding. I have walked your path, have I not?"

It was her turn to remain silent. Where was Luca? He cast an anxious eye down the creek. They should have returned by now.

"If I could only speak to my father—"

He shushed her with a quick sound, crouching and cocking his head to try and hear better. Then he bit back a curse word, pulled her back into his arms and scrambled for the far bank. Horses approached. Far too many to be Luca and Celso. He stumbled and Alessandra yelped, but he was on his feet immediately, as aware of the oncoming horses as if they were reaching out to nip his back and neck. They reached the far side and he swiftly made his way up the silty, crumbling soil, entering the trees just before the patrol pulled up right across from them.

Rodolfo kept moving, aware that if their path was discovered, the search party would reach them in seconds. He winced every time his boot met a pinecone or branch, cracking like an alarm bell, but he had to keep moving. He paused to listen, panting, when they reached a small meadow. Behind them, they still could see the dim glow of a torch outlining the trees in silhouette, but no shouts rose. He clenched his teeth and gazed cautiously around. Something was not right. Someone was near. Luca? Celso?

Slowly, he set Alessandra down. She was quiet, clearly recognizing his fear. She stilled, inches away from his chest, recognizing him as her protector now. How long had it been since he'd felt protective of a woman who trusted him?

A very long time. Gabriella…she'd never trusted him completely. And for good reason…

He saw the light to the right, first, and moved to pick up Alessandra. But when he did, he saw other torches coming from the left. He rose, slowly, looking across the small meadow. Two more. And from the back. They were surrounded.

Two men on horses entered the meadow. Then two more.

Alessandra clung to Rodolfo's tunic and he wrapped his arms around her as the eight men closed in. They would not take her away again, only to abuse her, use her. Not if he yet still lived. Mayhap he could make a way for her to run, to escape at least. "When I shout," he whispered. "You run, Alessandra. No matter what happens. Run and hide. Make your way back home. I pray your father can protect you."

She looked up at him, her big, pretty eyes round with fear.

But the nearest knight was upon them. "You disappoint me, daughter of Firenze," he said, dismounting and glowering at Alessandra. "Lord Barbato saved you, and you flee from his protection?"

Slowly, Rodolfo unsheathed his sword. But Alessandra stumbled toward the knight before he could move, sinking to her knees and clinging to his hand. "Brother, please, you must hear me. It was Lord Barbato who abused me, cut my hair. All to ignite war between Siena and Firenze again."

He shook off her hand. "Nonsense. Lord Barbato would never stoop to such things. He is far too powerful to use a mere woman to accomplish his goals."

"You are wrong," Rodolfo said. He stepped forward, and six knights all raised their swords, making certain he made no further progress.

"And you are?" asked the knight.

"Lord Rodolfo Greco."

The men all paused. One turned to his companion, eyes alight.

"'Twas Lord Barbato who proposed I force Lady Gabriella Betarrini to marry me in order to weaken Sienese morale. So you see," he said, tipping his sword into the soft soil and placing his hands on the hilt, "Lord Barbato is quite adept at using whatever resource he has to accomplish his goals."

The knight stepped forward, closer to Rodolfo, roughly hauling Alessandra alongside him. Rodolfo clenched his teeth, but forced himself not to react.

The man looked up at Rodolfo, feeling brave, backed up by seven others. That was when Rodolfo heard the owl call. *There was a chance...a small chance...*

"You abused this girl yourself," said the knight, looking her over.

"Nay," Rodolfo said, staring back into his eyes. "'Twas your lord. Think, man. Why would I—or any other man in Castello Forelli—bring harm to the woman? 'Twould only invite your wrath."

The knight glanced down at her, looking her over in a way that made Rodolfo again force himself to stay still. "She's comely enough. Before her hair was shorn off, I daresay she was a beauty." He turned a fierce stare toward Rodolfo.

Rodolfo nodded. "Yes. She is beautiful. But I belong among brothers who respect and protect women. Not use them."

The knight circled him, leaving Alessandra behind. "You are a traitor, Lord Greco. You abandoned those who trusted you to aid Lord Forelli. And by order of the Grandi, you shall meet your death this night.

Kneel and accept death, at least, with what little honor you have left."

Rodolfo considered the circle of men. "Is there not one righteous man among you? Not one who shall listen to reason? Why might I have turned away from all I loved, all I had in my coffers—"

"Because of your devil-born brotherhood oath," spat the knight. "Roll up your sleeves."

Rodolfo froze.

The knight's sword came up under his chin. "Your sleeve, Lord Greco."

Slowly, he pulled up the long sleeve, stained with blood and dirt, until his adversary could see the triangle.

"What does it symbolize?" asked the man.

"Honor. Service. Brotherhood. Things you apparently have forgotten."

The man struck, punching him in the gut. "I serve my *Fiorentini* brothers in such a manner," spat the knight. "Not my enemies."

"Are you not to take me back to Firenze for a public execution?" Rodolfo asked, when his breath returned enough to speak. The knight tossed his sword to another beside Alessandra.

"Nay, the Grandi demand summary execution. Your head shall suffice. Kneel."

"Please! Mercy!" Alessandra cried, as Rodolfo sank to his knees. But they ignored her.

"How many of you are there, Lord Greco? In the brotherhood?" asked the knight.

Rodolfo remained still, lips closed. He considered the distance between him and each of the others, calculated who might react first…

"No response?" the knight said with a scoffing laugh. "No matter. We shall eventually find every one of you. And then we shall kill every living family member. Our men began the process after the battle. We shall complete their task."

Rodolfo closed his eyes a moment and then looked back to the knight. "May God have mercy on your soul. For I certainly wouldn't."

"'Tis you who should consider what it will be to meet your Maker," he said, raising his sword, preparing for a death strike.

The arrow came then, singing through their group, striking the knight in the neck. Another right after it, hitting the man holding Alessandra.

Rodolfo rose, taking his gurgling, falling, accuser's sword in hand, and turned to meet the charge of a man behind him. He flipped the sword in his hand and rammed it through another man at his side. "Go, Alessandra! Run!" he shouted in her direction. But it took a few more parries and strikes for him to glance back and see that she remained, choosing to fight rather than run. She took down one—who still looked surprised as he fell to his face—then whipped around to meet the heavy sword of another, narrowly blocking it from her head.

Luca and Celso arrived then, and together, they first took care of the man who threatened Alessandra, then formed a wall between her and the rest of the Fiorentini, alongside Rodolfo, moving outward, taking on the remaining knights. Torches lit their small arena, smoldering in the green summer grasses. A man fell atop one and his clothes ignited. He screamed piteously until Alessandra turned him over and over, putting out the fire. But he was dead. She sat on her haunches, staring at him, at the other dead about them, tears streaming down her face.

Rodolfo clasped arms with Luca and Celso in thanks, then quietly moved toward her, sinking to his haunches. "Alessandra," he said lowly.

Her pretty eyes, wild and wide and distant, briefly focused on him, her long eyelashes fluttering in confusion. He thought her beautiful. And utterly lost. "What have I done?" she whispered.

"What you had to," he returned softly. "It will be well. Trust me,

Alessandra," he said, catching her trembling hands in his. "In time, it will be well again."

## –EVANGELIA–

"It's all right, Dad," I said. The four of us—me, my sister, Mom and Dad—were riding together, two by two, surrounded by twenty knights of Castello Forelli, closing in on Siena, at last, in the dark.

"Don't you see?" he said quietly, even though we spoke in English. "It won't be all right. Every time some new battle is incited because of our presence here, history takes a slight turn."

"Or a big one," Mom put in. "What happens if Galileo's great-great-grandfather dies in a battle he was never meant to be in?"

"But what if Mussolini's great-great does?" Gabi countered. "Boom. Hitler has no ally in Italy. Maybe." She groaned. "We could go crazy, thinking of all the changes we could set into motion. We just can't go there."

"These people would find any reason they could to go to battle," I said with a shrug. "I don't see how we can fight that—other than do our best to keep from inciting those battles. I swear, they need their own version of the '60s to change things up."

"Maybe we can get that rolling with a few bell-bottom jeans and fringed vests," Gabi said with a smile. "Give peace a chance, man."

"Big muumuu dresses with no waistband," I said, cocking my brow at her belly. Not that she had one yet. I was just teasing her.

She narrowed her eyes at me, apparently not quite ready to share any hint of the Big News with Mom and Dad. I didn't see the point. It wasn't like the longer she waited, the more ready for it they'd be. But then, maybe this wasn't the best night to lay it on 'em, when they were already feeling the weight of history on their shoulders.

"In time, with the Renaissance upon them, fighting will ease."

"And that's in what? A hundred years?" I asked.

"A couple hundred," Dad said.

"God chose to send us here," Gabi said. "He'll figure it out. We can't."

"Yeah, we can't," I echoed. "No matter how brilliant you two are, you can't think your way through this. It just…is."

"We can still make wise choices," Mom said, after a moment.

"The best we can," Gabi said. "Of course. But we also have to be free to live our lives…and fight for those we love. Lia's already tangled in so many knots she can't shoot an arrow. I don't need you two putting glue in my sheath, making me second-guess every enemy coming my way."

"Gabriella," Mom said in astonishment. "I didn't intend—"

"I know, I know," she said, lifting her hands. "You don't *intend* to do that. But you *have*, Mom. And that might put us in danger too. If we pause. You know how it is…when…" Her eyes swept toward me. She obviously didn't want to say too much, bring up too much. Make me relive our battles.

"We all know, Gabs," I said with a sigh. "And I get it. I have to get my fighting game back. I'm just not quite certain how to do that." Truly, the idea of me shooting anyone seemed like a distant memory. Like I was another person or something.

"Maybe you won't ever have to, Sweetheart," Dad said. "Maybe Marcello will think of a way out of this. Maybe Luca and Rodolfo will get back in time, hand off Alessandra, and all will be well again."

I looked north, beyond the torches of our party, then out into the deep dark night, and shivered. It was good Siena loomed in the distance, a late-night, faint glow about her, like the last vestiges of the sun. *I gotta paint that someday,* I thought. Because right then, settling into the armed palazzo, behind armed gates, far away from any battle *this* night, sounded just about perfect.

Just about. I looked north again. *Luca, be safe…*

## CHAPTER 13

I was still feeling that way as I sank beneath the lovely, soft covers of my bed at Palazzo Forelli in Siena, aware that there was a guard at my door as well as more on the roof and tower above me, and still others outside the front gates...and at the city wall...and still more beyond it. If I wasn't safe here in Siena, I wasn't safe anywhere. But thoughts of Luca kept me tossing and turning through the night, wondering where he was, if he was all right. If he'd reached Alessandra in time...

I kept telling myself he was safe, and would doze off.

Then I'd dream that his head was about to be chopped off by an enemy sword. I aimed at his enemy. I knew I could save him if I could simply let my arrow fly, but I felt immobilized, stuck, powerless as I watched the sword swing down, down, down toward his neck—

And woke up panting, sweating, a scream dying in my throat. I'd seen that Fiorentini's head roll and imagined it as Luca's. *No, no. You didn't see it happen. It didn't happen.*

I had to find my way through this. To get better. So if I ever was in that situation, I could save Luca. Or Gabi. Or Marcello. Or anyone else in the broader "Clan Forelli."

"Some She-Wolf you turned out to be," I muttered to myself. I padded over to the window and opened the shutter latch, pushing them outward. The faint pink of sunrise teased the sky, and never had I been so glad a night was over.

Nor feared the morning more.

Would Luca return to Castello Forelli with Alessandra in hand? Would the knights back off, with no reason to attack? Even now, the additional contingents of knights from Siena should be riding in, ready to join Marcello's men and turn away those of the north. But if they did not, Luca would be in the center of it all…

Agitated, I turned and threw on an older blue gown and dragged a horsehair brush through my hair, pinning it into a quick knot. I jammed my feet into tapestry slippers and went to the door, pulling it open so quickly that Otello jumped in surprise, quickly wiping away a trail of drool and blinking heavy lids. He'd obviously been sleeping against the wall.

"*Buon giorno*, Otello," I said with a small grin as the big man abruptly settled back into guard stance.

"*Buon giorno*, m'lady," he said. I was a few steps away before he began to trail me. "Up early this morning, are you not?"

"Indeed. Thoughts of our men meeting the Fiorentini…" I paused. "I thought it best I commit them to God's care rather than toss and turn, fretting." I turned left, heading toward the small palazzo chapel.

"Most wise of you, m'lady," said the man, following behind me.

"Wise or desperate," I muttered in English. I turned another corner and saw there were candles lit along this hallway, as well as in the chapel. Peeking in the door, I saw Father Tomas, kneeling, his head in his hands, praying.

Tentatively, I entered. And within a few steps he lifted his head, smiling when he saw me. "Lady Evangelia," he said. "Please." He gestured toward the kneeling rail beside him.

Feeling awkward, I took it. More than a year I'd been here—been here for good—and the priest and I had had a few conversations about faith. And while I attended daily mass with the rest of the castello—it was expected with a chaplain about, and actually, I'd come to kinda like the ritual of it—I'd not really pressed into it. That's what Father Tomas had told me once. *God is with you, m'lady. But until you press into what that means for you, it will mean little at all.*

"Are you in need of prayer, m'lady?" he asked gently, after we'd knelt there, side by side, for several minutes.

"I…I am not certain what I am in need of," I said. "I feel…at odds. Fearful. Wound up, here," I said, gesturing toward my belly. "Like wool wound too tightly around a spool to ever unwind again."

"Ahh," he said. He was as round-faced as my guard, who'd settled into keeping watch over me from outside the chapel door. The silly haircut he'd kept up—even though excommunicated from his order—only made its shape more pronounced. But his eyes were kind. And I knew he'd done much to save my sister, as well as try and aid Fortino as he languished on his deathbed. I trusted him.

He peered at me a moment and then looked up to the crucifix above the tiny altar. He stared at it, so I did too. Then he bent his head, staring at the wood planks. "'Tis fear that entraps you so," he said gently.

"Fear?"

"Fear. This is what God has told me." He looked me in the eye. "What do you fear?"

I cocked my head, suddenly wishing I could walk out. This wasn't really what I'd come here for—

"M'lady?"

"I know not," I said, dodging him.

"Why the untruth? Why do you fear telling me *what* you fear?"

There was no malice in his tone, no judgment. Only care.

"Very well," I said with a heavy sigh. "I fear that I shall never be able to shoot an arrow again, while I watch those I love cut down."

"Ahh, yes," he said, nodding, his hands clasped before his mouth. He tapped his lips with his knuckles, thinking. "Fear, of course, is not of the Lord. 'Tis of his nemesis."

I frowned in confusion.

"Other than fearing the Lord, respecting him, he is not a God of fear." Tomas said. "'Tis the enemy who preys upon our tendencies toward it."

"So…" I said slowly, "I'm in need of an exorcism?"

He laughed, a heartening, warm sound. "Nay, m'lady. Nay. But you are in need of a reminder of the God you serve. He is almighty. Beyond compare. Who can be against him?"

Tomas let that sink in a moment, then, "Consider how his enemy has tied your hands. If you cannot defend those you love, it may be he has more opportunity to take them down, yes?"

I nodded.

He watched me a moment. "Forgive me, m'lady. I know you are the gentler sex, and you have seen far more bloodshed than any woman is meant to see. But God has placed you here for a reason. For such a time as this. And to allow the enemy to bind you…" He shook his head.

"There were so many," I said with a shake of my head. "So many sons and brothers and husbands and fathers and uncles…" My voice cracked, remembering, remembering. *So many* I had killed.

He was silent a moment, then laid a warm, broad hand on my shoulder. "'Tis a burden for certain," he said. "You carry a warrior's weight. But consider this, m'lady. If you had not taken those lives, they would have done all they could to take down those around you. Other knights of Castello Forelli or Siena. Sons and brothers and husbands and fathers and uncles." He shook his head and pulled his hand away.

"Nay, war is not what God had in mind when he breathed Eden into existence. But we've wandered far from Eden, m'lady. Far from it. And we make our way through our days, the best we can. Fighting for good, not evil. Do you believe the Sienese or Lord Marcello or Sir Luca to be evil?"

I shook my head. "Of course not."

"Do you believe they battle for good, righteous causes?"

I thought about that. Since we'd returned, Marcello and Luca seemed content to keep the peace. To defend. Now that they'd reclaimed the land stolen decades ago and reestablished the old border... "Yes. I believe they fight for the right reasons."

He peered at me. "M'lady, I pray you can grow old in the gentle ways of women. But there is a reason the evil one has chosen to bind you," he whispered. "You and your sister have great power. The She-Wolves play handsomely to the crowds," he said with a smile. "But it is not mere legend. 'Tis truth. Fact," he said, a ferocity entering his tone. "And while you've had a time to hibernate, to heal, now you must prepare yourself to fight alongside your brothers, if called upon. Press into the One who calls you. He shall show you the way."

He stared at me for a long moment, as if willing me to accept it, then closed his eyes and began a long prayer, shoulder to shoulder with me. I closed my eyes too, leaning my forehead on my hands. I only remembered a little Latin, so I couldn't really follow it. But it wasn't the words that really hit me. It was the feeling of release that gradually stole over me.

An unwinding of the wool.

Freedom.

"I demand you grant my daughter freedom!" Signore Donatelli shouted up to the guards on Castello Forelli's walls, as dawn tinged the sky pink.

"Anything?" Marcello mouthed upward to the guards above him, on the wall. They each looked to the men at their other side, and then turned back to Marcello, with a shake of the head.

*Luca, Rodolfo,* Marcello groaned inwardly, internally looking over the land between here and the border. *Where are you?* What could have waylaid them? Were they lost? Captured? He paused. "Open the gates," he said to the men. Donatelli and his friend had arrived with but twelve Fiorentini knights. The others awaited word from them, just across the border.

"Lord Forelli!" boomed Signore Donatelli's big companion from outside. "Give us the girl, and we shall depart!"

"She is not quite ready to depart," Marcello said, as the gates opened between them. "If you would give us but another day or two—"

"No more time!" cried Signore Donatelli. "You swore upon your life—"

Marcello strode forward, four knights flanking him. "I swore upon my life that she would be delivered to you." He took a deep breath. "And it was my sole intention to do so—"

He glanced up as the big man lunged toward him, but two of his men stood in his way. Then he looked to Alessandra's father, lifting his hands. "Be at peace. She's well. At least she was. She made a remarkable recovery. And then a day past, she decided to make her own way home."

The older man's mouth dropped open. "She ran from you?" His look hardened. "What sort of ill treatment had she received to do such a thing?"

"She received no ill treatment," Marcello said. "We treated her as a guest. She wished to return to you, but I told her she had to wait until today, so that I could hand her over as promised." He stepped toward the man. "I gave you my word, upon my life. And I am a man of my word," he said fiercely.

The man turned partially away, hand on his head. "The girl can be headstrong…"

"Signore," said his big companion, struggling against the Fiorentini knights, "We must search the man's castle and be certain she is not held prisoner within."

Marcello shook his head. "Please," he said, gesturing backward. "Search it from top to bottom. The girl is fiercely for the Fiorentini, and headstrong. And I, truth be told, am eager to be done with her. But she is *no longer here.*"

Both men shared a long look, considering his words. Apparently it squared with what they knew of the young woman.

"So where is she now?" asked her father, suddenly looking more drawn and old.

"I know not," Marcello said. It would not do to tell them they'd sent men to fetch her from across the border.

A man whistled from atop the wall. "Sir Luca, on his way!" crowed the guard.

"Lord Greco too! Two more, accompanying them."

"The girl?" Marcello called up in agitation.

The guard frowned and shook his head. "No one in a gown, m'lord."

Signore Donatelli drew his sword, as did the Fiorentini knights behind him.

"Hold!" Marcello yelled, lifting his hands, keeping his own men from drawing. He stepped toward the older man. "We are not your foes," he said. "Do you not see? They are using your daughter as rationale to strike against us!"

"I called them here," the man said in agitation, waving behind him. "You Sienese cannot be trusted. I should never have left Alessandra in your hands."

Another whistle. "Fiorentini nobleman with a flag, m'lord!" called the guard.

Marcello continued to stare at Signore Donatelli. "I gave you my word. Your daughter was safe with us. Until she decided to leave the keep."

As the newcomers arrived, the entire company turned to watch.

"Papa!" Alessandra cried. She was in front of Rodolfo, wearing men's clothes, and in shocking condition. Hair shorn, bruising around one cheek. A split lip. And filthy.

"Al-Alessandra?" said the man, stumbling toward her. Rodolfo dismounted and moved to help her down, but she'd already slid off. She limped toward her father. She had no shoes. Her hands and feet were caked with blood and dirt...

Marcello groaned. Anyone might judge Castello Forelli if...

The Fiorentini stepped forward as Alessandra and her father embraced.

Marcello growled a command and his men drew their swords too. More came through the gate and then the beam slammed back into place. For better or worse, this initial battle would take place outside the castello, just as he'd directed his men.

Rodolfo and Luca came up to him and then he saw Celso. His mouth dropped open. "Celso? Celso Costa?" Marcello hadn't seen Celso for ten years or more. They clasped arms and grinned at each other.

"There you see, evidence of a traitor within my own ranks," Lord Barbato said as he rode up, flanked by four men and Lord Foraboschi.

He gestured toward Celso and Marcello. "How long had you planned this duplicity, Lord Forelli?"

Marcello let out a humorless laugh and cast a questioning look toward Greco and Celso. "Do you speak of Celso? I had no idea he was in your employ."

"They did not entice me to anything, m'lord," Celso said. "But I could not stand by and watch you—"

"Silence!" cried Barbato, his face reddening. "I see they managed to seize the girl again." He glanced to Signore Donatelli. "I regret, sir, that we could not rescue your daughter before she was so savagely abused."

"What nonsense is this?" Marcello cried. "She did not leave our household as such..." he said, gesturing to Alessandra. "Any abuse she suffered was in your own men's hands!"

The Fiorentini lord groaned and grimaced as if it were a tall tale. "Sadly, the girl has been ruined," Lord Barbato said. "Raped repeatedly."

"'Tis a falsehood!" Alessandra cried. "Papa, he was the one who beat me! He was the one who sent—"

"Poor child," Barbato interrupted, throwing up his hands. "Even her mind is gone."

"'Tis a falsehood!" she cried again, advancing toward him as if she intended to tear him from his horse. Knights closed in to block her way, and Marcello nodded to three men to protect Alessandra, trying to sort out exactly what had transpired.

"I am yet pure!" Alessandra cried, her father now holding her back. "But 'twas not Lord Barbato's intention," she spat out. "He wanted me ruined, so that he might blame it on the Sienese! And if it weren't for the only honorable man in his service, Celso...it would have been done as he ordered." Tears ran down her face.

Marcello glanced to his old friend and the man gave him a slow nod.

Barbato smiled, as if incredulous. "The girl is as mad as she is ruined. No man shall ever have her. Give her to us. We shall see her to a nunnery where she will be looked after. But then prepare yourselves for the wrath of Firenze to fall upon you. Already, we are at work, ferreting out any other sleeping brothers." He stared hard at Celso. "You are one of them, are you not? You've kept it covered for years, but you too, must bear the mark shared by the Forellis and Greco."

Marcello's eyes narrowed.

"He intends to find and kill the others!" Alessandra said, struggling out of her father's attempt to set her behind him, silence her. "Every one of the brotherhood who yet live, as well as every living family member! And Lady Gabriella and—"

"Witness it, Lord Forelli," Barbato said with a smile. "This is what complete and utter madness looks like. See what your abuse has wrought?"

Her father took a step away from her. "I am too late. My daughter is lost to me."

Alessandra whirled. "Nay! Papa, nay! Do you not see? Have you not heard? We fight for the Fiorentini, but these man…these men are evil! We do not wish to side with them. Lord Barbato has abused me. Attempted to use me in the most foul, despicable ways…"

She grasped hold of his hand, but he shook her off, as if she were unclean.

"I cannot find a husband for you. Not now. And you betray our people with your words, with your disrespect to Lord Barbato. You are not my daughter." He shook his head, his face etched in deep lines of grief and disbelief, as if he were trying to make out Alessandra beneath a mask.

The nobleman nodded soberly, pretending to share Signore Donatelli's pain. "It is an unfair hand you have been dealt," he said. "Your service shall not be forgotten. And I shall see to Alessandra's welfare myself."

She whipped her head around in horror. Then she began to tremble, violently.

"M'lord," Greco whispered, asking permission to go to her.

"Hold," Marcello whispered back. She must decide. Now. Decide who she was for, forever more. Only she could make this decision. There would be no turning back.

"Papa," she cried out, as he turned and walked toward his horse, his shoulders hunched in sorrow. He did not turn back around.

"Fear not, sweet girl," Lord Barbato said. "You are in my care now." He flicked two fingers in her direction, telling the knight to bring her.

"Nay," she said numbly, only making a half-effort to free herself of the Fiorentini knight's grasp upon her arm, looking confused, still glancing over her shoulder toward her father. The knight dragged her toward Lord Barbato, and her eyes widened in terror. "Nay!" she screamed.

Celso took a step forward but Marcello held up his hand. "Hold," he said lowly. "This must be her choice alone."

She screamed again when Lord Barbato grabbed hold of her wrist, preparing to lift her before him on his steed. She fought, dropping and dragging her nails down her captor's arm, drawing blood. Then she turned, her big, brown eyes searching the men beside Marcello, settling on Rodolfo.

"M'lord!" she beseeched him.

"Go," Marcello grunted.

Then he drew his sword and followed Rodolfo into the fight.

## CHAPTER 14

Alessandra stood there as Rodolfo pulled her farther away, toward safety, as the Fiorentini skirmished briefly with the Sienese, and then retreated. Two took off on a separate path, no doubt bent on alerting the rest of the troops on the border. But Alessandra could only watch her father looking sorrowfully over his shoulder at her, as if she were a mere ghost. Dead to him, already.

"Papa!" she cried, reaching out.

But when he turned away, disappearing among the oak and brush, she fell to her knees, weeping. How could he not believe her? Turn his back on her?

It hurt worse than the injuries she'd suffered at Barbato's hands.

The woods became eerily silent as the last of the Fiorentini disappeared, and Castello Forelli's men sheathed their swords.

"It won't be long," Lord Forelli growled. "Get her inside the gates."

"Yes, m'lord," Rodolfo said. He didn't pause as he turned to her. Didn't inquire of her needs. Simply picked her up and carried her inside the castello, even as she wept, his tunic soon growing damp with her tears. The gates banged shut behind her, and the crossbeam slid back into place with a metallic clang that echoed in her head. She thought she might forever carry the sound of it with the memory of when her life as a Fiorentini ended.

Rodolfo carried her into the small castello chapel, with its lovely, fresco covered walls, and sat down on the third bench. It was cool in the small building, even as the climbing sun warmed the courtyard. "Shh, shh," he said, settling her anew on his lap, cradling her. "I know, Alessandra. I know your pain. I'm so sorry you must bear it as I have."

"How could he..." she sniffed. "How could he not believe me? My own father?"

"Barbato and his ilk, they specialize in poisoning the minds and hearts of others. In time, mayhap we can reach out to your father. Make him see reason."

She clung to his words. Thinking of her father. Her home. Her neighbors. Never seeing any of them again...Which only made her weep with fresh pain.

"Shh, Alessandra. Shh," he said, rocking her a little, kissing her brow, her head, somehow able to ignore her embarrassing appearance. Only making her feel accepted. Cared for. Loved.

Who was this man? This man who had ventured across the border to save her? Who had freed her from her enemies twice over? She looked up at him, and saw that his own brown eyes were wet with tears.

Never had she been more drawn to him.

He looked down into her eyes, studying her, considering her. Then he bent closer, silently inquiring, his breath hot across her lips. Sweet. Inviting.

Tipping her chin up, she moved her lips across his, barely brushing them. She reached up and put her hand against his face and he closed his eyes, sighing, and covering her hand with his own, kissed her palm. Then he turned back to look into her eyes.

"Alessandra," he whispered, his voice ragged. "Could it be? That two Fiorentini find themselves within Sienese gates? So that we might find each other? To know love?"

"I am nothing," she whispered back. "I have nothing. No home. No family. No dowry. I am not worthy of you, m'lord."

"I am a man only recently given what he has by new friends and family," he said, his eyes covering her face. "So we find ourselves in similar circumstances. Alessandra, it is a grief to lose what you know and love. I understand. But you are a warrior, within, beaten as you now may feel. You shall rise again. I see it in you. And this castello, these people, celebrate warrior women, do they not? Far more than any others either of us have ever met, I'd wager."

His words held such promise, his handsome eyes twinkling with hope, that Alessandra felt the tiniest spark of light within her. "M'lord," she began.

"Rodolfo," he corrected.

"Rodolfo," she said, staring into his eyes, begging him closer.

And that was all the invitation he needed. He bent his head and gave her the most tender, sweetest, passionate kiss she'd ever known. She got lost in the comfort of it, the reassurance of his arms, the way he pulled her close—and it warmed her to the core, easing aside the bitter cold draft of her father's betrayal.

When he drew away, he looked again into her eyes. "Is it possible?" he whispered, giving her a gentle kiss on her cheek, her temple. "Is it possible?" he repeated in wonder.

And with each rendition of his question, she felt an incredible, mad hope surge, on the darkest day of her life.

## −EVANGELIA−

The messenger arrived late-morning, having ridden all the way from Castello Forelli. I saw him first and rose from my stool beside the easel and parchment upon it. Mom and Dad set down their books and leaned forward, waiting. Gabi turned from the other window and the messenger went directly to her.

"M'lady," he said, gasping for breath.

She turned and poured a glass of water for him, not bothering to ask a servant to do it. We all waited anxiously for him to get ahold of himself, and share what he must.

I wrung my hands, hating every drop of water he swallowed so greedily. Hating myself for begrudging his thirst, but just wanting the dude to *speak*.

"Quickly," Gabi said, losing patience. "What news have you? Are our men in good health?"

He nodded. "Yes, m'lady. Our lord bid me come with a most urgent message. He fears you have become double the target because of your..." He paused to clear his throat. "State of grace," he finally said. "And Lady Evangelia's hesitancy to wield her bow has become known as well, to our enemies. He wants to be certain that you shall remain here, within the palazzo, under guard. You are not to leave until he comes for you himself."

Gabi took a step back, hand at her throat. "What has happened to provoke the Fiorentini so? Did Lord Greco and Sir Luca not return with the girl?"

"They did, m'lady," he said with a polite nod, wringing his hands. "But the girl has plainly suffered abuse."

Mom turned away, groaning. We all knew what it meant.

"'Tis abuse the Fiorentini claim the men of Castello Forelli subjected her to," the messenger went on to say. He shook his head. "She's in poor form, m'lady. Her hair shorn. Beaten."

"At Lord Barbato's hands, of course," Gabi said, taking a step toward the window, remembering. "That man is capable of anything."

"All they need is another excuse," Mom said. "They'll say it's rationale to take you or Lia. Anyone, really."

"And publicly execute you. An eye for an eye, and all of that. He's right," Dad said, gesturing toward the messenger. "Under no circumstance are you two leaving this palazzo. Understood?"

We nodded, seriously freaked again. The Fiorentini had wanted us before, but now, if they'd gotten worked up into a frenzy…Memories of the assassins they'd sent to track down the brotherhood returned to me. I decided I was all for double-guard duty.

"Where is Alessandra now?" I asked.

"Back at Castello Forelli. Her father has disowned her for declaring it was a Fiorentini who abused her, and Lord Foraboshi declared her mad. He intended to put her away, into a nunnery, but she turned to Lord Greco for help."

Lord Greco. A smile edged my lips as I shared a look with Gabi. Maybe the girl hadn't been so Firenze-minded that she couldn't see the handsome former-Fiorentini who'd ridden to her aid. I was just glad she hadn't set her eyes on Luca.

Gabi shook her head, remembering herself, her responsibilities. "What else would Lord Forelli have me do, while I await him here?"

"M'lord bids you see to informing the rest of the Nine and send messengers to his brothers near Siena to bar their gates. He has sent word to those beyond Siena."

I shared a look with Dad, my hopes that our guys might soon be with us again crashing alongside Gabi's. If Luca were here, I might be able to draw a full breath…

That's when we heard the alarm bells. First one church's. Then another's. I went to the window, but could see little besides people scurrying out of the piazza below it. Sienese knights in formation trotted through the far gate.

Another stranger hovered at the doorway, accompanied by one of our men. "Permission to enter, m'lady?"

"Come," Gabi said, lifting her chin and waving him inward.

"News from Firenze, m'lady," he said with a nod. "I am to pass it along to each of the Nine."

"My husband is in battle on behalf of Siena. I shall receive it on his behalf," she said, all-stately-Don't-Mess-with-Me.

"The Fiorentini have mandated that each citizen's arm be inspected for the mark that your husband and his captain share with Lord Greco."

"It was one of the brotherhood who assisted Signorina Alessandra in her escape," interrupted the messenger, "reaching Sir Luca and Lord Greco."

Gabi paled and I rushed to help her to a seat, feeling more than a little queasy myself. "Not again…" She moaned. I felt as light-headed as she looked.

"They mean business, Gabs," I said in English, in her ear. "They want to finish what they started a year ago. We have to concentrate on those who yet live."

She seemed to gather herself then, nodding. "Is there anything else?" she asked the Sienese messenger.

"Nay, m'lady."

"Good then. Please. Carry on with your task and inform the others." She turned to the messenger from Castello Forelli. "If that is all, go to the kitchens. They'll see to you from there."

"Yes, m'lady," he said, giving her a bow and leaving the room.

Together, we slowly met our parents' eyes. "They're nothing but a bunch of thugs," Gabi grumbled. "Gang-bangers."

"Vendettas go way back," Dad said. "Fact of life, here." He leaned closer. "Now what did he mean when he mentioned your 'state of grace'?"

She abruptly stood. "We don't have time for this. I must see to getting word to the brotherhood."

I grabbed her arm and pulled her to a stop. "Gabi. Maybe it's time you tell them. Go on. Just do it."

She froze, a blush climbing her neck. "I don't know what he was talking about. Or what you are."

"I'll see about sending word to the brotherhood." I stared hard at her. *This was for her good, my little niece or nephew's good...* "You tell them."

"Lia..."

"Gabi's pregnant," I said.

And as my sister sputtered in rage, my mother gasped, and my father put his hands on his face, I walked out, in search of paper, pen and men to carry new messages of warning.

<hr />

By early afternoon, they were weary and frustrated. Every move they made, the Fiorentini countered. But they did not engage in full attack. They continually stabbed at Marcello's men, and then withdrew.

"They toy with us," Luca said, panting, rubbing the back of his hand over his sweaty lip and forehead.

"Indeed," Marcello said. He studied the retreating backs of a contingent of Fiorentini, as they crossed the creek bed, and Rodolfo and Celso came up on his other side.

He turned to wave over a scout, on horseback. When the man reached him, he said, "The Fiorentini resist full attack. Take another and circle around them. See if they await reinforcements."

"Yes, Lord Forelli," said the man, and immediately wheeled his horse around and galloped off.

"It makes no sense, though," Luca said. "We are as yet outnumbered, and they have the advantage of Alessandra's supposed abuse to fuel their men. Why not press in, now?"

"They know we can merely hole up in Castello Forelli. They're awaiting something else…" His chin lifted and his eyes whipped over to Luca's.

"Nay," Luca said, frowning, shaking his head. "They would not attempt it. The women are safe within Palazzo Forelli, in the heart of the city!"

"They might," Rodolfo said, miserably. "Lord Barbato tortured Alessandra. Made her tell him all she knew."

Luca and Marcello turned to face him. "And?" Marcello growled.

His miserable look told him what they feared most.

"So they know of Evangelia's hesitancy," Luca said, sounding as if he were trying to reassure himself as much as them. "Lady Gabriella and her parents will see Evangelia comes to no harm, to say nothing of the ample guards we assigned."

Marcello met his eyes. "'Tis that. They know she is weak. But they also know something of Gabriella."

Luca's sandy brow lowered. "And that is…"

"She carries a child."

His brows lifted and he whooped, slapping Marcello's upper arms as if he'd just heard the finest news all day. Which it was, of course. But Marcello waited for him to understand.

Gradually, the joy faded into understanding. "Ahh. But won't a She-

Wolf with child be all the more fierce in her defense? And the only men capable of reaching them would be of the likes of those that went after the brotherhood...We killed them all."

"Nay," Rodolfo said. "That is an elite force, the pride of the Grandi. They would have replaced them by now. And they'd be burning to prove themselves anew."

Marcello was already moving toward his horse, the men with him, studying the sun, now well on its way down. "They shall see her as twice the delectable target she once was, and Evangelia an easy conquest."

The muscles in Luca's jaw twitched as he ran toward their horses, slightly ahead of Marcello.

"The Fiorentini did not intend to fully engage us here today," Marcello said. "They meant to distract us. They gave up Alessandra, but intend to take our own." They doubled their pace, swinging up into their saddles. "Rodolfo, Celso, see to a full retreat of the men. Bar the gates of Castello Forelli and see to her as if she were your own."

"Yes, m'lord," Rodolfo said. Celso echoed his call.

Marcello turned to Luca. "You and I must ride, as fast as we can, to Siena."

"Right beside you," Luca said.

## CHAPTER 15

### –EVANGELIA–

I awakened from a nightmare in which I held Luca, bloody and wounded, in my arms as he gasped for his last breath. I sat up, panting, my face wet with tears and stared into the darkness. It's *just a dream,* I told myself. *Just a dream.* I threw off my sweat-soaked covers and on shaking legs, went to the window, unlatching and opening the shutters to allow the blessed cool of night wash into the room. I leaned out on the wide, stone sill and lifted my face, feeling the breeze dry my tears.

And when I opened my eyes, I saw a dark form swinging toward me. He hit my chest with his boots, knocking me to the floor, and my head bashed against the stone. I blinked, stunned and dizzy, then felt the blade across my neck, a man lifting me, behind me now, even as my guard knocked on my door. "M'lady? Is all well?"

"Tell him you are well, you only tripped," ground out the voice in my ear. He pressed the knife against my throat.

"Be at peace," I called out, my voice sounding strangled. My assailant eased his pressure a bit. "I only tripped in the darkness."

"M'lady, you sound…distressed. May I enter?"

"Tell him you have to get dressed first," whispered the man, lifting me to my feet. He was only a little taller than I, but strong, fiercely strong. And then I knew. The dark clothing, the ropes. More of Firenze's assassins. "Now," he said, pressing his knife in to my flesh. I could feel the wet trickle of blood as he dragged me to the window. "We have your sister."

*Gabriella.*

"M'lady?" called my guard.

"Let me only don a gown," I called out.

"Yes, m'lady," the guard said, sounding contrite for even pressing it now.

"I hear you can climb a rope," said the man in my ear, as he set me on the windowsill, my legs dangling over the edge.

"I have done so, yes," I whispered back, my heart pounding.

"Your sister has a knife to her neck. Cry out or try and escape and she'll be found dead on the palazzo steps come morning. Understood?"

I started to nod, but then realized I was likely to end up with my neck sliced if I did so. "Yes."

"Good," he said. "Grab hold of the rope."

Then, with no further warning, he shoved me.

I gasped and dangled there for a long moment, then began to slide downward, wincing as the passing rope burned my hands. The man climbed out of the window above me and I yelped as our rope swung, and prayed it wouldn't break. Where were the guards, stationed about the base of the palazzo? Or those above us? Had they all been killed?

My attacker came, faster than I, driving me toward the ground. As soon as I reached it, I stumbled, then was immediately grabbed, gagged, tied up and carried away.

We moved across the wide expanse of il Campo—Siena's main plaza—then down a street, a man carrying me over his shoulder as if I was nothing but a sack of grain. His shoulder drove into my belly, making it almost impossible to breathe, but I forced myself to concentrate. I thought there were five others with us.

How could this be happening? Did they not really have Gabi? Was it all a ruse to get me out of the palazzo in silence? I'd been such a fool. To open my shutters. But then he'd probably just have jimmied the latch and stolen in as I slept. I consoled myself with the thought that it was better, the way it had happened. If I'd been asleep when he entered, it would have freaked me out all the more.

The leader sounded a warning and they split up, sliding into hiding places, in doorways, behind a wagon, down an alley. The man set me down on my feet and I felt my knees give way, like they were jelly. Had I hit my head harder than I thought? My captor wrapped an arm around my waist, as if he sensed I was about to faint.

I briefly considered trying to make a break for it. If I could free my bleeding hands, take out the gag... But I first had to know if they told the truth—if they had Gabi. Had to help her, if I could. As if sensing my impulse, my captor wrapped a steely arm around my neck and we both remained still as two drunk men, swaying and singing, made their way past us and down the street.

His companion whistled, and we were once again on the move, this time with me running barefoot between two of them. We emerged in a small piazza they called "Pozzo Secco." *Dry well.* Siena was riddled with them—the city's one major drawback. She was too high and too often arid. It was a constant threat, because under siege, she'd not last longer than a month with every citizen inside her gates. Not if they wanted to drink water.

But I knew of this place. Marcello had come home from a meeting in which the Nine had discussed giving several *contrade*—the districts of Siena—new access to the city's aqueduct, allowing dry wells to again flow. "After four generations, Piazzetta del Pozzo Secco shall become Piazzetta del Pozzo Bagnato," he'd groaned, basically saying the piazza of the dry well would become the piazza of the wet well. "What do you wager that we'll get water to flow to those, and others will then run dry?"

One of the men tossed a rope over the edge, and a second later, we heard it splash. He sidled over the edge and slipped down the rope. I grimaced. My rope-burned hands were already split, bleeding and aching. Would they even hold me?

"Go on," said a man, lifting me up and over the side of the well. "Make haste." I didn't wait for them to shove me. I slid down. And at the bottom, I immediately bent and put my hands in the water slowly washing by us, as deep as our ankles. I closed my eyes in relief, but then I was roughly lifted upright again, rushed through a narrow tunnel, newly and roughly hewn, then into the big, barrel-vaulted ceiling of the *bottini*—the city's aqueduct. Dad had told me about it—how it connected all the *fonte*, or fountains, of the *contrade*. How it was an engineering marvel, *yada, yada*. Dad could yammer on for a good hour over such things. But one big factoid stuck out to me. The *bottini* was twenty-five kilometers long. A labyrinth webbing underneath the city.

*Twenty-five kilometers.*

About fourteen or fifteen miles of tunnel.

The water was deeper here, up to our knees, but the men rushed onward, following another with a torch. I heard the splash of the other men running behind me.

At the juncture of two tunnels, I saw her. Gabriella, between two men.

And I was both relieved and heartbroken.

Because they were doing it. Succeeding in the impossible.

Kidnapping the She-Wolves from their very own city.

Marcello and Luca cried out to the guards at the wall. "'Tis Lord Marcello Forelli and Luca Forelli! Open the gates at once! Make haste!"

A guard opened a small window and peered out at them. They lifted their faces to the torchlight, so that he might make a more ready identification.

"Open the gates!" the guard called tiredly. "'Tis indeed Lord Forelli!"

Despite their fears, they could not sound an alarm—not until their suspicions were confirmed. And as he paced, Luca prayed to God that their fears were unfounded. That they were merely two fools in love, desperate to protect the women they loved most. That this was simply a mad dash they'd all laugh about, come Christmastide. He almost smiled, thinking of Evangelia laughing. She was so beautiful when she smiled. And when she laughed…it was magical. He'd gladly spend the rest of his life trying to make her laugh, just for the sheer joy of it.

At last the gates opened, and Luca and Marcello quickly mounted, urging their tired steeds up the winding, cobblestone streets to the center of the city.

They knew as soon as they reached the palazzo that something was wrong. The guards were not at their posts, as Marcello had personally dictated. None answered his whistle. Luca unsheathed his sword and jumped to the ground even before his horse came to a full stop, Marcello beside him. Marcello went to the massive doors and rammed the metal knocker down, over and over. They could hear men inside, already shouting to one another. Were there intruders inside? Luca edged along the wall, sword lifted, looking for the men who would be stationed outside. They would never have willingly left their posts. Not for any reason. Especially after they'd heard Marcello's impassioned speech before they left.

He saw the dim form of a boot across an alley and groaned. He rushed past a wagon and saw the sprawled body of a Forelli knight, his head at such an angle that he was clearly dead. He swallowed hard and whistled an alarm to Marcello.

Marcello paused then shouted. "Siena to arms! Enemies among us! Siena to arms!"

A guard opened the palazzo door as Luca rejoined him, and they both brushed past, charging up the steps to the main floor, two at a time, then beyond it to the guest rooms. Clearly, the men inside were in an uproar. Four were running down the hall, swords drawn, opening doors without awaiting an invitation, shouting accounts to the others. "Lord and Lady Betarrini, accounted for!"

Luca drew up when he saw the guard at Lia's door, in the corner as if sleeping. But by the dark stain at his chest, he knew the truth. He moved toward him, lifted his head by the hair, and saw the deep red blood seeping across his tunic and neck. With a growl, he kicked in the door and saw nothing but the open shutters on the far side, a rope dangling at the center. "Impossible," he muttered. *"Impossible!"*

Marcello joined him, panting, sword in hand. "Gabriella, too," he growled.

Outside, bells were beginning to ring, the alarm spreading.

"Marcello, what is it?" the girls' mother asked. Ben wrapped his arm around her shoulder.

"They've infiltrated the palazzo and kidnapped your daughters. We're going after them."

"We'll go with you—"

"Nay, please," he said, going to them. "Let us do this. We'll move faster on our own."

Biting her lip, Adri agreed and Ben nodded. "Bar the doors again!" Marcello screamed to his men as he turned. "Three knights to each of the Betarrinis and Father Tomas! Better yet, all of you guard them together, in the Great Hall. The rest of you, with us."

"Yes, m'lord!" called one, clearly miserable they'd failed him.

"Come," Marcello said to Luca, and they ran down the stairs. Outside, they took a torch from the wall and ran down the street and into il Campo, to where they'd apparently brought Evangelia down by rope.

"Here," Luca said, bending. *Blood.* Was Evangelia wounded? Fury and fear warred within his chest. He'd kill every one of them— "And here," he said, pointing to the next stain on the cobblestones. They ran, following the trail, one drip of blood after another. Soldiers ran to them, and Marcello barely looked up as he commanded their captain.

"Look for men, all dressed in black. Small men. But beware—they are likely the fiercest enemies your men have ever encountered. They do not fight as honorable knights. They use any method at their disposal. And allow no one to depart the city gates. *No one.* Understood?"

"Yes, m'lord. I shall send others to your aid and you can direct them as you wish."

"Good," Marcello grunted. He looked up, and turned, running down a road, then looked about, the torchlight dancing across the stones in maddening splashes of light and shadow. "Do you see anything?"

"Nay," Luca said, searching the ground for any more blood, any clue as to where they'd gone.

"Here! Over here, m'lord!" cried a boy beside another, a hundred yards away.

Marcello and Luca shared a look and then ran to them. It was the little squires Ben had insisted on bringing with them, Pio and Sandro, small daggers in each of their hands. "We followed them," Pio said proudly, pulling at Marcello's sleeve.

"Well done, little man," Marcello said, relief in every word. "Which way?"

"This way!" Sandro cried, running ahead of them.

Luca's heart hammered in his chest, as they ran, eventually emerging into a small piazzetta.

"Piazzetta del Pozzo Secco," Marcello said, lifting his torch and looking around at the two-story buildings that surrounded it. All were dark and silent. As he turned, Luca saw it, on the wall of the well. A handprint of blood.

"Marcello…" He ran over to the well, touching the spot of blood, rubbing it between his fingers. Still wet. He peered down into the silent darkness below. She'd been there, moments before them. He cried out in frustration. They'd been so close!

But by the saints…if the Fiorentini had taken the women down into the maze of the *bottini,* how were they to find them?

---

–EVANGELIA–

We ran down the *bottini* as best we could, our soggy skirts clinging and slowing us down, to say nothing of the gags in our mouths, making it hard to breathe. But I didn't want them to carry us. If by some miracle Luca and Marcello could find us down here, it'd be best if they couldn't use us as human shields. At least, not immediately. Gabs and I were decent swimmers. We could disappear under the water for a moment, add to the confusion. But the thought of going under, my mouth gagged, my hands tied, made me choke with panic even before I'd tried it.

Six men ran in front of us, six behind. I didn't know if our guys had succeeded in killing any of them, but the bad guys weren't carrying any bodies. We paused at another juncture and as the two streams of water collided, Gabi stumbled against me, and I reached up to balance us against the curved ceiling. I gave her a questioning *Are you all right?* look before a man roughly pulled her away, setting off again. They were like spiders, I decided. Tarantulas. Scurrying. Eerie in their movements.

She looked over her shoulder at me, her eyes shifting to the ceiling, trying to tell me something, and I glanced up as two men dragged me forward, too.

I'd left a bloody streak on the ceiling.

And if my mouth hadn't been deformed by the gag, the spiders would've seen me grinning.

Because while we weren't much of a fighting duo at this point, there were others coming after us who were. *God willing...*

---

"God in heaven...Help us," Luca muttered, already over the side and lowering himself down the rope. It was slick with blood. *So it was her hands...Her beautiful, elegant hands...*

"They'll likely attempt to escape out the aqueduct," Marcello barked to a Forelli knight, above him, his voice echoing off the well walls. "They must have overcome the aqueduct guard, breached the wall, and with the low summer water, entered that way. Alert the city guard. Send several contingents there. Expect enemies when you arrive, even before these emerge. And take these boys back to Palazzo Forelli!"

"Yes, m'lord!"

Marcello came down, and after him, twelve knights—a few of the remaining Forelli guards, the rest Sienese in their red tunics, with white crosses. Four held torches and all drew their swords. Two archers led the way.

They ran down the slick-bottomed *bottini,* pausing at the first juncture. Marcello closed his eyes, as if trying to remember where they might be beneath the city, where their adversaries were likely to go.

*We should split up,* Luca thought. But then thought better of it. If the Fiorentini had been able to silently murder nine Forelli knights and take off with Gabriella and Evangelia, they'd need to stick together if they were to get the women back. *But what if they went the other way?* He wondered, as they splashed down a tunnel after Marcello. His heart hammered at the thought. Of losing Evangelia. Of failing her.

They reached the next juncture and Marcello lifted his torch and stared at a bloody streak on the wall. He reached up and touched it, rubbing the blood between his fingers. "Fresh," he said, looking to the channel to his right. "They intend to try to move upstream, out the aqueduct."

"That's madness. They'll drown!" Luca said.

"We have to gamble on something. We must double-back. Make our way to the next fonte entrance and come in above them. They've gone wider than necessary. And they have the women with them—which is likely slowing them down. If we can enter in front of them…"

Luca nodded. It was their only opportunity to surprise them.

As one, they turned and ran, praying they weren't already too late.

# CHAPTER 16

## –EVANGELIA–

The water was up to our thighs, the current stronger as we neared what had to be the walls of the city. Gabi fell again, and I struggled to haul her up, her head just clearing the rush of water. A Fiorentini spider took hold of her other arm and we got her to her feet, her breath coming fast and panicked through her nose.

"Their skirts threaten to sweep them away!" a man beside us called forward, to the leader.

"Take care of it, then," the leader returned, sounding irritated that they couldn't think of this for themselves. We were immediately surrounded, and separated, the men laughing. Memories of being tied up in the woods, swept over me, and I breathed fast and hard, fighting panic.

Two men took out long daggers and began cutting away at the fabric of my skirts, as I assumed they did to Gabi's, too. They laughed over the idea of the She-Wolves of Siena looking like nothing more than half-drowned harlots.

"If their people could see them now!" crowed one, reaching out for a handful of my long, wet hair. The other finished his task, his dagger carelessly jabbing me. I winced and sidled away, into another, who wrapped his arms around me.

"Mayhap later, girl," he said, as if I'd been throwing myself at him.

He shoved me away, and the others laughed. Ahead of us, I saw that Gabi suffered similar mockery. But as I stumbled and righted myself, I realized I was glad my skirts were gone. The water mostly covered my legs. And now it was far easier to move, as well as to remain stable. It left me less panicked about falling, since I had the use of my legs to kick and right myself.

Their leader awaited us, hands on hips. "Keep your hands to yourselves," he hissed. "We'll earn enough in reward for delivering these two to keep us in gold—and women—to the end of our days. But we must escape these cursed walls and deliver them to the Grandi. Only they can decide if the She-Wolves suffer our sister's fate. Not us."

I frowned at his obvious reference to Alessandra and the accusations that she'd been abused at our men's hands. Was that what they intended? Retribution in kind? I glanced over my shoulder, hoping against hope that I'd see a flicker of torchlight, know that Luca and Marcello trailed us…but there was nothing.

※

The man's voice easily carried to them, even over the rush of the water.

The Fiorentini were right around the corner, not twenty paces away. They could see the reflection of their torches on the wall. Marcello looked over at Luca, his face half-submerged. In his hands were two daggers, just as there were in Luca's. Three other knights who could swim were with them in the water, the others waiting in the other tunnel, awaiting sounds of battle.

The light drew closer on the wall, and Marcello lifted his chin, took a deep breath, then went under, as did Luca, a second later. They dived deep, not wanting a kicking foot or rising hand to alert the men that they approached. They'd gambled that the Fiorentini traveled up the center of the bottini, where it was least slick, and went to either side, leaving the men at the front for the knights behind them. Luca counted to thirty, hoping they had passed the leader, and then rose, just as Marcello did. They each took down their first man within seconds, then another, and Luca dived for Evangelia, dragging her underneath the water with him. But a man was immediately upon him, and then another, and Luca shoved her away, hoping he could stay between them.

He felt the pierce of an enemy's dagger in his thigh and rose, infuriated, intent on taking this one down, drowning him as a crocodile took his prey. As he went under, he glimpsed Evangelia in the torchlight, pulling the gag from her mouth, screaming for Gabriella.

When he rose, his enemy drifting away from him, dead, and, turning to take on the next, he saw Evangelia wade out into the bottini for a drifting bow, then run downstream after the drifting, dead body of an archer, intent on the quiver of arrows. "Evangelia! Stay with—"

He grunted and ripped the sword from his back, just barely stopping his adversary's strike at his neck. He roared and pushed the man back, but the man was quick, twisting, going under the water, and rising where he didn't expect him. He couldn't go after Evangelia...not if he wanted to stay alive to help her.

Luca growled in frustration, renewing his attack and then glimpsed where she was headed. Two men had Gabriella, and were dragging her with them, away. Marcello cried out, obviously injured, then roared as he attacked his adversary anew. Luca finally dispatched his attacker with a feint and plunged a knife into his belly, then turned and ran after

Evangelia, Gabriella, and the other two Fiorentini. He glanced over his shoulder at his cousin, pushing a Fiorentini underwater. Two Forelli knights hovered nearby.

*Marcello would want me to go after his wife. His baby.*

He turned back, chagrined that they were all out of sight again, and ran, as fast as he could, against the waters that seemed to fight him. *By the saints, Lord, don't let me have tarried too long. Please don't let me have tarried too long!*

Luca turned the corner and splashed to a stop, just shy of running into Evangelia, aiming down her bowstring at the running figures thirty feet away.

He held his breath. She'd shot nothing but a few targets a couple days ago. Over the course of a *year*. And he knew her hands were bloody, likely trembling, weakened. If her arrow went wide—

She let it loose, and it struck the man at Gabriella's left in the center of his neck. His hands went up, as if surrendering, just before he splashed face-first into the water. The other immediately turned, dagger to Gabriella's throat, dragging her backward, even as Evangelia strode forward through the water, nocking another arrow as she went.

"Stay where you are, or I'll kill her now!" cried the man.

"Nay. You shall not leave with her," Evangelia said, not stopping for another ten paces. Behind Gabriella and her captor, another assassin held a torch, leaving them in perfect silhouette.

For the first time, Luca smiled. "So...you only set aside your bow and arrow so that you could pick them up again in a way that would heighten your legend?"

A smile edged her beautiful face, but her eyes remained only on her prey. "I do adore a good dramatic moment."

Luca sucked in his breath. "You know that he'll likely kill her and then try and escape," he whispered. "Take the glory of the kill rather than be captured."

"I am aware," she said, aiming again.

"Cease your aim!" cried the man, panic edging his tone, taking a few more steps backward. "Put down your bow!"

"You did not hear what transpired for your brothers at the villa in Aquila last year?" Luca called.

The man paused, and Luca could almost see him frowning.

"Nay?" Luca called. "Ah well. It went something like this…"

And Lia let her next arrow fly, piercing Gabriella's captor in the eye a second later. Then another, taking down the man with the torch, who had turned to run.

They rushed forward as Gabriella was dragged under. She came up just before they reached her, pulling at her gag, choking. Marcello was right behind them, taking his wife in his arms, even as Luca cut her hands free. Two others came, with torches.

Luca turned Evangelia toward him, gently taking the bow from her hands, setting it adrift on the water, and lifted her palms to the light, wincing at the deep cuts and burns. He pulled her closer, wrapping her arms around him, and cradled her face, covering it with small kisses. "Ah, Evangelia, how I feared for you…"

"And I for you." But then she turned to her sister, as soon as she was in reach. They clung to each other for a moment, weeping, and Luca and Marcello each backed up, leaning against opposite walls, taking their first deep breath since their arrival. Marcello gave him a grateful smile.

"I could not have done it without you, Captain."

"Nor I without you, m'lord. Or our men."

Marcello nodded soberly. "Or our women." He stepped forward to wrap his arms around Gabriella, and Luca moved behind Evangelia, sliding his arms across her upper chest and kissing her beside the ear, as the remaining Sienese and Forelli knights rounded the corner and cheered.

"I'm beginning to believe that Lia and I must sleep with our weapons," Gabi said, with a wan smile.

"Not a bad idea, that," Marcello said.

"Speaking of weapons…" Luca said, turning Lia in his arms.

"We shall speak of it later, yes?" she said.

He nodded, and pulled her close again, kissing her on the forehead. "Whenever you are ready, m'lady."

# EPILOGUE

## –EVANGELIA–

It was as the guys suspected. The Fiorentini forces faded back across the border when the knights' mission failed in capturing me and Gabi, and our uneasy truce resumed. The guys relaxed a little, with Celso now in our company—the only one of the brotherhood that had remained behind enemy lines.

And Rodolfo…well, Rodolfo was like a new man, smiling all the time. Laughing, even. It turned out his laugh was pretty awesome, deep and warm, making us all smile when we heard the unfamiliar sound. He finally had somewhere to focus all of that mad intensity. And under his care and attention, Alessandra was blossoming…and gradually accepting our forgiveness, our understanding.

"That lone sunflower, on the next hill," Luca challenged, in my ear. My eyes moved to where he pointed, over my shoulder, brushing my ear with his lips as he withdrew.

It was impossibly far.

I looked back at him and cocked a brow. "You think I cannot do it?"

"On the contrary," he said, taking a step away, arms crossed, waiting.

"I believe you can."

I looked to the fat sunflower, feeling the breeze on my cheek, knowing how it increased the challenge. That was the thing about Luca. He thought I could do the impossible. And he made me think the same.

I glanced behind me, to Gabi, her eyes closed against the sun, her hand on her swelling belly. Marcello was on his side, beside her, playing with a coil of her hair. He smiled his encouragement up at me.

"Give it a try, Squirt," Dad said, handing Mom some grapes.

My eyes shifted across the rest of our party, spread over the hill near the castello, the new wall clearly taking shape in the distance. Some of the men were sparring with wooden swords, others wrestling, like the big boys they were, showing off for the few women in attendance. Celso, Lutterius and Patrizio were riding up the hill, allowing their horses to lazily pick their way up the trail. Father Tomas and Adela, back from Rome, were sitting, side by side, sharing a book. To my left, Rodolfo was halfway down the golden hill, standing beside Alessandra, fiddling with a piece of grass. Alessandra tucked her short hair behind her ear, smiling and laughing in response to what he was saying. He laughed too, and then gathered her in his arms, all tender and sweet.

I had a flashback to him in the rain, locked in the stocks, misery etched in his every word. And now, joy. Such joy.

How things had changed for us. For us all. I closed my eyes and felt the breeze across my cheek and nose, judging its speed. Smelling lavender and sage and pine and fresh cut hay. Felt the warm, Tuscan, August sun on my face.

"You with us still, Lia?" Gabi said, shielding her eyes with her hand and looking up to me.

"Oh, I'm with you," I said, eying the sunflower again, before looking back at her. "More than I've ever been. Here, with you. Luca. Marcello. Mom. Dad. For the first time, it feels like home to me, you know? Not just because I'm here with you." My eyes shifted to Luca. "But because it's where I belong. Because I couldn't..." my voice cracked, my heart filled with so many conflicting emotions. I took a deep breath and looked back to her. "Because I couldn't be anywhere else and feel this right."

She smiled with me. "I'm glad, Lia. I'm really glad." She rolled to her side and then up to her feet, walking over to me with a slight waddle. "Think it'll be a girl?" she asked, shoulder to shoulder with me, looking out across the rolling hills, hand resting on her baby bump. It really was all kinds of cuteness. "The littlest She-Wolf?"

"Could be. I could show her how to handle a bow and arrow."

"Oh, that'd be a requirement," Gabi said.

I turned and nocked my arrow, aimed at the sunflower, silently counting the yards between us, feeling the breeze again, watching as the fat, golden flower swayed.

And then I let my arrow fly.

## ACKNOWLEDGMENTS

Many thanks to Caitlyn Carlson and Lindsay Olson for editing these two novellas and being ongoing She-Wolf editors and River of Time champions. Special thanks also to Jennifer Crosby for the Italian help, and to readers who helped me proof the manuscript, especially Kristin, Amber, Karin, Julie, Serena, Jen, Britney, Asher, Katie, Kaitlyn and Rachelle.

## JOIN THE RIVER TRIBE!

Still want more River connection and news? Be sure to join the River Tribe on Facebook: **facebook.com/riveroftimeseries**.

## LISA T. BERGREN

You can find out more about Lisa T. Bergren and her latest projects at **LisaBergren.com**. She's currently at work on a Grand Tour series (Christian historical fiction), beginning with the just-released *Glamorous Illusions* and the upcoming *Grave Consequences*, and another general-market YA trilogy called Remnant, due to begin releasing Fall 2013.